spirit

gothika #4

eli easton
jamie fessenden
kim fielding
b.g. thomas

REAMSPINNER
PRESS

Published by
DREAMSPINNER PRESS

5032 Capital Circle SW, Suite 2, PMB# 279, Tallahassee, FL 32305-7886 USA
www.dreamspinnerpress.com

Spirit
© 2015 Dreamspinner Press.
Edited by Tricia Kristufek

Cover Art
© 2015 AngstyG.
www.angstyg.com
Cover content is for illustrative purposes only and any person depicted on the cover is a model.

ISBN: 978-1-63476-641-8
Digital ISBN: 978-1-63476-642-5
Library of Congress Control Number: 2015948191
First Edition October 2015

Printed in the United States of America
∞
This paper meets the requirements of
ANSI/NISO Z39.48-1992 (Permanence of Paper).

Table of Contents

The Mill

by Jamie Fessenden

Chapter One

"Was in the town of Hawley
When the people was burned and killed,
In a textile manufactory
Called as the Hawley Mill."

THE SECOND floor of the mill building was a cavernous space so large Frank Carter's flashlight beam nearly vanished in the darkness, casting only a vague blur of illumination against the far walls. The wooden floor had been replaced a hundred years ago, after the fire burned the first floor to ash in 1907, but the renovators hadn't refinished it yet. The floor was varnished, though the sheen had been worn off by eighty years of footsteps until the mill was shut down in 1989. Grooves in the oak and holes for bolts still marked where rows of massive cast-iron sewing machines once whirred and clattered, filling the chasm with an ear-splitting din.

Now every step Frank made in his sneakers could be heard, the slightest squeak of his rubber soles echoing back from the void. He switched on his night-vision goggles and pulled them down over his eyes. The entire empty expanse appeared in all its glory, as if it were bathed in a sickly greenish-gray light.

Hawley Textile Mill had been empty since the last serger was hauled out of the building in the nineties. There had been an attempt to renovate the property as a shopping mall, but a series of injuries, accidents, and overall bad luck plagued the construction crew until the investors withdrew. For almost twenty years now, the mill building had remained untouched.

"I'm not seeing anything on the infrared, Houston," Junior reported over the headset.

"Are you still on the fifth floor?"

"I'm just finishing my sweep."

"Where are you, Savannah?"

"Third floor."

"Anything on EMF?"

"Sure enough," she drawled, "if electrical wires get you all excited."

"We were warned the building still had juice to keep the security systems active."

"I know, sugar."

"If anyone's interested," Frank interrupted, "I'm currently on the second floor with the goggles. Not that it's important or anything. Maybe I'll just go stick my head in a bucket of water. Would you like me to go and stick my head in a bucket of water? God, I'm so depressed!"

Houston laughed at the *Hitchhiker's Guide to the Galaxy* reference. "Keep your head dry, Baba. You'll short out the headset if you get it wet. What have you got?"

"Nothing. Just checking in."

They'd all insisted on adopting ridiculous nicknames when they founded C-Troop Paranormal. Or more specifically, everyone but Frank had insisted on it. Frank thought it was lame. Savannah—Tamicka Jones—her nickname was pretty obvious. She wore her Savannah accent as a badge of honor. But Houston had never lived in Texas. His nickname came from manning the consoles for all the cameras and coordinating communications and data collection, as NASA's base in Houston did for the astronauts. Junior was fresh out of college—Frank's younger brother, Louis.

Houston had inflicted the name "Baba" on Frank, supposedly because he fussed over everybody too much. "Baba" was Russian for "old woman." Frank hated the name, but once Louis had gotten wind of it, there had been no escape.

"I'm on the fourth floor now," Junior announced. "I smell something."

"Did you fart?"

Junior snorted into the mic. "No, asshole. It smells like burning."

That was worrisome. The building had been inactive for almost two decades. The only thing Frank could think of that might smell like burning was faulty wiring. "Junior, are you sure you're smelling something burning? Maybe it's something else—cleaning chemicals or—"

"No, Baba. It definitely smells like… smoke. I don't think it's electrical…."

"Maybe it's an apparition," Houston suggested. "After all, there was a fire here in 1907."

Maybe. But Frank didn't like leaping to paranormal explanations when there might be something more mundane—and in this case, potentially more dangerous—causing it.

"Guys!" Junior exclaimed. "You should see this. The infrared's lit up like a Christmas tree!"

"What do you mean?"

"Everything is showing hot—*real* hot. All the walls, and the floor, and the sewing machines…. But I don't see anything when I look with the naked eye."

"Wait a minute," Frank said. "All the sewing machines were taken out in the nineties."

"That can't be right. I can see them right in front of me."

"Camera seven is pointed right at you, Junior," Houston interjected. "You're standing in the middle of a big ol' empty space."

"But I can *see* them."

"Child, what are you smoking down there?" Savannah asked.

"I've got the camera recording. You can see them for yourselves."

Frank was inclined to believe him. Junior had a good head on his shoulders, and a vision of something from the past was hardly unusual for the type of work they were doing. But Frank doubted anything would show up on the camera. Whatever Junior was seeing, he wasn't likely to be seeing it with his eyes—not directly.

"Hold on," he said. "I'm coming up there."

He strode across the empty expanse toward the stairwell at the back, but before he was halfway there, Savannah reported, "I'm in the stairwell, going down. I smell something too."

"What?" Houston asked.

"Junior's right. It smells like… something's burning. I could swear it's *smoky.*"

"You see smoke?"

"Well… I don't know. It just sort of… *feels* smoky."

Frank broke into a run. "Junior! You've got the infrared. Do you see any heat sources on that floor?"

No answer.

"Junior?"

Still no answer.

Houston said, "What are you doing, Junior?" A pause. "Junior!"

Frank heard a sound. It was incredibly faint, but he thought it might be a scream—a man's scream. Junior's scream. It wasn't coming over the headset but from somewhere high above him, muffled by distance and two floors. He ran harder and slammed through the door to the stairwell, smashing it against the wall.

Smoke. There *was* smoke in here. He could smell it too. "Goddamn it! What—"

He didn't get to finish the thought. A door slammed open high above him in the dark stairwell and Louis was screaming. Frantic footsteps stumbled down the metal stairs, and as if from a great distance, Savannah shouted, "Junior!"

Frank ran up the stairs as his brother's footsteps came clattering down toward him in the dark, dissolving into a cacophony of noise—the sound of a man falling down a flight of metal stairs amid shattering technical equipment. The agonizing scream ended abruptly as Louis's body crashed into the landing with a sickening thud. The fragments of his headset and camera rained down around him.

FRANK STAYED with Louis while they waited for the ambulance, clutching his hand to reassure himself that Louis had a pulse. He had no idea how to assess his brother's injuries. He could tell he was still breathing—that was it. Otherwise he was unresponsive. He was bleeding and it looked as if his leg might be broken, judging from the sickening way it twisted underneath him.

Please, God, don't let his back be broken....

Savannah turned on the lights in the stairwell and came to sit with him while Houston made the 911 call. He kept checking in with Frank while they waited for the ambulance.

"I don't smell it anymore," Savannah commented quietly, holding one of Junior's limp hands in both of hers.

Frank looked at her, uncomprehending. Then slowly it dawned on him. The smoke. He couldn't smell it either. Not a trace of it.

He tried to speak, found he couldn't, and then cleared his throat to try again. "His face looks burned." The side of it Frank could see was puffed up and red.

"He'll be all right, sugar. Just hang in there."

When the paramedics arrived with a stretcher, Frank and Savannah got out of their way. The only thing Frank could learn from them was that Louis didn't appear to have a broken back or neck, but he had several injuries to the head and body that were potentially life-threatening. And yes, his leg was broken.

Though he felt he was barely holding it together, Frank insisted on helping Houston and Savannah do a quick lock-up of the building while the ambulance took Louis to the Hawley Memorial Hospital. The team couldn't leave until everything was secure, and after what had happened to Junior—whatever *had* happened to him—Frank couldn't bring himself to leave anyone alone in the building. But as soon as that was done, they all piled into the company van and went straight to the hospital.

THEY SPENT the next three hours in the ER waiting room, hearing nothing about Louis's condition. Had Louis been conscious, Frank might have been allowed into the ER with him, since they were family. But with Louis unresponsive and possibly needing surgery on his leg, Frank had simply filled out reams of paperwork about Louis's medical and family history, praying he hadn't forgotten about any allergies to medications, and then been told to wait.

"I don't know what happened," Houston said, keeping his voice low. There was an old woman napping in a chair by the television set. "He was waving his hand in the air in front of him, like he was trying to touch whatever he thought he was seeing. Then he started freaking out—waving his arms around, hitting himself, and staggering back. He ran through the door to the stairwell."

"I know," Frank said. They'd been over it a million times. The camera equipment was packed into the back of the van, too difficult to reach without unpacking everything in the hospital parking lot. They'd have to review it later. But the three of them were all roughly on the same page. It appeared Louis had seen a vision of the fire—perhaps he'd felt he was *in* the fire. The way Houston described it, Louis may have thought his clothes were on fire before he panicked and ran for the exit. Then it appeared he stumbled blindly down the stairs and fell.

The camera footage might tell them more, but Frank doubted it.

Junior, Frank thought, *you'd better come out of this. I want a full report, you little pipsqueak! No lying down on the job.*

He didn't know what he'd do, if…. No. He refused to think about that. Louis would be fine. He had to be. He was the only family Frank had.

Around two in the morning, Savannah put a gentle hand on his arm to pull his attention away from an insipid miracle sponge infomercial. The doctor was approaching.

"Are you Frank?" the woman asked, smiling and extending a hand.

Frank shook it. "That's me. I'm Junior's—Louis's—older brother."

"I'm Dr. Khambatta. First, let me tell you your brother is doing well. He hasn't yet regained consciousness, but his condition is stable."

"Can I see him?"

Her smile turned wistful. "It's well past visiting hours, but I can take you back for a short time to see him. Your friends may see him during visiting hours tomorrow."

"Do you think he'll be all right?"

"Yes, I do. He has a mild concussion, and we had to operate on his leg to reset the femur—it was broken in two places—but he should recover fully."

"What about the burns on his face?" Savannah asked.

Dr. Khambatta appeared confused. "Burns? No, there are no burns. His face is fine."

Chapter Two

"At seven o'clock the firebells rang
But oh, it was too late,
The flames they were fast spreading
And at a rapid rate."

"THE TOWER signifies a massive change." Toby held up the tarot card, which depicted a tower being struck by lightning and collapsing while screaming people tumbled from it to their deaths. "It could be for the worse. It could be for the better. But in any case, it's likely to be life-changing."

Mrs. Hawley pursed her lips primly. "I don't like the Tower. It's such an unpleasant-looking card with all those poor people falling to their deaths, don't you think? Change it to something else, please."

Toby gaped at her a moment, uncertain whether she meant it or not. Mrs. Hawley did own half the town of Hawley, which had grown up around the mill that made her grandfather enormously wealthy in the first half of the twentieth century. She was used to having her way. But not even the wealthiest patrons could command the fates to obey their whims.

He caught the twinkle of mischief in the old woman's eye and realized she was pulling his leg. That was more in line with the woman he knew. "I'll have a stern word with the deck later, Mrs. H."

She'd insisted upon him calling her that after their first session together. For all her money, she was very down-to-earth and approachable. Though Toby had been warned by other people in town not to cross her. She wasn't above throwing her weight around if she was angered.

The woman reached out to pluck the card from his hand. "Reminds one of a mill fire, doesn't it?" she asked, examining the picture closely, her forehead creased in concentration.

"Yes, it does." Toby knew the history of the mill as well as anyone in Hawley did. "But this doesn't represent the distant past. Its position in the reading indicates something in the present."

"Is last night close enough?"

"What do you mean?"

Mrs. H. set the card down on the table. "A young man fell down a flight of stairs in the mill last night. He wasn't killed, thank the stars, but he's currently in ICU. His condition is serious but stable."

"That's horrible! How did it happen? Did he break in?"

She fluttered her hand in the air. "No, no. He was there because I hired him. Well, technically I hired his brother's... agency. The two work together."

"Doing what?"

"Well...." Mrs. H. glanced around as if to be certain they wouldn't be overheard. They were alone, of course—Toby had renovated the closet of his store specifically to provide an isolated, private space for readings. "I hired them to investigate for signs of spiritual activity in the mill."

Toby repressed a snicker. "They're ghost hunters?"

"Not the ones on television! The *last* thing I need is to have their investigation broadcast for the entire world to see. They call themselves 'paranormal investigators,' and they've promised to be discreet. I was hoping they'd conclude there was nothing there so we could release a report and quell the rumors. I need to sell that accursed building! Or renovate it as a shopping mall. It's been empty—and costing me money in property taxes—for far too long."

It wasn't that Toby didn't believe in ghosts. On the contrary, he frequently communed with the dead for his clients. But ever since the—admittedly entertaining—show *Ghost Hunters* took off, everybody who could afford to buy an EMF meter was out there claiming to be an expert. Now it appeared to have gotten someone seriously injured. "Is he going to be okay?"

"Louis? I'm afraid nobody knows for certain. I'm paying for any medical expenses not covered by their insurance, of course, and I'm allowing them to take as much time off from the investigation as they need—I'm not *entirely* without compassion, regardless of what the gossips in town may say." That glimmer of humor returned to her eyes. "But they want to cancel the contract!"

"I can't say I'm surprised, under the circumstances."

"I can't have that! I need the investigation completed so appropriate steps can be taken."

Toby doubted the wisdom of what he was about to say but decided a psychic needed to tell the truth, regardless of whether clients wanted to hear it. And that included advice. "Mrs. H.... there is always the possibility their investigation won't get the results you're hoping for. If the mill building *does* turn out to be haunted, what will you do then?"

"That's another problem with these investigators," she replied with a sniff. "They simply diagnose. They don't *cure*. They're so wrapped up in their scientific toys—meters and field readers and what-not—but there are no scientific methods for getting *rid* of spirits if they're found, are there? Of course not! That's where I was hoping you could help me."

Toby's eyes went wide and he straightened in his chair. "Me?"

"Yes, of course, dear," Mrs. H. told him sensibly. "You don't think I really came to get a reading, did you? I already know I'm a filthy rich bitch who always gets her way. I don't need the cards to tell me that."

Toby stared blankly at her a moment, until she went on without him.

"I was hoping to engage your services as a medium," she said. "Once his team succeeds in *finding* whatever spirits might be haunting Hawley mill, Frank— they all have silly nicknames I wouldn't be caught dead using—needs someone who can persuade them to *leave*."

Toby found his voice at last. "And you think that should be me?"

"Absolutely! Who in town is better qualified to commune with spirits?"

He would be able to talk to the spirits, if anyone could. Of that Toby had no doubt. Spirits had been visiting him since he was a child. But most were friendly. "I'm honored that you would consider me, Mrs. H., but was it the spirits who injured this poor man last night?"

Mrs. H. tapped her bottom lip with one beautifully manicured index finger. "I'm uncertain of that. Louis—that's the younger brother—apparently panicked and threw himself into the stairwell. Frank believes something in the mill convinced him he was on fire. So I suppose you could say, if it was a spirit, it caused Louis to injure himself."

"That's often the way spirits cause harm—by affecting our perceptions. Most aren't powerful enough to affect the physical world directly. Though poltergeists—"

"There!" Mrs. H. exclaimed, clapping her hands together in delight. "You see? I knew you would be the best man for the job! Please say you'll do it. I'll pay you handsomely, of course."

Toby's small New Age shop barely scraped by, selling books and herbs and the occasional psychic reading. Even Mrs. H.'s weekly patronage, while appreciated, didn't help much financially. Toby charged her the same rate as all his other clients, regardless of her wealth. This was the first time she'd tossed him a bone.

"How does…. Frank? How does he feel about me joining his team?"

"I'll have a word with him." Mrs. H. gathered up her purse and stood. Apparently the reading was over. "Truthfully, he might not be in favor of it. These scientific-types would rather depend upon electromagnetic readouts or whatever they call it. They're suspicious of old-fashioned mediums. And honestly, who can blame them with all the frauds out there today? But I trust you, dear. And so will Frank and his team, once they get to know you."

Toby wished he had her confidence. He moved to open the door for her and then escorted her through his shop to the front door. The place was empty, apart from the young woman attending the front counter.

This was moving awfully fast for Toby. He would have liked more time to think about it. But if he'd learned anything about Mrs. H. in her weekly visits, it was that she never hesitated once she'd made up her mind.

"If they agree to let me join them," he said, holding the door open for her, "I suppose I'm willing to do what I can."

"Wonderful! I'll call you later with the details."

And then she was gone, leaving Toby with the feeling he'd been fast-talked into something he might regret. He noticed Cassandra watching him from the counter. She was a tiny young woman—still in college, studying art—dressed all in black with heavy black makeup around her eyes. Even her fingernails were black. The only color she displayed was her bright red hair, wreathing her head in tight ringlets.

"Has anybody come in?" Toby asked, more for conversation than anything else. He knew what the answer would be.

"Nope. We did get a shipment of dried herbs. I already put them in their bottles."

"Great. Thanks."

Then, because he couldn't stand to leave a reading unfinished, Toby went back to the reading room. He drew the final card and placed it on the table in the position signifying the future. Then he frowned at it. Given the context of the reading and the discussion he'd just had with Mrs. H., it might not be a particularly fortuitous card—not for a woman whose family business had once been responsible for the deaths of ninety-seven mill workers, almost all young women.

It was Justice.

Chapter Three

"They were men and women there
And children too, I'm told,
Who might have been saved from out of the flames
If the truth was only known."

FRANK DIDN'T like psychics. He understood what he did was the same thing with different methods—communicating with spirits. But the field of parapsychology was attempting to gain credence in the scientific community using instruments to gather data and evaluate the evidence rationally. Every time he saw a television psychic tricking an audience member into giving him information to regurgitate back as "a message from beyond," Frank envisioned respect for his field going farther and farther down the toilet.

So he was less than thrilled when Celia Hawley called his cell phone to inform him she was sending over her personal psychic to assist with the investigation of the mill. He'd already told her he wanted to back off the investigation. One near casualty was more than enough for him. Junior still hadn't regained consciousness. Frank hadn't gone into parapsychology to get his brother or anyone else killed. But the woman was impossible! She told him what she wanted done and expected him to do it. No arguments. It was like arguing with his mother.

And that was how he found himself back at the Hawley Mill building on Tuesday morning with his crew—minus Junior. Dr. Khambatta had assured him Junior's leg was doing as well as could be expected, and the concussion.... Well, that could take anywhere from a week to three months to heal. But the MRI had found no signs of brain damage. Why he hadn't yet regained consciousness was a mystery. In the meantime, Junior was being moved out of ICU that afternoon.

The building loomed over them as they unloaded the van in the parking lot, its dark windows ominous even on that sunny July morning. The windows on the lowest two floors had long ago been boarded up to keep out people looking to steal what little had been left behind or see for themselves whether the stories of ghosts were true.

"We could just bail," Houston suggested as he helped Frank lower one of the heavy equipment cases to the tarmac. "She may be rich, but she's not gonna hunt us down, is she? It's not like we've stolen anything of hers."

Houston was Junior's age—they'd been best friends and roommates in college. His hallmark way of dressing—one Frank kept after him about, since it was unprofessional—was a pair of low-hanging jeans that revealed about two inches of his boxers and a baseball cap that never seemed to face front. He was full of attitude, but underneath that he was loyal and passionate about the team and what they were doing. It was hard not to feel protective of him, the same way Frank felt protective of Junior.

"You don't have to do this, Houston. Neither does Savannah. I'm going back in there because Mrs. Hawley said she'd help with Junior's medical expenses, and... well, the job just isn't done. But that doesn't mean I want anyone else hurt over it."

Houston snorted and punched Frank lightly in the upper arm. "Fuck that! We're a team."

"That's right," Savannah interjected from inside the van. "You don't seriously think we'd let you go back in there alone, do you?"

She was older—closer to Frank's age. Unlike the boys, who'd started tagging along with Frank on his investigations before he'd gone professional, Savannah hadn't fallen into his lap. She'd been working with another group down in Georgia and already knew her way around EMF readers and thermal imagers. She specialized in researching the histories of locations, which could be challenging for someone like Frank, who didn't know his way around town property records. He'd met her through an old army buddy, and it had taken a year of wooing and salary negotiations to convince her to come work for him.

"I won't be alone," Frank replied. "Not technically. Though God knows what good this so-called psychic will do me."

Houston laughed. "Maybe you can trip him when the monster is chasing you to buy yourself some time."

"Houston!" Savannah scolded. "There's no need to be mean-spirited. And don't think I didn't see you smirking, Baba."

"Who, me?"

Savannah raised a hand to hush both of them as a small dark blue Honda Civic pulled into the parking lot. The car looked as if it were on its last gasp, dented in places and sporting patches of Bondo. It parked near them and the driver climbed out.

He was beautiful. Frank supposed some might call him handsome, since he wasn't particularly feminine, but there was a softness to his features that made Frank think of silk sheets and languorous caresses. He was probably in his late twenties, with a head of wild, dark brown curls and a thin mustache and beard—not wispy, like a teenager struggling to grow his first facial hair, but he would probably never have a heavy beard. It softened an otherwise angular jawline and chin and emphasized his full lips. Most striking were his eyes, when he removed his sunglasses. They weren't brown as Frank had expected from his coloring, but a warm, emerald green.

This had to be the psychic. He confirmed it by looking directly at Frank and saying, "I'm Toby Reese. Mrs. Hawley said she'd tell you to expect me."

"*Ordered* is more like," Houston muttered as he pulled another crate out of the van.

Savannah glared at him, but Reese quirked up a corner of his mouth and said, "Yeah, she's kinda used to getting her way."

Frank stepped forward, offering his hand. "Frank Carter. They call me Baba. And this is Savannah. The kid with no manners is Houston."

FRANK CARTER was ex-military. Toby knew that from the briefing Mrs. H. had given him over the phone last night. It was obvious from his swagger—he had to be either military or police. What she'd neglected to mention was that he was gorgeous. Muscular and broad-shouldered, he had a slightly freckled complexion and short strawberry blond hair—though not a crewcut. It was just long enough to be sticking up in all directions, as if he'd crawled out of bed that morning and couldn't find a comb. It was adorable and an odd contrast to the neatly trimmed beard he sported. When he shook hands, he regarded Toby with wide, baby blue eyes.

Toby attempted to shake hands with the others. Savannah accepted his hand graciously, but Houston chose to act like a punk and pretend he hadn't noticed Toby's hand hanging pathetically in the air. The older members of the team frowned and exchanged glances, but nobody said anything.

Toby withdrew his hand and asked, "Do you need help unloading?"

"Nope," Houston said.

Frank overrode him. "Sure. You want to climb in the van and get the other end of this crate?"

"I'll get it!"

"You deal with the case you've got in your hands, Houston. Let Toby help me with this one."

Houston shot Toby a hostile look but did as he was told.

Oh boy. This is going to be fun.

When they'd unloaded everything and locked the van, Toby helped the team carry the equipment into the foyer of the mill building. Though he'd lived in this town for most of his life, driven past the sinister, abandoned building nearly every day, and even snuck peeks in the windows when he was a kid, he'd never actually been inside.

It was disquieting, even in daylight. From the empty foyer, he could see an enormous room opening up to the north, dark apart from slanting shafts of light coming in between the boards on the windows, and nearly empty. There were chairs strewn about and piles of debris nobody had thought worth salvaging when the mill shuttered its doors. The far wall was lost in darkness.

Worse than the way the mill appeared to Toby's physical senses was the way it *felt*. Even if he hadn't known the building's history, there was a sickness in the place. Toby had never experienced such a powerful sense of dread. It seemed to envelop him and settle into his body like a virus, making him queasy and disoriented. He gripped the wall to prevent himself from falling over.

"Are you okay?" Frank asked.

"This place… it's affecting me."

"Do you need to sit down?"

"Maybe you should go home," the punk muttered as he placed a large flat-screen monitor on what must have once been the receptionist's desk.

"Houston!" Frank snapped. "Just do your job, please?"

Toby was dimly aware Frank had him by the elbow. He waved the man off. "Thanks. I'll be all right. I just need to put my wards up."

He breathed deeply a few times to calm himself, then envisioned a beam of white light coming down from the sky and up from the earth, meeting in the center of his chest to form a glowing ball of pure energy. With each breath, he felt the ball expanding, pushing the darkness out of his body and beyond, until the oppressive sick feeling faded. In his mind's eye, he saw himself standing in the center of a protective sphere of clean, pure white energy that pushed the darkness of Hawley Mill away from him, keeping him safe.

When he opened his eyes, he found all three of the team members looking at him as if he'd just farted.

"Oookaaay…." Houston said, shaking his head in disbelief and turning back to the monitor.

"I'll get the extension cords," Savannah said. She seemed to be avoiding looking at Toby as she went outside.

Toby frowned at the sour expression on Frank's face. "I'm fine. I just needed to ground myself."

"What exactly do you intend to do here, Mr. Reese?"

"Toby," Toby insisted. "And Mrs. H. hired me to talk to any spirits your investigation turns up."

"What good will that do?"

"If I can establish communication, I might be able to persuade them to move on."

Frank made a low noise in his throat that sounded a bit like a growl. "Do you intend to 'communicate'"—he said the word as if it were something he found disgusting—"during our investigation?"

"No. I expect I'll just help lug things around and whatever else you tell me to do." He added, to make it clear, "Besides getting lost. She's not paying me to sit in the car outside all night."

Frank regarded him thoughtfully for a long, uncomfortable moment. Then he said, "I think we need to have a little chat—alone."

Chapter Four

"But oh, the villains that locked the doors
And told them to keep still,
It was the bosses and overseers
That burning Hawley Mill."

"WAIT HERE a sec."

Frank went out to the van to retrieve the small case containing the team's EMF readers. He might as well take one with him, if he was going through the building. He left the case in a corner of the foyer, grabbed one of the readers for himself, and then told Toby, "Follow me."

They entered the factory floor from the foyer entrance, and Frank led the way into the dark, ruined landscape. The light wasn't so dim he couldn't see his surroundings, but he was grateful for the button on the EMF reader that lit up the display.

"Have you been in the building before?" he asked.

"Never. I've only seen it from the outside."

"I assume you know about the fire?"

"Of course," Toby replied. "Everyone who lives in Hawley more than a few years hears about the fire, eventually. It's our... communal heritage, I suppose."

Frank and his team lived in Portsmouth, so they'd never heard the story before accepting the job. The mill had employed almost two-hundred-and-fifty people in 1907, almost all young women in their late teens or early twenties. Ninety-seven of those workers perished in the fire. There had only been two ways out of the building at the time, and the back exit had been locked for some reason—perhaps to prevent workers from sneaking out on unauthorized smoking breaks or union organizers from sneaking in. Most of those who exited through the front door made it out alive, but those who went down the back stairwell had been trapped.

The cause of the fire was still unknown.

"Savannah dug into the history of the mill before we came out here," he said, casually noting the EMF level on the factory floor as they strode across it. It was fluctuating a bit, but very low. It never rose above one milligauss. "There were some reports of workers sensing an angry presence after the damage was repaired and the building became operative again—about three years after the fire. But nobody took it seriously. Who works in a building where almost a hundred people died and doesn't feel creeped out by it, now and then?"

Toby snorted, but he didn't say anything, so Frank continued.

"Then when the mill shut down in the late nineteen-eighties, things heated up. It was as if the building no longer wanted people in it—or so the construction workers claimed."

"Maybe the spirits were disturbed when everything changed."

Frank stopped walking. Toby took a few steps without him, then noticed he was alone and turned to look back.

"What?"

"Houston is being kind of rude to you," Frank said. "I'm sorry about that. He's taking what happened to Junior hard—they've been best friends for a long time. But you should know he picked up a lot of that attitude about psychics from me. I don't really like... spiritualists."

Toby grinned at him, displaying some of the most perfect white teeth Frank had ever seen. "That's okay. I don't like parapsychologists much."

"Why not?"

"You first."

Frank had to smile at that. "Okay. Well... we can start with a very long history of fraud by people claiming to have the ability to communicate with the dead."

"Granted. The only response I can offer is that I am not a fake."

"So you say."

"Yes."

Frank continued walking toward the far end of the room, and Toby fell into step beside him. "So if you go into a room and get a sense of, say, a malevolent entity watching you, how can you prove it isn't your imagination?"

"Only by receiving information from it that can later be verified," Toby admitted.

"Exactly! But so often it's information you could easily have gotten from a little research, or people who knew the spirit when it was a living person. I have yet to see a psychic produce something that could only have come from a spirit—something verifiable, that is. What things are like in the afterworld doesn't count."

Toby laughed. "You have high standards! Something I couldn't have learned from books or talking to people, but can later be verified by reading books or talking to people? How is *that* supposed to work?"

He had Frank there. It would be nearly impossible. "What if it was something like the location of an heirloom nobody could find?"

"That's very precise. Would you accept that as verification of psychic ability?"

Frank shrugged. "Maybe."

"Then I'll do my best."

He was being condescending, which was irritating. But Frank had initiated this conversation—Toby hadn't asked for a professional critique—so he couldn't really blame the guy. "All right. But fair's fair. What's your beef with parapsychologists?"

"My 'beef' is mostly with the ghost-hunting variety of parapsychologist," Toby said with an annoying smirk.

Frank refused to take the bait. He raised his eyebrows as if to say, "And?"

"What you're doing is searching for physical anomalies," Toby went on. "Take that device in your hand—"

"It reads electromagnetic fields."

"Yes. So let's say you find a spot with a high EMF reading, and you're able to verify the spike isn't being caused by wires in the walls or a fuse box or anything like that. Why do you then conclude the EMF spike was caused by something paranormal?"

"I don't, necessarily," Frank protested. "But one theory is that EMF spikes are caused by the presence of spiritual entities—"

"Why? Where did that theory come from?"

"From reports. People who claim to have seen ghosts often report electrical disturbances accompanying the experience—lights flickering, batteries being drained, electrical devices turning on or off by themselves...."

Toby laughed again. "Anecdotal reports? From laymen? How can you base a scientific theory on those?"

"You have to start somewhere."

"So some people say they see ghosts while electrical anomalies are occurring near them, and you conclude electrical anomalies equal ghosts? What if electrical anomalies make people *think* they see ghosts?"

"It's a possibility," Frank admitted. "One theory is that the feelings of dread people often associate with a particular room or location might be caused by proximity to electrical transformers."

"So when your EMF reader finds an unexplained electromagnetic anomaly, it's possible there's no spirit presence at all—just some kind of natural, but unexplained, fluctuation in the electromagnetic field that could *cause* people to think they're seeing or feeling a ghost. In other words, you don't know whether you're finding the *result* of a haunting or the *cause* of a haunting."

Frank frowned at him. *Wiseass.* Though to be fair, he was more annoyed that Toby was better at this game than he was. "I'm beginning to think you're a plant."

"A skeptic sent here undercover as a 'psychic' so I can sabotage your investigation?" Toby didn't seem at all bothered by the insinuation.

"Maybe."

Toby spread his hands in a gesture of peace. "I'm not. You'll just have to trust me and Mrs. H. on that. But are we done calling each other frauds now? It's getting old."

"Agreed."

FRANK GAVE Toby a tour of the entire building, pointing out locations where people had reported seeing or hearing things in the past. Toby suspected the tour was as much to get him out of the way while Houston and Savannah set up the team's equipment as anything else. That was fine with him. He needed to get a feel for the building, in any event. And although he would never admit it to Frank, he was glad not to be wandering these cavernous rooms by himself. Up above the second floor, the windows weren't boarded up—except for some individual panes that had been replaced by wood after local kids used them for target practice—so there was more light. But it only helped a bit. There was something bleak and desolate about the mill. It wasn't merely the years of emptiness and neglect. Despite the wards he'd put up, Toby could still sense something foul in the building. There was something *wrong* there, something sick. It permeated the brick walls, the iron fixtures, the massive wooden crossbeams.

He didn't feel inclined to comment on his feeling about the place as they walked. He knew Frank's low opinion of psychics now, so there was no point in inviting his disdain.

The elevator—a rickety-looking thing with tarnished brass fixtures and a metal safety gate instead of a proper door—made him extremely uncomfortable. It felt almost as if it were angry at him. Fortunately he wasn't forced to step inside it. The electricity had been cut from all but the security systems. The elevator wasn't going anywhere, so they had no choice but to take the stairs.

On the fifth floor, Frank took him to one of the windows, a massive thing taller than a man with several glass panes set in an iron framework. On the other side of it was the fire escape. "So many people tried to climb down the fire escape," Frank told him, "it collapsed under their weight. It took out the fire escape just below it as it plunged to the ground."

"Jesus...."

"When the flames got too hot up here, workers just started leaping out to their deaths. I guess they thought it would be quicker than burning. Also, that way their families could identify their bodies for proper burials."

Toby made a face. "Ugh! That's okay. I don't need all the gory details."

"Sorry. But I wanted to point out that workers claimed to have heard the sound of the fire escape collapsing when they've been up here, along with the screams of young women. One man said the whole building felt as if it was shaking."

They visited the basement last, apparently because Frank thought it was the least interesting part of the building. It was dark enough down there to make Frank pull out his pocket Maglite to light their way. "Nothing's ever been reported down here," he said. "And our scanners haven't detected anything unusual."

But Toby sensed something *very* unusual. As they approached the mammoth furnace and boiler used to heat the mill—now stone cold and empty—he felt a wave of fear wash over him. He reached out to steady himself and take some deep breaths. After a moment he realized he'd grabbed Frank's forearm. The man hadn't shaken his hand off or glared at him. He was just watching Toby calmly.

"Sorry," Toby said, yanking his hand away.

"No problem. Are you… having another… attack or whatever happened in the foyer?"

Toby took another breath and wiped his palms against his shirt. They were damp with sweat. "I guess you could call it that. There's something here—something about this furnace. It was strong enough to break through my wards."

"Something like what?"

"Fear." Toby stepped forward, extending his hand out to touch the metal side of the furnace. But to his surprise, the contact didn't produce any strong sensations on a psychic level. "Something's weird, though. Is this the original furnace?"

It was the size of a small car and made of metal, but it seemed oddly modern. Toby would have thought a furnace from the early nineteen-hundreds might be coal-burning—not that he was an expert on that subject—but this appeared to be powered by propane.

"It isn't," Frank replied. He waved the EMF reader in the air around the furnace, pressing the button to illuminate the display. "The original had to be replaced after the fire. It's possible the cause of the fire was the furnace exploding or burning out of control. Nobody really knows. But the first floor above this part of the basement collapsed. Everything had to be replaced. The furnace you're touching is an even newer model put in place after the Second World War."

"Do you get a reading?"

Frank shook his head. "A bit higher, thanks to the metal, but not really significant."

"Something happened here."

"Like what?"

"I don't know. But I get a stronger sense of fear in this spot than anywhere else in the building."

Frank sounded a bit impatient when he said, "Savannah hasn't come up with anything about the basement. Nobody's known to have died down here, and none of the workers reported any phenomena here in the past."

"I'm telling you, something happened here," Toby insisted.

Frank shrugged, his expression noncommittal. "If you say so. Our equipment hasn't picked up anything. That's all I'm saying."

Chapter Five

"The first scene was a touching one
From a maid so young in years,
She was standing by a window and
Her eyes were filled with tears."

"HE'S A nutjob," Houston said for about the tenth time. "That's all there is to it."

He and Frank were standing in line at the Taco Bell down the road from the mill building, waiting for the food they'd ordered for themselves, Savannah, and Toby. Frank needed to check that the twenty-four-hour 7-Eleven nearby had a public restroom. There were no working facilities in the mill building, and this stuff tended to go right through him.

"Yeah, well… a lot of people think *we're* nutjobs."

"True," Houston said.

The team members had retreated to their hotel rooms for some naptime during the afternoon, and Toby had hopefully taken a nap at his home, wherever that was. It was going to be a long night.

"Just give the guy a chance," Frank said. "I don't think he's any happier about being shoved into the middle of our investigation than we are, but Mrs. Hawley is paying the bills. He doesn't seem so bad, really. He let you drive his car, didn't he?"

Toby had been more than generous about letting Frank and Houston use his car to visit the hospital and make a food run. The van was needed at the mill, since it contained an assortment of tools that might be necessary.

Houston grunted but didn't bother answering. That was probably the best Frank was going to get out of him. The guy was barely holding it together with Junior in the hospital and still unconscious when they'd stopped by an hour earlier. If he hadn't known Houston was straight, Frank might have thought their relationship was closer than he'd realized. He'd never really been sure about Junior's sexuality. Frank hadn't seen him date anyone since graduating college, and even then Junior had never brought any girlfriends or boyfriends home on the holidays. But Houston had dated a lot of girls in the past. Never for long, and they'd all been too busy for much dating since they put the team together, but still….

No. They're just really close friends. A lot of guys their age have really intense relationships with their friends.

As they carried the bags full of burritos, quesadillas, and tacos to Toby's little Honda, Frank's cell phone rang. He juggled the bags a bit to free up a hand and answered it.

"Baba," Savannah said urgently, "you might want to get back here."

"Is something wrong?"

She took her time answering. "I don't know. Your boy's acting… strange."

My boy? "You mean Toby? What's he doing?"

"I… don't know. He went out onto the factory floor. I can see him on camera one. He's standing there motionless in the dark—he doesn't even have his flashlight on. I tried to raise him on the walkie-talkie, but he didn't respond."

"We'll be right there."

TOBY STOOD in the middle of the factory floor, far enough away from the foyer that the lights of the monitoring station seemed as tiny and far away as stars, and the noise of the gas-powered generator outside the front door was a distant purr. He knew Savannah was worried, but he was still where she could see him on one of the cameras, though he'd turned off the walkie-talkie she'd loaned him.

He needed some time alone in the heart of the building before the team started wandering through and deliberately disturbing things. According to Savannah, part of their methodology was to shout things out—questions and insults—in an attempt to elicit a response. Toby supposed that made sense, if the goal was to document activity. They wanted to stir things up a bit, try to get something on camera.

But that wasn't *his* goal. He could already feel a presence in the mill. Angering that presence was the last thing he wanted to do. Mrs. H. had hired him to establish communication with it, and if possible, convince it to move on.

He wasn't afraid, though he could sense the terror and rage etched into the stone walls over a century ago. If the spirits here had any power at all, electric lights or even Frank and his team wouldn't protect him from them. The only thing Toby could count on were his wards. But he could feel them fluctuating as the pervasive darkness attempted to get at the tiny, frail human in its midst. In the back of his mind, it growled in frustration, low and ominous, like the sound of metal scraping brick.

This was what had gotten to Junior and to so many others over the decades. As he strained to listen, Toby heard the faint clattering of machines… of sewing machines. Not like the small one he had at home, but heavy iron things bolted to the floors, operated by broad foot pedals rocking back and forth, back and forth—

THE MILL | 25

hundreds of them churning out a chaotic symphony of pedals and pulleys and metal gears....

ChChChChChCh—

The sound came to him as if from far away... or long ago. It was elusive, like a half-forgotten memory he was struggling to recall.

ChaChaChaChaChaCha—

As if it were growing closer, the sound became more insistent. Toby closed his eyes and spread his hands wide like the branches of an old television antenna. The sound grew louder, more distinct. But it brought something dark and sinister with it—a malignant hitchhiker, writhing in the dark like an octopus in a cloud of black ink.

ChakChakChakChakChakChakChak—

Toby's wards began to crack like eggshells. He felt fear as the thing enveloped him, penetrating the depths of his mind with tentacles of smoke. He smelled burning—wood, hot iron, burning hair and clothes and flesh....

DjakDjakDjakDjakDjakDjakDjakDjak....

SAVANNAH WAS losing it when Frank and Houston hurried into the foyer. She was searching frantically though the equipment crates, but she abandoned that the moment she saw him. "Goddamn it, Baba!" she exclaimed, startling him with a rare use of foul language. "He turned off his flashlight! I can see him on camera one, but I can't go after him without night-vision goggles or a flashlight or... *something!*"

Frank held a hand up in an attempt to calm her. "What's going on?"

"Last I saw the goggles," Houston interjected, "they were still in the van, unless one of you guys moved them."

"Listen!"

Savannah reached over to one of the amplifiers and turned the volume up. That particular control was connected to the microphone near camera one, and it was extremely sensitive, so it could pick up even quiet noises within about a fifty-foot radius of the camera. The sound that came out of the speaker was quiet but distinctly human. It sounded like Toby, muttering under his breath. But it was disturbingly monotone and repetitive—and fast, like some kind of machine.

"DjakDjakDjakDjakDjakDjakDjakDjak...."

It went on and on without ceasing.

"What the fuck is he doing?" Houston asked.

"I don't know. He was quiet for a long time. Then he started making that noise."

"There was a Special Ed kid in my high school who used to go into these weird fits—"

"You two stay here," Frank interrupted. "I've got a flashlight. I'll go see if he's okay." Somehow he didn't think Toby would be making a noise like that if he was fine. Not unless it was some kind of meditation chant or something. It didn't sound particularly soothing, though. Toby was repeating the... word... in a rapid, agitated voice.

Frank walked out onto the factory floor, his flashlight illuminating a small circle of the foot-worn oak floor. Having a light with him did little to relieve the oppressive gloom of the place. It merely made everything outside the circle of light seem darker.

Toby hadn't moved. He stood with both hands splayed out, as still as a statue, and as Frank approached, the sound of his muttered chant grew louder.

"Toby?"

Toby's body remained motionless, but his head slowly turned as if to look at Frank over his shoulder. But his eyes were half closed, only the whites visible. "DjakDjakDjakDjakDjakDjakDjakDjak...."

"What are you doing, Toby? It's kind of weirding us out."

Toby's face contorted in anger, and he spoke more slowly, clipping the word until Frank could clearly make it out. "Jack.... Jack.... Jack.... Jack...."

"Who's Jack?"

"*Jaaaaaaaaaaaa....*" Toby shouted, the name dissolving into a scream.

Frank took a step back, uncertain how he should respond. Before he could make a decision, Toby threw his arms over his head and collapsed hard on his knees. He was silent for a few moments except for his ragged breathing. Then he took several long, tremulous breaths and toppled to the floor.

Frank rushed to his side, terrified Toby might be dead. His skin was cold and clammy to Frank's touch, though he was breathing faintly. But he was unconscious.

"What the hell are you guys doing here? This is the second time you've called us in a week!"

"We're doing what we were paid to do by the owner of the building."

"If there was another fall like that last one—"

"He didn't fall. He passed out or had a seizure or something."

"Guys! I think he's coming around. Toby? Can you hear me?"

Toby tried to answer, but he couldn't manage more than a thin rasp. He didn't recognize the voice of the woman talking to him. He heard Frank arguing with somebody—a man—but he didn't recognize the other voice. Somebody was touching him. He felt hands on his arms and upper chest. Something seemed to be strapped to his face....

"His pulse is stronger now. Can you open your eyes for me, Toby?"

It wasn't easy, but Toby managed to pry his lids open, even though they felt as if they were glued together. Judging by the heavy iron girders directly above him, he was still lying out on the factory floor. But somebody had placed a pillow under his head and another one under his legs. Everything was lit up, which seemed odd, considering the mill had no electricity.

A young woman moved into view over him. "Good! Now I'm going to shine a light in your eyes for just a second. Try to keep them open." She shined a penlight into each eye in turn, leaving spots in Toby's vision when she pulled it away. "Pupils dilating normally. Can you tell me what your name is?"

That seemed kind of silly. She'd just called him by name a minute ago. But he knew she was testing to see if he was lucid. He cleared his throat and was able to give her a muffled "Toby" from behind the oxygen mask—still—strapped over his mouth.

She held her hand in front of his face. "How many fingers?"

"Three."

This went on for a while, before Toby was able to convince her he was fully conscious. At last she removed the oxygen mask and allowed him to sit up. But she made him stay seated.

During this time, Toby heard Frank's phone ring and saw the man drift off out of the circle of light cast by four of the battery-powered high-intensity LED lanterns belonging to his team. He was gone for a few minutes while the EMTs continued to fuss over Toby. They tried to convince him to go to the hospital, but he was adamant in his refusal. He felt fine now. His knees hurt, but he could flex them. He had no desire to waste the rest of the night in the ER.

Frank returned and asked the EMT Toby had first seen upon opening his eyes, "Is it okay if I talk to him?"

"Go right ahead. He seems to be doing fine."

Frank squatted beside Toby and looked directly into his eyes. His reddish hair was sticking up in all directions, which was kind of cute, but his face looked haggard. "Do you remember what you were saying, just before you passed out?"

"I remember... a presence," Toby said slowly. "It felt like a man. I thought I could keep him out, but he was incredibly strong—boiling over with rage."

"What else do you remember?"

"Nothing."

"Do you remember a name?"

Toby concentrated. Gradually, something took shape in the back of his mind. "Jack," he said. "I think it was Jack."

"But you don't know who Jack is?"

"No."

"Nobody named Jack died in that fire. Savannah has a database she put together when she was researching it, and I had her check while the EMTs were tending to you. Only about twenty of the victims were men, and none of them was named Jack. There was a James. I suppose it's possible he was nicknamed Jack, but…."

Frank sighed and frowned, glancing down at the phone still in his hand. "Anyway, I might have brushed it off. You seemed kind of out of your mind while you were chanting. Maybe you were just hallucinating. Except Dr. Khambatta called me from the hospital. Louis—Junior—woke up about half an hour ago. But only briefly. He's unconscious again."

"I'm sorry to hear that."

Frank rubbed his chin with the back of his hand. "The point is… he said something when he woke up. Screamed it, really. It sounded like a name. He kept screaming it over and over again, until he passed out." He paused. "The name was Jack."

Chapter Six

"She cried, 'Oh, save me! Save me!'
She called her mother's name,
But her mother could not save her
And she fell back in the flame."

SAVANNAH HAD managed to find a list printed in the *Hawley Sentinel* of all who perished in the 1907 fire the day after the disaster, but not everyone who worked for the mill died. Some had escaped, and still others just hadn't been in the building at the time. But those names weren't a matter of public record.

Still, a company as large as Hawley Mills had to keep books. Federal regulations in 1907 were largely nonexistent—income taxes weren't in effect at the time, and there were few safety regulations—but the company itself would have tracked payroll. More than a hundred years later, those records might have been destroyed... if it hadn't been for William Ezra Hawley, Celia Hawley's grandfather, the man who built the factory. He'd been meticulous about the bookkeeping, and he'd kept all the records.

His son hadn't shared his obsession for storing everything, so he'd destroyed most of the older records. However, he'd been contacted by a man from Maine, Thomas Deacon, who had a fascination with the old New England industrial mills of the late nineteenth and early twentieth centuries. Thomas purchased many of the old records, particularly those around the time of the fire, which had been a memorable event in New England—memorable enough to have had a folk ballad written about it, in fact.

Celia had apparently been in contact with Mr. Deacon for a number of years, since he was always interested in gathering more information. She told Savannah he'd passed away in 1994. But he willed all of his papers, everything he'd collected over the decades, to the town library historical room where he'd lived.

It was because of this chain of events C-Troop Paranormal found themselves on a long-ass road trip to Boothbay Harbor, Maine—about three hours. Frank chose to ride with Toby, despite his concern Toby's car might fall apart en route, while Houston and Savannah took the van. Technically there was a third seat in the van—an extra one Houston had rigged up just behind the driver's seat—but it was uncomfortable and more than a little risky with all the team's equipment packed into the back.

"I apologize for not having a working radio," Toby said as they pulled onto Route 27.

The lack of air-conditioning was more of an inconvenience than the radio, but Frank merely rolled down his window and said, "That's not a problem. I don't really like listening to it, anyway."

"I didn't think so. I pictured you as more of an I-spy-with-my-little-eye kind of guy."

Frank gave him a sour look, but the smirk Toby was wearing made it obvious he was pulling Frank's leg. Frank snorted and settled back in his seat. It was going to be a long ride.

They'd already had a discussion about the stupidity of Toby wandering out onto the factory floor by himself in the dark. He'd surprised Frank by admitting he'd misjudged the danger, and then apologizing for what he put the team through. So... fine. No point in harping on it. At least it had produced an interesting lead.

Searching for something they could talk about, he settled on, "So what made you go into your line of work?"

"Running an occult bookstore and herb shop?"

"I guess I meant doing psychic readings," Frank amended.

"I don't know. I've always felt a connection to the spirit world, ever since I was a boy. We had an elderly neighbor who passed away. I was too young to fully grasp what death meant, at the time, and I was puzzled that everybody acted sad about it. Because I still visited with him in his garden every day."

Frank laughed. Then he quickly stopped himself, afraid he might have offended the guy. "Sorry."

But Toby didn't seem offended. He smiled and said, "A lot of people might say I was just fantasizing, the way a lot of kids do, but I'm convinced I was really talking to Mr. Paulsen. He was happy to be reunited with his wife. I'd never met her, since she died before I was born. And he said he just wanted to make sure his son and others who loved him would be all right, now that he'd left."

Frank wasn't sure that was convincing. Those were typical sentiments people always claimed to hear from the dead—things are good on the other side, people are reunited with loved ones, but they're concerned about those they left behind. Stock psychic mumbo-jumbo. He didn't feel Toby was trying to scam him, exactly. He liked the guy. He seemed okay, for the most part. But was he fooling himself about his ability to commune with the spirits? Maybe.

Except he got a name for us. One that could pan out.

They'd just have to wait and see on that, Frank supposed.

"What about you?" Toby asked. "What got you into ghost hunting?"

There was a note of humor in his voice that Frank found irritating. "I know what you're thinking," he said. "I watched one too many episodes of *Ghost Hunters* on television and thought, 'Gee willikers! I could do that!'"

Toby laughed. "Well… maybe."

"No. What really happened was Louis and I lost our mom to cancer when he was just five years old."

"I'm sorry."

The stricken look on Toby's face was almost funny. Frank waved a dismissive hand. "We were both devastated, of course, but Louis was falling apart, and I knew I had to be strong for him."

"You couldn't have been more than ten yourself."

"I was eleven." Frank shrugged. "Anyway, one of the ways I dealt with it was reading him ghost stories. Not scary ones, but cute ones about ghost families and children who are ghosts like *Ghosts Who Went to School*. It made him feel better to think about Mom becoming a friendly spirit who might be looking over us. As we got older, we started reading about real-life hauntings and poltergeists. It just kind of developed from there."

Toby gave him a quick smile before returning his attention to the road. "That's really sweet. You're always looking after everyone, aren't you? Not just Louis, but your whole team."

Frank was a bit embarrassed by that, so he just grunted noncommittally and glanced out the window at the passing greenery. Route 27 was just a two-lane road carved through the forest—paved but not exactly a highway. At this time of year, it was a nice drive.

"Normally," Mrs. Montgomery said, setting the heavy bound volume on the table with a *thud*, "we only allow one of these to be checked out at a time. But I suppose, since Celia Hawley called on your behalf…."

"It would help us a lot if we could each look through one," Savannah told her sweetly. "We've only booked into the B and B for one night."

The elderly librarian smiled and nodded. "I'll bring out the others."

It was boring work. Toby was used to keeping the books in his shop, but that was child's play compared to going through the seven bound volumes of paperwork from Hawley Mill. Most of it was handwritten, faded, and illegible, and it was only roughly ordered by date. No attempt had been made to separate payroll from receipts or shipping invoices.

Frank and Savannah dug into the task like the professionals Toby now considered them to be, but Houston quickly got on his nerves. He had the attention span of a gnat. His constant fidgeting and talking finally got so annoying, Frank snapped at him. "Houston! If you can't focus on what you're doing, find something else to occupy yourself."

Houston looked wounded. "Like what?"

"I don't know. I'm starting to get hungry." Frank looked at Toby and Savannah. "You guys want some food?"

"Sure."

"I guess so."

Frank pulled out his wallet and fished out a couple of twenties. He handed them to Houston. "Go find a McDonald's and get us each a cheeseburger meal or something. You're not vegetarian, are you?" The last was directed at Toby.

"No. Triple cheeseburger for me, Baba."

Houston looked offended by his use of Frank's nickname, but he merely gave Toby a sour look. He took Frank's and Savannah's orders and left.

"If looks could kill," Savannah muttered under her breath.

Toby smirked and shook his head. "So much for the slumber party I had planned tonight. I'd been counting on doing our hair and painting each other's toenails." When Houston had booked rooms at the Briarwood Bed and Breakfast, only three had been available. So he'd given Frank and Savannah their own rooms and booked himself and Toby into the room with two single beds.

"Aw."

Frank sighed. "I'm getting tired of his attitude. He can have my room tonight. I'll room with you."

"Okay."

"Unless you want the single."

"No," Toby said quickly. "I don't mind sharing a room with you." He was surprised at how pleased he was to learn Frank would be bunking with him. It might not be such a good thing, considering Frank was straight. He'd have to stay on his best behavior.

Mrs. Montgomery would have a fit if they ate McDonald's food in the historical room, so they'd all have to take a break when Houston returned. That meant they needed to focus while he was gone, so they stuck their noses back in the books. Fortunately, without Houston distracting them, things went much easier.

"I've got something!" Savannah exclaimed about a half hour later.

"An employee list?"

"No. But we're looking for a 'Jack,' aren't we?" She slid the book across the table to him. "Take a look at this."

It was a handwritten note, addressed to someone named Mr. Roberts and signed with an almost illegible signature. It might have said, "Stephen Latimer." But the text of the note was fairly easy to read.

Mr. Roberts,

We may have to do something about Miss Quinn. There are rumors around the floor that she's taken up with the new shift supervisor, Jack Bishop. Have a word with the man, please. If he and Miss Quinn have been sneaking off together, fire the girl. Mr. Hawley does not want his reputation tarnished by that sort of thing among his seamstresses.

Cordially,
Stephen Latimer

The note was dated just two days before the fire.

"Fire the girl, of course," Toby muttered. "No word about disciplining the boyfriend."

Savannah leaned across the table to flip the page. "Then there's this."

Mr. Latimer,

I've spoken with both Bishop and the young woman in question. She insisted that she is not involved with Bishop in any way. I have to say, I found her convincing. I shall leave the matter to your judgement. Please advise.

Cordially,
Henry Roberts

"That one's dated the morning of the fire," Frank observed. "Was that the end of it?"

"Apparently," Savannah said. "I don't see any more notes about it. And there was a Rosaleen Quinn on the list of those who died in the fire, so the poor girl wasn't dismissed—not that day. It's too bad. It would have saved her life. She was only eighteen."

Frank looked at Toby. "Does that name sound familiar? Jack Bishop?"

"I don't know," Toby replied. Truthfully, he didn't remember much about what had happened the evening the name "Jack" surfaced. "I could try to contact him. Or Rosaleen."

Frank shifted uncomfortably and glanced away. "If you think that'll work."

Chapter Seven

"The next scene was a horrible one
Just as it caught my eye.
They were leaping from a window
From up so very high."

THE BRIARWOOD B and B turned out to be very quaint. It had a common area downstairs that reminded Frank of his grandmother's house—lace doilies and antimacassars draped over all the chairs and couches and an absurd number of porcelain figurines taking up every available inch of shelf space. His grandmother had been partial to rabbits, but the owners of the Briarwood obsessed on seagulls, lobster traps, buoys, and an infinite variety of seashells. Beyond the living room, a breakfast area with three small tables looked out upon the harbor.

The owners, Mr. and Mrs. Libby, had a sixteen-year-old son—a thin, shy boy named Gale who spoke in a quiet mumble. He escorted the visitors upstairs to their rooms, dropping Houston and Savannah off on the second floor, then continuing up to the third floor with Frank and Toby in tow.

Houston had looked irritated when Frank informed him of the room change. It wasn't because he had any desire to room with Toby, Frank knew. But Houston had specifically given Frank the largest single room. Frank was the boss, and in Houston's eyes that made him the most important member of the team. He was very big on people respecting the boss, which Frank often found cute—not that he'd ever said that to Houston. But Toby had been hanging around with them for almost a week, and apart from taking a risk he shouldn't have, he'd been cooperative and friendly the entire time. Houston's automatic dislike of the guy was getting old.

Frank could have insisted Toby take the single room, but he knew that would *really* get Houston's goat. No need to stir things up that much. Frank had roomed with less pleasant guys in college, and it was just for one night. Hopefully Toby didn't snore.

The room was small, but not uncomfortably so. In the front, where the roof slanted down, two dormer windows looked out upon the bay. The beds were to the left of the door, one flush against the wall, and the other more or less in the middle of the room. In keeping with the general décor of the B and B, the beds had old-fashioned metal frames painted in white enamel, and were draped with white crochet bedspreads covered in rows of... whatever those raised patterns were called. Frank knew next to nothing about crochet. The patterns were diamond-shaped, if that meant anything.

"There's a bathroom across the hall," Gale said, almost inaudibly. "Just a toilet and sink. If you want to shower in the morning, you'll have to use the bathroom on the second floor. Mom doesn't like it if people run around in towels or their underwear, so make sure you're dressed when you go back and forth."

"Okay, we will. Thanks."

Gale backed out and closed the door, leaving Frank and Toby alone.

"Do you want the wall or the middle?" Toby asked cheerfully.

"Take your pick. I'll be fine with whatever."

Toby dropped his travel bag near the foot of the bed near the wall. He flopped down on the mattress, causing the frame to creak ominously. "Oops! Guess we'd better not get too athletic."

Frank had never seen a man blush before, but he did now, as Toby grasped the implications of what he'd just said. He gave Frank an embarrassed smile and then quickly looked away.

God, you are too cute.

Frank hadn't seen any indication Toby was gay, so he figured it was best not to let his thoughts stray in that direction. He set his bag down in the corner, out of the way. "So how do you plan on contacting Jack Bishop? Do you just go off and meditate like you did the other night?"

"That sometimes works," Toby answered. He shrugged. "Or sometimes I hold a more formal séance, if others are interested in participating."

Franked huffed out a laugh. "Jesus! Don't let Houston hear you say that. He'll flip."

"Why?"

Frank came over and sat down on his bed across from Toby. "The thing you might want to keep in mind is... we started this whole thing, C-Troop Paranormal, as a scientific endeavor. Yeah, I know some people would think that's funny, maybe even you—"

"No," Toby said sharply. "I know you take yourselves seriously, and you're trying to be scientific, even if I'm not convinced on the science."

Frank nodded. "Well, good. But your... methods... are different. I'll be honest. Before I met you, I wouldn't have wanted our group associated with a psychic."

"But you do now?"

Toby was looking at him with that wry expression he wore when he was yanking Frank's chain. But Frank didn't rise to the bait. He just smiled.

"Maybe. I guess I've taken a liking to you, at least."

"Thanks."

"But Houston hasn't."

"No shit."

"And talking about séances and channeling and shit like that.... It's just gonna make him nervous about where things are going with our group."

Toby raised his eyebrows and nodded slowly. "Okay. Good to know. What about you? Do those things make *you* nervous?"

You *make me nervous.* "I'm still trying to make my mind up on that subject."

"Fair enough."

Frank glanced around uncomfortably, not knowing where to take the conversation next, until his eyes settled on the alarm clock—a baby blue relic from the fifties with hands coated in a yellow-green paint he hoped was phosphorous instead of radium. Just past nine thirty.

They'd stayed at the library for another hour or so, hoping to find more information, and then wandered along the wharf for a while. Frank's grandparents had lived in York, so being near the ocean didn't seem like a big deal to him. But Savannah had never seen the area. She'd dragged the boys to every silly bric-a-brac store she could find—not to shop, thankfully, but just to do the tourist thing. She'd finally insisted they stop at a place that sold lobster, because she'd never tried it. And wasn't that what tourists were supposed to do in Maine? Eat lobster?

Frank hated lobster. But he indulged her.

"I think I might turn in," he said. "All that running around wore me out."

NO! DON'T! Stop it! Stop it! Stop it!

Help me!

I can't breathe! I can't breathe! Oh God!

"Help me!"

"Toby! What is it?"

He thrashed about, his arms caught in the bedsheets, until strong hands gripped his shoulders. But that just made him panic more. He punched at the blankets and kicked his legs, trying to free himself. "No!"

The hands released him. "Toby! It's just me—Frank. I won't hurt you."

"Help me," he sobbed.

"It's okay. You're safe. I'm gonna turn on the light."

The room lit up with a click from the small table lamp between the beds.

Even as he became aware of the room, Frank, where he was, Toby couldn't stop sobbing. He finally freed his hands and brought them up to cover his face.

He felt the mattress sink as Frank sat on the bed beside him. "Are you okay?"

Toby tried to answer, but he couldn't. His entire body was trembling. He'd never been so frightened, so lost.

Frank touched his shoulder again, tentatively. When Toby didn't resist, Frank gathered him into his arms and held him tight against his broad chest. He was bare-chested and the warmth of his skin was soothing. He smelled good, a combination of the musky scent of his skin, Old Spice, and the fresh smell of sea air he'd picked up on their walk that day. Toby lowered his hands and instinctively pressed his face into the comfort of Frank's embrace.

"Did you have a nightmare?" Frank asked.

He finally found his voice, saying weakly. "More than that."

"Do you want to talk about it?"

"Tomorrow." Toby felt exhausted. His body wanted to drift off again, yet he was afraid to give in to the weariness—afraid of what might be waiting for him in the darkness.

To his surprise, Frank lifted a hand to stroke his hair. "Can you go back to sleep?"

"Don't leave me." He sounded so pathetic. But he felt so vulnerable right now, he hadn't been able to stop himself.

Frank said, "How about if we just lie down for a bit?"

He shifted his body around so he could lie back against Toby's pillow. Toby was embarrassed to hear himself whimper as Frank moved him, but the man didn't release him from his arms. He adjusted their positions until they were lying side by side with Toby nestled against him, his face pressed snugly against Frank's warm side and Frank's arm draped protectively around his back.

"Do you mind if I get under the covers?" Frank asked quietly. He sounded embarrassed. "It's kind of chilly."

"No."

Frank arched his back to lift the blankets out from under him. A moment later he was in the bed, his hip against Toby's crotch, and Toby finally registered they were both in their underwear. No wonder Frank had been self-conscious. Toby prayed he wouldn't get a hard-on, since it would be obvious in this position.

"You want the light on?"

"No. You can turn it off." He felt safe now.

Frank stretched and a second later the room was dark, except for the pale glow of moonlight filtering in through the windows.

"Good night," Frank said.

Then he kissed the top of Toby's head.

Chapter Eight

"And the only means of their escape
Was sliding down a rope,
And just as they were half way down
The burning strands they broke."

THE MORNING was embarrassing.

Frank was a bit disoriented, at first. There was a naked man lying against him, warm and smooth in his arms, making his body tingle. Frank's cock was hard in his underwear, straining against the fabric, and the man was grinding his crotch against Frank's hip as their legs intertwined and caressed each other.

Then his memory came back to him, and he realized just who he was in bed with.

Oh shit!

He stopped his legs from their unconscious attempt at morning frottage, but Toby whimpered in his sleep and continued dry humping his hip. Fortunately, now that Frank was fully conscious, he could feel Toby's underwear rubbing against his skin—he wasn't completely naked, after all. He was, however, very erect. And as good as it felt to lie with him like this, Frank needed to put a stop to it.

"Toby," he said gently. "Toby. Wake up, man."

Toby made a sound that shot straight through Frank's throbbing cock—a sensual moan like a man being caressed—and slid his hand down Frank's belly until his fingers were cupping Frank's erection through the thin cotton of his briefs.

"Okay, that was really not what I was hoping for." Frank groaned. He reached down and pulled Toby's hand off his crotch. "Toby! Wake up!"

Toby started and gasped. "Wha…?"

"It's morning. We fell asleep."

The poor guy seemed really out of it. He looked up at Frank with his face scrunched up like an adorable child, his dark brown curls a tangled heap on top of his head. "Did we have sex?"

Frank's eyes opened painfully wide. "No! You were upset. I just… you didn't want to be alone…."

"Oh. I remember now."

The way he'd asked about having sex was so casual, as if he wouldn't have been surprised. *Is he gay?* The thought did nothing to ease Frank's state of arousal. But he couldn't think of a way to ask without sounding like he was making a pass.

"I thought I'd get up in a few minutes," Frank said, "once you'd gone back to sleep—go back to my own bed. But I fell asleep too."

"It's okay." Toby rolled away from him, and Frank lifted his arm to let him free.

Frank took that as his cue to get the fuck out of the bed. He slipped out from under the sheets and stood up, only then remembering he had a huge hard-on. He covered his crotch with his hands and was surprised when he brushed against a wet spot on his hip. He looked down at it. "Um... did you come on me?"

Frank watched in fascination as Toby slid his hand down underneath the covers and felt his crotch. His face flushed crimson as he withdrew it, glanced at the palm, and then wiped it on his chest. "Uh... not exactly. I just... leak a lot. Sorry."

"Oh. Well... that's cool. You know, it happens. Can't really control morning wood...." *Or morning dry humping.*

"Christ, this is embarrassing."

Frank laughed nervously. "I had a boner too, bud. It's okay. We're just lucky nobody was here to film it and put it on YouTube." *And you have no fucking idea how much I want to crawl back in that bed with you, right now.*

"I'm really sorry about how I behaved last night," Toby said, rubbing his face with one hand. "I'm not usually such a baby about bad visions. This one just kind of snuck up on me in a dream...."

"Do you want to tell me what you saw?"

"It was too chaotic to make much sense of. There was fear and anger and... someone forcing me down onto a cold, cement floor.... Oh God! I was raped!" Toby's hand trembled as he lowered it. He took several deep breaths and blinked his eyes rapidly. "I mean... *she* was... I... I need to get up."

He seemed to be having trouble sitting up, so Frank held out a hand and half lifted him to a sitting position. Toby let go and sat on the edge of the bed, hugging himself and rocking slightly.

"I'll be all right. I just need to...."

Then he was sobbing, and Frank had no idea what to do. He wasn't sure if he believed in the "vision" Toby had had, but it was clearly real to him, and it had traumatized him severely. It tore Frank up inside to see him like this. He knelt in front of Toby and placed a tentative hand on his forearm. "Toby...."

"Jesus, Frank! I *felt* it! I felt him slamming into me! I had no idea it could hurt so much! And... *ugh*... she *trusted* the fucker! She thought he cared about her!"

"Do you know who she was?"

"Rosaleen," Toby said, clutching at his hand. "Rosaleen Quinn. She didn't die in the fire, Frank. She was raped in that basement—and I think she was murdered!"

"I WENT online last night to see if I could find any more information on either Rosaleen or Jack," Savannah said at breakfast.

The four of them were eating downstairs in the Briarwood's dining area. The food was good—pancakes, bacon, and eggs prepared by Mrs. Libby and served by Gale. The orange juice wasn't exactly fresh-squeezed, but it was a decent brand. And the toast used fresh bread from a local bakery. The windows presented them with a gorgeous view of the harbor, sparkling in the morning sunlight.

Toby had filled Savannah and Houston in on the details of his vision the night before. Thankfully it was already beginning to fade, or at least to become more distant. It no longer felt as if the rape and murder had happened directly to *him*, though it was still difficult to talk about. In a way, this made it clearer. He could now recall details about the events he'd witnessed—details he'd been too emotional to think about earlier.

Still, he knew he'd never forget what he'd experienced. He didn't want to. *Someone has to remember.*

"The *Hawley Sentinel* is archived back to 1900," Savannah went on. "But I couldn't find any obituaries for them. No funeral notices, nothing. That isn't really unusual. The families were probably too poor to be putting paid notices in the papers. They'd let their family and friends know by word of mouth."

"Where does that leave us?" Frank asked.

"Nowhere, really." She placed a hand over Toby's where it rested on the table. With his nerves as badly frayed as they were, he was grateful for the comfort. "I'm not saying I don't believe that vision you had, sugar, but... if her body wasn't found until after the fire—or never found at all—there won't be any record of a murder anywhere."

Houston glanced up from his pancakes and asked with his mouth half full, "How could they say she was killed in the fire if they never found her body?"

"Oh, sugar, they never found most of those poor girls' bodies. Only the ones who jumped out windows or asphyxiated from the smoke in the stairwell. Most were burned up. It was like a furnace in there."

"Jack might have survived," Frank insisted. "What if he killed her and took off? The fire started later that morning, and it covered his tracks. He would've gotten off scot-free. He'd have to be dead by now, unless he's almost a hundred and thirty, but he could have died any time between then and, say, 1997."

"So you just want me to search eighty years of archives for the name 'Jack Bishop'?"

"No," Frank said, giving her a wry smile. "Jack may have moved away. That seems likely."

"Ah, I see. You want me to search the archives of *every* newspaper in the United States over an eighty-year time period for what is probably a fairly common name." Then she added with a sweet smile, "Aren't you just precious?"

Frank grinned back at her, but he was saved from answering by the ringer of his cell phone. He pulled it out of his pocket and glanced at it, his smile vanishing. "It's the hospital."

They all froze and looked at him in trepidation.

"Frank Carter." He listened a moment, a scowl coming across his handsome face. "Another one?" Pause. "Well, what's his condition now?"

The conversation went on for a minute or so, during which Toby watched Houston out of the corner of his eye. The young man swallowed his food and stared hard at Frank, his knuckles whitening as he clutched his fork tightly. For the first time, Toby sensed something from him—a powerful anxiety radiating from his body like heat.

He's at the breaking point, Toby realized.

When Frank hung up, Houston pounced on him. "What did they say?"

Frank seemed weary as he slowly set the phone down and glanced across the table at him. "Nothing's really changed. He's still unconscious. Though she said it was odd—his brainwaves are very active, like a man in REM sleep. Not typically what they would call a coma. But he won't wake up."

"If nothing's changed," Houston persisted, "why did they call? What did you mean when you said 'another one'?"

Frank sighed. "He had another episode around two o'clock in the morning." He looked pointedly at Toby. "Which was the time the clock read when you had your nightmare."

"An episode?" Toby asked, almost afraid of what the answer might be.

"He started shouting. Something like, 'You fucking got me in trouble, you stuck-up bitch!'"

Chapter Nine

"Christ, Christ, what a horrible mess,
They were mangled, burned, and killed,
Six stories high and falling from
The burning Hawley Mill."

FRANK'S MOOD was dark as they finished their breakfast and packed for the trip back to New Hampshire. Louis's brain being in REM, instead of a comatose state, seemed like a good thing. But it made no sense he was even in a coma to begin with. Sure, he took a bad fall down the stairs, but the MRI hadn't shown any sign of brain damage. He should have been on the mend already.

His mood didn't improve any when Houston took him aside just as they were about to head out.

"You and I need to talk."

Shit. What fresh hell is this? "What is it, Houston?"

The young man frowned as he fidgeted with his jacket zipper. "Savannah and that Toby guy have been talking about doing a séance to learn more about 'Jack and Rosaleen.'" He said the last two names in a mocking tone of voice.

Fuck. Frank had warned Toby about letting Houston hear about that. "And?"

"Are you fucking kidding me? A séance, Frank?"

Frank shrugged and spread his hands. "I know. It's not scientific. It may not produce any data we can verify—"

"We don't even know if there ever was a Jack! He's not in any of the records. And yeah, sure, there was a Rosaleen, but we can't verify anything but her name. Toby's making all this shit up, Frank! You know he is!"

"No, I don't know that," Frank said. "I know it's tenuous, and we might ultimately have to throw it out, but from what I've seen, I think he's a decent guy. I don't think he's a fraud. At least, not a deliberate one. *Deluded,* maybe. He could be wrong about these 'visions' he claims to have—"

"Did you sleep with him?"

That caught Frank off guard. He stared at Houston in disbelief for a moment. Then shock was supplanted by anger. "I don't recall prying into your sex life, so what the fuck makes you think you can pry into mine?"

Houston flinched as though he'd been slapped. He tugged at his zipper and looked at the ground like a chastised puppy. But he wasn't ready to give up just yet. "He's fooling you. That's all I have to say."

Frank bit back an angry retort. Houston was acting like a child, and Frank wasn't in the mood. But he took a breath and forced himself to say calmly, "If you don't want to participate in the séance, you don't have to."

"I don't. I want to go to the hospital. Louis needs me."

That curtailed Frank's anger. He nodded. "Maybe you're right. We haven't had much time to sit with him since the accident. If you go, you can try reading to him or something. It might get through."

"You'll let me go?"

"Of course."

"Can I stay the night with him?"

That request was a little surprising, but Frank saw no reason Houston couldn't, if the hospital allowed it. He clapped a hand on the young man's shoulder. "I'll call the hospital and see if I can arrange it."

As he turned to go back to the car, Houston dropped the bomb on him. "I love him, you know."

Frank turned slowly back to him. "Love? As in *love*?"

Houston nodded, holding his chin up as if he expected Frank to rail at him.

"I thought you were straight."

"So did I," Houston said uncomfortably. "Until a year or so ago."

"What happened then?"

"I don't know. I just realized I didn't want to be with anybody but him."

"Does Louis know that?"

Houston shook his head, and Frank thought he might be tearing up. "I was afraid to tell him. I kept putting it off. I didn't expect...."

Frank took a hold of his jacket and tugged on it. Houston put up no resistance as Frank pulled him into an embrace. "Tell him when you sit with him," Frank said quietly into his ear. "They say people in comas can sometimes hear you. I don't know if he feels the same, but... don't count on getting another chance."

FRANK SEEMED to be brooding when he got into the car for the trip home, so Toby let him ride in silence for a while. But when they passed Gardiner, Frank said, "When you woke up this morning, the first thing you wanted to know is if we had sex...."

"Oh," Toby said. "Are you about to tell me we *did*?"

He certainly couldn't remember it, if they had. All he remembered was Frank holding him after the nightmare. Though Frank had kissed him....

Frank looked at him closely. "You think it's a real possibility?"

"What are you asking, Frank? I wasn't trying to imply anything about you, if that's what you mean."

Frank grunted and shifted in his seat. "Sorry. I don't do this very much. The thing is... I *am* gay. And I was wondering if you might be too."

Toby suppressed a laugh at his seriousness. "Yes, I am. And if your next question is, 'Do I find you attractive?' then the answer to that is also yes."

"Oh. Okay." Frank glanced out the window. "I think you're attractive too."

Toby did laugh at that. "Now I'm regretting letting you escape from my bed this morning."

"Yeah, me too."

They rode in companionable silence for a few miles, neither bringing up the possibility of something happening between them now. Toby was certainly open to the idea. He found Frank sweet and interesting and adored the way he looked after everyone in his charge—even an uninvited psychic having nightmares at two in the morning. He was a good man, solid, dependable... and cute as hell.

Toby wasn't sure what he could offer in return, though. Oh, he was decent-looking. He was vain enough to acknowledge that. He could probably offer Frank a good time in bed. But beyond that? They had a shared interest in the occult, but they were coming at it from opposite directions.

Well, we'll just have to see how it goes.

"So," Frank said, breaking into his thoughts, "do we want to take this somewhere?"

"I certainly do."

Frank gave him an adorably shy smile. "The team should probably have some downtime tonight. Houston... has some things he needs to work out. And Savannah would research till she dropped, if I didn't order her to take a night off now and then. What are you gonna be doing?"

"I'm hoping to have dinner with you."

AFTER CHECKING in on Junior at the hospital and making sure Houston had whatever he needed, Frank went back to the hotel to shower and dress. Then he drove the van to pick Toby up at his apartment—a nice little space he rented above his shop. Frank had been both curious to see it and dreading it. What if it turned out to be some kind of psychedelic pad with a shrine to the Fox Sisters or something like that? There was only so far Frank was willing to bend on the "psychic" thing. But it was just an apartment, neat and sparsely furnished. There was what looked like a Wiccan altar on the dresser in the bedroom, but Frank could handle that. A man's religion was his own business. As long as he didn't worship the Cottingley Fairies.

They'd have to have a talk about that at some point.

But it was hard to give the apartment much more than a glance when his tour guide was looking so incredible. Toby had showered, so his loose curls were a bit wet, which Frank found surprisingly sexy. He'd dressed in a pale blue button-down shirt that hugged his torso deliciously, complemented by tight gray slacks that displayed a perfect, tight ass to magnificent effect. Frank was already sporting a semi and they hadn't even begun the evening.

Hawley wasn't exactly known for its gourmet cuisine, but Manchester was only a half hour away. Toby directed him to a Nepalese restaurant called Café Momo on Hanover Street.

Frank's eyes went wide when he looked over the menu—not because of the prices, though they were steep, but because of the food itself. "Boar?" he asked. "Goat? Buffalo? Where the hell do they even *find* those around here?"

Toby laughed. "There's a buffalo farm in Dover, about fifty miles from here. And goats are everywhere."

"Wild boar?"

"I think they get that from a ranch in Texas. We don't have to eat here, if you don't want to."

Frank shook his head. "No, I didn't say that. I just… don't recognize anything on the menu."

"To me, it tends to taste like an interesting combination of Indian and Chinese. A 'momo' is a lot like a Chinese dumpling. Some of the chicken dishes taste somewhat Indian, but the spice isn't quite the same. They also have fantastic mojitos. Go figure."

Frank passed on the mojito, since he was driving, and the company van was finicky enough to handle sober, but he couldn't pass up an opportunity to eat buffalo momo and something called "Lamb Nepali Way." He was delighted to discover they had mango lassi on the drink list.

After they'd ordered, he looked across the table at Toby's beautiful features illuminated by the candle in the center of the table, and couldn't help saying, "You look incredible."

Toby smiled shyly. "So do you."

"I'm all right, I suppose." He'd showered, trimmed his beard a bit, and put on some clean clothes. Nothing fancy. "But I've been wanting to tell you ever since I first saw you getting out of your car—you are a beautiful thing to look upon."

"Thing?"

"Sorry, I'm not very good at expressing myself."

Toby's smile broadened, and he reached across the table to slide his fingers over the top of Frank's hand. "I'm teasing. It's been a long time since anyone's said anything that sweet to me. And I find you very handsome… and dead sexy."

Frank looked away, embarrassed. Fortunately the waiter arrived with their drinks and saved him from having to come up with a response. He was out of his element here. He was used to telling people where to go, what equipment to set up, what data to collect. The last time he'd dated was… he couldn't remember. A long time ago. And even though this date seemed to be going pretty well, he was still afraid he'd screw it up somehow.

"Thank you," Toby said when they were alone again, "for what you did last night."

"What? Oh… that." Frank shifted self-consciously in his seat. "It wasn't very professional."

Toby gave him a sour face. "It was what I needed, at the time. And what was unprofessional about it? You didn't grope me or try to take advantage of me."

"I should have put my pants back on." It had been so… *erotic*.

"Please," Toby said. "It was two o'clock in the morning. We were both awakened from sleep and we just wanted to get back to sleep. Don't make it sound sordid. You were taking care of me, like you take care of everyone."

Frank didn't know what to say to that, so he withdrew his hand from under Toby's fingers—it hadn't occurred to him to break the contact before then, even as the waiter had deposited their drinks—and fiddled with the cloth napkin in his lap. "You have a nice place," he said, trying to divert the conversation.

"Thanks. Where do you live? Is it far from Hawley?"

"Only about an hour away from here, in Keene. Louis and I still live in the same house we grew up in."

"That doesn't surprise me."

Frank looked up sharply. "Why not?"

"I just mean you seem like a very… settled person," Toby responded. "Most of us are drifters. We live in one place for a year, move to another, live there for a year or two…. We keep hoping to find a place we can settle in, but there are always jobs or other circumstances forcing us to move on. You're not like that."

"Well… after I got out of the service, I had to take care of our dad. He'd been kind of… frail… ever since Mom died, but he had a stroke while I was in Iraq. Louis took care of him as best he could, but he was going to college—still living at home, but you know, he couldn't be around all the time. So I did my stint and came home, worked nights doing security when Louis was home. After Dad passed away, Louis and I just kind of kept going the way we'd been. I never even thought about moving out. I don't know about Louis."

"How long ago was that?"

Frank had to count back. "About five years, I guess." It didn't seem like much of a life, now that he'd summed it up. But he didn't regret any of it. And he'd been happy, more or less—still was.

As long as Louis wakes up again. Frank had dropped Houston off at the hospital that afternoon and made arrangements for him to stay the night. Fortunately the other bed in the room was empty at the moment. But Louis's condition hadn't changed.

"How do you find time to do the paranormal investigation?" Toby asked.

Frank shrugged. "It's usually just a night here and there, when I'm not working. We don't charge, generally, so I pay Savannah out of my own pocket—she has a day job at Barnes & Noble in Portsmouth. Plus we got a little bit of inheritance from Dad. It's not much, but we get by. Louis and Houston are willing to work for meals. Houston stays in one of our spare rooms."

"Mrs. H. is paying you, isn't she?"

Frank laughed. "Oh yeah. I didn't even have to ask. She just had her secretary call me and dangle a wad of cash in front of me, plus expenses. I feel like a gigolo."

"Don't," Toby said seriously. "That mill is a dangerous place. You've already seen how dangerous it can be."

The smile faded from Frank's face. "Yeah. I have."

DINNER WAS wonderful. Despite Frank's initial hesitancy over the food, he seemed to enjoy it. After dessert, he took Toby back to his apartment, parking in front of the shop.

"I had a good time," Frank said, smiling.

Toby didn't like the sound of that. It sounded like a prelude to "Good night," and he wasn't in the mood to end the evening just yet. "Would you like to come inside for a bit?"

"What for?"

Toby blinked at him. Nobody had ever asked that before. "For a drink?"

"I can't. I have to drive."

"Yeah…. Maybe we could just talk for a while?"

"That would be awesome, but I should probably get back to the hotel."

Was that a brush-off? Maybe. "I guess…." Then, almost without being able to help himself, Toby blurted out, "Why?"

Frank looked puzzled. "Well… it's getting kind of late."

"I mean… you could always stay here tonight."

"I don't want to put you out—"

"Oh, for fuck's sake, Frank! I'm offering you sex! Do you want it or not?"

Frank's baby blue eyes went wide, as if he'd just realized a train was coming and he was parked on the tracks. "Sex?"

Toby suddenly wanted to run upstairs, crawl under his bed, and die of embarrassment. What had possessed him to blurt it out like that? Now Frank probably thought he was the kind of guy who spread his legs for every man who bought him a mojito. "I don't… I mean—"

"Okay."

They regarded each other in silence for a long moment. Then Toby opened his door and climbed out of the van. He waited while Frank did the same and then checked all the doors to make sure the van was secure for the night.

"Is it okay to leave it here?" Frank asked. His voice seemed a little shaky.

"Sure, it's fine." Like most of Hawley, the road in front of the shop was unmetered.

He led the way into the entry next to the shop door, and up the stairs to his apartment. Inside, he went straight for the small rack on his kitchen counter that had a couple of bottles of decent wine in it. "Red or white?"

Frank hesitated a moment, perhaps debating whether he should still refuse a drink, then replied, "White."

"Well, it's actually pink."

"Fine."

Toby retrieved wineglasses from the cupboard and poured for both of them. When they each had a glass, he took a sip and said, "I made things really awkward. I'm sorry."

Frank sipped his own glass—or rather, downed half of it. Then he took a deep breath. "If you hadn't, I'd be on my way back to an empty bed at a cheap motor inn and pissed off at myself for not having the balls to make a move."

"Really?"

"Really."

"You can make a move now, you know."

Frank took Toby's wineglass, set both glasses on the counter, and then pulled him into his arms to kiss him. Toby was amazed at how soft and warm his lips were, despite the prickling of his beard. They were close to the same height—Frank was maybe an inch taller—but Toby felt as if his entire body was wrapped in Frank's embrace. He'd never felt so safe and protected.

They explored each other's bodies, caressing every inch of their backs and sides through the cloth of their shirts, then yanking the shirts up to touch hot, bare skin. Frank was wearing a simple brown T-shirt under an open flannel shirt, and it looked incredibly sexy on him, but now Toby wanted it *off*. Frank put up no resistance as Toby slid the flannel shirt off his shoulders and let it drop to the floor.

"Take it off," he murmured into Frank's mouth.

Frank laughed but stepped back long enough to remove the T-shirt and reveal a tight, muscular torso. He had a fine dusting of reddish chest hair and a delicious trail leading down into the waistband of his underwear. "You too."

"Let's go into the bedroom," Toby insisted, reaching down to caress the growing bulge in Frank's jeans. Frank growled in frustration but followed him out of the kitchen.

In the bedroom Toby allowed Frank to unbutton his shirt and slip it off. Frank groaned when he saw Toby's chest and stroked the skin of his abdomen while he dove for Toby's left nipple. Toby had never had a guy pay much attention to his nipples before, and it surprised him how good it felt to have a hot tongue tickle the sensitive nub. When Frank bit it gently, he arched his back in surprise and gasped. "Ah! Jesus! Do that again."

Frank moved to the other nipple and showed him why it was good to have two. After a minute Toby was dry humping his crotch against Frank's thigh. Before he could suggest they try something else, he found himself lifted off the floor by Frank's strong arms and spun around so Frank could lay him out on the bed.

Frank was on top of him in an instant, kissing his way up Toby's neck to claim his mouth once more. He was a damned good kisser, and Toby opened himself to Frank's probing tongue with enthusiasm. Then Frank slid his mouth over to Toby's ear, nipped his earlobe, and growled, "I want you naked."

"Yes!"

Toby didn't have to do a thing. He lay there entranced as Frank stripped him. Then, when he was stark naked, his achingly swollen cock jutting up obscenely between his open legs, Frank stepped back to look at him. His expression was admiring, lustful, as he yanked his belt open and shoved his jeans and underwear down. His cock stood almost straight up from its nest of red-gold pubic hair.

Toby didn't usually like to be fucked. Half the guys he'd been with didn't do it right and he just ended up sore afterward. But looking at that cock, he knew he wanted it inside him. Now.

"Will you fuck me?" he asked breathlessly.

"Do you have condoms?"

He did. And lube, of course. He retrieved them from his nightstand and sat on the edge of his bed, pulling Frank in close. Before he put the condom on, he couldn't resist taking Frank into his mouth. Frank didn't seem to mind the detour. He groaned and stroked Toby's hair while Toby worshipped him, exploring the length and breadth of that beautiful cock and teasing the tip with his tongue, tasting the sweetness there. Toby himself was leaking pretty severely now, as he'd done when they were sleeping together. He could feel it as the head of his cock moved against his inner thigh, leaving a trail.

At last Toby pulled away, ripped open the condom wrapper, and rolled it onto Frank, stroking him as he gently urged the condom down his shaft. Then he dabbed some lube on it and watched Frank shudder as he coated its length.

Toby lay back on the mattress again and urged, "Fuck me, Frank. Please."

Frank growled again as he climbed onto the bed and positioned himself between Toby's thighs. He took some of the lube onto his index finger and for a couple of delicious minutes, Toby luxuriated in his gentle probing. But it wasn't enough, and Toby soon pleaded, "Do it."

Frank entered him then, slowly, filling him up. Then he leaned forward and merged his mouth with Toby's as he gently began to move within him. Toby whimpered, but when Frank hesitated, he whispered, "Don't stop. That's just the sound I make when I'm in heaven."

Frank chuckled. "Well, then I hope to hear more of it."

He did. A lot more.

Frank came first, since Toby had largely forgotten about his own cock. All he cared about was what was happening in his ass. He felt Frank shudder and his entire body stiffen. Then his cock seemed to grow larger inside Toby, and Toby felt it bucking over and over again with his release. Frank let out a long, shuddering sigh when it was over.

Toby was unhappy for a moment when Frank pulled out of him, but Frank slid down his body and drew Toby's neglected cock into his mouth. "Oh God!"

Frank was good at that too, it turned out. Toby felt the head of his cock engulfed in warmth and started when he realized just how deeply Frank was taking him into his throat. He shuddered and came while Frank swallowed again and again, not pulling away until Toby was completely spent.

Then Frank crawled back up his body to kiss him. Toby could taste his own come in Frank's mouth, and he found it an incredible turn-on. He wondered how soon they might be able to go at it again.

At last, Frank broke the kiss to say, "I hate to spoil the mood, but I really gotta take a leak."

Toby snorted. "Charming. It's behind there." He pointed to the bead curtain that covered the entrance to the bathroom.

Frank climbed out of bed and pushed it aside. He peered into the small space on the other side. "No door?"

"'Fraid not. The previous tenant kicked it in—God knows why. My landlady has been saying she'll replace it for the last five years."

"You should sue."

"I should, but she knows I won't. If you have to do anything you're embarrassed about, I'll leave the room for a few minutes."

Frank quirked an eyebrow at him. "If I had to do *that*, I'd... never mind. I don't. Be right back."

He slipped into the bathroom, did his business, and returned. But to Toby's disappointment, he didn't come back to the bed. He wandered naked around the room, taking in Toby's poster of *The Lord of the Rings*, his small rock waterfall, and his collection of meditation CDs. Eventually, he came to the Wiccan altar on Toby's dresser—two small statues of a naked, horned god and a similarly naked goddess, a chalice, and a ritual knife, all laid out on a blue cloth with a gold pentagram printed on it. Toby held his breath. Not everyone understood Wicca. Frank might think he was into black magic or Satanism.

Frank turned to him and raised that eyebrow again. "How do you feel about the Cottingley Fairies?"

"You mean those fake photos of fairies two Victorian girls took, using cutouts from magazines?" Toby asked.

Frank smiled and slid back onto the bed. "We might be able to make this work, after all."

Then he kissed Toby long and passionately, until they were both worked up enough to go for another round.

Interlude

"SHOULDN'T HE be on a feeding tube or something?" Houston asked.

The nurse smiled sympathetically as he made up the other bed in the room for Houston to sleep in and said, "You see that tube going into his nose? That goes all the way down to his stomach, and that's how we get food in. It's not as efficient as the large feeding tubes you might have seen on TV, but it's safer, for a lot of reasons. Especially if he might wake up at any moment."

Houston took a deep breath, held it, and let it out slowly. Maybe this wasn't such a good idea. Louis looked awful lying there, his skin pale and waxen, his hair greasy and messed up. It was a horrible thing to look at. But Houston knew this was where he belonged.

"If you need anything, there's a buzzer right here," the nurse said, indicating the small button hanging from a cord on the bedframe. Then he laughed and added, "Don't get carried away. The bathroom is right over there and you can get your own glasses of water. It's for emergencies."

"Got it."

"You have a good night."

"Thanks."

Then, at last, Houston was alone in the room. He tried to tell himself he wasn't really alone. Louis was right there. But it didn't feel that way. It felt as if Louis were on the other side of the moon.

"I've got something to tell you," Houston said to the unconscious figure. "It seems kind of pointless, since you can't hear me, but Frank says I should tell you." He slid the uncomfortable plastic chair he was sitting on closer to the bed and reached out to take Louis's hand in his. There was no response. The hand was warm, but otherwise there was no indication at all it was alive.

"We've been friends a long time," Houston went on. "Like.... Jesus. Eight years or so. You never made a secret of the fact that you were bi. You used to tease me—tell me I had a cute ass when I was in my underwear, shit like that. I never knew if you were serious. It didn't matter. I had my girlfriends, and you had a couple too. But you remember when you slept with Rob that night our senior year? And we got into that huge fight the next day? Well... I didn't get what was going on with me then—why I was so pissed off."

He paused, afraid to go on, even knowing he was probably just talking to himself. "I finally pieced it together about a year ago—sometime last summer. Maybe that night we went skinny dipping at Otter Brook Dam. The way you looked, naked in the moonlight.... You were so... fucking... beautiful, man. Or maybe the night we fell asleep on the couch together watching that stupid horror movie...."

He took a breath, held it a moment, and then let it out in one big huff. "So this is the way it is. I'm in love with you. I've been trying to think of a way to tell you all year, but... well, I kept chickening out. I mean, sure, we're best friends. But you've never really acted *interested*. But.... Frank says I should tell you now, so I'm telling you. I love you."

Louis's hand flexed in his, the fingers closing slightly.

"Louis?" Houston stood and peered down into his friend's face. "Louis? Can you hear me?"

But there was no response. Louis's fingers stayed curled around his, but there was no other movement, and Louis didn't open his eyes.

After a few moments, Houston removed his baseball cap and placed it on top of Louis's head. "Here, you need this more than I do. Loser."

He sat back down, lifted Louis's hand to his lips, and kissed it. Then he settled back, wondering if he'd remembered to pack his Kindle. It was going to be a long night.

Chapter Ten

"But I hope their spirits has fled
To a better place far still,
Up high, up high, up in the sky
Above the Hawley Mill."

TOBY AND Savannah seemed to have decided the matter of the séance, whether Frank was on board or not. He didn't put up a fight. Maybe they'd learn something; maybe they wouldn't. There was no harm in trying—he hoped. The last thing he wanted was to have to make another 911 call. But Toby insisted he could guard against that.

Famous last words.

Just before sunset, while Frank and Savannah were unloading equipment from the van—just enough to cover the foyer tonight—a car drove into the lot. Frank looked up from his work, expecting to see Toby's Civic, but was surprised to see a brand new BMW instead. Mrs. Hawley was at the wheel. Toby was in the passenger seat, and a young woman with scarlet hair was in the back.

"Frank!" Toby called with forced cheerfulness the moment he was out of the car. "I hope you don't mind me inviting Mrs. H. along."

His anxious expression suggested he'd done nothing of the sort.

"A séance!" the old woman exclaimed, clapping her gloved hands together in delight. "I haven't been to one of these since my second husband died without telling anyone where he'd hidden the safety deposit key, the paranoid old fool."

Toby came close to Frank and said under his breath, "She called me to check on progress, and I made the mistake of mentioning my plan."

Frank smirked at him. "I forgive you."

"*You* can try talking her out of it, if you like."

"Not on your life."

"Am I allowed to kiss you in front of Savannah?"

"Go for it."

Toby kissed him tenderly on the mouth, enough to get his motor revving but no more, and then turned to introduce the red-haired girl. "This is my assistant at the shop, Cassandra."

"Pleased to meet you, Cassandra."

"Mr. Carter." Out of the car, Frank could see she was dressed all in black—even her lipstick and fingernails—and she had sort of an Egyptian kohl thing going around her eyes. She accepted his outstretched hand with a limp wrist, as if she expected him to kiss it, and an air of Victorian affectation he found amusing.

"Cassandra's Wiccan, so I invited her to assist with casting the circle and setting up wards."

Ah. Magic. That was Toby's plan for protecting everyone. It made Frank distinctly uncomfortable, even while he acknowledged that his belief spirits *could* attack wasn't far removed from Toby's belief that a Wiccan circle casting could protect them from those attacks. They both believed in psychic energy. It was whether living humans could consciously control it that they differed on.

Give it a chance, Frank reminded himself.

"We're going to be recording the whole thing on video and audio," he said. "We'll also be monitoring EMF and thermal in the room. Our team still has to document any activity."

Toby didn't seem to have any issues with Frank's setup. "Good. No Houston tonight?"

"He'd rather chew broken glass," Frank replied. "But that's fine. I told him to keep an eye on Junior at the hospital and text me during the séance if he says anything or reacts in any way."

Toby nodded. "Sounds like a plan. But please keep your phone on vibrate, so it doesn't completely yank me out of trance."

The thought of Toby going into a trance state made Frank a bit uncomfortable—less out of fear than because he was growing fond of the guy and didn't want to watch him make a fool of himself—but all he said was, "Will do."

As he turned to lead the way into the building, Frank caught Savannah watching the two of them with a knowing smile.

"Did you have a comment to make?" he challenged her.

"Me? I would *never*."

TOBY KNEW casting a circle would be the best way to protect all of them from whatever malevolent force had attacked him—and probably Frank's brother, as well—a few days earlier. It invoked forces more powerful than anything he could raise on his own. But he fretted about Frank's reaction. The man seemed to understand Wicca was simply an alternative religion, and not something evil or Satanic, but that didn't mean he was really cool with it.

Still, Toby knew what had to be done.

"I'm going to draw a circle in chalk inside the reception area," he announced to all present. "If you need to bring in more equipment while I'm doing that, go right ahead, but please try not to smudge the circle. When we actually cast it, everyone will need to be inside the boundary I draw and stay there until the séance is done."

The floor of the reception area was carpeted—a short pile with an ugly brown pattern that had faded over the past few decades until it was nearly indistinguishable. It also smelled of mildew, now that he was close to it. He drew the circle by hand with pastel blue "lecturer's chalk," the kind used in street painting. It didn't need to be geometrically perfect. Technically the circle didn't even have to be drawn, since the actual circle was created from psychic energy, but Toby wanted something concrete to give Frank and the others a clear idea of the boundary.

While Frank and Savannah set up their own equipment at the receptionist's desk, Cassandra and Mrs. H. brought in the supplies Toby needed. He was going all-out this time, and he couldn't deny it was partly for show. Not only did it need to be impressive enough to convince everyone present the circle was real, but it also needed to convince the spirits of the mill he meant business. Magick—even real magick—took place where the human mind interfaced with the Universal Mind, and therefore was always part psychological.

Cassandra used a compass to determine the four directions and placed colored candles at each point: yellow in the east, red for the south, blue in the west, and green in the north. The candles were jar candles, for safety. Since there hadn't been room for a folding table in the trunk of Mrs. H.'s BMW, they would all be sitting on the floor. He did, at least, put down a heavy blanket and meditation pillows for the five of them. He'd been a bit concerned about Mrs. H. having to sit on the floor at her age, but she'd insisted she was in perfect health and could manage.

They brought in a few more accoutrements, and then there was nothing to do for several minutes but wait until Frank and Savannah had everything running on their end.

FRANK KNEW he was dragging his feet, taking more time to get setup than he really needed. He wasn't thrilled with this whole séance thing. But after he'd tested the sound on the mics for the tenth time, he glanced up to find Savannah watching him, arms crossed like an irritated parent. He turned around and saw that *everybody* was waiting for him.

Oops.

"Sorry. I guess I'm a little nervous."

Toby gave him a knowing smile and extended a hand. "If both of you can come inside the circle, we'll begin."

Savannah smiled and cocked her head at a jaunty angle, crooking her arm at him. She tended to wear her thick, jet black hair pulled back in a tight bun to keep it out of the way as she worked, but in that pose, she suddenly looked like a debutante waiting for her date to escort her onto the ballroom floor. So Frank stood, bowed, and escorted her into the circle.

Watching Toby go through the casting was… challenging. Intellectually he knew it was just another religion. Instead of one god, Toby and Cassandra worshipped two. Instead of saints, Toby called upon "elemental spirits." But even though he wasn't particularly religious, Frank had been raised Catholic, and this was decidedly not Catholic—or even Christian. It would definitely take some getting used to, if they decided they wanted to keep this thing between them going.

Cassandra lit the last candle—the green one—and intoned, "Guardian of the North, element of earth, power of strength and endurance, we call upon you to bless our circle and protect us during our working. Please join us!"

Toby was standing behind her, a small knife pointed at the edge of the circle with his right hand, crossed in front of his body so he could walk clockwise. In his left hand, he held a censer up high, burning frankincense and myrrh. He claimed those were for protection. But there was also something called elecampane in it. Frank wasn't familiar with that herb, but Toby told them it aided psychic ability. Whatever. The whole mixture was pretty overpowering in the closed room. By the time Toby reached the east again and declared the circle complete, Frank was feeling a bit nauseated.

"Sit, please," Toby said, indicating the small circle of cushions on the floor.

Frank offered a hand to Mrs. Hawley, who seemed a bit creaky, despite her insistence she could run circles around all of them. Then he took his place between her and Savannah. Toby settled into a half lotus position, his back straight and his hands in his lap.

"I'll ask you all to remain as quiet as possible until I come out of the trance. Cassandra will be asking me questions, and you may hear Frank's phone buzz. If it does, he'll relay what the text message says. But apart from that, please don't say anything… unless the spirit asks you a direct question. Otherwise it may bring me out too soon."

Frank quietly took his phone out and placed it on the carpet in front of him.

Toby watched him, nodded slightly, and then closed his eyes. Nothing much happened for a long time. Toby breathed slowly and evenly while the others tried not to fidget.

At last his eyelids flickered open part way, but not enough to reveal his pupils.

Cassandra quietly reached out to an unlit candle in the center of their circle and lit it with a butane lighter. "Spirits of this place, we welcome you in peace. May the light of this candle guide you to us. Come speak with us."

There was a long silence. Then Toby asked in a slow, quiet voice—almost a whisper, "Who… are… you?"

Cassandra seemed to be considering her answer carefully. Then with a glance at Mrs. Hawley, she said, "The current owner of the mill."

Toby jerked his head to face Mrs. Hawley, though his eyes were still nearly closed. "A woman?"

"Yes."

Toby turned slowly back to face the candle. "Why do you bother us?"

"Us? How many are here?"

"Many."

"Is one of you Rosaleen Quinn?"

"She is here."

"And Jack Bishop?"

Toby let out a sharp, unpleasant laugh. Frank didn't believe in demons, but the malevolent grin Toby wore as he continued to chuckle at some private joke chilled him to the core. "Not here. But near. He tries and tries to escape… but we will never… let… him… go…."

HOUSTON HATED this. He couldn't believe Frank had fallen for all this psychic medium bullshit. Sure, Toby was a good-looking guy, and kind of nice. But he was either a nutcase or manipulating Frank for some reason. Money, most likely. Mrs. Hawley was paying him, wasn't she? Maybe he had plans to write a book. *The Hawley Mills Horror*. Catchy. He might even get a movie deal.

And he's gonna make us all look like fucking idiots.

Still, in the back of his mind he wondered. *If Toby's a fake, why does Louis shout things every time he goes into a trance? How could he fake that?*

Well, that's what Houston was there to find out. Frank had just texted him they were beginning the séance. The doctor had been notified, and even though she was reluctant to go along with it, she'd agreed to let the on-call nurse know not to interfere if Louis started talking—not unless his heart rate shot through the roof or he was otherwise in danger.

Several minutes had gone by, but all was still. Junior appeared to be sleeping peacefully. Houston kissed him gently on the forehead—that was okay, wasn't it?—then opened his Kindle and went back to rereading *Firestarter* by Stephen King. He'd been reading *Doctor Sleep* before Louis's accident, but… he just couldn't deal with that one right now.

Just when Houston had convinced himself nothing was going to happen, he heard something. Something like heavy breathing.

He looked up, startled, and found Louis *watching him*. Well, he couldn't actually be watching—not with his eyes rolled back like that so only the whites were showing. But his face was turned toward Houston.

"Louis," Houston gasped before he remembered he wasn't supposed to interfere.

Louis didn't appear to hear him. He "stared" at Houston for a moment longer. Then his face contorted in anger and he hissed, "Let... me... go...."

FRANK'S PHONE buzzed, and he glanced at the text message from Houston. Even though he'd been expecting it, it still disturbed him to read *Louis awake but not awake. "let me go."*

"Junior just said 'Let me go,'" he told Cassandra quietly, trying to keep his voice from shaking.

Toby was still grinning in that disconcerting way. He laughed again and shook his head.

"Is Jack with Louis?" Cassandra asked.

"Part of him...."

Cassandra's eyes widened. "Where is the other part?"

Toby—or whatever was speaking through him—seemed to find that uproariously funny. When it finally stopped laughing, it replied, "Where it should be...."

SHE WASN'T dead—not yet. He'd left her unconscious on the cold cement floor of the basement, perhaps thinking she was dead. But she awoke, coughing and gagging for breath. The air there was always difficult to breathe because of the smoke from the massive coal-burning furnace, but never had she found it so painful to open her throat and take in air. The pain was the worst she'd ever felt—her neck, between her legs, all over her body where it had been scraped and bruised against the floor.... She tried to cry out, but she couldn't. She couldn't move or make a sound. For a few seconds, she had hope she'd survive, that she'd be able to crawl up the stairs to safety. But then she heard him returning.

"Christ! You're still alive?" He kicked her.

She cried out, though she knew it would do no good. She knew how loud the machines were when they were all going at once. Even now, she could hear their endless clattering through the heavy oak floor over her head. Nobody would hear her.

"I'm not havin' you go whining back to Roberts." He grabbed her wrists and pulled, dragging her across the floor, scraping her hip and leg across the cement, shredding the already worn fabric of her dress. She whimpered for him to stop, but he ignored her.

She felt the heat of the furnace and saw how the floor was blackened with soot and coal dust before she realized where he was dragging her, what he intended to do.

"No! Jack! You can't!"

He kicked her face hard, and she tasted blood.

It was impossible to open the cast-iron door without first donning the heavy canvas gloves used by the maintenance workers, and while he was searching for these, she attempted to crawl away. But she didn't get far before he came after her and dragged her back. She heard the scrape of the massive latch and the squeal of the door as he opened it.

The heat forced him to step back a moment. Then he lifted her, in those strong arms she'd once admired, while she struggled and screamed—

"NO! ENOUGH! *Enough!*" Toby screamed.

Frank couldn't help himself. He leaped forward, toppling the candle and the bowl of water in the middle of the circle in order to catch Toby as he fell over backward, his fists digging into his eyes. "Toby!"

He was vaguely aware of Cassandra making sure the candle was out, but he was focused on the man in his arms.

"He killed her!" Toby gasped. "Stuffed her into the furnace! But then he stoked the furnace too high to make sure… everything burned. The flames got out of control, climbed up the chimneys. It's what started the fire."

"Jack Bishop?"

"Yes."

"Frank," he heard Savannah say, but he ignored her.

"Where was he when the place went up?" he demanded.

"On the first floor. He made it out alive."

Figures.

"Oh God! He left by the stairwell exit… and *locked it behind him*!"

"Frank!" Savannah shouted.

He looked up and saw instantly what she'd been trying to draw his attention to. Through the glass doors that led to the factory floor, something was moving. It was still dark in there, but there were shafts of moonlight coming through the gaps in the wooden boards, along with light from the halogen lights in the parking lot. And against this dim backdrop, Frank could see shadows, as if people were moving about… walking slowly toward the foyer.

Frank struggled to lift Toby to a standing position. "We need to get out of here. Now."

"They're coming closer," Cassandra said, her face ashen.

"I see them. Try to take some of the equipment with you."

They grabbed what they could—laptops, cameras, monitors, microphones. Other things, like power supplies, cables, and surge protectors, Frank ordered them to leave behind. Toby could barely walk on his own—the séance seemed to have drained him of all his strength—so Frank just shoved him out the door.

When they were loading things into the van, Cassandra asked, "Where's the old lady?"

They all froze. Mrs. Hawley was nowhere to be seen.

"She must still be inside," Savannah said.

"Goddamn it!" Frank growled. "Get everything packed up. I'll go back for her."

He ran back to the foyer, but Mrs. Hawley was nowhere to be seen. With a growing sense of dread, he walked to the glass door leading onto the factory floor. The shadowy forms were still there, still indistinct in the dimly lit interior. But they'd stopped moving. They seemed to be focused on a single point a hundred feet or so away from the door, a tiny form standing alone in their midst—Mrs. Hawley.

Frank tried the door. It was locked.

"Mrs. Hawley!"

LEANING AGAINST the side of the van, barely able to stand, Toby could feel the evil of the mill radiating off the building. Or perhaps not evil, but *anger*. And hatred. Hatred for Jack Bishop, for what he'd done to Rosaleen, for what he'd done to *all* of them when his violence against her expanded to take almost a hundred other innocent lives.

But something didn't add up. Jack had survived the fire. Why was his spirit tied to this building? Guilt? But he was apparently trying to escape. How did he get trapped there, if he hadn't *died* there?

Because he *did* die there. Somehow.

But Toby had seen him leave the building in his vision when the fire alarm was first sounded.

He's there. I know it!

Toby pushed himself away from the van, staggering but managing not to fall—barely. Savannah and Cassandra moved toward him, but he waved them away. "I need to go back inside!"

FRANK WATCHED in dismay as the heavy UPS bounced harmlessly off the glass door without even cracking it. Did he have anything heavier? The chair? Not likely, but he'd try it. Mrs. Hawley hadn't moved, as far as he could see. He wasn't even certain the spirits could harm her directly. But what if they possessed her as they had Louis?

He reached for the chair just as Toby staggered through the front door. Or rather he was half carried through the door by both Savannah and Cassandra, one arm draped around each of their shoulders.

"Jesus Christ!" Frank snarled. He dropped the chair and moved forward to take Toby's arm from around Cassandra. The girl looked relieved to be out from underneath his weight. "I told all three of you to get the fuck out of here!"

"He insisted," Savannah said, rolling her eyes.

"I've got him."

Savannah relinquished Toby's other arm. "Cassandra can go back outside, if she likes. I'm staying as long as you two are in here. And Mrs. Hawley. Did you find her?"

"Yes and no," Frank said. He nodded in the direction of the factory floor.

"Why haven't you gone after her?"

"Because the goddamn door refuses to let me through. You try it!"

Savannah gave him a puzzled look, then walked over to the door and pulled on it. It didn't budge. "Is it locked?"

"No. If you look closely, you can see the bolt isn't engaged." The door lock was a simple mechanism. Turn the key to the right and a metal bolt slid into place; turn it to the left and the bolt slid back. There was empty space where the bolt would have been, if it had been locked.

"Help me get near it," Toby ordered him.

Frank didn't want to obey. He wanted to drag Toby's sorry psychic ass back outside and toss him into the van. But he did as Toby asked.

When they were near the door, Toby extended his hand and pressed it against the lock. That was all. Then he grabbed the door handle and pulled.

The damned thing opened.

"What the fuck did you do?"

"Take me in there, please. Now."

Frank growled and hoisted Toby's arm to a more secure position over his shoulder before moving forward. "You keep bossing me around, I might develop a fetish for spanking you."

Out of the corner of his eye, he caught Toby smirking. But they didn't have time for that now. Frank helped Toby cross the distance between the door and Mrs. Hawley's position. To his annoyance, Savannah and Cassandra flanked them.

Goddamn it!

Well, he supposed he had to respect them for not being afraid—at least, no more than he was. The shadows were still there, impossible to see clearly, but moving around them silently in the darkness. In his peripheral vision, Frank glimpsed what looked like women in drab, dark dresses, but they were never there when he tried to look at them directly. He could *feel* them, though. Their anger seemed to radiate off them, making the air feel hot and suffocating. It was hard to breathe.

"Mrs. H.," Toby said quietly.

The old woman turned to them, apparently surprised to see them there. "I've been trying to reason with them, but they won't listen."

"Reason with them how?"

"I've told them if they don't want the building turned into a mall, I'll just tear the monstrosity down! It's no use to anyone as it is. And I certainly can't subject others to what we've gone through." She looked pointedly at Frank. "You'll still get your pay, dear, but I don't think we need bother with your final report. I have no doubt the building is indeed haunted."

Cassandra snorted, then looked apologetic and quickly covered her mouth.

"Mrs. H.," Toby said, "They don't want the building torn down."

"Whyever not?"

"Because they've committed a murder, and they don't want it discovered."

Frank looked at him, puzzled. "A murder?"

"Jack Bishop. He returned here, years after the fire—perhaps after the mill was shut down in 1989. That would make sense. Nobody reported much psychic activity here until then."

"Why would he come here?"

"Well... not guilt. I don't think he had much of a conscience. Perhaps just curiosity. And the spirits who'd more or less lain dormant here for over seventy years were enraged by his presence. It isn't easy for a spirit to move objects in the physical plane. But ninety-seven angry spirits could manage it. They killed him. And they know if the building is renovated or torn down, his body will be discovered."

Frank could have sworn he felt a ripple go through the air surrounding them, as if the spirits were disturbed by what Toby had just said.

But Celia Hawley scoffed at it. "If they *did* kill Bishop, why on earth would they care about his body being discovered? It's not as if they can go to prison."

"They've been holding him prisoner," Toby responded. "If his body is discovered, his spirit will be free. And they can't stand it!" He raised his voice, looking around at the restless shadows. "But Jack isn't the only prisoner here, is he? You've all been trapped here for more than a century! Your families, your friends— they've all passed on. But you're still here, trapped in your worst nightmare, with the monster responsible." He paused, and Frank could feel how near he was to collapsing. "This is hell. But it's a hell you've created for yourselves. It's time to set yourselves free...."

For a long time, nothing happened. Then Frank felt the darkness easing. The air no longer seemed as oppressive. He could see into the darkness, where the shadows had seemed too deep just moments before.

Something metal crashed, and they all jumped. A whirring noise drew their attention to the far wall. The elevator safety gate was open. As they watched, the elevator moved upward until it was almost out of sight, revealing the gaping black hole of the elevator shaft underneath.

"That's it," Toby whispered. "They frightened him and he ran. They herded him right into the elevator on the fourth floor, and he was so terrified he didn't see until it was too late."

"He's at the bottom of the elevator shaft?" Savannah asked in a frightened voice.

"Yes."

Chapter Eleven

WHEN THEY were back outside in the relatively cool—and certainly less oppressive—evening air, Frank's cell phone buzzed. He looked at the text messages and found: *Come to the hospital. Now.*

Shit.

Frank tried calling Houston's cell, but it just rang a few times and went to voice mail. "Houston, this is Frank. We're on our way. Call me when you get this message."

He tossed his phone to Savannah. "Hold on to this, please. Answer it if Houston calls back."

"Will do."

Cassandra and Mrs. Hawley were helping Toby into the backseat of the BMW. The guy still looked awful. Frank waited for the women to step aside, then leaned in and gave him a gentle peck on the cheek. "Are you gonna be all right?"

"I'll be fine," Toby assured him. "I just need to sleep for a few days."

"Houston texted me to go to the hospital. I don't know what's going on."

"Then go! Mrs. H. will take me home."

Frank kissed him once more—on the lips this time—and ran back to the van.

IT WAS past visiting hours, but the nurse at the front desk had been flagged to page Dr. Khambatta if Frank showed up. A couple of minutes later, the doctor was hurrying down the hall toward him and Savannah, and Frank's heart started beating again—she was grinning.

"Your brother is awake!" she exclaimed. "He woke up about a half hour ago, and he seems very lucid. All of his vitals are good."

"Oh my God."

He had to extricate himself from Savannah's embrace before he could follow the doctor down the hall to the elevator. This time nobody seemed to mind Savannah tagging along. Frank doubted she'd listen if they tried to keep her out, anyway.

They entered the room and found Houston leaning over Junior's bed. Frank didn't know much about medical stuff, but he was pretty sure what he was doing wasn't CPR.

"That explains why you haven't been answering your cell phone."

Houston jumped a mile. Then he had the good grace to look sheepish while he wiped his mouth with the back of his hand.

"Hey, Frank!" Louis said cheerfully. "Savannah! How's it going?"

"It's going all right. Some of us have had to work while you've been napping."

Savannah practically shoved him out of the way to get to Louis's bedside. She gave him a warm embrace. "Oh, honey child, you have no idea how much we been missing you!"

Louis put up with her hugging him and roughing up his greasy hair with good humor, but to him it probably felt like the day after he'd fallen down the stairs. If he even remembered that much.

Suddenly Savannah pushed him away, holding him at arm's length. "So what's all this we just walked in on?" She cocked an eyebrow at Houston.

Junior grinned and looked up at Houston. "I don't know. I woke up, and the first thing I thought was, 'Houston loves me!' I didn't even get a chance to say much. He started hugging me, and the next thing I knew, we were making out."

Houston blushed. "Yeah, well… I *must* love you to kiss you with that week-old morning breath."

Dr. Khambatta interjected, "We broke up the make-out session so we could examine Louis. Though it certainly didn't take them long to get back to it."

"What about Casanova's broken leg?" Frank asked wryly.

"Still broken, of course. And he still has a minor concussion, though everything is healing well. The nurse put something in his IV for the pain after we examined him."

"Yeah, I'm feeling pretty good," Junior said cheerfully.

"No wonder Houston's looking good to you." Frank clapped a hand on Houston's shoulder to make it clear he was teasing. The poor guy looked like he might pass out from anxiety. Then Frank sat on the edge of the bed and took Louis's hand. "You had us worried, Junior. You had *me* worried. I wouldn't know what to do with myself if anything happened to you."

Louis squeezed his hand back. "I had a lot of… fucked-up dreams. Nightmares. About the mill, and the fire, and… some stuff I don't want to talk about right now."

"It can wait. I think I know some of it."

There was a quiet knock on the open door and a young man in a nurse's uniform addressed Dr. Khambatta. "I was told the patient needed a bath."

The doctor nodded. "I think he'd appreciate that. A bath, a shampoo. And he needs to brush his teeth."

"Sponge bath?"

"You can take him into the shower."

"This promises to be totally humiliating," Louis said. Then he smiled up at Houston. "But I should have fresh breath soon, if you want to stick around."

TOBY STAYED in bed for a couple of days. He felt like a total slouch, but whenever he tried to get out of bed longer than it took to go to the bathroom or eat some yogurt, exhaustion overtook him and he had to lie down again. He knew he wasn't ill in a physical sense. But psychic work often took a toll on him, and this had been a very rough ride. Fortunately Cassandra was more than capable of running the shop. She had to expand her hours to cover both days, open to close, but Toby fully intended to give her a bonus for that, as well as the work she'd put in at the mill. Regarding the latter, she seemed to have enjoyed it. The exact phrase she'd used was "bang up to the elephant"—not that he had any idea what that meant.

The best part was when Frank came by to tell him the good news about his brother, Louis, waking up out of his coma. Not only was Toby delighted to hear that—and the bit of gossip Frank dropped about Louis and Houston somehow stumbling into each other's arms—but Frank stayed with him for a couple of hours, cuddling. Toby hadn't had a boyfriend who enjoyed cuddling since college. It was… nice. Very nice.

On the third morning, he was able to drag his ass out of bed and shower, then wander downstairs to see if Cassandra might like a break from manning the cash register. He stumbled across Mrs. H. grilling the girl about which essential oils were best for arthritis.

"There you are!" the old woman exclaimed when she saw him.

"Good morning, Mrs. H. If you need something for arthritis—"

"Never mind that now," she said, waving a hand dismissively. "I have something to tell you. The police have been to the mill. Guess what they found at the bottom of the elevator shaft?"

"A body?"

"Well… a skeleton. And rotten clothing, plus a wallet with identification. It was Jack Bishop, all right!" She seemed delighted. "Miss Jones—Savannah?— she did some more research and managed to track him down. He'd been living in Manchester until he was reported missing in July of 1990—right around the anniversary of the fire. Now listen up, both of you. This is very important. If anyone asks, Toby did *not* know where the body was. We were all doing some ghost hunting and someone shined a flashlight down the elevator shaft. It looked as if there might be something down there. That's all. Got that?"

"Why?" Cassandra asked.

Mrs. H. sighed and crossed her arms, tapping the gloved fingers of one hand against her elbow. "So that Toby isn't accused of murdering Mr. Bishop, my dear, and leading us to the scene twenty-five years later. That's why. The police aren't very imaginative when it comes to the workings of the psychic plane."

"I appreciate you looking out for me, Mrs. H.," Toby said.

"Think nothing of it. Now, I must run. I have a meeting with my stockbroker. But I'll see you at the usual time on Monday for my reading?"

Considering how much trouble her last reading had resulted in, Toby had to suppress a shudder at the thought of doing another one. On the other hand, it had led him to Frank. He smiled and gave her a nod. "I'm looking forward to it."

Epilogue

THE MILL was torn down that August, and by early October fresh turf had been laid down to convert the grounds into a park. In the center, though the pipework was still being installed, a marble fountain had been erected with brass plaques at intervals around it, listing the names of the victims of the fire on July 17, 1907. One woman, Rosaleen Quinn, had a plaque of her own, though the reason for this was known to only seven people—seven people sworn to secrecy.

The discovery of Jack Bishop's body made the local papers, and there was much speculation about how it had ended up at the bottom of the elevator shaft. Where it had ultimately been laid to rest, Frank didn't know... and didn't much care. That monster's fate was in the hands of God or karma or whatever controlled men's destinies after death. Though he technically died in the mill, his name was not listed on the fountain plaques.

"I need to rest," Louis said. His arms were trembling as he hobbled over to a bench near the fountain on his crutches. Houston guided him down into a sitting position.

"You shouldn't push yourself so hard," Houston said.

"Oh, come on! It's barely a hill."

"The doctor said the leg needs rest in order to heal."

"I'm resting right now. See?"

Houston groaned but apparently decided he couldn't win this argument, so he just kissed Louis to shut him up.

Frank watched the exchange with amusement. It had been wonderful to see the two boys so happy over the past two and a half months. Savannah had declared that, between them and how sickly sweet he and Toby could be, she was going to have to get her blood sugar checked. Frank glanced at his boyfriend and thought she was probably right. He'd started singing along with the radio whenever they were in the van. He'd never done that. Not before Toby.

Toby had picked out the flowers he and Savannah were planting around Rosaleen's plaque today—heather for protection and white roses for love. The chrysanthemums and other decorative flowers Mrs. Hawley had ordered for the fountain would be planted by the florist later that week. Technically the park was still closed for construction. It would open in another week.

"May you find peace at last," Toby murmured when they were finished, placing his hand on the plaque.

Savannah added, "You'll always be in our hearts, honey child."

It was good to watch the two of them together. They'd grown fond of each other over the past several weeks, whenever the C-Troop team was able to visit Hawley and hang out with Toby and Cassandra. Even Houston seemed to have gotten over his initial dislike of Toby.

Frank and Toby had talked about doing more investigations together, with Toby as part of the C-Troop team, and Cassandra had been pestering both of them to bring her along too. Frank had been hesitant to propose the idea to the others, but they surprised him by approving of it. Oh, sure, Houston was still uptight about keeping things scientific, and Frank kind of agreed with him. But maybe they could find room for both approaches.

Savannah and Houston were family to Frank, almost as much as Louis. It would have been difficult to keep seeing Toby if they'd disapproved. He would still have done it, of course—nobody told Frank Carter who he could or could not love. But it was nice to have everybody on the same page. His and Toby's jobs kept them apart during most of the week, especially since Frank tended to work nights, but Keene was only a bit more than an hour's drive from Hawley. It hadn't been too difficult to arrange time together.

Frank came up behind them and wrapped his arms around Toby's middle. "We're gonna have to head back soon. We have an investigation in Peterborough tonight. Do you want to grab something for lunch?"

"Mmm. That sounds nice." The way he was caressing Frank's forearm made lunch sound like a dirty proposition. Maybe it was.

Apparently Savannah thought it might be. She gave the two of them a smirk and said, "You two go on. I'll watch after the Hardy Boys."

"Sounds good."

As they walked across the grass to where Toby's car and the van were parked, Toby asked, "Hardy Boys? Do they have another nickname now?"

"Who knows?" Frank said. "This group comes up with nicknames at the drop of a hat. At least they seem to have given up calling me 'Baba.' God, I hated that name!"

"They haven't proposed any nicknames for me, have they?"

"They're tossing some around." Frank gave him a mischievous grin. "'Psychic,' 'Psychicboy'…."

Toby groaned. "Gods, it makes me sound like a superhero!"

"I've seen you in the bedroom," Frank laughed. "It might apply."

"Me? You're the animal in the bedroom. Maybe I should come up with some nicknames for *you*. How do you feel about 'Tarzan' or 'Deep Throat'?"

Frank snorted. He reached out to pull Toby close and glanced back over his shoulder to make sure nobody could overhear them. "How about we keep that one to ourselves?"

Author's Note

THE HAWLEY Mill fire is based upon real events that occurred not once, but several times in New England at various textile mills—the Granite Mill in Fall River, Massachusetts in 1874, the Cocheco Mill in Dover, New Hampshire in 1907, and most famously the Triangle Shirtwaist Factory fire in New York City in 1911, which cost the lives of 146 people, mostly young women between sixteen and twenty-three-years-old. And there were other similar tragedies. The lack of safety precautions in these mills often meant it was impossible to escape if fire broke out.

The verses heading up each chapter in this story are taken from a ballad originally written about the Granite Mill fire sometime before 1890. There were many variations on it, so I don't feel I'm breaking with tradition by adapting the verses to my fictional Hawley Mill. But here is the original ballad in its entirety.

The Granite Mill Fire

Was in Fall River City
When the people was burned and killed,
In a cotton manufactory
Called as the Granite Mill.
At seven o'clock the firebells rang
But oh, it was too late,
The flames they were fast spreading
And at a rapid rate.

They were men and women there
And children too, I'm told,
Who might have been saved from out of the flames
If the truth was only known.
But oh, the villains that locked the doors
And told them to keep still,
It was the bosses and overseers

That burning Granite Mill.

The first scene was a touching one
From a maid so young in years,
She was standing by a window and
Her eyes were filled with tears.
She cried, "Oh, save me! Save me!"
She called her mother's name,
But her mother could not save her
And she fell back in the flame.

The next scene was a horrible one
Just as it caught my eye.
They were leaping from a window
From up so very high,
And the only means of their escape
Was sliding down a rope,
And just as they were half way down
The burning strands they broke.

Christ, Christ, what a horrible mess,
They were mangled, burned and killed,
Six stories high, and falling from
The burning Granite Mill.
But I hope their spirits has fled
To a better place far still,
Up high, up high, up in the sky
Above the Granite Mill.

JAMIE FESSENDEN set out to be a writer in junior high school. He published a couple of short pieces in his high school's literary magazine and had another story place in the top 100 in a national contest, but it wasn't until he met his partner, Erich, almost twenty years later, that he began writing again in earnest. With Erich alternately inspiring and goading him, Jamie wrote several screenplays and directed a few of them as micro-budget independent films. He then began writing novels and published his first novella in 2010.

After nine years together, Jamie and Erich have married and purchased a house together in the wilds of Raymond, New Hampshire, where there are no street lights, turkeys and deer wander through their yard, and coyotes serenade them on a nightly basis. Jamie recently left his "day job" as a tech support analyst to be a full-time writer.

Visit Jamie: jamiefessenden.wordpress.com
Facebook: www.facebook.com/pages/Jamie-Fessenden-Author/102004836534286
Twitter: @JamieFessenden1

By JAMIE FESSENDEN

Billy's Bones
The Christmas Wager
Dogs of Cyberwar
The Healing Power of Eggnog
Murder on the Mountain
Murderous Requiem
Saturn in Retrograde
Screwups
Violated
We're Both Straight, Right?

GOTHIKA
Claw (Multiple Author Anthology)
Stitch (Multiple Author Anthology)
Bones (Multiple Author Anthology)
Spirit (Multiple Author Anthology)

Published by DREAMSPINNER PRESS
www.dreamspinnerpress.com

Dei ex Machina

by Kim Fielding

One

THE GHOST perched atop the tall limestone walls of the palace, gazing down at the colorful crowds that strolled the Riva promenade. Beyond the cafés and vendors, the harbor sparkled in the bright sun and the distant islands floated like clouds in the Adriatic Sea.

On the bad days, the ghost had no sense of self. He floated in an inky soup, grasping desperately for anything at all: a sensation, a memory, a thought. Sometimes his efforts were fruitless for a very long time, and then he was lost, he was nothing, he was—

No. Today was a good day; he remembered. Once—a very long time ago—he had been a living man, and his name had been Sabbio. He'd been able to smell the salt air and the fish at the market, to taste the tang of an olive and the sweetness of a fig. And gods, once he'd been able to feel the breeze against his skin and the touch of a hand. People had *seen* him and spoken to him, had listened to his accented Latin. Once he'd been real.

Now he was only a ghost.

He'd been a phantom long enough to see civilizations die and new ones born. He'd eavesdropped on a basketful of languages, sometimes only turning the strange words over in his mind, other times listening long enough to understand what people said. He'd witnessed a cornucopia of clothing styles, some odd enough to make even a dead man laugh. He'd viewed some wondrous machines that he never could have conceived of when he was alive. But for all these centuries, even on his best days, he'd been simply an observer. Seeing, but never seen.

The Riva was paved in big marble blocks that gleamed like glass. People walked slowly with their lovers, their children, or their friends. They sat on benches under the palm trees or at tables shaded by sail-like canopies.

It pleased Sabbio to know that people still treasured the palace, especially since its construction had cost him his life. He'd been nothing but a slave, one of hundreds killed in the rush to erect Emperor Diocletian's retirement home. But however insignificant he once had been—and he was far less significant now—at least he had helped create something of lasting value.

He felt the emptiness growing inside him and knew his good day would soon end and he'd fall back into that endless pit. As always, he feared he'd never claw his way back out.

At least he could make these moments count.

Using only effort of will, Sabbio descended from the palace wall and drifted over the promenade. He watched as a proud young couple bought their young child a dog-shaped balloon from a vendor's cart, and he listened as an older couple on a bench argued in Italian over where to eat dinner. He liked Italian because it was so close to Latin and because the syllables rose and fell like music. Even a disagreement sounded like a song.

He wafted over to the busy cafés. There had been no coffee when he was alive, and anyway, slaves were given nothing to drink but watered wine. He wondered what coffee tasted like and why it was taken in such tiny cups. Some café patrons drank rakija instead—he imagined it tasted like very strong wine—or beer, which he'd smelled so very long ago.

He hovered for a time near a group of young men who discussed sports and boasted about women they'd slept with. They were handsome. And although they spoke Croatian and wore sunglasses, T-shirts, and track pants, they were not very different from the older boys he'd admired in his village before he was captured and enslaved. He watched them wistfully.

In a shadowy spot near the wall, a beautiful man and attractive woman sat silently, watching the people around them. He was younger than she was, with dark hair, and her chestnut tresses cascaded over her shoulders. Something about them unsettled Sabbio, so he avoided passing too close.

A few tables away, tourists conversed in German about the city of Dubrovnik, farther down the coast. They thought it was beautiful. Sabbio had never been there, of course. It hadn't existed when he was alive—not that he would have been free to travel in any case—and now he couldn't go far from the palace. Still, it was nice to hear about the other city, just as he'd heard about so many places over the centuries.

Not far from the Germans, an older woman sat with several young people, telling tales in English of the emperor Diocletian and his palace. Not all of what she said was accurate, but Sabbio knew he wasn't the only one who forgot things as time passed. Entire nations forgot—and were forgotten. He enjoyed listening to her anyway, especially because she so obviously cared about her subject. Not all of her students were as rapt as Sabbio, however; two teenaged girls flirted with each other, brushing their knees together under the table where nobody but Sabbio could see. He smiled. Many things changed, but human beings remained essentially the same. That was a comfort.

The group three tables over also chatted in English. Sabbio had been surprised at the speed with which English seemed to take over, and although he was more than a little hazy about politics, he assumed the English empire must have exceeded the old Roman one. Strange, that. In his day, the British Isles were populated by barbarians in mud huts. Or so he'd been told. In any case, he liked the way the language itself seemed to gobble up other tongues, using their words as it saw fit.

These English-speakers—four men and a woman—were drinking wine. They looked relaxed, as tourists ought to, but one of the men toyed with his glass, a faraway look in his shadowed brown eyes. He was very tan, as if he spent long hours under the sun. Even though he looked slightly underfed, he was still very nice-looking, with pink lips and honey-colored curls.

Ignoring the lively conversation of his friends, the handsome man glanced up. For a moment it was almost as if he stared straight at Sabbio. Sabbio swallowed and reached for him. But then the man's gaze shifted to the side and he sighed, slumping in his seat.

A gaping chasm as big as the heavens tore through Sabbio's middle, and he fell into himself, into the eternal dark.

Two

THERE WAS an art to catching the eyes of Croatian waiters, and Mason Gould had not even begun to master it. When he first sat down at a sidewalk café, the waiter would always come promptly to take his order, and the drink would arrive soon afterward. But good luck trying to get your bill. Ordering a second round was even more impossible. The upside was that you could park your ass in a chair for hours without the waitstaff sending you dirty looks. The downside was that you could get really thirsty.

"Nicole," he said, interrupting his sister-in-law's speculation on the number of shoe stores per capita in Split.

"What?"

"I want another glass."

She rolled her eyes, but not very emphatically. She was the only one among their party with a knack for flagging down waiters. It probably helped that she was gorgeous, blonde, and busty. The previous week she had the Italian men practically throwing themselves at her feet, even when she was holding hands with her husband—Mason's brother, Adam. Croatian men were slightly quieter in their admiration but nearly as obvious.

Now, when Nicole swiveled toward the nearest waiter and smiled, the guy came scurrying over like his shoes were on fire.

"More, uh, vino please," she said, smiling. "For the guys. Espresso for me, please."

The waiter nodded, still ignoring the male contingent at the table. "No problem."

Adam was used to people ogling his wife. Hell, a lot of women ogled him. He was ripped and tattooed, and he somehow managed to pull off looking like a bad boy instead of a bank manager from Modesto. Mason used to be jealous of his younger brother, but nowadays he didn't have the energy for it.

The waiter brought a fresh round. Mason drank his quickly, then played with the stem of the glass. Adam was trying to convince the gang to take a ferry to one of the islands the next day, but Mason's friends, Doug and Pete, lobbied for finding a beach instead.

"Or we could rent a car," Doug offered. "There's a peninsula south of here. Uh, Pel-something. Lots of wineries."

Mason kept out of the conversation. He stared at the Adriatic, wishing it was the Pacific and Carl was at his side. For just a moment, he thought he saw something wavering in front of him, and then it was gone. A trick of the sun reflecting off the bright pavement and blue-green water. Maybe he ought to go lie down and rest his eyes.

He started to stand, but Doug, who was sitting next to him, caught his arm. "Are you okay?"

Suddenly without the energy to walk to their apartment, Mason collapsed back into his chair. "Fine," he mumbled unconvincingly.

"You look a little…." Doug shook his head slightly. "What do *you* want to do tomorrow?"

"I don't care." They could get on a plane and head back to California, for all it mattered to him. His friends and family had meant well, dragging him along on a trip to ease his mourning, but it hadn't worked. He was just as ravaged in Europe as he'd been in the States.

Doug gave him a worried look, one Mason was familiar with—he'd been on the receiving end of that expression a lot lately. "It's only been eight months," Mason said, trying to explain himself. "He was the love of my life and he's gone and I didn't even get to say good-bye, and it's only been eight fucking months." He kept his voice flat and toneless.

"Honey, we know," Doug said. He patted Mason's shoulder. "And for God's sake, nobody's telling you not to be sad about it. But you were always…. One of the things Carl loved about you was your energy. Your zest. You know he'd want you to move on a little, to enjoy life. He'd hate to see you so miserable."

He can't see me at all because he's fucking dead! With an effort, Mason bit back his retort. Carl's death had hit Doug hard too—the two of them had known each other since they were kids. Carl had introduced Doug to his husband, Pete. And Doug was right. Carl's pet name for Mason had been Spark. "My firecracker," he used to whisper fondly as he stroked Mason's flank. But Carl got killed and Mason's spark had extinguished, leaving only ashes.

Clenching his jaw, Mason looked away. At a table several yards down the Riva, a man and woman stared at him. She was gorgeous, with a curvy body that reminded him of a 50s movie star, long red-brown locks, and the kind of face that would be beautiful no matter her age. Her younger companion was pretty in a goth kind of way, with pouty lips, bedroom eyes, and almost preternaturally dark hair. The woman leaned over to say something to the man, and Mason was quite certain they were talking about him. Usually he didn't give a crap what other people thought, but there was something odd about those two, something he couldn't put his finger on. Their regard made him uncomfortable.

Mason stood, and this time Doug didn't grab him. He dropped some kuna onto the table to pay for his wine. "I'm going for a walk," he announced. Maybe a ramble through the old town's narrow streets and alleys would clear his head a little.

"Do you want company?" Doug asked, still frowning with concern.

"No. Don't worry, I'm not going to throw myself off the cathedral tower or anything. I just want a little exercise. I'll meet you guys back at the apartment for dinner, okay?"

Although nobody else at the table looked especially pleased, they nodded. Mason gave them the shadow of a smile and wandered off.

As he stalked through the palace, he thought maybe it would have been better if his friends had taken him somewhere else. Somewhere new and shiny, without a hint of history. Vegas, perhaps. Because Carl would have *adored* Split. He would have read a dozen books about the old city, bored them all with lectures about why and how it was built, and stopped to inspect every ancient stone. By the time they headed back to California, Mason would have been the reluctant recipient of an encyclopedic knowledge about the crumbling Roman Empire and the Croatian wars. Carl would have taken about a million photos and browsed every goddamn shop, until Mason was about ready to strangle him. And when they packed for the return home, Carl's suitcase wouldn't have fit all the shit he'd bought, so he'd have stuffed Mason's bag full too.

Mason found himself stalled in front of an ice cream stand, blinking back tears. If he'd only had the chance to say good-bye. Hell, he'd barely glanced up from his coffee when Carl left for work that morning. Mason had been sitting at the kitchen table, deep in thought over his new landscaping project. He was trying to talk the client out of redwoods, which would grow fast and soon overpower the small front yard. Mason might have mumbled "Haveagooddaybabe" as Carl hurried out the door, but maybe not.

Shit. Maybe he should have had another glass of wine.

He wandered an erratic path through the old town until his feet grew tired, then found himself in a large square just outside the palace, surrounded by newer buildings that still predated any California structures by several centuries. Picking one of the many cafés at random, he plunked himself down. The waiter materialized almost at once, took Mason's order for coffee, and strolled away. He returned quickly, bearing coffee and a glass of water. He never once smiled. Mason had concluded that Croatian waiters smiled only at Nicole.

He was halfway through his coffee when he rubbed his face tiredly. Hiding behind his palms felt so good that he stayed that way, like a young child frozen in a game of peekaboo. He startled when he heard someone sit across from him.

The man looked a few years older than Mason—perhaps late thirties—and he was big. Broad-shouldered, muscular, and tall even when he was sitting down. He was handsome too, in a slightly brutish way, with a strong jaw, prominent nose, and pale blue eyes. His brown hair was cut very short. He wasn't smiling as he assessed Mason, but he didn't look hostile either.

"Um…," Mason said, unsure how to react.

"I am Viktor Lulić. Where are you from?" Lulić had a thick Croatian accent.

"Um, California. But—"

"American. I thought maybe you were English." He nodded slightly, as if he were pleased with the discovery.

The guy definitely wasn't trying to pick Mason up. For one thing, gay life in Croatia tended to be somewhat subdued. Doug had said that thousands of antigay protestors had turned violent just a few years ago during Split's first pride parade. Doug and Pete had been careful about public displays of affection, and Mason hadn't exactly been flying the rainbow flag since he arrived. Lulić didn't seem to be sending any subtle signals that he wanted to get into Mason's pants. At least, Mason didn't think so. He hadn't flirted with anyone since he met Carl almost ten years ago; he was pretty rusty.

Maybe Lulić wanted to sell him something. A room for the night, a guided tour. The locals didn't seem especially pushy, but this guy could be an exception.

"What can I do for you?" Mason asked. He would have just walked away, but he hadn't paid yet—and, of course, his waiter was nowhere in sight.

Lulić quirked the corner of his mouth. "I think I can do for *you*."

Drugs, maybe? Mason hadn't seen evidence of anything harder than rakija, but maybe the locals figured Americans were a bunch of stoners. "Whatever you're selling, man, I'm not in the market for it."

"I am not selling. I am making free offer. I heard you and your friends at café on Riva."

Mason tensed as he tried to remember what they had talked about. Had this guy been stalking him all afternoon?

Probably sensing Mason's unease, Lulić sighed and set his hands on the table, palms up. "I am sorry. I know it was rude, but I try to practice my English. But now I can help you."

"Help me how?"

"You said someone you love died. I am sorry to hear this. And I know…. My wife, she died too. Three years. Cancer." If the grief on his face was fake, he was a hell of an actor.

"I'm sorry. But, um, my someone was a man. My husband."

Lulić shrugged. "This is not important. Pain in heart is same, yes?"

"Yes," Mason murmured.

"I was with Ivana when she was in hospital. I held her hand when she died. This… this was very hard. But also good, to say I loved her. You did not do this with your husband?"

"He was murdered. He was walking across campus, and some psycho just opened fire. Carl didn't know him—the bastard wasn't even a student there. He was just having a really bad day, I guess, and decided the university made for easy pickings. He killed four people before he turned the gun on himself."

"Guns," Lulić said grimly. "My father died in Homeland War. It is not same as murder, maybe, but still...."

"The pain in the heart is the same," Mason said.

"*Da*. But *your* pain, maybe I can help."

Mason leaned back and crossed his arms. "Unless you can turn back time, Viktor, I doubt there's much you can do for me."

For a moment or two, Lulić rubbed his jaw and looked at Mason. His fingers were broad, the knuckles scraped and calloused as if he worked with his hands a lot. But his fingernails were clean. After a decade as a landscaper, Mason had dirt permanently embedded under his. Carl used to claim that Mason's work-roughened hands were one of his best features.

Apparently reaching a decision, Lulić leaned forward and dropped his voice slightly. "My mother is... I do not know English word. She can talk to, ah, *duhovi*. How you say...." He scrunched up his face as he tried to remember.

"I don't understand," Mason said.

Like many Croatian men, Lulić carried a man-bag. He rummaged in it for a moment and then pulled out a phone. He poked at it as he said, "I have translation app. Ah! Spirits. My mother talks to spirits."

Well, that was a surprise. "Mom sees dead people?"

Unexpectedly, Lulić grinned. "*Sixth Sense!* Bruce Willis. I am fan. *Die Hard.*" Then he grew serious again. "My mother is like this. She talks to spirits. She has done this since she was young. She says it is like turning radio to right station. Most of us cannot get this station, but she can."

Hands down, it was the weirdest conversation Mason had undertaken in years. He wondered if he should check Adam's copy of Rick Steves's guidebook to see if this was some local scam. But Viktor seemed earnest enough, and he hadn't yet asked for a thing. And, well, at least Mason would have a good story to take home with him.

"That's an interesting hobby your mom has, but I don't see how it helps me."

"Maybe she can talk to your husband. Say good-bye for you. This will give you some peace."

Mason felt as if his heart were bathed in acid. "Carl died six thousand miles from here."

"Yes. But maybe this does not matter. My mother's spirits are from everywhere." He chuckled. "She understands only those who speak Croatian or German, though."

"Carl only spoke English. And ancient Latin and Greek." Because if you taught classical history, you pretty much had to. Sometimes Carl would recite ancient poetry to Mason, who didn't understand the words but was always turned on by them.

"I can translate," Viktor said. "If she can find him. I cannot promise she will, but she can try."

The guy's entire story had to be bullshit from top to bottom. This was not an M. Night Shyamalan movie, and nobody could tune in the dead. Viktor was either crazy or a slick scam artist. People who were shattered by loss made the perfect marks. Mason knew all of this. But God, it was so tempting to believe! Just the idea of a few final words with Carl, a chance to let him know how much Mason loved him, how much he missed him....

"I don't have the money to pay for anything like this," Mason said with a sigh. It was true. On Adam's insistence, he'd invested most of the money from Carl's life insurance in a retirement account, because Mason was self-employed and wouldn't have a pension. The remainder had gone to paying down the mortgage so the bills would be less tight on a single income. The European trip had been a splurge that ate up a lot of his savings account.

"This is not for money," Viktor said.

"Then why?"

"Because... you are so sad. In Dalmatia, you should enjoy sea and wine and delicious food. You should not be sad." He smiled and waved his hands to indicate the entire square, as if he were saying, *How can anyone mourn in a beautiful place like this?*

"You don't even know me."

"True. But in one year I will end my job—I am mechanic for trains—and I will start tourist company. This is why I practice English. And you will be so happy with me, you will send many friends to Split. I will be rich." Viktor grinned widely. It was really hard not to like him.

"Fine. Send my message to your mother, and if she dials up Carl, you can text me to let me know."

"She will have to see you in person. Because he was your husband. You will be like...." He poked at his phone again. "Like antenna for radio."

"Thanks, but—"

"Tomorrow. Now she cooks dinner, I think. Tomorrow I meet you here, and I will take you to her. It is not far. Ten?"

Although it was insane, Mason found himself nodding. Hell, at the very least he was curious to know what the scam was. Probably nothing violent. Despite a recent civil war, Croatians were a lot less likely to kill people than Americans were. He was willing to bet not a single Croatian professor had been murdered while walking from his office to the library.

"Okay," Mason said. "Ten o'clock."

Three

"YOU ARE out of your fucking mind," Adam said with complete conviction.

They'd picked up a prosciutto pizza for dinner—Croatians were very fond of the stuff and made it as well as the Italians—and brought it back to their apartment, where the five of them sat around a dining table that looked as if it came from Ikea. In fact, all the furniture looked to be products of an umlaut-riddled warehouse, which was a bit incongruous with the apartment's ancient stone walls, curved archways, and hand-hewn ceiling beams. The building itself was about a block from one of the palace entrances, in a part of town that had been built around the time Columbus was looking for India. It was a comfortable apartment, with three bedrooms and two baths, located above a street-level bar and an ice cream place.

Mason took a bite of pizza, chewed, and swallowed. "Probably," he admitted.

"So you'll come with us to Hvar in the morning? We're taking a catamaran." Adam navigated his pizza slice through the air as if it were a boat.

"Nope. I'm going to meet Viktor at ten."

"But that's nuts! We're going to be exploring a beautiful island while you're having a séance with a serial killer."

Chewing thoughtfully, Mason tilted his head. "I wonder if serial killers would attend séances. Would it bother them to chat with their victims, or would they get a kick out of it?"

"Mason!" When Adam got exasperated, he sounded remarkably like their father. Mason considered telling him so.

"I think you should go with Viktor," Pete said quietly, and everyone swiveled their heads to stare. Pete was brilliant but spoke little outside the classroom. He was the kind of guy who watched everything, missing nothing. When he did offer advice, his words carried a lot of weight. Plus, Mason reminded himself, this trip had been organized on Pete's behalf too. That same sunny morning eight months earlier, Pete had walked across the quad just in time to see a kid with a gun mow down two students, the Dean of Humanities, and the man who was one of Pete's colleagues and closest friends.

"Why do you say that?" Doug asked, resting his hand on Pete's shoulder.

"Because it's pretty unlikely this Viktor guy really is a serial killer. And because maybe whatever his mother does will help Mason feel a little better. Help him heal." He offered Mason a small, apologetic smile.

Adam snorted dismissively. "Don't tell me you believe in that crap!"

"Spiritualism? I'm neutral on the subject. The null hypothesis has never been disproven to my satisfaction, but that doesn't mean there's no afterlife, or that communication with those who've passed on is impossible. I've been studying the human mind for almost twenty years, and it's an astonishing phenomenon. It wouldn't surprise me if it transcended and even survived the physical self, if some part of us lasted beyond death. A spark." He smiled at Mason again.

The conversation moved on to everyone's theories about life and death and heaven and hell, and Adam stopped arguing about Mason's plans. Later that night, though, while Adam and Mason took their turn washing the dinner dishes, Adam leaned in close. "Don't get yourself hurt, big brother. Mom and Dad will kill me if I bring you back to the States in pieces." And he ruffled Mason's hair with his soapsudsy fingers.

IN THE morning, Nicole made a last-ditch effort to get Mason to see sense. Adam had probably put her up to it. But Mason dug in his heels, and eventually the gang left for the harbor without him. It was too early to meet Viktor, so Mason emptied his pockets of everything except a hundred kuna—less than twenty bucks—his phone, and a photocopy of his passport. If Viktor did turn out to be a robber, he wasn't going to get anything out of the deal except a smartphone two generations out of date and enough money for a pizza and beer.

Mason spent over an hour wandering the old city aimlessly, stopping once for a piece of cherry strudel. As he walked, he sometimes let his fingers sweep against the palace's stone walls, thinking about the many thousands of people who'd brushed against them over the years.

At ten to ten, he found yesterday's café in People's Square. His previous table was occupied, so he sat next to it. The same expressionless waiter took his order for cappuccino.

Viktor arrived almost fifteen minutes late. Mason had already learned that Croatians in general—and Dalmatians especially—took a more southern European approach to punctuality, rather than emulating some of their prompter neighbors to the north. That didn't bother him. There were a million worse places to spend time than in a café a few blocks from the Adriatic, sitting and watching people stroll by.

When Viktor finally plopped down across from Mason, he looked happy. "I did not scare you away."

"Not quite. My friends think you might be Hannibal Lecter, though."

Viktor grinned. "Not possible. I drink žlahtina, not Chianti. So you will come with me?"

"I guess so."

"Good. My mother wants to meet you. She likes Americans. She says you are loud like Italians, but you are friendly and you, um, like old things very much."

"I'll try to keep my voice down," Mason said with a chuckle. Then he attempted to catch the waiter's attention and failed spectacularly.

Apparently realizing the problem, Viktor turned his head, and as if by magic, the waiter sauntered over with the bill.

Impressive, Mason thought as he set a few coins on the plastic tray.

Viktor led him out of the old city, but not far. His mother apparently lived in a nondescript socialist-era building just a few blocks from the Riva. "I live in second-floor flat with my children," Viktor explained as he unlocked the front door. "My mother lives upstairs. Is good for children to be near their grandmother, yes? And train station is only short walk from here."

"How old are your kids?" Mason asked.

"Ten and twelve. They are in school now. Too bad. They could practice English with you."

The building's common area was somewhat dingy and hadn't been updated since Tito's days. There was no elevator. Mason was puffing slightly by the time they arrived in front of Mrs. Lulić's door—which was actually on the fourth floor by American counting. He used to be in really good shape, but he'd let that slip after Carl's death. The only exercise he'd been getting lately was at work, digging and planting.

Viktor rapped twice but didn't wait for an answer. He opened the door and ushered Mason inside. The apartment interior was bright and cheery, with modern furniture in the living room and a few abstract paintings on the walls. After the shabby common area at street level and the gloomy stairwell, Mason was pleasantly surprised.

Mrs. Lulić, when she came bustling in, was a surprise too. Mason had vaguely expected a witchy-looking old lady wearing a babushka and lumpy sweater, but Mrs. Lulić was tall and elegant, with carefully styled blonde hair and a flattering green dress. "Hello," she said, smiling at him and holding out her hand.

"Uh, *dobar dan*, Mrs. Lulić." *Good day* was almost the limit of his Croatian, but she seemed to appreciate his attempt as they shook. Then he realized that he'd never told Viktor his name. "I'm Mason Gould. Thank you for letting me come over."

Viktor murmured softly in translation.

If the Lulićes were up to no good, they were certainly going about it oddly. They sat Mason in a comfy chair, and Mrs. Lulić brought him tea and some kind of custardy cake, and then Viktor translated as she asked gentle questions about the US.

"I have always wanted to visit New York," she said via her son.

Mason grinned. "Me too. I've never been to the east coast."

"Yes, America is very big. Tell me, is California like we see in movies?"

"Parts of it, sure. Not where I live. We have cows. And strip malls."

Viktor had to use his phone to figure out how to say *strip mall* in Croatian.

She recommended a few of her favorite restaurants in Split and told him he really ought to see at least one of the islands. And, she said, if he planned to travel inland, he needed to go to Plitvice Lakes National Park.

Viktor seconded that endorsement. "Most beautiful place on planet."

"Thanks. I'll keep that in mind." Mason and his gang were bound for Vienna next because Doug was a cellist who thought everybody ought to be subjected to a lot of Mozart.

Eventually the tea and cakes were polished off. Mrs. Lulić did not take out a crystal ball or Ouija board. She just sat in an armchair with her hands clasped in her lap. "Tell me about your husband," she said softly. She didn't wince over the words or indicate in any way that she was disturbed that Mason was gay.

How do you summarize the man you love in a few simple sentences? Mason looked at his feet. "His name was Carl. He was smart and funny and kind. He didn't care that he was a professor and I'm just a landscaper—he always made me feel smart too. He liked to watch boring news shows on TV. He snored really loudly. He was a terrible dancer. He cried at sappy movies and always claimed it was just allergies. He… he loved me." Mason managed to keep his voice even, but his throat felt thick and congested.

He waited while Viktor finished putting Mason's words into Croatian. And it was strange, because even though he'd spent plenty of time talking about Carl over the past several months, he suddenly felt a little lighter. Maybe because these two complete strangers from a country far from the US now knew about Carl, and they both nodded solemnly over Mason's description. They'd remember Carl long after Mason was back in California. And wasn't that a type of afterlife—having a presence in people's hearts and minds even when your body was ashes?

Memory was a kind of spark too.

Mrs. Lulić spoke quietly to Viktor, gazing at Mason during the interpretation phase. "Mama will try to talk to Carl in Latin," Viktor said. "She is doctor and had to learn at university. But her Latin is very bad, so you should choose easy words."

A doctor who talked to ghosts.

Why not?

Mason nodded, and Viktor picked up a nearby pencil and pad of paper.

"I don't have anything fancy to say. Just… I love him very much. I'm sorry I didn't tell him that more often when I had the chance. And I hope he's happy, wherever he is. I hope someday I'll meet him again." Strange, how the emotions that swirled within him—which felt as if they could fill a library's worth of volumes—could be distilled into just a few brief sentences.

Viktor passed the paper to his mother, and she took a moment to read it. When she was done, she gave Mason a sweet, encouraging smile. She closed her eyes and murmured haltingly in something that was not Croatian. Latin, Mason supposed, although the only words he knew in the language were botanical names.

After Mrs. Lulić stopped talking, the room was quiet. Mason heard his own heart and lungs busy working, the whir of a fan somewhere, the faint rumble of traffic wafting through an open window. Mrs. Lulić kept her eyes shut, but she cocked her head slightly, as if she were listening for something. Viktor watched his mother closely, a proud smile playing at the corners of his mouth.

And Mason…. He didn't see anything out of the ordinary. Certainly didn't hear Carl or anyone else. But he had that itchy shoulder blade sensation, as if someone were staring at him from behind. The feeling was so strong that he turned around to look. Nothing there other than a sleek china cabinet, but the feeling didn't go away. He *smelled* something too—just a whiff of dust and sweat that didn't fit at all with the immaculate apartment.

Power of suggestion, he told himself. But the hairs on the back of his neck stood, his breathing quickened, and the air seemed thick. He was absolutely positive that someone besides him and the Lulićes was in the room. Not Carl—Mason was sure of that.

It was like one of those stupid magic picture things. Something was right there in front of him, and if he only focused his eyes properly, he'd see it. But he couldn't, no matter how hard he squinted and blinked.

"Who's there?" he whispered. He wasn't frightened.

Mrs. Lulić answered—"Sabbio"—but Mason didn't know what that meant.

Still twisted around in his chair, he slowly lifted one hand and reached forward. For an extremely brief moment, there was pressure against his fingertips. The smoothness of skin.

Then the tension popped like a bubble, and he was alone in the apartment with Viktor and Mrs. Lulić.

"What was *that*?" Mason breathed.

Mrs. Lulić shot him a sad smile before saying something in Croatian to her son. Viktor turned to Mason when she was done. "Mama says she is sorry. She did not hear Carl. But he maybe heard her. Sometimes connection is not so good. But it is not so sad he did not come. Means he is far away, with peace, yes? Closer spirits are ones who cannot rest."

Mason couldn't help but smile. "Figures. He always sucked at answering my text messages too. I'd send him, like, a dozen. He always claimed he read them, but he'd wait until he got home to talk to me."

"I think he knows you love him."

Oddly, Mason thought so too. He couldn't explain why, but he felt much better. God, he still missed Carl, in the same way that he'd miss a severed limb. But the ache had faded to manageable levels.

"There was.... I felt...." Mason struggled to put his question into words.

"A spirit," Viktor said, nodding. "Yes. It was here."

"It wasn't Carl."

"I know. It was.... One minute." Viktor had a short conversation with his mother. He had to consult his phone before providing an interpretation. "Some spirits do not rest. They are angry or sad, maybe. *Uznemiren*. Unsettled. Although Mama called Carl, unsettled spirit heard and came for visit. Do not worry. They cannot hurt you."

"I didn't get a wanting-to-hurt-me vibe. I think it was just...."

"Lonely," Viktor finished for him. "Yes."

"Can we do anything to help it?"

After Viktor translated, Mrs. Lulić gave Mason the same wide smile as his mother had when he'd informed her his landscaping company was operating solidly in the black. *You did good*, that smile said. It was nice to receive it. Mrs. Lulić said something to Viktor.

"Mama says you are good boy."

"I'm thirty-three."

Viktor shrugged. "She calls me boy too. *Dječak*. It means she is happy." He grinned. "When she is angry she calls me other things."

Well, Mason's parents referred to him, Adam, and Nicole as *the kids*. Carl had been one of the kids too, even after he got tenure. "I'm glad your mother likes me."

"She says unhappy spirits can be settled. They want only to know someone cares, maybe."

"Can she do this for whoever showed up today?"

"Maybe. But now... maybe you can call it. It came to you."

Mason nodded at the truth of that. "So I just...."

"Be open. Welcome it, like guest in your house." Viktor pointed at the dishes on the coffee table. "Give it tea and cake."

"Great. Ghost snacks. And then it will... rest?"

Viktor conferred with his mother before answering. "It might rest. Maybe it has problems, you can solve them. Unfinished business. You find what it wants."

Mason didn't know why this prospect energized him instead of freaking him out, but he nodded. "Okay. I guess I can try that if I get the chance." He stood, and his hosts followed suit. He walked to Mrs. Lulić. "*Hvala*. Thank you. This was very nice of you."

Instead of shaking his hand, though, she embraced him and gave each of his cheeks a kiss. "*Dobar dječak*," she said. "*Nadam se da ćete naći ljubav ponovno.*"

"She hopes you find love again," Viktor said.

Viktor walked Mason down the stairs and out to the street. They stood awkwardly for a moment before Viktor clapped Mason's shoulder. "You have phone? I give you my number. You can call if you need me."

"Plus I'll be able to pass on your info to any friends who visit Split. I'll tell them your tourist services come highly recommended." Mason handed over the phone.

Laughing, Viktor punched his number into Mason's contacts before returning the device.

"Thanks," Mason said. "For everything. I'm sorry I thought you might be a serial killer."

"I think only America has serial killers. We are too simple for this in Croatia. We would rather sit in cafés all day."

"Wise choice."

"You know how to get back to palace?"

Mason pointed. "That way, right?"

"Yes. Now go. Visit island. See Plitvice. Have good holiday." He patted Mason again. "*Sretan put.*"

"What does that mean?"

Viktor's eyes sparkled. "Bon voyage."

The walk back to the old city came easily; Mason felt newly buoyant. And he was hungry, so he grabbed a sandwich at one of the places that also sold pastries and slices of pizza. He carried his lunch back to the apartment, intending to eat quickly and head back out for a while. But by the time the sandwich was gone, he felt tired. Not unpleasantly lethargic, the way he had for months. Just sleepy, as if he'd accomplished a major task. Maybe he had. For reasons that didn't make any sense to him, he'd somehow found closure. He'd ask Pete about it later. The guy had a doctorate in psychology, so maybe he could explain.

Yawning and stretching luxuriantly, Mason wandered to his bedroom and closed the door. Thick walls kept the apartment cool, and the bed had a fluffy comforter, so he stripped naked before climbing between the sheets. The smooth cotton was nice against his skin. He spent a moment or two rearranging the pillows to his satisfaction, and then he quickly fell fast asleep.

Four

LATIN WAS not his first tongue, just as Sabbio was not his original name. But he had been young when he was captured—barely more than a boy—and his new masters had quickly beaten their language into him. He'd resisted for a short time, but soon realized it brought him only fresh welts and bruises. And besides, Latin words were generally the only ones he and his fellow slaves had in common. Once his heart acknowledged that he'd never be free again, he found servitude was easier if he forgot his old ways, his old name.

Latin became his adopted tongue, but not long after he died, he stopped hearing it. The palace was abandoned only a few years after being built. New people entered the safety of the walls a few hundred years later as they fled invaders, and they spoke another language entirely. Nowadays, he sometimes heard Latin within the Italian that visitors spoke, or scattered in French or English, or intoned by a priest in the cathedral, but the language was not far from being the ghost that he was.

But now, as he floated in the cold depths of the pit, he heard Latin. *Veni nobiscum loqui, phasma. Verba habemus pro vobis. Veni, phasma. Come speak with us, spirit. We have words for you. Come, spirit.* It was poor Latin, but understandable. And while few sounds ever made their way into the chasm, these words rang clear.

Sabbio clung to them. Like the toy balloons that sometimes escaped from the children along the Riva, the words carried him upward and outward until he broke free of the hole altogether. He found himself in a bright room where a handsome older woman spoke and two men listened. It was she who had called him.

For the first time in eons, he was filled with joy. Someone knew of him! Someone talked to him! But as he listened more, he realized the words were addressed not to him, but to another ghost. He was so bitterly disappointed that he very nearly tumbled back into the abyss.

As he teetered on the edge, though, he recognized one of the men. Sabbio had seen him sitting at a table on the Riva, toying with his wineglass as his companions chatted in English. He was handsome but sad, and Sabbio regained his balance and remained in the room, standing behind the familiar man.

The man suddenly turned around and looked at him. "Who's there?" he whispered.

It was the first time in seventeen centuries that anyone had addressed him. "Sabbio," he answered. He didn't think the man heard him, but the woman did. She repeated his name.

The man reached for him.

Even though he knew nothing could come of it, Sabbio mirrored the gesture. Their fingertips met—and for the briefest of moments, Sabbio *felt*. Pressure, heat, the steady beat of a pulse.

It was too much. He fled, sinking through walls and down to the street. Stunned, he hunched in a passageway. Someone had *touched* him.

His mind was still whirling when he heard laughter nearby. He turned the corner and found the two men from the apartment standing on the sidewalk and talking. The one with the very short hair touched the other man's—*Sabbio's* man's—shoulder, and Sabbio momentarily seethed with jealousy. But then he calmed enough to scoff at himself. He'd had nobody even when he was alive; he certainly couldn't claim anyone now.

Still, when the men parted, Sabbio followed the handsome one as he walked quickly toward the palace. The man stopped at a *pekarna* to buy some food, but instead of eating it right away, he carried it a few blocks into one of the buildings near the palace. Sabbio had watched with great interest as those buildings were constructed, not by slaves but by freemen who joked with each other while they worked, who took long breaks for meals, who went home at night to lie with their wives.

Now the man entered a large apartment, and although he closed the door, Sabbio easily slipped inside. While the man ate, Sabbio floated, examining the rooms and their contents. He didn't often go indoors, and when he did, he was always amazed at the sheer number of things people owned—far more than even the wealthy possessed when he was alive. And some of the items were so strange: a box that heated food almost instantly, a kettle that boiled water without a fire, a big glassy tablet on the wall that showed moving images and played sounds.

After eating, the man stood to stretch. Abandoning his food wrappers and dirty plate, he entered one of the bedrooms. Feeling guilty yet aroused, Sabbio watched the man strip. His torso was ladder-ribbed and pale, a contrast to his deeply tanned arms and legs. Although he was thin, he possessed wiry muscles. He had little body hair aside from the nest of dark gold curls at his groin, and he was circumcised. *A Jew?* Perhaps.

It was barely past midday, but the man climbed into bed, pulled up the covers, and sighed deeply. He was asleep within minutes.

Sabbio crept closer. He studied the man's face, even more handsome now that slumber had banished his sorrow and fatigue. He'd mussed his hair on the pillow, and Sabbio desperately wanted to tame the curls with his fingers. Without conscious intent, he raised his hand. And when his fingers touched the man's head, Sabbio fell inside.

Five

MASON DREAMED he was naked, walking through Split. No big surprise, considering he was already in Split. But in the dream, all the modern buildings were gone. Where the medieval ones should have been, tents and campfires clustered near piles of building materials. The palace itself was only partially constructed, its marble and limestone gleaming in the bright sun. Where the Riva belonged, water lapped against the foot of the palace's southern façade. Boats floated in the harbor, but they weren't modern cruise ships or Jadrolinija ferries. Instead, they were narrow vessels with high sterns and large square sails.

Hundreds, maybe thousands, of people scurried around the palace. Most of them wore nothing but ragged tunics or dirty loincloths. And they worked *hard*— laying stones, pulling carts, digging holes. Mason winced when he heard the crack of a lash.

He saw two men nearby who weren't working. They wore uniforms, with swords at their hips and whips tucked into their belts. They reminded him of every road construction supervisor he had ever seen, just standing there while everyone else labored, talking with each other and laughing.

Talking in Latin, he realized. Which he didn't speak. So maybe his dreaming mind was making up gibberish and calling it Latin, or maybe his subconscious had learned a thing or two from botany lessons and from Carl.

Mason approached the men. Soldiers? Guards?

"Hey. I'm pretty sure this worksite is not gonna pass OSHA inspection," he said. But neither of them even glanced his way. Based on their gestures and guffaws, he would have bet a thousand dollars they were talking about getting laid. "Yeah, I know guys like you. Probably can't even get it up. Or if you do, you're a thirty-second wonder."

Behind him, someone laughed.

Mason spun around and found himself face-to-face with a naked man. He was probably in his late twenties, a couple of inches shorter than Mason's five ten but very muscular. His brown hair was severely shorn, his wide eyes were brown shot with green, and his cheeks and chin were lightly stubbled. Even through the thick hair on his chest and belly, Mason saw scars and welts. His uncut cock was soft and plump.

In a raspy voice, the man said something. A question of some kind.

"I can't understand you," Mason replied.

The man staggered back a half step. "Can you... can you see me?" Good old English, but heavily accented.

Mason had never dreamed with such clarity. "Who are you?" he asked, because although he didn't recognize the man, there was something familiar about him.

"I'm called Sabbio." He looked as if he might be about to cry. "Gods, you can hear me!"

"I... yes. Sabbio. That's what Mrs. Lulić said. Were you.... Am I dreaming about the spirit she summoned?"

But Sabbio was shaking his head—not in denial, but disbelief. He dropped ungracefully to his knees, exclaiming quietly to himself in Latin. For some reason, Mason wanted to hold him and give him comfort.

Instead, he crouched down. "I'm having a dream about Roman times." He didn't know why he needed to explain the dream to a ghost.

"I was alive then," Sabbio said, his voice cracking. "I died here. And now I am in your dream."

Mason let out a long breath. According to Adam's tour book, over two thousand people had been killed in the rush to complete the palace. "You were a slave?"

"Yes. But... please. Your name?"

"Mason Gould."

Sabbio frowned slightly. "Mason? Like a stonemason?"

"I guess so." His parents had picked the name because they liked it. His father, who had a penchant for terrible jokes and puns, liked to refer to him as *my son Mason*.

"I was a mason. A stonesetter." Sabbio gestured toward the half-built palace walls.

"How did you die?"

"I... it was an accident. I fell and broke my leg, and then I grew ill with fever."

Mason shuddered at the thought of a slow death from infection without antibiotics or painkillers. "I'm sorry. You were young."

"Slaves like me did not live long."

Sabbio had apparently found a bit of his equilibrium, because he rose slowly. Mason followed suit. They stood very close—near enough for Mason to smell Sabbio's odor of sweat and dust, which wasn't unpleasant, and to see the wrinkles that had barely begun to form at the corners of his eyes.

"This is a very weird dream," Mason said.

"Please! Do not wake up! Not yet. I have not.... It has been so long since anyone...."

It was strange to feel sorry for someone you'd dreamed up, but Mason did. "I'll try to stay asleep."

Sabbio smiled and ducked his head slightly. "Thank you." When he looked up again, he was frowning a little. "Why are you sad?"

Mason watched as slaves sweated in the unforgiving sun. One of them stumbled on the uneven ground; a guard flicked him with a whip and then laughed at the resulting yelp. Jesus. "My husband died," Mason finally said.

"You... you can marry a man?" Sabbio asked, eyes wide.

"In California, yeah. We got hitched as soon as it was legal." He smiled at the memory—Carl dropping down on one knee within minutes after the Supreme Court decision was announced, the rush to get a license in case the law somehow changed again, the ceremony a few weeks later. Carl's dumbshit parents boycotted the event, but Mason's parents had hugged Carl so tightly that he later said he'd been almost unable to breathe.

"You were trying to speak to him, were you not? When that woman called?"

It took Mason a moment to make sense of the question, and then he nodded. "But she said she couldn't hear him."

"Was his death fast?"

"Yes." Almost instant, the medical examiner had said. Lucky shot.

"Even if he was young, a fast death is good. And I think he must be at peace. Nobody haunts you now but me." Sabbio's smile was wistful. "He has you to remember him well, and that is important."

"Who remembers you?"

"Nobody. Nobody mourns a slave."

Mason's stomach twisted uncomfortably. This figment seemed so real. When Mason reached out to settle a comforting hand on Sabbio's shoulder, the skin was warm, the muscle and bone solid.

Sabbio closed his eyes and gave a small whimper, which undid Mason completely. He clutched Sabbio in his arms, and Sabbio melted against him almost at once, returning the embrace and burying his face in the crook of Mason's neck. "*Ne dimittas*. Please. Do not let go."

It had been eight long months since Mason had held anyone. He had no intention of letting go as long as his dream continued. And damn, he'd never had such a *real* dream, one that made such coherent—if not rational—sense, one so detailed that he could see ants crawling around his bare feet and feel the thump of Sabbio's heart. When he smoothed his palms along Sabbio's strong back, Mason felt the ridges and furrows of old lash scars, which made him want to cry.

Instead, he kissed the soft bristles of Sabbio's hair.

Sabbio looked up at him with startled eyes. His mouth hung open slightly, and he was breathing very fast. "Yes. Please, yes, Mason."

This time, Mason kissed his lips. Sabbio moaned and eagerly accepted Mason's tongue into his mouth, grabbing at Mason's hips as if to hold him in place. Mason kissed him again, harder, so his head swam and his nerves sang. His cock stiffened—rubbing against Sabbio's answering hardness—and Mason grasped handfuls of Sabbio's glorious ass to draw their bodies tightly together. He stopped worrying about how odd this dream was and concentrated instead on the lovely rush of his senses and the delicious, hungry noises coming from Sabbio's throat.

"I want you," Mason whispered into Sabbio's ear, although nobody else could hear them. He hadn't wanted much of anything since Carl died, and it was wonderful to feel need again. He'd ignore for now that the object of his desire was imaginary. "Can I fuck you, Sabbio?"

Sabbio shuddered. "Please."

They collapsed to the ground together, Sabbio sprawled beneath Mason and still holding him as if to keep him from escaping. As Mason kissed and licked his jawline, his neck, his collarbone, Sabbio writhed, arching up with his hips as far as Mason's weight allowed. And Sabbio muttered urgently in many languages— some Mason recognized and some he didn't. The words all seemed to have the same meaning: *yes, more, please.*

"Have you done this before?" Mason asked, fully aware it was crazy to question the virginity of his apparition but needing to know. Sabbio seemed willing enough—desperate, even—but Mason didn't want to hurt him.

Sabbio looked at him solemnly. "Not in hundreds of years. And never with someone like you."

Mason wasn't sure how to interpret that last part. He knew from Carl's frequent lectures on the subject that the Romans hadn't thought about sex the same way modern Americans did. There was no real concept of homosexuality. Fucking was all about power, and nobody back then would frown on a free man who stuck his dick in a man of lesser status. A man who was penetrated, however, was considered weak, emasculated, perverted.

Of course, this used to both piss off and amuse Carl, because he was the pushiest bottom imaginable.

"You can say no, Sabbio." Didn't matter if he was a slave and a creation of Mason's brain—Mason wouldn't force him.

"I am saying yes." Sabbio smiled and wiggled beneath him. "I am very much saying yes."

Thank God. Mason resumed what he'd been doing—licking, nibbling a bit here and there, tracing Sabbio's body with tongue and lips and fingertips. Sabbio responded beautifully to every touch. When Mason mouthed his taut brown nipples, Sabbio groaned and gripped Mason's hips so hard it hurt. But Mason didn't care. He would have happily withstood a goddamn whip if it meant he got to keep touching Sabbio.

Slowly, torturously, he worked his way down the firm abdomen, tracing every ridge of muscle, knowing their strength had been earned through brutal work instead of hours at the gym. He played with Sabbio's dark treasure trail. And he nosed at the creases of Sabbio's legs, at his balls, at the tender skin behind them, inhaling sweat and a deeply masculine musk that reminded him of rich soil ready for planting. He lavished special attention on Sabbio's cock—not especially long, but thick, the damp red crown peeking from the retracted foreskin.

He hadn't dreamed any lube, which was a shame. Spit and precome were going to have to suffice. As Sabbio rocked his hips upward, Mason stroked the length of his shaft and watched pearly droplets appear at the tip. He was just going to use his finger to gather some of the fluid when a loud noise intruded on his senses. It was a musical twang that didn't belong in Roman Split.

"No!" Mason cried when he recognized the sound: his goddamn phone was ringing. "Not yet!"

But it was too late. He and Sabbio cried out together as everything—the half-built palace, the slaves and guards, the sandy ground, and Sabbio himself—faded away to mist and was gone.

Six

Mason woke up achingly hard and really pissed off. He fumbled at the bedside until he found his phone. "What!" he growled.

"You okay?" Adam sounded concerned.

After a few steadying breaths, Mason managed a single syllable. "Yeah."

"I've texted you about a zillion times. I was worried. We all were. I mean, you were going off with the crazy ghost guy and—"

"I'm fine. Viktor and his mother gave me cake and tea. They didn't kill me."

"Then why the hell didn't you text me back?"

"I was asleep." And dreaming. Fuck. A renewed sense of loss tore at him—this time not for Carl, but for a man who didn't even exist.

"Oh. Um, sorry. I was just… worried."

Mason made an effort to sound normal. "Aren't you supposed to be lazing around an island or something?"

"I am. We've been walking around, and we had this amazing lunch with fresh sardines and local wine." He started going on about castles and lavender and beaches, but Mason didn't really listen. He was thinking about the taste of salty skin, the tang still lingering in his mouth.

"Hell of a dream," he muttered.

Adam stopped monologuing. "What's that?"

"Nothing. I'm… still sleepy, I guess."

"Okay. Look, it turns out Hvar has a good club scene. We're gonna take a late boat back. Is that all right?"

"Sure. Have fun."

"I mean, we could take an earlier one instead." Adam paused a moment. "If you want."

"Party the night away. It's fine with me. I'll dig up something for dinner and probably turn in early."

Mason ended up having to assure his brother two or three more times that everything was hunky-dory, but eventually Adam hung up.

Sitting on the edge of the bed, Mason wanted to cry. But his stupid dick was still hard, so with a defeated moan, he fell back onto the mattress and stroked himself. With his eyes closed, he imagined the hand was Sabbio's instead of his own. Mason's palms and fingers were calloused from years of hauling wheelbarrows, wielding shovels and rakes and spades, manhandling rocks and pots and various landscaping materials. But Sabbio was a stonesetter, and his hands were even tougher. Mason could still feel the way they had dragged over his shoulders and hips.

"Sabbio," he called out as he came.

Afterward, he tried to fall back asleep. He wasn't optimistic about being able to resume the dream but wanted to try. Sleep eluded him, and with a disgusted growl, he eventually hoisted himself off the bed and stomped to the bathroom. A shower felt good but didn't really calm him, so he decided to spend some time outdoors.

Walking around the palace was an odd experience. On the one hand, he saw weathered limestone, crowded cafés, and shops selling shoes and neckties and trinkets. But at the same time, like a hazy overlay, he saw the walls half-built and freshly white; ragged men labored hard as whip-wielding guards yelled at them to work faster. He felt dizzy and a little lost, and when he staggered his way to the Riva, he saw ghostly water washing over his feet.

He collapsed on a bench and spent a very long time staring out to sea.

By the time he stood again, the sun had set and his legs were stiff. He was hungry but not especially in the mood for a restaurant meal. He strolled to the grocery store—incongruously located adjacent to the ancient palace wall—and bought a roll, a little prosciutto, and a packaged salad. He picked up some dried figs too. Back at the apartment, he supplemented his light dinner with a bottle of wine.

After picking at his food, he sat in front of the television for a while, flipping through American shows with Croatian subtitles, Croatian programs with terrible production values, and something puzzling in German that he thought might be a game show. He went to bed early, before the rest of his group reappeared.

He didn't dream.

"ARE YOU *sure* you're okay?" Adam sat on the edge of Mason's bed, looking bright-eyed and bushy-tailed, despite his late-night clubbing.

"You're going to drive me nuts if you keep on asking that."

"I know. It's just... there was that whole weird séance thing you did yesterday. And now you're sleeping a lot."

Mason glanced at the bedside clock. "It's not even nine yet."

"But you're usually up before dawn."

"Sure, when I want to get to work before it's a zillion degrees out. I'm not working today, Adam. I am on vacation, remember?" He poked Adam's knee.

Adam scooched slightly away. "So does that mean you'll do something with us today? We only have two days left in Croatia."

Mason rubbed his head. "Somebody told me we should really see Plitivice Lakes."

As it turned out, Plitvice was over two hours away. But for some reason, Adam seized the idea like a bulldog, and less than thirty minutes after Mason woke up, all five of them were squeezing into their rented car for the drive north. Mason didn't even have time for a shower or coffee, and he breakfasted on slightly stale bread as they drove.

It was worth the trip, though. The scenery was breathtaking, with wooden walkways snaking over crystal-clear water, trout floating right underfoot, and waterfalls you could walk behind. Mason could have sworn certain shades of green and blue existed only in the park, and he wished he knew more about the native flora. He recognized many of the plants, but others were new to him.

By the time they got back in the car, he was making mental notes for future landscape designs that might incorporate some of the park's elements on a much smaller scale. As wonderful as the day had been, though, he'd never quite stopped thinking about Sabbio and that realistic dream.

They went out for a seafood dinner. Mason ate squid ink risotto and drank a little too much wine, but that was okay. He bantered lightly with his friends and family. On the way back, they all paused for a while to listen to an a cappella men's group singing in the peristyle. Mason couldn't understand the words, of course, but they sounded mournful.

"Who wants more wine?" Doug asked when they returned to the apartment.

Everybody said yes except for Mason. "I'm gonna shower and then hit the sack," he announced. "And yes, Adam, I am perfectly fine. Just a little grungy and tired."

He liked the bathroom. It was nicely tiled, with sleek fixtures and a large, slightly complicated shower stall. Tonight, though, he kind of wished there was a bathtub instead. A soak would have felt nice.

"Spoiled," he chided himself as he stripped.

As he reached to turn on the water, he caught sight of his reflection in the full-length mirror—and he froze. Each hip was imprinted with five small, oval bruises, arrayed exactly like someone's fingerprints.

He stared dumbly at the purple marks, then poked at one experimentally. It was slightly sore.

As he was digesting that development, he took a closer look and found similar marks on his shoulders.

He tried, but no matter how he twisted his wrist or splayed his fingers, he couldn't duplicate the marks with his own fingertips. He obviously hadn't caused the bruises by gripping himself.

"Psychosomatic," he whispered, collapsing onto the closed toilet. God, he really *was* going nuts. Or maybe the Lulićes had drugged his tea with something to make him very suggestible. The problem with that theory was that he'd felt pretty clear-headed during and after his time in Mrs. Lulić's apartment. Besides, why would they bother? They hadn't asked anything of him apart from a recommendation for future tourists.

His life used to be really simple. He dug in the dirt for a living, which he loved and which earned him enough to pay his share of the bills. He had a nice little house and a decent pickup truck. And he had a husband who was brilliant and cute and loving. All it took to change that was one little bullet. And now here he was, naked in a bathroom in Croatia, mysteriously bruised and haunted by a dream.

Pete had a doctorate in psychology, was right in the other room, and wouldn't make Mason feel like a weirdo. As Mason stood, he decided to consult with him as soon as he could get him alone. In the meantime, he used his phone to snap a couple of photos of the marks. The images could double as proof *and* as a really bizarre Grindr profile pic, he thought sourly as he got into the shower.

Seven

THE GHOST floundered in the pit for an eternity. He'd been torn apart somehow and couldn't remember even enough to put himself back together. *Maybe this is hell*, he thought vaguely. He'd heard the Christians preach about it enough times. Had he really been so evil as to deserve this? He couldn't remember that either.

But even as he screamed and flailed, an image came to him. Stone. Big and solid, weathering over the years but enduring. Shaped by time, by water, by human tools, yet always strong. Yes, stone. He thought very hard about it, and eventually he could feel it between his nonexistent hands. He'd held stone many times before, he realized. He'd carved it, carried it, placed it.

He'd been a mason.

The memory brought an enormous rush of relief—he'd feared he'd never find himself again. His name was Sabbio and he had been a mason. But even as he grasped that precious knowledge, he remembered something else. Another mason. No, a man *named* Mason. Who was sad and lovely, who'd welcomed Sabbio into his dream and held him, who'd lavished Sabbio's body with so much care, he'd almost felt alive.

Sabbio mentally transformed a stone into a ladder, and he used it to climb out of the abyss.

He emerged not near the edge of the palace as usual, but in a small room illuminated only by the glowing numbers of a clock. He'd been in the room before. And that sleeping figure huddled under the blanket—oh, gods, that was Mason. He was still here.

Sabbio settled himself on the bed where he could see Mason's face. He was thankful his ghostly eyesight was better than it had been when he was alive. Mason's even breathing soothed him, and the memory of what those full lips had done to his body made Sabbio feel warm. He wished he could sit there forever, just watching. But lives were so fleeting. And Mason surely didn't live in Split. He'd be gone in the blink of an eye.

One more chance, Sabbio thought. It wouldn't be enough, but it would have to suffice. Just a few more stolen minutes.

He reached out—and then fell into Mason's dreams.

He found himself somewhere unfamiliar. A wooden fence surrounded him on three sides, while the white stucco wall of a house encompassed the fourth. The ground was nothing but fine dirt spotted with a few scraggly weeds. Overhead, the sky was vivid blue. Mason stood several paces away, naked, his back to Sabbio. He was a little too thin, Sabbio thought, but very fine nonetheless, all long limbs and wiry muscle.

Sabbio made a soft noise, and Mason whirled around. "You're here!" Mason exclaimed. He rushed forward and grasped Sabbio's shoulders. "I didn't know if I'd see you again."

Grinning at being welcomed—being wanted—Sabbio settled his hands on Mason's waist. "You are not angry that I visit you?"

"No! But…. Jesus. You seem so real. Look! You left bruises." He looked pointedly at his shoulder and hip, where fingerprints had turned the skin purple.

"I am sorry! I did not mean to hurt you."

"It's fine. It's… damn, it's weird, but it's fine." He pulled Sabbio a little closer. "I'm glad you're here."

Sabbio allowed himself a moment to rest against Mason's chest. "Where is this place?"

"My house."

"In California?" Sabbio had heard people speak of the place over the past century or two. He'd gathered it was filled with palm trees, like the ones along the Riva, and famous people in fashionable clothing.

"Yeah. But it doesn't look like this now. When Carl and I first bought the place, the back yard was a mess. Broken cement, ugly plantings, too much grass. I had to start the landscaping from scratch. This is what it looked like after I'd stripped the crap away. It looks a hell of a lot nicer now."

"You love this place."

Mason nodded, which Sabbio felt instead of saw. "I do. I xeriscaped. That's, um—"

"Dry," Sabbio finished for him. "I know a little Greek."

"Of course you do. Anyway, I put in some cacti and succulents, a lot of stone. And a bunch of Mediterranean natives, like lavendula, artemisia, and santolina. I planted a couple of olive trees too, but the fruitless kind because I didn't want a mess. And I built an arbor with grapevines on it, which was nice for shade. Carl and I would sit there most evenings. He said my garden made him feel like a Roman emperor."

Sabbio could picture it quite well. "Diocletian liked to garden. Even before the palace was finished, he planted things. I caught glimpses of him sometimes." He'd wondered then what it was like to be emperor. Better than a slave, of course, but still human, still carrying sorrows. At least people rarely plotted to kill a slave.

Mason made a satisfied grunt and kissed Sabbio's hair. "You feel so real," he murmured.

"I am. No, I was real. Now I am only a ghost."

"You're a hallucination."

Sabbio had never heard that word in English before, but it closely resembled a Latin term. "You think you only dream me."

"There's no such thing as ghosts." Mason sounded sad, and he moved one of his hands down between Sabbio's shoulders. It felt good—warm and solid.

"Of course there are ghosts. A body dies and the spirit must go somewhere." Sabbio sighed. "Most move on, like your Carl. I did not."

"Why not?" asked Mason. He kissed Sabbio again, as if to soften the question.

"I do not know. I think… I was lonely. I never had the chance to love someone. And wherever spirits go when they move on, nobody waits for me there. I was young when I was taken. My family forgot me."

Mason petted him soothingly. "I'll remember you. Even if you're a figment."

With a gasp, Sabbio stepped back. "That… that is it!"

"What is?"

Sabbio was filled with such excitement, he couldn't remember the words in English. He paced back and forth over the soft soil, muttering to himself in Latin as he thought his idea through. Yes, the concept made sense.

He stopped in front of Mason, who'd been watching curiously. "I think you can help me," Sabbio said.

"With what?"

"It has been so very long. And until you, nobody has seen me or talked to me. Nobody has *touched* me." He gave Mason's chest a tentative stroke. "It has been a very difficult way to exist."

Mason nodded, which gave Sabbio courage to continue.

"I do not want to be such as this anymore. I have wished for… for an end almost since I died. But I cannot end myself."

"I guess a ghost can't really commit suicide," Mason said.

"No. But I think that if you believe in me, if you know I existed…." He fought for the right words. "Once a man named Sabbio lived, and he was a good stonemason. He liked to listen to the sea, but he always got ill when he was put in a boat. And he wanted to love. You will remember this and I will end, or perhaps I will move on. It will be very good." He was crying a bit, the tears burning his eyes, but that was a joy because he hadn't been able to cry since he died.

"You're breaking my heart," Mason said, raspy-voiced. "God, I wish I could help you. But I can't just force myself to believe in ghosts. I need… proof, I guess."

"Bruises," Sabbio said, pointing.

"Psychosomatic."

Sabbio puzzled over that term for a moment. "Spirit body?"

"Um, mind body, I guess. It means I created the bruises with my overactive imagination."

That was a very odd idea, but Sabbio didn't argue. Modern people were far more complicated than ancient dead slaves. But if physical marks on Mason's body weren't enough to convince him, what was?

Sabbio walked restlessly back and forth, his feet sending up little puffs of soil. He felt as he had when he was first captured by Roman soldiers so many years ago—trapped, half of him convinced he could escape if he could only figure out how, half already acknowledging he would be consigned to a life of slavery. Of course, the latter half had been right. He'd never spent another minute of his life free. But gods, he couldn't let this last opportunity slip away. He might have to wait millennia for the next chance.

"I can tell you things in Latin," he said. "Things about life in the Roman empire. You can check and see these things are true. That will be proof."

But Mason shook his head. "Carl studied ancient Rome and he knew Latin. I could have filed all that stuff away in my subconscious."

"I...." Sabbio stood very near the house; he turned to the wall so Mason wouldn't see his face. "I do not know other things to tell you. I was only a slave." He brushed his fingers along the rough stucco, enjoying the slight discomfort because even pain was a rare sensation, and he wondered who had built this house and how.

Mason came up behind him and set a hand on his shoulder. "I'm sorry. I want to believe. I can even.... When I was with the Lulićes, something was there. I'm sure of it."

"I was there," Sabbio whispered.

"I can't make that leap, though. I guess I can believe in spirits. I even.... Deep in my heart, I know that Carl still exists somehow. Somewhere. But I can't believe that a ghost could appear all flesh and blood in my dreams." He sounded as upset as Sabbio felt, which was oddly comforting.

Abandoning hope of anything but a brief respite from his suffering, Sabbio turned and leaned against Mason. "I am not flesh and blood."

Mason held him. "Then what are you made of?"

Sabbio had to think only a moment before the answer came with complete certainty. "Want. I am made of nothing but want." Nothing but unfulfilled hope.

With a soft grunt, Mason tightened the embrace. "I'm sorry. I'm so sorry. I wish I could help you." His heartbeat was like a great drum, and his skin was warm. And his arms—longer than Sabbio's—were strong and solid.

"You can help," Sabbio whispered. And he sucked on Mason's tender neck. Sex wouldn't save Sabbio from being a phantom, wouldn't keep him from tumbling again into the pit. But it would be something precious he could remember for a very long time, a bright light to help keep him intact. And Mason would be gentle with him—Sabbio knew that already. Nothing like the masters who'd used him now and then when he was a slave. None of them had been especially cruel, but they certainly hadn't been caring. To them, Sabbio was a convenient hole to be filled.

But now Mason kissed him so sweetly while petting his back—as if to smooth away the scars—and Sabbio inexplicably felt like a youth again, untouched, innocent, yearning. He wanted to laugh and cry at the same time, but instead he focused on kissing Mason back. He tried to memorize the way Mason tasted, the feel of his teeth against Sabbio's tongue.

Although Sabbio knew he'd be clumsy due to inexperience, he intended to worship Mason's body as he'd worship a god. But he didn't get that chance— instead it was Mason who licked and sucked and nibbled, who petted and stroked, until Sabbio's knees went weak and they both collapsed to the soft earth. Mason spread Sabbio's pliant body as if he were an artist arranging a model and then proceeded to explore every inch of Sabbio with his lips and fingers.

Sabbio touched whatever bits of Mason he could reach, and he stared up into the clear blue sky with wonder. Whether he was a boy in his long-gone village or a slave laboring for his Roman masters, he'd never imagined he'd remain on earth for hundreds of years. He'd never imagined that one day he'd visit the dreams of a man from far away, and that the man would make his body sing with pleasure.

When Mason cradled Sabbio's balls in one hand and kissed the tip of his cock, Sabbio very nearly came.

"No!" he said, pushing Mason away.

Mason knelt over him, frowning. "Did I hurt you? I'm sorry, I didn't—"

"You did not." Sabbio took a few calming breaths. "I don't want it to be over yet. Please."

"I could wake up again," Mason said.

"Not yet. Please." He would beg a million times if it would help.

A small smile curled the corners of Mason's lips. "I turned my phone off this time." Then he bent over and returned to his exquisite torture, making sure to balance Sabbio at the edge of climax.

By the time Mason moistened and stretched Sabbio's passage, Sabbio had forgotten all languages and could only moan and plead incoherently. Mason's eyes had shed their earlier shadows and now gleamed like flames, and his lips were beautifully swollen. He could be a god, Sabbio thought. Or at least the son of one.

Vulcan, perhaps. When he had breath again and mastery of his tongue, Sabbio would ask Mason about his parents.

"You're gorgeous," Mason said, gazing down at him in wonder. "I dream big."

Feeling valued, Sabbio smiled.

Then Sabbio bent his knees and hooked his arms around them, giving himself as an offering. Mason positioned himself carefully before sliding slowly inside.

Sabbio was stretched and filled, and as he arched his back and groaned, he knew for now his body contained life, even if this was only a dream. And gods, it felt so good! Whatever existence remained to him—the netherworld, a Christian heaven or hell, eternity as a ghost—it would never be as good as this moment, when he was overcome with bliss and Mason whispered Sabbio's name with every long thrust.

When the sensations became almost too much to bear, Sabbio tilted his head back and cried out, and his untouched cock erupted like Vesuvius, spewing hot come over his belly and chest.

Mason sped his movements, and within moments he jerked, froze, and then collapsed atop Sabbio, sweaty and breathing hard. Sabbio expected him to roll off and stand, but instead Mason kissed him again, deeply and thoroughly, hands smoothing along Sabbio's arms.

"I'm going to wake up to sticky sheets," Mason chuckled. "Haven't done that since I was a kid."

Sabbio relaxed his legs and set his hands on Mason's ass. Mason was still inside him, and neither of them moved enough to dislodge him. Sabbio wanted to stay this way for eternity.

"I want you to be real," Mason said. "And not a ghost either, because... I can't have a future with a ghost."

A future. *No*, Sabbio thought. *I'm all about the past, aren't I?*

As if sensing this, Mason kissed his cheek. "I'm impressed with myself, you know. I didn't think I was capable of imagining something as amazing as you. I'm just a guy who plants stuff, you know?"

"You make things grow," Sabbio said.

After several more kisses, Mason finally did pull himself away. He held out a hand to help Sabbio to his feet, which was good because Sabbio was a bit sore. Not that he minded.

"Is California a good place to live?"

"Yeah, sure. Good weather. My part isn't all that exciting, but it's affordable. And we can grow almost anything here." He waved his arm, and as Sabbio watched in fascination, the bare earth sprouted plants. The leaves were all shades of green—from dusty gray through fresh grass and into the deep colors of a forest—and scattered flowers added accents of pink, yellow, and orange. The arbor that Mason had mentioned supported fat clusters of grapes hanging within reach of two shaded chairs. A small fountain tinkled pleasantly nearby.

"Does it truly look like this?" Sabbio asked.

Mason looked around. "More or less. Real life has more weeds and ants. Do you like it?"

"Even Diocletian would approve." And would likely recognize most of the plants. It was nice to know these familiar things grew so long after Sabbio's death and so far away from his home. It made him feel as if *this* place could be his home, even though he knew it was impossible.

Mason slung his arm around Sabbio's shoulders. "Anything you'd change?"

Sabbio thought a moment before answering, then pointed to the house. "The sun is very bright there."

"Yeah, we get a lot of sun."

"I would extend your roof over columns to make a portico. It would be a good place for you to sleep in the afternoons."

The corners of Mason's eyes crinkled. "So I could dream about you?"

"I do not believe I can enter your dreams when you are so far from Split."

Mason looked serious again. Sad. "I'll miss you."

"Even if I am not real?"

"Even if."

They were kissing again when the landscape evaporated. Sabbio tried to keep hold of his lover, but Mason disappeared too. All that remained was a ghost in the abyss.

Eight

MASON WOKE up with a kiss-swollen mouth and sticky sheets. His bruises ached. So did his heart.

He showered and dressed and emerged into the large common room. Pete sat alone at the table, sipping tea and reading his Kindle. He gave Mason a slightly distracted smile. "Morning."

"Where is everyone?"

"Nicole dragged Adam shopping—shoes, I believe. Doug's meeting with those musicians he's been corresponding with. I think they're trying to lure him back for some kind of music festival."

Mason poured coffee from the pot someone had thoughtfully brewed, grabbed a plateful of prosciutto from the fridge, and joined Pete at the table. "Reading something good?"

"Spies. My guilty pleasure." But he put down the Kindle and cocked his head slightly to examine Mason.

"What?"

"I've been teaching for over fifteen years. I recognize an unasked question when I see one."

"Oh." Mason squirmed uncomfortably and stared into his mug. Stuff that seemed reasonable when you were alone in a dark room—or dreaming in your bed—sounded pretty lame over a sunlit breakfast. Lame and kind of crazy, actually. But Pete still waited for him to say something. "I, uh, had this dream. After I visited the Lulićes."

When Mason paused, unable to spit out anything more, Pete smiled. "I'm feeling very Freudian now. Good preparation for Vienna. Did your dream involve trains and tunnels?"

"I thought tunnels were for straight guys."

"Maybe you're just a repressed heterosexual."

That made Mason chuff a laugh. "*Very* repressed. Anyway, it was a sex dream, but there was nothing symbolic about the sex. I mean… there were genuine man-parts involved."

"Does that bother you?" Pete asked, in true Freudian fashion.

"Not the man-parts per se. But…." And since there didn't seem to be any way around it, Mason told him what had happened with Mrs. Lulić, and the two dreams that had followed. He showed Pete the photos of his bruises and even pulled off his shirt so Pete could see firsthand the ones on his shoulders.

Pete did not call the Croatian men in white coats. He listened closely and peered at the bruises, his mouth squished up in thought. Even after Mason stopped talking and put his shirt back on, Pete was silent.

"Am I losing it?" Mason finally asked.

"I don't think you're ready for a padded room."

Mason exhaled gratefully. "Okay. That's good, I guess."

Pete reached across the table to pat his hand. "People handle grief in a variety of ways. You've been pretty private about it, but we can all see how much it's been tearing you apart. And there's nothing wrong with grieving, Mason. Nothing abnormal or unhealthy. But it's also fine to move on when you feel ready for it. That's healthy too."

Picking at the prosciutto, Mason frowned. "So is that what Sabbio is? Some kind of weirdo coping mechanism to help me move on?"

"Maybe."

Mason groaned slightly and rubbed his face. He didn't want to be nuts, but he also… well, he wanted Sabbio to exist.

Pete stood, walked to the counter, and plugged in the electric kettle. He whistled quietly—one of Doug's pieces, probably—while waiting for the water to heat. Then he refilled his cup and returned to the table, where he dipped the teabag into the water several times.

"Mason, I think I've already hinted at what I think is the best standard for judging your own behavior: is it healthy? For the past months, you've been neglecting yourself and your friends and family, and that's not good. But you agreed to come on this trip—"

"Yeah, I've been the life of the party."

"You've been here, with us, and that's what counts. That *is* good. And as for your ghost…. It sounds as if your experiences with Mrs. Lulić have helped you deal with Carl's loss. You believe he's in a good place now, right?"

Mason nodded, then looked up at Pete. "Do you?"

"Yes. I'm agnostic, but I am convinced that Carl is beyond suffering. If you think that too, then meeting with Mrs. Lulić was a healthy thing."

"Okay." Mason could get behind that. "But now I'm fixated on a hallucination. Fixated enough to bruise."

Pete sipped his tea, wincing as he probably burned his tongue.

Mason wondered how anyone could be so perpetually calm and patient. He'd learned several weeks after the shooting that when the gun had gone off, Pete had been among the first people to rush forward to aid the wounded. He'd called

911 on his phone even as his dear friend Carl lay dead in his lap. And if he'd lost his composure even once, it had been in the privacy of his own home, perhaps with Doug there to comfort him.

He gave Mason an encouraging smile. "What's bothering you most about those dreams? Do you feel unfaithful to Carl?"

"No," Mason answered honestly. "It's just… not knowing."

"Not knowing what?"

Mason sighed. "Whether he's real. I mean, my head knows he can't be, but my heart disagrees. I wish I could have proof and shut one of them up."

"Okay, then. You've already established that your dreams themselves can't prove anything. So what might?"

Licking his lips, Mason considered. He was positive there would be no paperwork to research—if there had been any Roman records of slaves in Split, they would certainly be long gone. And a slave probably had no grave, no headstone. "Mrs. Lulić," he said at last. "Maybe she can help."

"Maybe. But, Mason, I want you to think about something else. Suppose you become convinced Sabbio is real. Then what? Will you be satisfied to leave him here?"

"I…. No. I'd want to be with him. Or at least find a way…. He's been alone for seventeen centuries. Christ, I'm a mess after eight months, and I still have friends and family. He can't even have a conversation with anyone." And as he spoke, he realized he'd already made a decision. "I need to talk to Mrs. Lulić again."

To his immense relief, Pete smiled and patted his hand. "Then I think that's what you ought to do."

VIKTOR ANSWERED his phone on the second ring, sounding faintly out of breath. "*Molim?*"

"Uh, hi. This is Mason Gould. The guy you—"

"Mason! It is good to hear from you. Already you want tour?" In the background, something clattered noisily. A train, maybe. But Viktor sounded jovial.

"Actually, I was hoping your mom might be willing to talk to me again. I know I'm being a pain in the ass, but I have some questions."

"No, no, you are not pain in ass. Mama likes you. I finish work in three hours. Meet me outside my building."

Relief loosened the tight bands around Mason's chest. He hadn't exactly expected Viktor to refuse, but the Lulićes didn't owe him anything. "Thanks, man. I'll see you then."

AT THE agreed-upon time, Mason stood anxiously outside the ugly socialist building, pretending to admire the shoes in the shop window next door.

Viktor came loping up the sidewalk wearing a blue workman's jumpsuit. He grinned at Mason. "Flowers for me?"

Mason looked at the bouquet in his hand. "For your mom. I brought this for you." He handed over the paper bag from his other hand.

Viktor pulled the bottle out. "This is very good wine!"

"Good. My brother bought a bunch of it the other day at the winery."

"It was not necessary for you to bring gifts."

Mason shrugged. "You guys are doing me a big favor."

As they went inside and tromped up the stairs, Viktor apologized for his work attire. "It is dirty," he said, scowling at a grease spot on his knee.

"Hey, I'm a landscaper. You should see me when I'm done with work. At least you don't smell like composting chicken manure. Carl used to drag me to the shower as soon as I got home."

"Ivana, she did this too," Viktor replied with a soft smile. "She told me every day, no getting finger marks on walls."

Mrs. Lulić must have heard them coming, because she was waiting for them at her open front door. She seemed pleased with the flowers, bustling away to put them in water. She returned with a tray laden with tea and cookies and motioned for Mason to sit. Judging by the expression on her face, she warned her grubby son not to follow suit.

Viktor laughed and kissed her cheek.

"How can we help?" Viktor asked. "Mama does not think she can talk to your husband."

Mason took a polite sip of tea, even though his stomach felt a bit queasy with nerves. "I know. I'm.... After visiting the other day, I feel pretty much okay about Carl. I mean, I still miss him like hell. But the wound's not so raw, you know?"

Viktor did know; he nodded thoughtfully before translating for his mother. She sat next to Mason on the sofa and patted his arm kindly. She had lost loved ones as well. Hadn't Viktor mentioned his father died in the war? Loss was an injury nearly every human being experienced.

"I didn't actually come here today to talk to dead people," Mason explained. "I was just hoping for advice. And I don't know if you're gonna be able to help me, but I don't know who else to ask. It's... it's about the ghost who was here the other day."

Mrs. Lulić waited for Viktor to interpret. Then she said something back, and Mason caught one familiar word: *Sabbio.*

"Mama says do not be afraid of Sabbio. He cannot harm you."

The laugh that escaped Mason's throat sounded slightly hysterical. "Fear isn't the problem." And then he told them what had happened. He kept it G-rated but couldn't stop an embarrassed blush, and he was fairly certain the Lulićes knew his dreams were a lot more NSFW than he was letting on. But neither Viktor nor his mother seemed shocked or upset by his story.

When he was done, Mrs. Lulić patted him and said something in Croatian.

"You like this Sabbio," Viktor said, his brow furrowed with concern.

"Yeah. He's... I can't really explain it. Ever since he first appeared, even before I saw him, I was drawn to him. And he's sweet, and so lonely, and I keep thinking how great it would be to...." He bit his lip instead of continuing.

But after hearing the translation, Mrs. Lulić smiled at him and gestured for him to continue, so he did.

"I want to make him stop being lonely. I want to take him to California and let him build a portico for my house, and I want to hear all about what he's experienced over the centuries, and I want... I want to hold him in my arms every day." Which would be stupid even if Sabbio was real and alive, because Mason barely knew him. But it was true nonetheless. And he admitted the dumbest part. "I don't think I even believe in him, but I'm kind of falling for him anyway."

Mrs. Lulić gave him a long look before asking a question.

"What would prove to you that he was real?" Viktor translated.

"I don't know. I have bruises from his fingers, but... I guess if he was there while I was awake, and if other people could see him too."

"And then what would you do with him?"

"I couldn't just leave him here. I'd want to find a way to bring him home."

Viktor and his mother chatted for a moment or two. It sounded to Mason as if she was trying to convince her son of something. Finally, Viktor shrugged and turned to Mason.

"Are you Catholic?"

"Nope. Dad's Jewish. Mom is crystals and incense and New Age. I'm undeclared."

"We are Catholic," Viktor said with a small grin. No surprise; about 90 percent of Croatians shared that faith. "But this land has room for other religions too. You can visit museums and see that people lived here thousands of years. In Krapina—to north, yes?—they find bones of, er, Neandertal. In cave. And also, Mama say priests do not always know truth."

Mason didn't understand the twist their conversation had taken. He ate a cookie and sipped his tea, then hazarded a question. "Does she know how to help me?"

"Not… exactly. But she thinks maybe this is problem for older times. Older gods. You should ask them."

"Like…. Jupiter?" Mason found it much easier to believe in Roman ghosts than thunderbolt-throwing deities.

"It is all…. Ah, I cannot say this in English. I do not know how to explain. If you believe one thing strong enough, maybe that thing is true for you." Viktor ran fingers through his shorn hair. "Once I was only mechanic for trains. Is good job, important, but not where my heart wants to be. Ivana, she said save money and learn English and you will have job you love. She told me this even when she was very sick. She told me so many times, I listened. And now it is almost true."

There was a difference, Mason thought, between having optimistic career goals and sacrificing goats to Apollo. And there was sure as hell a difference between playing tour guide and bringing a ghost back to life.

Perhaps seeing his skepticism, Mrs. Lulić said something gently. Mason looked expectantly at Viktor, who was smiling.

"Mama says maybe fate brings Sabbio to you. If this is fate, things will work some way." Vague consolation at best, yet the words brought some peace to Mason's unsettled mind.

One time over dinner, Carl and Pete had gotten into a friendly argument over fate versus free will, with Carl coming down on the side of destiny. A lot of the discussion had been over Mason's head—of the three of them, he didn't have a doctorate tucked away anywhere—but he'd enjoyed the banter anyway, and he and Doug had traded amused looks over their partners' enthusiasm.

If destiny was true, maybe fate had led Carl to go off in search of a library book just as a mentally unstable and well-armed young man was making his way to the quad. And if that was true, the same winds might have made Adam suggest a trip to Europe, made Doug ask for a stop in Split, and brought Mason to a café on the Riva, where Viktor overheard him mourn.

It was enough to make his head hurt.

"I have to think about this," he said quietly.

Nobody disagreed with him. Mrs. Lulić fed him more cookies and told a few stories about some of the enterprising ways she and her family had acquired goods during the socialist era. Viktor gave more tourism tips. "Go to Istria," he counseled. "Is like Italy, but better." And before Mason left, he was given a jar of homemade ajvar relish, a packet of dried figs, and a lot of well wishes. Mrs. Lulić kissed him once on each cheek.

Back on the street, Viktor shook his hand. "Come back. Even if you do not find your ghost, come back. World is very big place with many things to see, but at end, all *best* things are here in Dalmatia."

Mason was inclined to agree.

With the figs in his pocket and the jar cradled in his hand, Mason walked to the palace and wandered its streets. He paused in the peristyle. Diocletian was buried there, and although he'd once slaughtered Christians, they'd had the last word, building a cathedral right over his final resting place.

Mason found a quiet spot nearby and sat on some worn limestone steps, the sun warm on his face and a few lizards skittering nearby. He liked lizards. He often saw them on his fence at home. Maybe if he placed some flagstones near the arbor, they'd come closer to the house to sun themselves.

"All right," he murmured quietly. He looked around to make sure nobody was near enough to hear the crazy American talking to himself. He pressed his fingers to his shoulder and felt the fading ache of the bruises. "Sabbio is real. A figment could never hurt my heart like this." Yes. That was the truth. And if a Roman ghost was real, why not Roman gods?

He whispered. "I don't speak Latin, but I guess deities can manage English. Look, if you're there, please. Help Sabbio. He's suffered far too long. Give him a body or give him peace—just don't make him be alone anymore. I don't... I don't know what would please you. I don't even know who I'm talking to. The Fates? Just... please."

He had no more words. With a deep sigh, he stood and made his way back to the apartment. It was time to pack—they'd be leaving for Vienna early in the morning.

Nine

THE GHOST watched as Mason put his things into suitcases. Mason couldn't see him, although he kept looking nervously over his shoulder as he worked. It hurt Sabbio to be unable to touch him or speak to him, especially because he wanted to thank Mason for giving him so much. When Mason fell asleep, Sabbio found himself unable to enter his dreams. Perhaps that was just as well; Sabbio had tormented him enough already.

But in the morning, it was Sabbio who was tormented as Mason packed up the last of his belongings and looked around the bedroom. "I'll miss you," he whispered.

"I will think of you," Sabbio replied. But of course Mason didn't hear.

Shortly afterward, Mason and his companions left the apartment. Their suitcases bumped along the stone street until they left the pedestrian zone and piled into a waiting taxi van. Mason was looking out the window as they pulled away. Even though he obviously couldn't see Sabbio, Mason gave a small wave.

Seventeen hundred years ago, when a youthful Sabbio was taken from his home in chains, he'd learned that crying was useless. But now he floated to the top of the palace walls, faced the sea, and sobbed. This time when he fell into the pit, the emptiness was almost welcome.

HE STAYED in the nothingness longer than usual. It didn't seem worth the effort to fight his way out. Sometimes wispy memories floated by—a gentle touch on his skin, a kind voice in his ear—but he didn't try to claim them. Those memories were no more alive than he was.

Eventually, though, he grew afraid that if he stayed in the pit much longer, he'd never find his way out again. And even viewing the world as a perpetual observer was better than viewing nothing at all. Slowly and laboriously, like Sisyphus rolling the stone uphill, Sabbio climbed up and out.

He didn't know how much time had passed, and it didn't really matter. It had been early summer when he met Mason, and although he couldn't feel the chill, the light jackets and earlier sunsets told him autumn had arrived. Perhaps it was the same year, or perhaps not.

Sabbio spent the daytime hours atop the palace walls, watching the boats come and go. Or he wandered the Riva, eavesdropping on conversations in many languages. Sometimes he descended to the vaulted rooms of the palace cellars. He would inspect the stonework—still sturdy—and wonder which ones he had set.

Ghosts didn't sleep and couldn't dream, so at night he huddled in the darkness near the greenmarket, waiting for the merchants to make their predawn appearances. He liked watching them set up their booths, and he wondered what their fruits and vegetables tasted like.

One afternoon when the ache threatened to consume him, he floated to the apartment where the woman had called in Latin. She sat at her kitchen table with coffee and a book, but looked up as he entered. She wasn't alarmed, only curious.

"Who is it?" she asked in Croatian. Her gaze didn't focus on Sabbio, which meant she couldn't see him. But she listened.

"Sabbio. I was here once—"

"I remember." She smiled warmly. "Are you well?"

The question confounded him. "I'm dead."

Her laughter was kind. "I know. But you still feel."

He did, and that was both a blessing and a curse. He crossed the room and perched on the chair across from her, pretending he'd been invited for tea and sweets and soon they might chat about the weather or complain about politicians, just as he'd heard so many people do over the centuries.

"I'm lonely," he admitted.

"I know. And not for an old lady's company."

"You're not old. And you're very beautiful."

"And you are a flatterer. You're welcome to stay as long as you like, dear, and visit often. But it's not me you're pining for, is it?"

He didn't answer, which made her frown.

"Are you still there?"

"Yes."

"He came to see me before he left Split. Your American man. Did you know that?"

"No," Sabbio said, surprised. "Was he angry that I'd come when he wanted his husband?"

"No, dear. He's at peace with losing his husband. He came to talk about you. He hoped I knew some way to prove you were real. He wanted to find a way to help. He cares a great deal about you."

Sabbio opened his mouth and closed it again, unsure of what to say. He'd felt so close to Mason during those dreams, but he'd been sure it was only due to his own desperation and Mason's grief. He hadn't expected Mason to spare him much thought once he awakened.

"Sabbio?" Mrs. Lulić asked.

"Sorry. I…." He tried to collect himself. "What did you tell him?"

"Nothing very useful, I'm afraid. I said perhaps the Fates had brought you together. I suggested he…." She shrugged. "Faith. Sometimes it can work miracles."

"Faith in *what*?"

"Yourself. And love." She said it first in Croatian, then in Latin, as if wanting to make sure he understood.

He had to steer the conversation away from Mason at that point because he was too overwhelmed. So he asked her about herself and her family, and she asked him about his life, and they had a very pleasant chat. But the hour grew late, and he knew she had things to attend to.

"Thank you," he said as he moved toward the door.

"You can stay."

"I won't haunt you. You have grandchildren to spoil." He had a small, unexpected pang of loss. He would have liked to have had children, grandchildren. A family.

"I meant what I said before, Sabbio. You're welcome here anytime. I like your company."

That made him smile. "Thank you," he said again before leaving.

The next morning he skulked around the peristyle, considering her advice. A klapa group stood near the cathedral, singing about grapevines while tourists snapped photos. Sabbio listened to them for a while. He liked music. It was one of the constants of human beings. Even slaves had used music to lighten their burdens a little. Every spring, Sabbio and several of his fellow stonemasons would save a bit of their meager rations to make an offering to Minerva, and they'd sing in her honor.

Offerings to the gods. But which gods would Sabbio entreat? Gods of death? Fate? Love? They hadn't listened to him when he was alive, so why would they heed him now?

Still, he found a quiet place near the cathedral and looked up to the sky. "I have no offerings for you," he said, spreading his arms. "I had little when I was alive, and I possess not even a body now. But please, hear me. Grant me peace. Or… love. Just a little. Please."

Nobody answered—but then, he hadn't expected a response.

A FEW days later, Sabbio floated around the old part of the city, thinking about paying Mrs. Lulić a visit. Knowing that someone nearby could speak with him was a big temptation. And she'd said he was welcome. But maybe she was just being polite. He'd wait a few weeks longer, just in case.

He made his way to Narodni trg—People's Square—where the locals had whiled away the hours since the fourteenth century. It was an even better place than the Riva for listening in on conversations. Today he smiled at a young man who was trying to convince a girl to go dancing with him that night instead of attending a family function. She was going to say yes eventually, Sabbio thought, but not until she'd made the boy plead. Sabbio moved on to an old couple bickering over whether to replace their bedroom curtains, then to some mothers cooing over their babies.

After a while, listening without being heard and watching without being seen became too painful. He was about to leave for his usual spot high atop the palace when he spied two people sitting at a table nearly hidden behind a wall. One was a beautiful woman with an ample bust and cascades of chestnut-colored hair, and the other was an equally beautiful youth. He had raven hair and mournful brown eyes. They were both looking at Sabbio.

Sabbio's first impulse was to disappear. But he couldn't make himself move; he seemed made of the stone he'd once hewn. Then the woman beckoned to him, and he had no choice but to approach.

"*Salve*, Sabbio," the woman said when he reached the table. Her smile was enough to stir his cock, which was embarrassing since he was naked, but she only smiled wider, as if the sight of his erection pleased her. Her voice was like a lyre, and her eyes were the colors of the sea.

"You… you can…." He fumbled over the Latin.

"Of course we see you," said the youth. His voice was a raspy whisper, as if he didn't use it often, and his dark eyes were much older than his face. "And now we've permitted you to see us."

"Who?" Sabbio managed.

The youth shook his head slightly. "You know."

Sabbio looked at him long and hard, and he saw himself falling from a half-built limestone wall; saw himself lying sweaty and alone on a dirty pallet in a dark tent, moaning in agony; saw himself closing his eyes and gasping his final breaths. He turned his head slightly to see the woman, and what flashed before his eyes was Mason crouching between his legs, kissing Sabbio's balls.

"I know," Sabbio said. Mors and Venus—god of death and goddess of love. He fell to his knees.

Venus clicked her tongue at him. "Don't do *that*. It's tedious. We want to talk to you, not watch you grovel."

Sabbio stood on shaking legs. He kept his gaze trained on the ground. "I… I…."

"You called us, didn't you? So we came." Venus tucked her hair behind her shoulder.

"But you're—"

"Retired," Mors interrupted. "Everyone stopped believing in us. They moved on to other gods." He gestured in the general direction of the cathedral. His face seemed permanently set in a frown, but lack of current worshippers didn't appear to especially upset him.

Sabbio blinked a few times. He wouldn't have thought that after nearly two millennia he'd still be capable of astonishment, but here he was. "Retired?"

Venus laughed. "Like your emperor Diocletian. We putter around here and there, keep ourselves busy. I've been especially enjoying the Internet. So much sex! *He* likes to take broody walks through industrial zones." She waved her hand dismissively at Mors, who twitched his shoulder.

Sabbio was dizzy. Could a ghost faint?

Mors pulled out a chair that had definitely not existed a moment earlier. "Sit," he commanded.

As Mors lit a cigarette and took a deep drag, Venus enjoyed a forkful of pastry. Sabbio had always preferred men—not that he'd had any choice in the matter—but he couldn't stop watching as she swiped her pink tongue across her full lips. She winked at him. "Retired," she said again.

"Then why are you here now?"

"After Diocletian retired, what did he do?"

"Garden?" Sabbio said uncertainly. He'd been dead by then and not very tuned in to current events.

"Yes, he gardened. But not all the time. He also advised his successors. In between growing cabbages, he kept his hand in politics. And that's what Mors and I are doing now. Dabbling in our old professions."

Sabbio shook his head in bewilderment, making Venus sigh.

But it was Mors who spoke next, and his eyes were surprisingly compassionate. "I remember when you died. You suffered. But when your body was done, you refused to move on. Why?"

"I don't know."

Mors narrowed his eyes. "You do know."

"I…. It's stupid."

"Everything humans do is foolish," Venus said. "That's what makes them so entertaining."

Sabbio had been watching people for a long time, and he was inclined to agree with her. "I wanted someone to love me," he said quietly. "Nobody could, not when I was nothing but a ghost. But I wanted it anyway."

Both of the gods nodded at him. Mors even smiled a little. "Death is necessary. But so is love." And he reached over to stroke Sabbio's cheek with ice-cold fingers.

"People talk about us all the time," Venus said. "Even now. They paint us and sculpt us and name all sorts of things after us."

"Nobody names anything after *me*," Mors said morosely.

She patted his hand. "Because you're dreary, darling. But my *point* is that they talk about us, but they don't talk *to* us. Not anymore. But you did. And Mason does, which is very sweet."

"Mason talks to you?"

"He's built us an altar! Can you imagine? And he leaves little things for us—flowers, fruit, a glass of wine. He feels silly about it, but he does it anyway. And he begs us to help you."

The dizziness increased, and Sabbio would have fallen into the pit if Mors and Venus hadn't each grasped one of his hands. They were strong. There was no way he could fall with them holding him in place. "He remembers me?"

Venus looked older now—more like a mother than a lover—but still stunning. "Of course he does, baby. Mors and I, we were playing around a little when we brought you together. But you know what? I think those Parcae bitches got involved."

"The Fates?" Apparently Sabbio could speak only in questions.

Mors grunted. "They like to stick their noses into human affairs. And Morta, well, I think she feels a little bad over the death she chose for you. It was cruel of her. It was probably her idea that you and Mason should be together."

"We should be together." Sabbio managed to make it a statement, because it was important. "But I'm dead."

"Bah." Mors waved his hand. "We can fix that. We may be retired, but we haven't given up all our powers."

For the moment, Sabbio dismissed the ridiculous notion of being brought back to life. He shook his head. "Mason didn't ask for any of this. He didn't choose—"

Mors interrupted rudely. "Bah! Not *that* old tripe again. The discussion's deader than you are. Free will, destiny… what difference does it make? Mason wants you. You want Mason. You'll be much happier together than apart. So why should you care whether you *chose* each other or whether the whole thing was the Parcae's idea?"

And this must have been a favorite topic of his, because he continued, pointing a long thin finger at Sabbio while he spoke. "Humans blather on about making choices. But you can't choose the most important things—when and where you are born and to whom, or when, where, and how you die. They happen. *You* didn't choose to be a slave. It's not about making decisions, Sabbio. It's about dealing gracefully with what you've been given. It's about finding joy where you can."

Sabbio wasn't about to argue with a god, retired or not. And anyway, Mors made good points. "I want Mason," Sabbio said firmly. "And I want to make him happy. I think I could do that."

Venus leaned over and kissed his cheek, making his skin tingle. "We think so too, darling."

"What… what do I have to do?"

"Hold our hands. Close your eyes. Promise to honor us now and then. And have faith."

Perhaps Mason had difficulty believing Sabbio was real. That was understandable. Sabbio would believe enough for both of them. He took the hands of Mors and Venus and squeezed his eyes shut.

Ten

As Doug poured three glasses of wine and Pete relaxed on a kitchen chair, Mason chopped chicken for the stir-fry. He was hungry. He'd put in an especially long day at work—trying to finish a job before a storm hit—and he was looking forward to dinner and a quiet evening with his friends.

"So how come no date tonight?" Doug asked, leaning against the island.

"Because I'd rather hang with you guys."

"What about, uh, Colton?"

"Carson." Mason tossed a handful of chopped meat into a bowl and grabbed another breast. "He's a nice guy and everything, but we kinda… fizzled."

After returning from his European trip, Mason had decided it was time to jump into the dating pool. He'd seen a few guys—real dates, not hookups—but nothing had clicked. He hadn't disliked any of them. They were fun and good-looking, and he'd even seen a couple of them more than once, hoping mutual interest would grow. It didn't. There was no spark. Not like he'd had with Carl and not, gods help him, like he'd had with Sabbio.

Doug sipped his wine. "I could introduce you to a bassist. Giovanni. He's Italian, obviously, and he—"

"Thanks, but I really don't want a matchmaker."

Over at the table, Pete hummed the corresponding tune from *Fiddler on the Roof.*

Mason dumped the last of the chicken into the bowl and used his fingers to work the spice mixture into the meat. He was trying a new recipe, and he hoped it would turn out all right. "I think this spring I'm going to redo some of the backyard," he announced.

"Yeah?" said Doug. "How come? It looks really nice."

"I'm having some irrigation issues because of that slope near the back fence. The higher ground never holds enough water, and the lower gets too soggy. I want to do a little terracing and build a retaining wall." He'd have to hire someone for that part. Despite his name, his masonry skills were limited. Hell, maybe he'd have a portico added while he was at it, just as Sabbio had suggested. The extra shade would be nice, and the back of the house was architecturally bland.

"Terraces would look good," said Doug, and Pete nodded his agreement.

Deciding the meat was adequately mixed, Mason washed his hands, poured a little oil into the wok, and turned on the flame. While he was at it, he turned the jasmine rice down to a simmer. It was already smelling pretty good.

While he waited for the oil to heat, he grabbed his wineglass and took a taste. Not bad. "So tell me about this trip you guys are planning."

"Doug's been invited to play at a festival in Helsinki," Pete said, his voice full of pride.

"Hey! That's great! Congratulations."

Doug beamed. "And since we'll be in Finland anyway, we thought we'd visit some nearby countries. We're torn between Scandinavia or the Baltic states. My vote's for Sweden."

"And I think Estonia sounds really interesting," Pete added. "Want to join us? Your vote can be the tiebreaker."

"Thanks, guys. I appreciate the offer, but my bank account's still crying after last summer's trip. Unless I strike gold while I'm digging up the yard, I'm gonna be stuck in California for a while." And, he didn't add, if he *did* go abroad, he'd head straight to Split.

"Well, the offer stands if you hit the mother lode," Doug said.

Mason grinned at him before pouring the chicken into the pan. The meat began to sizzle at once—and then someone knocked on the door. "Damn!"

"I'll get it," Pete said, standing.

"Thanks." Mason stirred the food. "For some reason, solar panel and satellite dish salesmen can never find my doorbell. Don't know why. I mean, it's right there next to the door, and it looks exactly like a doorbell."

"What about UPS and FedEx?" asked Doug.

"They use the bell. They're fancy that way."

"Jehovah's Witnesses?"

"They—" Mason interrupted himself when he heard Pete returning. "Who was it?" he asked, glancing over his shoulder.

Pete had a very odd expression. "There's... somebody here to see you."

"Who?"

"I think you'd better come to the door."

Mason would have argued, but Pete's normally placid face was pale, his eyes extra big. He didn't look scared, just freaked out. And as far as Mason knew, Pete didn't do freaked out.

Fuck.

"Um...." Mason could have asked Doug to man the stove, but he didn't trust him, not with a mystery in progress. So instead, Mason turned off the stove and hoped dinner wouldn't be ruined. "Okay." With his friends in tow, he hurried into the living room.

And came to a screeching halt halfway through. Pete had left the door ajar, so the visitor on the doorstep was easily visible.

It was Sabbio.

"Oh gods," Mason whispered.

Sabbio wasn't naked this time. He wore perfectly ordinary modern attire—a pair of jeans and a plain white tee that hugged his muscular torso and upper arms. His hair was longer than before, curling slightly around his neck. He was chewing his lower lip and clenching his fists. "Mason?"

Mason whirled around to face Doug and Pete. "Can you see him? Is he there?"

"We see him," Pete answered quietly.

"And I'm not.... Jesus, this isn't a dream, is it?" He pinched his arm to make sure; it hurt very realistically, and he didn't wake up. Yet he felt as if he were sleepwalking as he moved slowly to the door. He reached out and placed his hand against Sabbio's chest.

Sabbio shuddered slightly but didn't disappear. Beneath his palm, Mason could feel Sabbio's heart beating and his chest moving up and down as he breathed. "Real?"

"Alive."

"How?"

Sabbio gave a tiny, nervous smile. "*Ex deorum donum.* A gift from the gods."

It didn't make any sense, and it couldn't be true. But here Sabbio was, with the porch light turning his skin golden and his eyes shining with unshed tears. And Mason wanted more than anything in the world for him to be there, so he didn't care if it was impossible. He was going to believe.

He gathered Sabbio tightly into his arms.

With a soft cry, Sabbio embraced him back.

They may have both wept a little. They may have exchanged whispered endearments in several languages. They may have squeezed each other so hard they could barely breathe. Didn't matter. Because Mason was positive about one thing: the man he held was as real as he was.

Eventually Mason released Sabbio from the hug, then immediately grabbed his hand and pulled him inside the house. Turning to look at his friends, he said, "Guys? I'd like you to meet the only living man who makes me spark. This is Sabbio."

Eleven

MASON GRIPPED Sabbio's hand so tightly it hurt, but Sabbio didn't mind. He'd held Mason's just as tightly as their airplane lifted into the air—and for most of the long flight from San Francisco to Frankfurt. He'd done it again when their second, smaller airplane took off. He couldn't help it. It was easier for him to believe in gods than to believe giant metal machines full of people and suitcases could fly like birds.

But now they were safely on the ground again, and it was Mason's turn to need comfort. Their hands were clasped under the café table, where few people would notice.

"I am not going to become a ghost again just because we have returned to Split," Sabbio said.

"I know. It's just… sometimes I'm afraid I'll wake up and find out the last two years have been a dream."

Sabbio smiled. "If so, it has been a wonderful dream."

It had. They'd spent every day working together, Mason teaching him planting and Sabbio instructing Mason on how to build walls. Laboring under the sun as a freeman—with his lover at his side—was marvelous. Even better, though, were the evenings they spent alone together, cooking, eating, leaving small gifts on the altar, watching TV, or practicing Sabbio's reading skills. And then they tumbled into bed, making love and falling asleep in each other's arms.

"I don't know what I did to deserve you," Mason said.

"Nor I you. But the Fates have been very kind."

When Mason smiled like that, he was more handsome than any god.

A moment later, a man approached their table, and Mason stood. "Viktor! It's good to see you."

Viktor grinned. "I am so happy you called me." He shook Mason's hand and looked curiously at Sabbio. "You have brought friend?"

"Viktor Lulić, meet Sabbio Gould."

Viktor's eyes went wide when Mason said Sabbio's name. "Is this your *sablast*? Your ghost?"

"Not anymore. Now he's my husband."

Recovering unexpectedly quickly, Viktor sat and gave Sabbio a hearty handshake. "*Predivan*! Wonderful! I have never seen ex-ghost before. How is this possible?"

Mason answered simply. "We believed."

That must have been good enough for Viktor, because he smiled again and leaned back in his chair. "I am no longer mechanic. Now I show Dalmatia to tourists almost every day."

"Do you have room in your schedule for us?" Mason asked.

"Always for you! But, Sabbio, you do not need guide."

Sabbio shrugged. "I know the palace and the old city. But when I was alive the first time, nothing else was here. And when I was dead, I could not move far beyond the walls."

"Ah." Viktor stroked his chin. "Then you must visit islands. I will take you. But also we will go to Dubrovnik and Ston. And I will show you best wine, best seafood, best everything."

Mason turned to Sabbio. "Sound good?" Over the past two years, he had taken considerable delight in introducing Sabbio to the wonders of America. They'd visited mountains with towering trees older than Sabbio, deserts full of darting lizards and prickly plants, cities with buildings so high they reached the heavens. And he asked Sabbio about all the ancient things he'd seen, which made Sabbio feel treasured and wise.

"It sounds very good," Sabbio said. And it did. But in the end, he and Mason both knew that where they went and what they saw was far less important than the fact that they were together.

Viktor slapped the table enthusiastically. "*Dobro*! Stay here. I will make one phone call. My cousin Frano will take other group today. His English is better, but I know more about Split. And we will begin our tour. I think… this is special tour. We begin with Mama, who will be very happy to see you both." And without waiting for their response, he scurried away from the table, rummaging in his man-bag as he went.

"He is happy to see us," Sabbio observed.

Mason took Sabbio's hand. "Without him, we'd never have met."

"The Fates would have found another way, I think."

"Maybe. Whatever. But I still think we owe the Lulićes at least a really nice dinner out."

"At least."

Sabbio and Mason sat at the café on the Riva, looking out at the blue-green sea. The air smelled of salt, the breeze tickled their hair, and if Sabbio licked his lips, they tasted of Mason's kiss. Today was a good day.

The gods had given him a young body, and since Mason was young too, they'd have many years together if they were lucky. But even if their luck ran out— even if one of them died early—Sabbio knew they would both pass peacefully into the afterlife, secure in having been loved.

"*Gratia, dei,*" Sabbio murmured.

Mason squeezed his hand and repeated the phrase in English. "Thank you, gods."

And perhaps Mors and Venus heard them and were pleased to be remembered. In any case, two men who had been born seventeen centuries apart now sat in front of an ancient palace—and simply enjoyed being in love.

KIM FIELDING is very pleased every time someone calls her eclectic. Her books have won Rainbow Awards and span a variety of genres. She has migrated back and forth across the western two-thirds of the United States and currently lives in California, where she long ago ran out of bookshelf space. She's a university professor who dreams of being able to travel and write full time. She also dreams of having two perfectly behaved children, a husband who isn't obsessed with football, and a house that cleans itself. Some dreams are more easily obtained than others.

Blogs: kfieldingwrites.com/ and www.goodreads.com/author/show/4105707.
Kim_Fielding/blog
Facebook: www.facebook.com/KFieldingWrites.
E-mail: kim@kfieldingwrites.com
Twitter: @KfieldingWrites

By KIM FIELDING

Alaska
Animal Magnetism (Dreamspinner Anthology)
Astounding!
The Border
Brute
Don't Try This at Home (Dreamspinner Anthology)
A Great Miracle Happened There
Grown-up
Housekeeping
Men of Steel (Dreamspinner Anthology)
Motel. Pool.
Night Shift
Pilgrimage
The Pillar
Phoenix
Rattlesnake
Saint Martin's Day
Snow on the Roof (Dreamspinner Anthology)
Speechless • The Gig
Steamed Up (Dreamspinner Anthology)
The Tin Box
Venetian Masks
Violet's Present

BONES
Good Bones
Buried Bones
The Gig
Bone Dry

GOTHIKA
Stitch (Multiple Author Anthology)
Bones (Multiple Author Anthology)
Claw (Multiple Author Anthology)
Spirit (Multiple Author Anthology)

Published by DREAMSPINNER PRESS
www.dreamspinnerpress.com

Among the Dead

by Eli Easton

1

THE FIRST time I saw the dead man in the bowler hat, I was on the Number 34 bus heading downtown.

It was the first Tuesday of the month, and I had to go into the office for my one-on-one with my boss, John Shaler. I hated first Tuesdays with the heat of a thousand pissed-off suns. But it was little enough forfeit to pay for having a steady job I could work from home the rest of the month. Thank God I'm the best dev Hora Systems has, or they would have kicked my agoraphobic ass to the curb a long time ago. I haven't exactly been the ideal employee AC.

AC—After Concussion. My life is pretty much defined by Before Concussion and After Concussion.

That particular first Tuesday, I left my basement apartment on Capitol Hill with the usual vein-thrumming mix of nerves, terror, and utter dread. As soon as I got on the bus, I saw a dead woman. She was up front, in those seats that face the aisle. She'd probably gotten hit by a truck or some kind of machine. Her body was sliced into thirds like she'd been through a giant Veg-O-Matic. She sat close to the oblivious driver, a purse primly clutched in her lap, while blood pooled under her seat. I walked past, pretending I didn't see her. My stomach threatened to toss up the Eggo and peanut butter I'd had for breakfast. I fucking hate blood. If I had my way, I'd never see it again.

A few stops later, an old couple got on and sat in the laps of two teenagers. Their lined faces were pinched into bitter, sour masks—the old couple, not the teenagers. They said nothing to each other, didn't even look at each other, but their movements were perfectly in sync: scratch of the nose, shaking finger and mouthing something angrily, rock in their seat, gnash teeth, sigh. There they remained for three stops and then they hobbled off, each step perfectly mirrored.

Interlocked spirits liked that were particularly horrifying to me. The idea of spending eternity with someone you hated in life—it's so unfair. You'd think that, in death, you could escape the commitments you regretted. Right? I mean, what else is death for? It ends all corporeal pleasure and shit, so there should be an upside. Debts cancelled, enemies escaped, mistakes left behind, and all that. But that's not how it is. I've seen a lot of spirits who were stuck together. And let me tell you, it's rarely down to true love.

I'll take my loneliness, thanks.

Despite my commitment to being single, I found myself craning my neck when we drove past Volunteer Park. But I didn't see the beautiful boy in the red hoodie. I hadn't seen him in a long time.

See, a few years ago, BC, I used to ride my bike to work, and my daily route went past the park. I often saw a young guy at the entrance on the corner of 15th and Galer. He was maybe eighteen, wore a red hoodie and jeans, and had blond hair, a pretty face, and sad blue eyes. His clothes were always the same, rumpled and dirty. I thought he might be a street kid, but he could have just been dedicated to the Seattle grunge thing. He was always alone. I called him Red Riding Hood in my head, and I always looked for him when I rode past.

I wished I'd had the nerve to stop and talk to him back then, but I never did. He was long gone now, maybe away at college somewhere. He could have ditched the grunge for a suit and tie for all I knew.

The bus passed Volunteer Park and then Broadway, the main shopping drag on Capitol Hill.

At the Swedish hospital stop, *he* got on. The man in the bowler hat.

To be honest, my first reaction was to check him out. He was handsome—dark-haired and slender, with an intelligent, soulful-looking face. Besides the bowler hat, he wore a three-piece tweed suit, looking very genteel for the bus and a bit old-fashioned. It took a second glance to realize he was also, unfortunately, not alive.

I stared down at my shoes. The floor of the bus was fairly clean, with it being just after seven in the morning. The slightly bubbled blue flooring looked bright around my scuffed brown leather shoes. It was a bit embarrassing, as if to say, *Even I, the floor of a public transit vehicle, am better groomed than you.*

I was about to tuck my neglected shoes under my seat in shame when a pair of pointed, black boots stepped in front of me. The legs were covered in dark brown tweed pants and almost completely solid, but the prickling hair on my arms and the back of my neck told me what I knew anyway. It was him.

I swallowed and raised my eyes. I expected him to be staring straight out the window or perhaps around the bus. But no, his warm brown eyes were looking into mine.

My heart pounded, and fear slicked through me in a black, oily tide. I closed my eyes and counted to ten. *Oh, God. Oh, God. Please be gone.*

When I opened my eyes, he'd moved. He was now across the bus, a few feet away, as if backing off. But he was still staring at me. *Shit.* I took calming breaths and pretended I didn't see him.

I glanced at the old lady sitting next to me to see if she'd noticed my freak-out, but she just sat reading her book.

When I got off at First and Bell, Bowler Hat followed me. He walked five steps behind me for the three blocks it took me to get to the Hora Systems offices, a dead man reflected in shop windows and the shiny surface of a black limousine. And when I passed through the revolving door at our building and signed in at reception, I risked a casual glance around.

He was there. He stood against the glass front of the building, his eyes fixed on me. He opened his mouth as if trying to speak.

"Hi, Joe," I blurted out to the security guard, just to act normal, like nothing was wrong.

Joe grunted, not looking at me.

I headed to the elevators.

"So HOW'S it going, Neil?" John asked.

Hora Systems was on the seventh floor of a black high-rise, and John's office had a nice view toward the Sound. It was a cloudy Seattle Tuesday, dreary despite being technically spring.

"Fine. I'm fine," I said.

"Yeah? How are the headaches?"

"Headaches" was my usual excuse for turning into a freak who never wanted to leave his apartment. I'd had a bad concussion, so people understood and accepted the idea that I might have terrible headaches as a result. Seeing dead people, not so much.

"About the same. But it's cool. I'm good enough to work. I prefer to work, actually." It was true. Working filled a lot of hours when you were stuck in your apartment.

"Good. Catch me up-to-date on the Gravalu project."

So I did, describing the inventory check system I was currently working on. Hora Systems converted traditional businesses to paperless. Most of our clients had systems so complex, they required custom coding, which gave plenty of work to me and the three devs who worked in the office. One of our big clients, Gravalu, was a bio-tech company. I'd been working on their system exclusively for some time.

"I feel like this project is taking too long," I said apologetically, "but it's not because I'm not cranking on it. It's the most complex system we've done. There are so many different chemicals and compounds. And this inventory check thing… I have to check the amount of each chemical in inventory against all the ways it was used in the lab, which all have their own logs. If there's more than a variable percentage difference in the amount, I put up a flag. I guess some of that sh—er, stuff can be dangerous, so they want to make sure no one's walking off with it."

"It's okay, Neil," John said with his usual boredom-masquerading-as-patience. "The client's paying for your hours. As long as they're happy with your progress, I'm happy."

"Good." I still felt a little nervous about it. I didn't know what I'd do if Hora Systems ever handed me a pink slip.

"So…. You ready to come back into the office again? Maybe start with two days a week?"

John asked this same question every month. And every month I said the same thing. "Not yet. Maybe in a few months."

John was polite enough to pretend he believed me.

THE ONE-ON-ONE with John was the easiest part of my first Tuesdays. Once I was in John's office, a dead-free zone, it was fine. I liked seeing the view out his window, drinking the company coffee, and talking to a real live person. I liked John. He was a good boss and a nice guy. And God knows I so seldom had a chance to talk to anyone. But after John, I had to face the trip home.

I took the elevator down to the lobby and stuck my head out warily. There was no sight of the dead man in the bowler hat. Cautiously, I ventured out of the elevator and then out of the building. I must have looked like a mouse sneaking around so timidly. Pause, dart, pause, dart. I didn't see him on the street. I was relieved, but still looking out for him nervously until I was on the bus and it was moving.

Bowler Hat never did reappear, but there was a big, ugly dead man who got on the bus while we were still downtown and rode all the way up to 15th on the hill. He made his way down the aisle, looking at every person with intense interest before plunging a large butcher knife into their chests or stomachs. Down the aisle he went, like some hellish inspector, one person at a time. None of the living saw him, of course, but they would rub a hand where he'd struck, as if suddenly feeling a pain, or go pale and sick-looking. One woman leaned forward and nearly put her head between her knees as if light-headed.

I didn't know what to do. If I tried to escape the guy, he'd know I saw him. That would be the *worst* thing I could do. Then maybe he'd follow me and keep stabbing. So I forced myself to shut my eyes and pretend to be asleep, despite the fact that my heart slammed in my chest and every nerve urged me to run. *Please let me get home. I just want to get home. Oh God.*

I could sense him getting closer, and when he was in front of me, I felt his legs brush my jeans. They feel solid, you know. Ghosts do. Which is weird, but I guess if you can see them, you can feel them. I kept myself from moving or opening my eyes. He must have stared at me for a long time. Just when I was hoping he'd move on without stabbing me, I felt the knife plunge into my chest with a heavy thrust. It didn't hurt as much as a real knife would, but it was still shocking. It was like a ghost echo of the way it would really feel—deep and sharp, violent and invasive.

I couldn't hold back a cry, but I covered it with a jerk of my body and then relaxed again, as if I'd just had a bad dream.

Butcher Knife moved on.

By the time I got off at my stop at Volunteer Park, walk-ran the three blocks to the house where I had my basement apartment, got inside, and locked the door, I was drenched with a stinking sweat born of anxiety and terror. God, I hated the bus! I vowed to get my bike out of storage. Fuck the consequences. I wasn't supposed to ride because my head injury was bad enough that any fall or knock could really hurt me now. But fuck it. I'd die before I rode the bus again. I promised myself I'd never have to.

And that's how your life narrows, incident by incident, vow by vow, until your world is the size of a one-bedroom basement apartment.

But at least in my eight hundred square feet, I was safe.

THE REASON Bowler Hat freaked me out so much was because, as a rule, the dead don't notice you. They're set on their own paths, and the less you interfere with them, the better. Maybe they assume I can't see them any more than the other living walking through their world can. Drawing their attention, letting them know you can be messed with? Very. Bad. Idea.

Yes, I'm a selfish bastard. But here's the thing: you can't help the dead. Forget Haley Joel Osment and the fucking *Ghost Whisperer*. That's all bullshit. Talking to the dead is like listening to a scratchy record in a language you don't speak—with intermittent power failures and creepy shades of *The Omen*. It's like playing charades with a madman. It's scary and depressing and it's dangerous.

Fuck it. I tried, okay? After I got through all the denial and shit, I tried.

The first year after the accident, also known as AC 1, I tried to fix myself. I'm a programmer, after all. I have a logical brain. I'm used to problem-solving. Well, there may be a Google page for just about everything, but there isn't one for how to stop seeing the dead. I worked with my doctor in the regular hospital where I recovered from the accident. He sent me to a psychiatrist, Dr. Able. I gave Dr. Able the old college try. At first he was very interested in my case, and I believed he could help me get back to the way I'd been before.

Dr. Able taught me some interesting things about the brain, about how the swelling caused by a concussion, if not fatal, can damage some areas and reroute others. He'd had patients who suddenly had amazing math ability or the ability to pick up a new language in weeks. He'd had others who thought their wives were aliens or couldn't process words starting with *D*. He'd seen people gain synesthesia, the ability to see odors or feel colors. But he'd never had a patient whose brain had rewired to see the dead.

We tried all the treatments. I went through twenty or so different meds, some of which made me sick or so tired I could barely open my eyes. We tried hypnosis. We even tried ECT, electroshock therapy.

Yes, they still do that. No, it doesn't hurt when they jolt you because you're under anesthesia. But it does hurt like a bitch when you wake up—lots of sore muscles from the seizures the electricity causes. My jaw had clenched so tight around the rubber insert they put in your mouth, it hurt like a bitch to move it. I could hardly talk or eat for a week.

Dr. Able had described ECT to me as a "hard reboot of the brain." That made sense to me, being a computer guy. But when my brain "rebooted," my ability to see the dead came back online even before I remembered my own name. So yeah, pretty much a complete failure.

By the end of that first year, I finally accepted that I really could see the dead and it wasn't going away. I began to ask the nurses about the people I was seeing, describe them. Turns out the dead people I saw at the hospital matched descriptions of people who'd been patients who had died in that ward.

Dr. Able told me my belief that I was *actually* seeing the dead was a worsening of my "damage-induced hallucinatory condition." I told him to watch out for the dead guy with the frizzy red hair and the hatchet. That guy really fucking hated Dr. Able. Then I checked myself out.

After that, at the start of AC 2, I tried to do something with this "gift." I was going to make a difference in the world! And, not coincidentally, I'd get rich. I'd be like one of those mediums on TV who see ghosts for a studio audience and bring everyone to tears of happiness and spiritual wonder. I was gonna be a hero, a Batman for the dead. But the few times I tried to communicate with them, it was a disaster.

There was one guy, typical *Mad Men* 50s father-type, with horn-rimmed glasses and a suit and tie. He paced in front of an apartment building not far from where I live. I talked to him, asked what was wrong. When he finally noticed me, his face got all angry, and he yelled at me in gibberish and smacked me upside the head. It felt like a scene he'd played out before, like he thought I was his son and we were arguing and he was hitting me. All day that guy followed me around, smacking me upside the head and yelling at me. The blows didn't hurt exactly, but I got a massive headache from all that negative energy. And I got drained too. Not to mention it's really unpleasant to have a man in your face screaming at you and hitting you.

I finally knocked myself out with a bottle of wine and a couple of "happy pills"—pills I'm supposed to take if I get too fearful. When I woke up later that night, Dad of the Year was gone. Thank God!

Makes you wonder, right? Was that the thing that haunted the guy? The way he lost his temper with his kids? Was that what he would obsess over in death—on and on and on, forever? Lovely.

The second time I tried to reach out to a dead person went even worse. I tried to help this sweet-looking old lady ghost I found wandering around downtown. She had on a print flower dress and wore her hair in a bun. I talked to her on the street, asked if she was able to move on, "go to the light," and all that crap, or if there was a message she wanted me to give to someone.

Long story short: she moved in with me for six weeks, convinced I was her son. She had dish-throwing tantrums over my meal choices, disconnected all my cell phone calls, turned the channel away from my favorite TV shows to *Sesame Street* and *National Geographic*, went *apoplectic* over Grindr, and stared at me in the shower with this disdainful moue, just *daring* me to touch my willy. Every. Single. Day.

Her name was Margaret, by the way. The dead old lady. I got rid of her by visiting the most expensive Jewish assisted living facility in the Seattle area. I pretended I was shopping for my real mother and got a tour of the place, with Margaret trailing along behind. Last time I saw her, she was happily waiting in line at the spa with three other old lady ghosts.

In the six weeks Margaret lived with me, I never figured out her real son's name, nor any pressing "unfinished business" I could help her with. I never convinced her to "go to the light," which, as far as I can tell, doesn't even exist. I changed nothing.

Now I just ignore them. And they ignore me. But Bowler Hat had seen me, followed me, watched me. I really wanted to know what that meant.

2

THE SECOND time I saw Bowler Hat, I was in Cafe O Late, the little bakery-slash-coffee shop down the street from my apartment. It was one of the few places I felt safe, and I came here when I couldn't stand staring at the same four walls of my apartment anymore.

I'd been searching for the error that was screwing up the formatting on an output string, and the screen began to bother my eyes. I looked up to gaze out the window at the street, and that's when I saw him. He was standing just outside the window, watching me.

I hastily looked back down at my screen, my heart pumping like it could bust out and run away all by itself.

I sensed his presence before I saw him, in the fresh wave of tingles that ran through me and raised all the hair on my body. I peeked up from under my eyelids, my head still lowered toward the computer, as if that would fool anyone. He was sitting in the empty chair opposite me at my little table. *Fuck.*

Once I looked at him, I couldn't look away. He sat there very calmly, gazing at me. I knew the gig was up. He knew I could see him. There was no point in pretending otherwise. And I couldn't have stopped staring if I wanted to.

Bowler Hat had lived in the early 1900s, I guessed. His brown tweet suit jacket wasn't too out of date, but the fabric was heavier than in our time. He had a matching vest, and his shirt had a stiff, tall white collar. The brown bowler hat was small and rather dashing. His hair was thick and a bit on the long side, curling at his collar. His dark brown eyes were soft and pleasant. Those eyes, his expression, were that of a man at least twenty-five, but there was a boyish frailty about him, as if he'd been sick for a long time.

I glanced at the handkerchief sticking out of his breast pocket. It was white and splashed with red, the color more vibrant than anyother color on him. Coughing up blood. Consumption, I guessed, now called tuberculosis. A lot of people his age died of it around the turn of the century.

I met his gaze again, astonished at how sane and calm he appeared. His eyes were clear, like it was not just that he saw me, but that he *saw me*—Neil, from 2015—and not some imagined relative or enemy from his past.

My heart was still beating dangerously fast, and I felt a little faint. His brow creased slightly in a worried frown, and he gave me a tiny smile. He slowly held up his hands, palms up, as if to say, *You're so afraid. Don't be. I won't hurt you.*

I huffed in disbelief and looked around the café to see if anyone was watching. The last thing I wanted was for someone to see me acting like a psycho: looking at, and talking to, someone who wasn't there. But this was their midmorning lull, and there were only a few other customers. No one in the café was watching me.

I looked at Bowler Hat again. "Look," I said, as quietly as I could. "I can't help you. There's nothing I can do for you. So just… leave me alone."

He looked sadder. He opened his mouth and his lips moved as if he were trying to speak, but nothing came out. He tried harder, his face going tense with the strain. It was both creepy and sad.

"I can't hear you. We can't communicate. So just… please. I'm sorry, but you're dead and I can't help you."

He stopped trying to talk, his shoulders rising and falling with a huge sigh. He stared at me, frowning. He was so normal-looking that it made me feel guilty for being rude. But I was still a little afraid of him too.

"Look, I have to work. I'm sorry, really I am." I used my firm voice. *Class dismissed.* I looked back down at my computer and forced myself to edit a line of code, though I hardly knew what I was doing. When I looked back up, Bowler Hat was gone.

I felt relieved, but a moment later, I felt something like disappointment too. I'd never seen a ghost like him. And he didn't seem threatening. There was a… pleasant feeling surrounding him, for lack of a better word.

He's dead. You can't be pals. There's no point.

I got up to buy another cup of coffee, needing a breather. When I returned to my seat, I went to grab a sugar packet from the little holder. That's when I saw it.

There were several ripped and emptied sugar packets littering the table and a heap of sugar on the fake oak surface. It was a haphazard mess—lines and blobs, like a toddler had been playing in it and pretending at writing. Maybe the dead man had been trying to leave a message, but I didn't understand it. I wasn't sure I wanted to. There was something about those squiggles that chilled me to the bone.

I hurriedly brushed the sugar onto a plate with my hand as if it were poisonous, and dumped it in the dirty plate bin.

I WAS drinking a beer and watching a horror movie on TV. I had to keep the sound down because my landlady, who lived in the main house upstairs, was an old woman who disliked disturbances. I got the feeling she didn't even want a tenant, honestly. Too much bother. But I figured as long as I was quiet and slipped her a rent check under the door upstairs once a month, we had a mutually beneficial arrangement. The place was dirt cheap for a one-bedroom apartment on Capitol Hill.

You may be wondering why I would watch horror films when my life is what it is. There's something about a horror movie that distracts and relaxes me. Maybe it's because with a movie, I'm in control. I have a pause button. And maybe I'm looking for answers. Not that I've ever found any answers in a horror movie.

Anyway, I was watching *The Dead Zone*, again. In case you aren't familiar with it, it's about a guy, Christopher Walken, who has a car accident and is in a longass coma. When he wakes up, he has psychic ability and can "see" things when he touches people. And he does not have a good time of it, let me tell you. I liked the fact that the movie dealt with this kind of "gift" realistically—that is, it's fucking horrible—as opposed to making it sound like larks and fairies. Eventually Christopher Walken does something important and awesome with his gift, because otherwise the movie would suck.

Unfortunately, real life is not a movie.

It had just gotten to the part where Chris wakes up in the hospital, when I felt familiar goosebumps sweep over my body. The hair on my arms and the back of my neck creeped and crawled their way to fully erect.

I'm very protective of my apartment. It's a ghost-free zone, and I do everything in my power to keep it that way, especially since the Margaret incident. But I felt a presence, and I knew who it would be.

I hit the Pause button on the remote and slowly turned. My couch was perpendicular to the door, and when I looked at it, there he was. He stood just inside the closed door, hands down by his sides. His face was calm, and he gave me that tiny smile again. He shrugged as if to say, *I know I shouldn't be here, but is it all right?*

I was still afraid of him, but less so than I'd been before. To be honest, he'd been on my mind since I'd seen him in the coffee shop. I was curious as to why he could see me and what he wanted. Not that I trust ghosts. I didn't trust that, at any moment, he might not turn into the sort of manic, ugly, screaming thing I so wanted to avoid. But I guess curiosity won out, or maybe it was the appealing look on his face. Or maybe I was fucking lonely.

I swallowed down my nerves. "You can come in," I said firmly, "but only for one hour. This isn't an extended invitation. I don't want you haunting this place. You got that?"

He nodded, his smile getting just a bit more pronounced, and then he did something odd. He folded his hands in front of him and tipped his head toward me. *Thank you.*

I rubbed my face. I was going to regret this, I just knew it.

He crossed the room in that creepy, too-fast way of theirs. In a blink, he was sitting in a chair across from the couch. With Christopher Walken frozen on the TV screen and the apartment silent, we looked at each other. He appeared pretty much the same as he had the other two times I'd seen him, except more tired. Maybe he wasn't getting enough eternal rest.

Dead jokes. Ya gotta laugh, you know?

I sighed. "Did you die of consumption?"

He looked a little surprised at my guess. He nodded. One of his hands rubbed around his chest to indicate his lungs, his brow furrowed. Yeah, I bet it was a painful way to go. His hands were very white and long-fingered. Soft-looking. He must have been a bookkeeper, I thought, or a musician or something of that sort. He hadn't done manual labor.

"1880s?" I asked.

He tilted his head to the side as if considering it. He raised a hand, palm up, and motioned up with his fingertips. *Higher.*

"1890s?"

He nodded.

"Huh." I wasn't sure what else to say. Weirdly enough, he felt like a visitor, like I had to make conversation with him. He looked so real, not obviously dead like most of them do. If not for the paleness of his skin, the slight trace of blood around his lips, and the fact that I could vaguely make out the pattern of the chair through his body, he could have been alive. He clearly wanted to make contact with me. And I felt sorry for him, I did. But, really, what was the point? It's not like we could hang out and play Ticket to Ride. Or anything else my body might have suggested, if he were alive.

"You do know you're dead?" I asked, trying not to sound mean about it.

He tilted his head again, as if considering it. Then he nodded it slowly.

"Do you know what year this is? This is 2015. Look." I pointed to the TV to indicate our advanced ability to induce a vegetative state. I fished my cell phone from the sofa beside me and waggled it. "See—2015. Did you know that much time had passed since... er... since you passed?"

He just looked at me, frustrated. He opened his mouth and tried to speak again, but nothing came out. So much for conversation.

"Look, I don't know why ghosts roam the earth, but if you know of a way off this pony ride, you might want to take it. I can't imagine you still have any unfinished business after a hundred and twenty years. Let it go, man. Other than that, I've got nothing to offer you."

He ignored me. He looked around the room, a thoughtful frown on his face. I got the feeling he was looking for something, maybe some way to talk to me. His eyes landed on a light fixture. He stared at it. It flickered.

"Hey!" I said, alarmed. "Do *not* blow a fuse. Please. The fuse box is upstairs and I have to bug the landlady and it's a total pain." I knew because blowing a fuse was one of Margaret's tricks when I tried watching porn. Poof went my power grid.

He looked at me, obviously displeased, but the lights didn't flicker again. After a moment, he waved at the TV, rather imperiously. *Go ahead, then, watch you drivel since you won't let me try to communicate.*

"Do you, um, know what TV is?"

His flat stare told me I was an idiot.

"Fine! I just didn't want to alarm you or anything, wondering why there was a man stuck in that little box."

He rolled his eyes. Seriously. A sarcastic ghost. That was a first.

I huffed, rewound the movie a bit, and turned off the mute.

He watched *The Dead Zone* with me, and then I decided to put in *The Sixth Sense*. I thought that might send a subtle message, that seeing the dead isn't really any living person's idea of a good time.

Halfway through, I looked over at the chair and he was gone. I felt a little guilty, but I told myself it was for the best. I really didn't want a dead guy hanging around my apartment, even if he wasn't scary or threatening.

But then, why did my little hermit hole suddenly feel so empty?

MY ENCOUNTER with the dead man left a heavy feeling in my chest that wouldn't let up. Two days later, I still felt miserable. I wasn't sure why he affected me that much.

What had I expected? For him to come back? Hang out?

I was lonelier than I'd realized. I needed to make an effort to be with real humans again. So that Friday night, I went to Monrose's, the least scary gay club in the area.

Gay clubs are full of the dead, and it's not a pretty scene. At the hip clubs on Broadway, there are so many dead gay men in the crowd, overlapping the living, that it hurts my eyes and brain trying to sort it out. Sometimes I can't even tell who is who. And it's pretty damn hard to have a good time with the evidence of lifelong debauchery and/or desperation in your face.

The young ones, dead of drug overdoses, car wrecks, or suicides, party a little too maniacally. The older ones look so gut-wrenchingly sad and alone. Their eyes stare like black holes at the good-looking, living guys at the clubs, longing personified. I guess those are the ones who never found love in their lifetime, or maybe guys addicted to sex who can't let it go.

Yeah. So. It can kind of spoil the mood.

Monrose's is on 15th, and it's more of a neighborhood pub. Its dead are mellower, like the guy who sits in the back booth nursing an invisible beer. He just seems happy to hang out forever. And the live guys are lower key too, lots of blue-collar guys, some gay, some straight ones looking for easy sex, some gay-friendly types just hanging out.

I sat at the counter and ordered a beer on tap. After a few minutes, a guy sat next to me.

"Hi, I'm Jess. Want some company?"

Obviously, I did, or I wouldn't be there. But did I want *his* company?

I looked him over. Jess wasn't bad-looking. He was maybe a few years older than my own twenty-eight. He wore a button-down shirt and slacks, like he'd just gotten off a desk job. He had pale skin, unremarkable brown hair and eyes, but a nice quirk to his generous mouth and heat in his gaze that was promising. I felt a twinge of interest below the belt. He would do.

"Sure," I said. "I'm Neil. Can I buy you a drink?"

Jess smiled, looking pleased. "I'd like that. Then maybe you'll let me buy you one."

"Cheers," I said, raising my glass of pale ale.

AN HOUR after Jess sat beside me at the bar, we were in the men's room. Signs said No Drugs but didn't warn patrons about anything related to the exchange of bodily fluids. There were three enclosed stalls, and it wasn't unusual for one of them to be occupied by two parties at any given moment.

Jess drank fast and got buzzed and increasingly flirtatious. A half hour ago, his hand had landed on my thigh and stayed there. I'd whispered in his ear, close enough to tickle. He kept moving that hand until he was practically touching my junk, and I figured we'd get arrested if we stayed at the bar. So here we were.

Sex had been pretty unremarkable AC. Meds will do that to you, not to mention fear and depression and, of course, hardly leaving the house. I didn't have as much sensation as I did before, either—another happy gift of the brain trauma. But Bowler Hat had stirred something inside me, a renewed desire for life, for reaching out to another human being. I was really looking forward to getting off with someone else. Jess's boring conversation—tax accountant—made it clear he was never going to be the love of my life. But he was a warm body, and he seemed to need this getting-off business much as I did.

His hands were all over me as we went into the last stall and locked the door. I went in for a kiss, but he turned his head, going for my neck instead. I liked kissing a lot, but some guys didn't. Fine. I can live with that.

My hand roamed to Jess's zipper and his to mine. Fabric gave way to flesh on flesh, our hands pumping each other. He was only half-mast, despite the needy feel of his hands, and I wasn't exactly rock hard either. *Damn alcohol.* Sometimes too much Dutch courage can put a finger in the dyke, and not in a good way.

"I want this. I want this," Jess muttered imploringly, making me feel a bit sorry for him, which did nothing for my boner.

I was about to get discouraged with the whole thing when something changed. It was like a current of electricity swept the room. The hairs on my arm stood to attention and so did my dick. I probably should have been a bit worried, but I was just honestly relieved. I could feel Jess firm up in my hand too, and he groaned against my neck.

"That's it," I said. "That's a lovely cock." I figured he could use some verbal encouragement.

He moaned and tugged me. It was a bit rougher than I would do, but it still felt amazing to have someone else touch me. Bowler Hat came into my mind, and I mentally pushed the image away. *Not now. Focus.*

"Want me to suck you?" Jess asked, his voice slurred.

It sounded good, but I was afraid to move and lose the momentum. Besides, his hand was doing the trick, and I liked feeling him pressed against my chest and neck. I needed the physical contact almost as much as the sex, and I wasn't ready to give it up.

"This works for me." I slicked my thumb over his slit to convince him to forge ahead.

"Oh God. Okay. Yeah. This is good."

And it was. I pressed him into the side of the stall so I could get my shoulders and chest fully against him. There was barely room between our hips for our hands to maneuver, but we managed. The head of my dick was more sensitive than usual, and the waves of pleasure were delicious. It wasn't long before I felt my balls tighten. I was close. Thank God. Fuck, I needed this.

"I'm almost there," Jess said into my neck.

"Me too," I answered. Then I shot. Jess followed, shuddering against me.

We both stayed in place for several moments, breathing heavy. Then Jess pushed me gently away. We cleaned up with toilet paper and flushed it down the john.

That's when Bowler Hat appeared. He was suddenly in the stall with us, pressed up against the back wall. His body went right through the back of the toilet like it wasn't there. He was just transparent enough for me to see the lines of the tiles through his body.

Shit.

I froze, a slick of mixed emotions rushing through me. Had he been here all along? Maybe outside the stall? Now that I wasn't in the middle of a sex act,

I remembered that sweet tingle of energy that had made me hard. Maybe he had appeared then. I had been secretly hoping to see him again, but here? I was embarrassed. Nothing like getting caught with your pants down—or unzipped, anyway—the smell of come fresh in the air. It flashed through my mind that Bowler was from 1890—not a lot of good PR on gay men back then.

I zipped up fast, my hands shaking.

Jess tensed. "What's wrong, baby?"

My eyes were fixed on the dead man. There was no shock or disapproval on his face. In fact, his eyes were warm, like he was pleased for me, albeit sadly. Maybe he was envious? Dear God, was Bowler Hat gay?

"Nothing." I forced myself to look away from the dead man's eyes and back at Jess.

Jess wore a sad smile. "Thank you. I haven't... that was really nice." He hesitated. "Would you...." He dug a card and a small pen out of a back pocket. "I'd like to see you again. If you want to. You can call me, that is."

"Sure," I said, though I knew I wouldn't call.

He put the card up against the wall and wrote on the back. The pen moved slowly, his tongue sticking out in concentration. I felt a tingle, and the hair on my arm went stiff again. My eyes went to the back of the stall, but Bowler Hat was gone. *What is he up to? What does he want?*

"Here." Jess handed me the card and shifted on his feet, uneasy.

I looked at the card. The back showed shaky handwriting with old-fashioned flourishes. *Edward Cleary. Chicago. d. 1898*

Holy shit! Jess didn't write that. I stared up at Jess in shock.

He fumbled for the latch on the stall door and opened it. "Thanks again, Tony. I'll see you soon?" He attempted a cheery wave, raising his right arm and waggling his fingers.

I was about to gently remind him my name was Neil when I saw it. The cuff of his sleeve rode up and on his wrist was a deep, open gash. It was so deep I could see bone, but the ripped-open flesh was colorless, not bleeding at all. In the light coming in the stall door, I suddenly saw clearly how very, *very* pale he was.

Jess turned, and I heard the door of the restroom open and close.

I sank to my knees in front of the toilet and vomited up everything in my stomach.

OF COURSE, I researched Bowler Hat.

Edward, that is. His name was Edward Cleary. It didn't take me long to find him. An hour with Google, and I found a brief mention of an Edward Cleary on a website that documented 19th century Spiritualism. Edward Cleary, b. 1869, d. 1898, had been a medium.

Wow. That explained a lot. Or maybe it explained nothing. It was interesting, though. I wanted to know more.

There were no pictures online, and I could only find that single-sentence entry. I decided to go to the main Seattle library, even though I had to ride the bus to get there. I debated with myself about it, but finally decided I was determined to go. I couldn't afford to let my world get any smaller.

As it turned out, the bus trip was less dreadful than usual. Mr. Stab-o-matic was thankfully absent. I saw numerous dead people, some quite gory, but they felt less threatening to me. Maybe it was because I didn't feel threatened by Edward. Or maybe I was so distracted by thoughts of him and why he was trying to contact me that I didn't have the mental space to get too upset about it.

I made it to the library without incident. It was the first time I'd been inside the massive downtown Seattle library. In case you're interested, yes, there are dead in the library, but they aren't the violent ones, praise Jane Austen and Zane Grey. Several wandered the stacks, perhaps seeking some elusive title for all eternity. Others were reading shadow books with utter focus in chairs or at tables.

A search of the library's card catalogue did the trick. There was a book published in 1887 about mediums of the day. It was written in a wordy, flowery style by a male Spiritualist named Dennings. There were no photographs, but it had a short chapter on Edward.

Edward Cleary was born in a small Illinois town. His family moved to Chicago when he was five years old. His father, a salesman, worked long hours representing a factory that made shoes. He traveled a great deal, leaving his only child, Edward, and his wife at home. Supposedly, Edward and his father did not get along, and his father never approved of Edward's "calling" as a medium.

If I was right and Edward had been gay in his lifetime, being a medium probably wasn't the only thing his father had disapproved of.

Edward claimed to have been able to see spirits from a young age. He was considered highly eccentric, according to the author. Whereas most mediums held séances in their own rooms, Edward claimed he had to "go where the spirits are," so he would either visit a client's home or sometimes public locations in order to "find" the spirit. His clients were often disappointed. Sometimes Edward never found their deceased loved one or couldn't communicate with them when he did. Nevertheless, he had enough successes to gather a devoted following who considered him the most genuine psychic of his day. He'd even solved a murder once by talking to a dead girl.

He died of consumption at age twenty-nine on November 21, 1898. There was a photograph of a young Edward looking very stiff and unsmiling.

Yes, he was Bowler Hat. And by God, he was so young and handsome in an ethereal way, probably thanks to his illness. How many ladies in Chicago had tucked away that page of newsprint and dreamed of the young psychic?

Was that why Edward was so rational in his afterlife? Why he could really see me? Did his gift—*our* gift—transcend even death? Once I passed over, would I be able to see the living clearly, the way Edward did?

I wasn't sure if I should feel grateful or horrified.

I GUESS I should tell you about the Accident. The one that scrambled my brain. It happened in March, a little over two years ago now. I'd only been out of college and working for Hora Systems for a couple of years when I met Shawn.

Shawn was my first real boyfriend, and he was the one who brought me out of my shell. I'd been pretty shy and tried to stay under the radar in high school, knowing I was gayer than a pink birthday cake. I was the only child of older parents, and we didn't do much together as a family, never went on trips and such. I came out in college and fooled around some, but I was still shy. Shawn was drop-dead gorgeous and a total live wire. We met when I went out for after-work drinks with some people at Hora Systems. Shawn was a good friend of a girl who worked with me. It was lust at first sight.

Shawn got me to get out and do things, physical things. He hung around with a group of guys, mostly straight, who played together on the weekends. Hang gliding, mountain climbing, windsurfing… nothing was too adventurous for Shawn. And he got me to try most of it. I fell in love with windsurfing. There's nothing like the freedom of zipping across the water on the Sound, controlling that board and sail with strength and, in my own mind at least, gracefulness.

I got tan. I got fitter than I'd ever been in my life. For the first time, I felt like an athlete, like someone who was cool. It was a heady feeling.

Shawn and I lasted a full year before he decided he was too young to be serious. He wanted to play the field. I was devastated, but that group of guys had become my social life, so I tried to act like I was cool with it.

A few weeks after the breakup, we all went windsurfing. I guess I was trying too hard to show off for Shawn, or maybe I was upset and my head wasn't in the game. It was a windy March day and Puget Sound was very choppy. It was cold and the water was freezing, but we were wearing wet suits.

I went out farther than I should have. The waves and wind jarred me this way and that, nearly yanking the sail out of my hands. I got a bit frightened. Before I could turn around, I caught the wake of a passing speedboat and lost hold of the sail and my balance. The front of the board went up, my feet slipped the straps, and I went down. The edge of the bow struck me hard on the head.

Fortunately, I didn't lose consciousness. I was able to drag myself up onto the board again. I remember lying there with bright red blood inching along the white deck as it rocked in the water. Another passing boat saw I was in trouble and helped me aboard and took me to shore.

It was weird having an ambulance pull up on the sand and load me in. Honestly, I only remember bits and pieces of it. I was seeing double when I bothered to open my eyes at all. It hurt so fucking bad. I got sick in the ambulance. And then I don't remember much else until I woke up a few days later in a hospital bed. And I could see the dead.

I HARDLY even noticed the trip home from the library. I was so consumed by questions, excitement, and a nausea-inducing mix of disappointment and hope.

Edward had been a medium. And not a fake one either. He'd been like me. He'd really seen the dead.

Seeing spirits from a young age. Going out to find them instead of pretending to "call" them during séance. Not always able to communicate with them.

That wasn't the way fake mediums operated, but it was in line with my own experiences. And the murdered girl... I could believe that. The dead aren't easy to communicate with, but they do tend to obsess on things they're upset about or things left unfinished. Murder would be one of those things. I'd never tried solving murders, never wanted anything to do with the ones who were gory or violent or weepy. But I thought it could be done.

So Edward had been like me. Was that why he was trying to communicate with me?

I grabbed some Thai to go from my favorite place on 15th and made it back to my apartment. I bolted the door and stood there, forehead on the wall. But the locks didn't give me the sense of safety they usually did.

I stuck the food in the fridge and grabbed a beer. I sat on the couch and picked up the remote, but I didn't turn the TV on. A moment later, I found myself crying.

I don't cry. I've been through a lot, and tears never solved a damn thing. And you become numb over the years, you know? But fuck it, Niagara Falls.

For the first time since the accident, I'd met someone who might have been able to understand, who might not think I was a total freak, someone to talk to about it. God, you have no idea how lonely it is not to have a *single person* to talk to about something so profound. Not to be able to say "hey, guess what I saw today" or "why do you think we hang out here after we die?" or "why does God allow this" or any of the other million questions and thoughts that go through my mind. People my age, living people, don't think about shit like that. And I don't blame them. If I could go through my day ignoring death, I would in a heartbeat. But I can't ignore it. I really wish I understood what it was about, what it was all for. Because, from where I'm standing? Our eventual fate is depressing as fuck.

I finally wiped my eyes and looked up, sick of myself. That's when I saw Edward. He was sitting in the chair. His hands were folded in his lap, his face was soft, and he looked at me with silent patience that went beyond mere understanding. It was pure observation, like he was my higher self watching my lower self lose it without judgment or any need to stop or sooth me.

Jesus, I was really getting poetic in my insanity.

I cleared my throat. "Hey."

He smiled.

"Had something in my eye." I laughed before I even got the words out. It was such a stupid excuse.

His smile grew bigger too.

"So, um, I looked you up. You were a medium when you were alive?"

He nodded slowly, his smile fading.

"And you were able to make a living at that?" I was genuinely curious.

He made a universal sign with his hand for so-so.

"Ah. It is pretty hard to get anything useful out of the dead. No offense."

He huffed, silently, but with clear irritation, as if to say, *Tell me about it.*

I sighed. "So... can I make it stop? Because I see them everywhere, and I hate it. It's turned me into a hermit. And... I'm tired of being afraid all the time."

He looked at me for a long moment, then gave a regretful shake of his head. *No. You can't stop it.*

Crap. I swallowed my disappointment. I hadn't really thought Edward could "fix" me, but still.

I had plenty more questions, of course. But how could he answer anything that required a more complicated response than "yes" or "no"?

"Have you... have you ever talked to a living person before? Before me?"

He nodded his head.

"Have you ever met anyone like you and me? Someone else who can see the dead?"

He tilted his head and considered me, his expression growing perplexed. After a moment, his face cleared, like he had figured something out. He smiled sadly, maybe even chuckled, even though I couldn't hear it. He nodded again, his dark eyes sparkling. He held up a single finger.

"One? You've met one other person who can see the dead?"

I wasn't sure if I'd guess right or not. He didn't answer. Instead, he got up and paced eagerly, paused to look at me expectantly, as if asking permission.

I shrugged. "You got an idea, go for it."

He walked over to my desk and looked at it. He seemed frustrated over what he saw or didn't see. He looked at me and mimed something with his hands, one hand posing above the flat of his other palm. *Writing.*

I sat up straighter. Oh, yeah. He'd managed to take over Jess's hand when he was writing on the card. That's how he'd left his name for me. Of course, Jess was dead. Would it work with me? I hesitated. Did I really want Edward taking over my body, or even just my hand? But it was a momentary thought. I trusted him and was eager to be able to learn more from him.

I got up, went to my desk, and took out a fresh notepad and pen. Edward nodded, his eyes glowing. I sat on the couch, pulled the coffee table closer, and opened the pad to a fresh page. I posed the tip of the pen over the blank page. Waited.

Nothing happened. I looked up at Edward. He stared at my hand, his face a mask of concentration, but I didn't feel any urge to write.

As I said, I watch a lot of horror movies, and I've read a lot on ghosts, most of which was crap. What we were attempting to do was called "automatic writing." That's when a ghost takes over as a psychic medium writes on paper. Apparently, we were doing it wrong. A memory tugged at the back of my mind. It was a scene from *The Changeling*. The woman medium had used automatic writing to communicate with the ghost. But she hadn't just sat there. She'd....

"Let's try this," I said. Blowing out a nervous breath, I felt the edge of the notepad with my free hand while my pen hand skimmed the pen over the page, back and forth. I closed my eyes and continued to move the pen slowly, relaxing my hand. When I felt I'd reached the end of a page, my free hand flipped the page over, and I began again at the top. I tried to let go of my muscles and my mind, just let it flow, not think.

I don't know how long this continued. I went through a lot of pages. Finally, I became aware that it wasn't working and it wasn't going to work. I stopped and opened my eyes slowly. The light in the room was bright and I felt dizzy. Wow, I'd really let go, hadn't I? I felt like I was coming out of a deep hypnosis session with Dr. Able.

Yes, they did that to me in the hospital too. No, it didn't help.

Edward was still sitting on the floor on the other side of the coffee table. He looked a little weak. He was more transparent than he'd been before, and his eyes were exhausted.

"Sorry," I said, disappointed. "I don't know what else we could try."

Edward looked surprised for a moment, then gestured at the notebook. I looked down. There on the page were heavily lined scribbles—and a word in Edward's shaky, old-fashioned handwriting. *HIM.*

I shivered as fear and amazement rippled down my spine. The notebook was almost at the end. I flipped pages back, scanning through all the scribbling for the message.

TRIST LASSITER. VOLUNTEER PARK. RESERVOIR. HELP HIM.

I looked up, astonished. But Edward was gone.

I HAVEN'T found a lot of joy in life since the accident. And it's not just the actual sight of the dead that's funky. It's what it means.

I read a book once called *Evolution of Evil* in which the author posits that all of the evils we endure are the result of evolution. Every time we adapted to survive, like learning how to stand on two legs to reach fruit in the trees, there's a price to be paid, like back pain. The biggest disservice evolution did for us, according to the author, was making our brains supersmart so we could outthink predators. That's all well and good, but as a result, our brains are sophisticated enough to understand the concept of death. Animals don't have to go around thinking "what a nice day, look at that green grass, and, oh yeah, someday soon I, and everyone I love will be a rotting carcass." Understanding we will die can cause psychosis and depression and generally stupid behavior.

Still, most people manage to *not* think about it, to stick their head in the sand. But it's hard to ignore the fact of death when you're standing next to a bug-eyed man with a rope around his neck. Know what I mean?

Also, it's not even just the constant reminder of death that's depressing. It's knowing what happens next that gets to me.

What is the point of it all? I ask myself. We live. We die. Then we wander around the planet Earth in our own little tormented world. What kind of a fucked-up system is that? Where are the Elysian Fields? The streets paved with gold? Hell, the twelve virgins? Or even a nice, restful oblivion. I'd take that in a pinch.

Seriously, it's horrible. Are we just energy waves after all, with no rhyme or reason to our existence, and once dead, do we just continue to echo around, obsessing on the shit that bothered us?

I wish I didn't worry about it, but I do. And that makes any chance of a relationship with a normal, healthy, twentysomething pretty remote. Even if it weren't for, you know, the agoraphobic thing.

That's me, Neil Gaven, a bundle of laughs.

4

TRIST LASSITER. Volunteer Park. Help him.

Great. I pondered the message, picking it apart like code I had to debug.

Edward wanted me to help someone named Trist Lassiter. Apparently Trist was to be found in the park near the reservoir.

How did Edward know about Trist? And who was this Trist guy anyway? Was Trist someone Edward talked to? Could Trist be the one person like me? Is that why Edward was trying to get me to help him? And what sort of help did Trist need? A Band-Aid? Stock market advice?

Could Trist be like me? It stood to reason that someone else out there could see what I saw. Concussion McSchmussion—if my brain could do it, it had to be a thing other brains could do. How amazing would it be to know someone like that? To no longer be alone? To have someone living to talk to about it?

But I was getting ahead of myself. I didn't know jack about this Trist person.

Sure, I could just stroll down to the park and check it out. It was only three blocks from where I lived. But it was *the park.*

I used to love Volunteer Park, but that was BC. It has huge trees, a lot of wide-open green lawns, a dahlia garden, a little outdoor stage, a view of downtown, a stone donut, and, yes, a reservoir. The Asian art museum is there too. I still ride by the place when I have to take the bus.

But driving past it on the street and walking into the heart of it are two different matters.

During the day, Volunteer Park is a safe place for families and kids. But after dark, it's… not. Being the biggest park on gay Capitol Hill, it's a hot hook-up spot, and sometimes by people who are a little scary. Then there are the drugs—doing them, selling them. And there had been quite a few murders in Volunteer Park over the years.

As for me, I saw the dead at all hours of the day the few times I dared venture inside. I guess ghosts prefer a nice green environment just like we do. There are dead murderers, dead victims, dead druggies, the old dead, and the very young in the park. Three ghost children hang around near the kiddie pool. Scary little fuckers, like *Ringu* scary. I stay far away from Volunteer Park.

And Edward was telling me to go into it. The reservoir was in the middle of a lot of green.

Of course, I didn't have to. I was under no obligation to follow Edward's orders. For all I knew, Edward was mixed up and there wasn't even a Trist there. Or maybe Trist was a dead guy. Or maybe he didn't want any help.

Or maybe he was young and lonely and scared and didn't know why he saw dead people.

Help him.

Damn it.

5

I RODE my bike. I pedaled around the outside of Volunteer Park and approached it from the far side, the side closest to the reservoir. That side was also farthest from the kiddie pool and the three demon spawn, which was a good thing. I was still nervous and dreading every second of this little Edward-inspired adventure.

I locked my bike at a rack, pulled down my hat, stuffed my hands in my pockets, and walked slowly into the park. The reservoir was straight ahead. I could already make out the chain-link fence that surrounded the concrete basin. This side of the reservoir wasn't far from the street and had good visibility. But the reservoir was a large structure, and the far side—back and beyond—was sketchy. That side was hidden from view by the concrete wall of the reservoir, trees, and scrub. If there was something vile and secret going on in Volunteer Park, that's where you'd find it.

Unfortunately, I didn't see anyone who might be Trist on the nice side of the reservoir. Of course, it wouldn't be that easy. But as I walked around the outside of it, I realized I didn't see any dead either. None. That was strange. In fact, the park was abnormally quiet, even for a Tuesday morning at 9:00 a.m. There was a woman jogging with a baby stroller and several other living people, but they appeared to be just passing through the park and gave the reservoir a wide berth.

The farther I walked around the reservoir, toward the trees, the more the hair on my arms stood up, and the hair on my scalp too. So even though I didn't see any dead, I knew they were there. And I was getting closer to them.

I told myself I would only go far enough to get a glimpse of what was going on. I could always turn and run. But despite those mental words of reassurance, I felt compelled to move forward, as if I was being pulled on a string. I was still a hundred yards away when I felt the first wave of nausea. I paused and took a breath. A few steps later, I broke out in a sweat, but the itchy sense of urgency pushed me on. Then I saw them.

Through the trees, I saw a group of dead people. There had to be twenty of them. Some of them were milling around rather aimlessly, but most of them were bent over something on the ground.

Shit. *Shit.* I could guess what that something was.

I broke into a run. I should have been afraid of them. Ordinarily I would have been. But in that second, all I felt was rage. *Those fucking bastards.*

I ran as fast as I could and plowed into them with an angry scream. "Get the fuck off! Get off!" They were solid when I hit them, but they gave away in an instant, unlike living flesh. Nausea and chills swept over me hard as I ended up in the middle of the pile. I swung my arms in all directions, pushing at old cloth and misleadingly solid torsos. "Go away! Get out of here, you fucking corpses. Leave!"

I don't know what all I screamed, but adrenaline carried me through the nausea and what should have been fear. And the ghosts, startled and angry at first, were suddenly gone. They evaporated as if they'd never been. I looked around, ready to fight the bastards, but I couldn't see a single one.

Except Edward. He stood a few feet away, watching me. Edward gave me a look I could only interpret as relief and approval, and then he vanished too.

That left me with the huddled figure on the ground. He had on a grungy hoodie and jeans and tennis shoes, and he was curled into a fetal position.

"Trist?" I plopped to my knees on the ground beside him. "Hey, can you hear me?"

I couldn't see his face because his hood was up. *A red hoodie.* His body looked tall and thin lying on the ground. He was definitely not a child. I suddenly was certain who it was. I tugged his shoulder gently to roll him onto his back so I could see his face.

His eyes were shut and his skin was so pale it was almost blue-white. But I still recognized him. He was the guy I'd dubbed Red Riding Hood, the cute, serious blond grunger I used to see when I rode my bike to work.

"Trist?" I said again, louder. I forced one hand under the hoodie so I could feel his neck. God, he was so cold. "Can you hear me? I'm going to call an ambulance."

He opened up his eyes and looked at me. His eyes were blue and struck me as being super clear. Amazing, really. Dusky red-blond lashes surrounded them. "You're real," he said. His voice was soft and weak, despite the alertness in his eyes.

I felt a hysterical giggle in my throat. I swallowed it. "Sure am. I'm Neil. Edward sent me to help you."

"Neil." He smiled. "Yeah, Edward told me about you."

He did? Christ, this was weird. "You need an ambulance, Trist. Okay?"

"No!" He moved then, struggling to sit up. I helped him to sit. He clutched my wrist, his expression desperate. "Don't want to go to the hospital. Please don't call. I'll run if you do."

I didn't think he could run far, but that wasn't the point. "But you're hurt. You need help. Fluids, probably. Meds. They were attacking you!"

"No." He looked as young as he had when I'd noticed him a few years ago, probably twenty at most. His face was round and sweet somehow, even though he had a jaded air. "No hospital. I'll be okay if I can just get away from the park for a little while. Please."

I couldn't blame him for wanting to avoid the hospital. Hospitals were filled with the dead. And after what he'd just experienced, he honestly needed to be as far away from them as possible. But there was something I needed to confirm first.

"Trist—*is* it Trist?"

He nodded.

"Um… did you see the people that were attacking you? What I mean is…." I took a shaky breath. In for a penny…. "Do you see dead people?"

He looked surprised. "Yeah. Don't you?"

I laughed. Like, bust-a-gut laughing. Which was pretty rude after what Trist had just been through, but I found it hysterical. *Don't you?* Like it was a perfectly normal thing.

Trist looked confused but slightly amused by my ludicrous outburst. He collapsed back to the ground, though, as if he wasn't strong enough to keep sitting up. And that reminded me that I needed to stop chortling like a hyena and help him.

"Let's get you out of here." I put my hands under his shoulders and helped him to sit up, and then get to his feet. He was heavy, as if he had hardly any strength to move on his own.

"I'm sorry," he said.

"It's okay. If I'd been through what you'd been through, I'd be weak too." I wasn't sure what the dead people had been doing to Trist, but I knew it wasn't good. Draining life force? Eating energy? Do they do that? I'd never let one touch me long enough for me to find out.

I helped him walk, with one arm around his waist and his arm over my shoulder. I held that hand so I could keep it in place. God, it was like ice.

"Where are we going?" Trist asked as I walked him back toward my bike.

"My apartment," I answered. "But I need you to help me get you there."

I worried that it wasn't a good idea. Trist, my Red Riding Hood, was sick and filthy, and I didn't even know him. My apartment was my sanctuary. But despite that, I had no doubt in my heart. Trist needed someone to help him, and I was going to do it, no matter the risk. I'd finally found someone else like me, and I was going to hang on for all I was worth.

"Thank you," Trist said with shaky relief. "Edward said you were good. I recognize you, you know. You're, um, Bike Guy."

"Bike Guy?" I smiled. We were out of the trees now and moving haltingly toward the place where I'd parked said bike. I wished it were closer. Trist was leaning most of his weight on me, his legs moving haltingly, as if they resented it.

"You used to ride by on your way to work in the mornings."

"I remember. I noticed you too."

"I thought you were cute," Trist admitted with a self-deprecating laugh.

Oh Lord. A thrill went through me. I already knew Trist was going to be important in my life because of the gift we shared. But the possibilities just moved ahead a few dozen notches. *Get him home. Get him safe.*

I'd have to think about the fact that our attraction was mutual later.

THE TRIP back to my place was awkward. Since I had my bike, and Trist was so weak, the only possibility was to put him on the bike and steer it while I walked beside him, like a father teaching a child how to ride. It was difficult, but we made progress block by block. Fortunately, we didn't run into any dead people, and we finally made it home.

I helped Trist off the bike and into my apartment. I was worried that he needed more medical help than I could give him, but I plowed ahead. At least I could get him safe inside and lying down so I could assess his condition.

Trist's head was hanging low by the time I got him inside, his body draped heavily over my shoulder. But he managed to look around with wonder when we got into my place.

"Oh my God! There's no one here! Do you have wards or something?"

Strangely enough, I knew exactly what he meant. It made me smile like a loon.

I propped Trist against the closed door and started to unzip his hoodie. Because, yeah, it was *rank.* I could see the dirt crusted on it, and for once I was grateful my sense of smell wasn't all that great since the accident. "I don't have any wards. There just aren't any dead here, and they don't follow me home as long as I pretend I can't see them."

He went still, his hands coming over mine to stop them and his face displaying a weird stunned amazement. We stared at each other for a moment, and then his face crumpled and he blinked as if he might cry.

I figured the shock was wearing off and it was finally sinking in that he was safe and with someone who understood. My heart melted right then, and who knew a melting heart hurt like a son of a bitch? My throat went all hot and tight. "Yeah. I see them too."

"I haven't… it's been… I never…."

"I know."

I wouldn't have imagined there was someone who had it worse off than me, but poor Trist! He saw what I saw, but it looked like he was homeless. He had no way to get away from them. If that resulted in getting gang-attacked like I witnessed today, how could he bear it?

I wanted to hug him, but I figured he might not want quite that much of an acknowledgment of his emotion, so I rubbed his shoulder instead. He swayed on his feet and closed his eyes. He seriously needed a shower, but he looked so exhausted. I decided it could wait.

"Listen, Trist, I'll let you sleep, but you should eat and drink a little something first. All right? I'm still worried I should call an ambulance. I don't want you getting any sicker on me." *Or dying*, I thought.

"No ambulance," he said again sternly.

I helped him to the bedroom and got him out of his hoodie, shoes, and jeans, leaving him in a T-shirt and horridly dirty white briefs. God, I was going to have to fumigate my bed, maybe the entire apartment, but c'est la vie. I helped him get under the covers.

"I'll be right back with some juice."

I went into the kitchen to hastily pour a large glass of orange juice and make him a peanut butter sandwich. I slathered butter and jam on the bread too, for the calories—he was terribly thin—and carried them back into the bedroom. I expected him to be asleep, but he wasn't. He was on his back looking around the room, his eyes bloodshot but still that startlingly lucid blue, like they were in 3D in a 2D world.

"This is a nice place," he said, like he felt unsure of his welcome. "I'll get your bed dirty."

"Don't worry about it. Can you get this down?" I handed him the orange juice. He paused for a moment, glass in his hand, as if assessing how he felt. I wondered if he'd felt the same nausea I felt in that park when those ghosts were attacking him. Mine was gone now.

Seeming to decide he felt well enough, he sipped the juice and put it on the bedside table. I handed him the sandwich. He looked it over, both sides, as if he'd never seen a sandwich before, then ate it quickly. "Thanks," he said when he was done.

"Okay. I'll be right here. And I'm going to check on you a lot. Make sure you're not getting worse. If you do, I'll have to call the ambulance."

But maybe he'd figured out by now that I wasn't really going to. He sank back into the bed and looked up at me. With his hoodie off, I could see his hair was a dirty blond, long, and in serious need of a wash. His face was round in shape, pretty, and he had naturally flared nostrils that I thought were super hot. They gave him a bad boy look. Even sick and covered in grime, he made my chest hurt. I could hardly believe he was my Red Riding Hood, and that he saw the dead too. What if we'd made friends earlier? What if I'd stopped one day a few years ago and just chatted with the guy? He could have helped me a lot that first year. We could have helped each other.

Thank God for Edward. Trist and I could have existed in the same neighborhood for years and never met.

"You don't mind? My staying here?" he asked me, hopeful, like he couldn't believe it.

"Of course not. I want you to stay. You're safe here. And if anyone comes, I'll handle it. Okay?"

He just stared at me. And yawned. "The attack you saw…. Normally I can avoid them, but not when I get too down. I think negativity upsets them."

I swallowed hard. "I get it. But you won't ever need to get that down again. Right?"

He smiled, and it was so bright and unexpected, it was like waking up from a nightmare. "Going to sleep now."

"Okay."

He closed his eyes.

I had a ridiculous urge to kiss his forehead or something. Idiot. Instead, I left him to sleep.

TRIST SLEPT and slept and slept. And then he slept some more. I checked on him often, to make sure he wasn't getting worse. But he seemed to be okay. He still felt a little cold to me, but I tucked the covers up high around his neck, added another blanket, and his color got rosier in the warmth of the bed. His skin felt soft under my palm, not too dry or sweaty. So I let him sleep.

I tried to get some work done on the Gravalu code and failed miserably. I couldn't stop thinking about how Trist had been so surprised about my apartment.

There's no one here!

How long had the dead been tormenting Trist like that? What if they followed him here? I didn't want to be forced to move because my place got infested.

Don't be stupid. Trist sees the dead; he's not a fucking psychic magnet. If you spent all your time on the streets or in a homeless shelter, you'd think they were everywhere too. Maybe he's never had the luxury of a private place like this.

It was true. I'd had this same basement apartment since I graduated from college, well before the accident. I was just lucky the house didn't have any ghosts in it. How awful to never be able to get away from them. The thought make me sick.

But anyway, it would take a hell of a lot for me to want Trist to leave. Even though I'd only spent a few minutes with him, there was something there. I liked him even way back, when I just saw him at the park. He was attractive, of course, but it was more than that. We had a connection. He seemed vulnerable and honest and tough, but the kind of toughness that was a scab over a wound, not cruelty. And he had the most amazing eyes I'd ever seen, almost magical or something.

And he thought I was cute too. There was that, my dick reminded me. *Stop. Give the poor guy a break.*

I WAS asleep when rustling noises woke me up. My first thought was that I had a mouse in the kitchen. Then I heard the fridge door and remembered. *Trist.*

I got up from my makeshift bed on the couch and pulled on my jeans as fast as I could, hopping on one leg.

The kitchen was dark except for the light from the open fridge. Trist looked up at me, guilty. "Sorry. I didn't mean to wake you up."

"What time is it?"

"A little after six a.m. I wasn't going to steal anything. I was just curious." He was wary, like I might be pissed off.

"Dude. You're welcome to any food I have. Are you hungry?"

"I wouldn't mind having something." He bit his lips as if embarrassed.

"That's good, right? You must be feeling better. Are you? Feeling better?" God, I wasn't awake enough for this shit.

But my stumbling made him smile. "I feel *tons* better. I can't remember the last time I was able to just rest like that. I owe you. Also, I used some toothpaste you had in the bathroom and a washcloth. Hope that's okay."

His face and hands did look cleaner, now that he mentioned it. "Of course! Help yourself to a shower too." I looked at the clock on the microwave: 6:15. "Jesus, you slept for fifteen hours."

"Sorry—I didn't mean to take your bed all night and make you sleep on the couch."

"No, it's cool. I'm just glad you're better." That reminded me of the way I'd found him, with all those dead people hanging over him. A thrill of fear had me walking to the wall and flipping on the light. In the 100-watt glare, the kitchen was comforting in its ordinariness. I tried to look cheerful. "I don't have any eggs or bacon, but I have cereal. And I can make some coffee."

"That would be amazing. Thank you," Trist said with the resignation of the endlessly indebted. I didn't want him to feel that way, not with me. But it would take time to work on that.

WE ATE cereal, and Trist was on his second cup of coffee before I finished my first. As soon as he finished getting every drop of milk from his bowl, he took it into the kitchen and rinsed it. He came back ready to talk.

"So how did you find me?" he asked, folding his legs to sit on the couch.

"Edward. He told me where you were. You mentioned him too. Do you know who I mean?"

Trist nodded. "Yes." He bit his lips—they were naturally quite dark pink. He seemed hyper now that he wasn't exhausted. Or maybe he was just excited to be here, the way I felt right now. I had a million questions and only one ordinary drip of space/time in which to express them.

"What does Edward look like to you?" I asked.

"Um, tall. Dark hair. Handsome. Maybe late twenties? Brown suit with one of those old-fashioned high white collars." Trist's clear blue eyes suddenly narrowed doubtfully. "Is that who you mean?"

"Yup." I felt a grin split my face. "That's him exactly. I can't believe you see him too."

Trist's face grew serious. He studied me as if he felt sorry for me, which was amazing considering what he'd been through. "How long has it been, Neil? How long have you been able to see the dead?"

I took a calming breath. Even with Trist, it was hard to talk about it. "You remember when I used to ride past the park on my way to work? That was a little over two years. I stopped biking to work because I had a windsurfing accident and hit my head. I had a serious concussion. When I woke up, I could see the dead. What about you? Have you always seen them?"

One corner of Trist's lips quirked up wryly. "I think I've been half dead my whole life. But no, not the way you mean. That happened about a year ago."

"What do you mean, you've been half dead?"

Trist shrugged. "Just… on the fringes, you might say. My mom was a single mother, and she died of breast cancer when I was thirteen. The state sent me to a foster home, but I hated it. The guy was a perv, so I ran away. I've been on my own ever since."

"That's awful."

He shrugged. "I've had jobs before, worked at restaurants and stuff, even rented a room for a while. But rent's expensive and jobs don't always stick. The park isn't that bad."

I managed not to argue with him. Sure, the park was pretty enough in the daytime, if you didn't see the dead. But even then, it wasn't a place I'd want to live. "What happened a year ago?"

Trist pressed his lips together and stared off toward the window, like he didn't want to look me in the eye when he said it. "I got beat up by a couple of guys. They hit me in the head with a big wrench. It was a really cold night. They left me for dead in the park, not far from where you found me."

"Oh, Trist."

I had about a million more questions. Had Trist had a concussion too, from being hit in the head? Did he start seeing dead people right away? Had *his* doctors ever heard of anyone else like us? Had he even had doctors?

But at that moment, when I could so easily picture Trist attacked and bleeding, nothing seemed more important than comforting him. I scooted toward him and, when he didn't seem alarmed or move away, pulled him into a careful hug.

I didn't want to make him feel trapped, or like I was coming on to him. He didn't know me at all. But instead of being wary of my touch, he turned in to my hug and put his arms around my back. He was a little taller than me, but he managed to put his forehead on my shoulder.

"Why did you come to find me?" His voiced was muffled against my shirt.

"Edward said you needed help."

"Yeah, but why did you care? You don't even know me."

"I…." God, how could I put it into words? "I liked you even before, Trist. When I used to ride by the park. But now that I know that you…. These past few years have been hard. They've sucked ass, if you want to know the truth. I've been so alone with this. And I think you've been alone too, and…. Maybe we can help each other."

Trist brought his hands up to clutch at my T-shirt. I'd changed into a plain white one last night to sleep on the couch, but his hands grabbed it like it was a saint's robe. "Do you mean that? Because… I'd really like that." His voice was wobbly.

"I do mean it, Trist. God, I've been living shut up in here like a hermit. I've been so afraid."

Trist give a tragic little laugh into my shirt. "This is the first time I haven't been scared shitless in so long. You have no idea."

I hugged him even tighter. Despite the fact that we hardly knew each other, I felt close to him, like I'd known him forever. We were two children holding hands, facing a monster together.

Then Trist brought his head up and kissed me.

It was needy and desperate, and I was so surprised I didn't know how to react. He pulled me in tighter with those fists in my T-shirt and opened his mouth against my unresponsive one, sucking at my bottom lip when I didn't open to let him in.

I pulled back hard. Though he had his fists in my shirt, he was still weak, and I broke away easily but more harshly than I meant to.

The vulnerability on his face closed like the eye of a camera clicking shut. He turned to the side so I could only see his profile and gripped his knees with both hands. "Sorry. Sorry."

"Trist, it's okay."

"I fucked up. I don't even know if you're—forget it, please? Or I can leave if you want me to."

I don't know why I'd pulled away from him, except that it had been unexpected and I wanted him, *him*, not just sex. It felt like I'd be taking advantage. He was young, yes, but not that young. He was, however, vulnerable, and he was one good sleep away from being badly hurt.

"Listen," I said as calmly as I could. "I am gay, and I do like you. A lot. You just surprised me. And this isn't about a quick hookup for me, okay? I want to… be your friend at the very least. Like I said before. I think we can help each other. So maybe we can take it slow?"

He shot me a wary look and gave a bitter laugh. "Sure. I get it." He looked down at his bare feet on the floor, twisting them this way and that. They were covered in dirt streaks. "Fuck. I'm filthy. Yeah. Real attractive." And then he gave a big yawn, looking suddenly exhausted again.

Right. That was enough of that.

I slapped my hands on my thighs and stood. "How about a shower, then?" I asked cheerfully. "You can take one while I'm making up the bed. And then I think after that, another nap wouldn't hurt."

Trist perked up like a kid spotting Santa Claus. "Seriously? I'd kill for one, if you're offering."

I loved seeing that light in his eyes. "Right this way."

I showed Trist the shower, shampoo, and spare toothbrush, nabbed a fresh towel from the closet, then left him to it and went to check the bedroom.

His hoodie, shoes, and socks were on the floor. They needed to be burned, honestly. In a hazardous waste facility. But I didn't want to piss him off, so I shoved them in the closet where I had a compact washer and drier. I'd deal with them later.

I stripped the bed and remade it with fresh sheets. I brought a glass of water and a bottle of aspirin in and put them on the bedside table. Then I stood there listening to the water run in the bathroom and considered what to do next. I was tired too. I'd only gotten a few hours of sleep. Should I leave Trist alone and go back to get a few more hours on the couch?

I didn't want to. It was like I was eight years old and my favorite uncle had come to visit. I couldn't force myself to let him be. I hadn't been very successful at it last night, checking on him constantly. Now that I knew him a little better, it would be worse.

I wanted to sleep in my own bed, with Trist.

But Trist had already kissed me, insulted when I pulled away. If we shared a bed, sex was liable to come up. Literally.

I knew in my bones what the answer was. I wasn't going to initiate it, but if Trist asked me for sex again, I wouldn't push him away. I meant everything I'd said on the couch, about wanting something more from him than a quick hookup. But I wasn't going to force us into unwanted abstinence on principle. Maybe sex was the way Trist knew how to communicate. Or maybe he needed touch, needed the closeness of it. God knows I craved it myself. I wasn't going to deny him or me. But I wouldn't let him bolt afterward either. I wanted Trist in my life for some time to come.

I contemplated the irony that the guy I'd fantasized about several years ago turned out to be Edward's Trist. *My* Trist. And he turned out to have the same weird gift I did. What were the odds of that? Dr. Able had never heard of another patient like me. What did it mean?

I knew what it felt like: fate. The sort of interesting story you tell your grandchildren.

Dear God, don't let me be hallucinating Trist too.

But Trist came out of the shower, clean and wet, his long dark blond hair sending trickles of water down his back. He had a towel around his waist and another in his hands, and he shivered in the cool air of the apartment. I couldn't help but stare at his bare chest. His skin was pale, and he was so thin, his collarbones and ribs stood out. Worse, he had dark bruises on both sides of his body, like someone had kicked him in the ribs. The bruises looked fresh. Had the dead people who'd attacked him done that damage? Or had he been beaten up recently by living punks? How many times had that happened to Trist?

He held the spare towel in front of his chest, self-conscious. I silently cursed myself for my staring and forced a smile, no matter that the abuse to his body made me sick. Far from putting me off him, though, it made me want to hold him and make it better and protect him so it never happened again.

"The bed's all freshly made. I thought I might grab a quick shower too."

"You didn't have to change the sheets. I'm sorry I got them dirty before."

"Trist, you were barely conscious when we got here. It's no problem."

He seemed to accept this, his brow clearing. He looked at the turned-down bed with longing. "I can't remember the last time I've been clean and slept on clean sheets too." He shivered again and hugged himself.

Damn it, where was my head?

"Let me get you something clean to put on." I opened up the bottom drawer of my dresser where I kept sweats and older T-shirts. The apartment was a bit on the cool side, being in the basement. I preferred to layer rather than turn the heat up too high. But Trist was so thin and he was recovering from trauma. I pulled out a comfortable gray sweatshirt and pants, some clean underwear, and thick socks. I grabbed a clean T-shirt and boxers for me too. "Here you go." I put his items on the bed.

"Thank you." Trist picked up the sweatshirt and held it against his chest as if he wanted to wait 'til I left to put it on. He seemed shy now, or maybe just overwhelmed.

"Do you… do you mind if, after my shower, I sleep in here too? The couch isn't great."

Trist looked surprised. "Oh. Sure. I can take the couch."

"No, I mean, we can both share the bed. If you don't mind. It's a queen, so we don't have to get too cozy if you don't want to."

Trist blinked in surprise. "Okay."

Before I could say or do anything else to botch it, and to give the poor guy the privacy to dress, I left the bedroom, shutting the door behind me. I turned up the thermostat near the front door and headed for the bathroom. I washed quickly, brushed my teeth, and contemplated whether or not to shave, standing at the sink and running fingers over my jaw.

The bathroom mirror was cloudy from Trist's hot shower and mine, so I couldn't see the stubble I was feeling. That was fine with me. I didn't much care for looking in the mirror these days. It's not that I have scars from the accident. There is a scar and a permanent hard lump on my noggin, but they're hidden under shaggy brown hair. It's just… looking myself in the eyes, facing what I've become, what I've lost… it isn't pleasant. I avoid it.

I decided not to shave. My stubble wasn't that bad yet. But I put on some deodorant and lotion. In case. I already had a semi at the mere prospect that sex might be happening in the near future. And if I let my mind linger on the image of Trist—sitting on my couch, standing in the kitchen, in nothing but a towel, all vulnerable and self-conscious—it threatened to become a full-blown erection.

This is about Trist, not you. Figure out what he needs.

When I finished and slipped into the bedroom, Trist was in bed but not asleep. The sweatpants and socks were folded neatly on the floor by the bed, but he had the sweatshirt on and, I couldn't help but ponder, probably the underwear too.

I went to the far side of the bed and paused to look at him. "Sure you don't mind?"

His Adam's apple bobbed as he swallowed. "I'd feel a lot better if you were here, Neil. I'd sleep better and all." He raised a hand to his mouth and bit at a thumbnail as if he was nervous.

So I climbed into bed. He turned on his side to face me, and I lay on my side, facing him. We looked at each other. Now that I was in bed with him, sleep felt as far away as it ever had. He didn't look particularly tired anymore either.

"We need some real food," I said. "How about we sleep for an hour or two, then I can get Thai delivered. Do you like Thai? There's also pizza."

"I love Thai," he said, giving me a smile. It faded quickly. "I don't know how I can pay you back for all this."

I grunted in frustration. "You pay me back just by being here. I told you, Trist. I haven't been able to have friends since my accident. No one would understand. But you do."

He studied my face as if judging my sincerity. He shifted his hand forward to touch me, but then stopped as if remembering how I'd reacted last time. His hand ended up stranded between us, lying curled on the sheet.

I looked at it, then covered it with my own. "You're still cold." I said, rubbing his hand. "Didn't the hot water warm you up?"

"It did, but I got cold when I got out."

Those crystal blue eyes of his looked at my lips and then my eyes. He bit his own lips as if he was holding back. Tension spooled between us like a tiny storm, complete with little jolts of lightning. His hand unfolded and he interlaced his fingers with mine, but he made no move to come closer. His eyes said he wanted to, though.

It was my move. I was the one who stopped last time.

"Would you like me to hold you and warm you up?" I offered. No, it wasn't the most sophisticated line, but it had the advantage of being a very practical offer. That's my programmer's brain.

He didn't answer, just scooted his body toward me until we were almost touching. I put my arms around him and pulled him in the rest of the way. I rubbed my hands on his back over the sweatshirt to warm him up. Our hips weren't flush, but he must have ditched the underwear after all because I felt his hard tip graze my stomach. *Shit.* The feel of him made me spontaneously combust. Lust made me feel hot from head to toe, and I went rock hard.

"I don't want to screw this up," Trist whispered in a conflicted voice.

"Don't worry. I think we both want this too much for that to happen," I reassured him. Then I kissed him.

I craved being close to him. That was the bottom line. And I sensed that he needed it as much as I did. Human connection. Touch. I hadn't so much as jerked off since that encounter with Jess at the club. I got sick even thinking about it. But my need for Trist overwhelmed that memory, thank God.

He kissed me back like he was sucking oxygen, forcing one arm under me so he could wrap both arms around my neck. He pressed fully against me and, yeah, he was naked except for that sweatshirt. One of my hands found his ass, which was small but nicely rounded, his bare skin cool to the touch. I suddenly remembered the way his body had looked in the light.

I pulled away from the kiss. "Are you okay to do this? I saw those bruises. You were really hurt."

"I can't feel any of that right now. Please don't stop." He sounded 100 percent certain.

"Okay, but let me know if anything hurts you. Promise?"

"Promise," he muttered, before taking my mouth again.

Amazingly, I still had a few brain cells I could dedicate to the question of how best to do what we both wanted without hurting him further. I figured lying on his side had to be painful, even if he was currently high on endorphins, so I pushed him gently onto his back. He'd slept on his back all night, so it had to be the best position for him.

I relinquished his mouth with regret and kissed my way down his neck and onto his pale chest. His nipples were peaked with eagerness—or at least I like to flatter myself that it wasn't because he was still cold. I sucked and licked them gently, getting his hips arching into the air to find contact. He was silent, though, probably a lesson hard-learned from having no privacy.

Ignoring that seeking part of him for now, I moved a bit lower and kissed the bruises on his ribs, pushing the covers down as I went. As I gently brushed my lips over those large, purplish marks, my heart grew heavy. I rested my forehead lightly on his stomach. "You should never have been hurt like this. No one deserves to be beaten."

If only I'd talked to him sooner; back then I was still capable of a full life and he was not yet so brutalized, before we'd both entered this nightmare.

"I don't want to think about that now," Trist said fiercely. "Please don't stop."

Of course he didn't want to think about it. Way to kill a mood. To make it up to him, I went to the primary target, nuzzling and licking the slightly loose skin on his shaft. He'd softened a bit, but with just a little attention from my mouth, he was stiff and plump under my tongue.

"Yeah," Trist said in a breathy voice when I gently sucked on the head. "God, yeah. Turn around, Neil. I want you too."

I hesitated. Part of me wanted to give this to him without reciprocation. But, honestly, what he was suggesting was one of my favorite positions. I found it incredibly sexy to have a cock in my mouth while I was getting a blow job. It was the best twofer on Earth. I pushed the covers all the way down and swung my body up and over him so I was above him on all fours, my junk rather ingloriously in his face. He didn't seem to mind. Immediately, both of his hands were on me. He tugged at my cock with one hand while he sucked at my balls.

I groaned and faltered in my own ministrations, pulling off and mouthing in an uncoordinated fashion along his length until my body adjusted enough to the sensation that I could function again. I did my best to give Trist the blowjob of his life, but I probably wasn't going to win any awards, not when he took me fully in his mouth and encouraged me to pump by putting his hands on my hips. He drove me insane, sucking and using his tongue around my stuttering thrusts. It felt amazing. I was so sensitive—my libido had returned with a banners waving.

I didn't last long. I came first, but he wasn't far behind. His semen was thick and bitter, probably from dehydration. I made a mental note to get him to drink more before collapsing in a puddle at his side. That's me, romantic fool.

Trist curled into me like a bug in a leaf. "I know I shouldn't say this, but I'm going to anyway. I want to stay with you, Neil. Please don't leave me."

"I won't leave you, ever," I said, absolutely meaning it.

And then, in true postorgasm fashion, we both slept.

6

IT CAN be awkward the next day when two people who hardly know each other make extravagant promises like that. And it was awkward at first. But Trist stayed.

Two weeks went by. I never thought I'd say this after the accident, but they were the best two weeks of my life.

I'd never felt as close to anyone, not even Shawn. With Shawn, there was always a distance he put between us, like he was with me, but he always had one foot out the door. We'd connect for sex or a few good hours together, but then he'd disconnect, pull away.

It wasn't like that with Trist. I worked on the Gravalu code while he cleaned around the apartment, read from my shelf of fantasy novels, or watched TV. He touched me frequently, passing by to give me a hug around the shoulders or kiss my cheek. And if he was on the couch, I'd take my laptop over there so I could sit with the sides of our bodies close together while I worked, or one of us would end up with his feet in the other one's lap.

We went out too. It wasn't bad going out, not with Trist along. We started walking down 15th to grab lunch most days. The dead felt less threatening at high noon. And when we did see them, we'd compare notes, even make fun of them sometimes.

"Half head ahead," Trist said one day, as a dead man with half his head missing crossed the street in front of us.

"He's got really good left leg control for a guy with no right brain," I pointed out appreciatively. "Ten o'clock, woman with a fox corpse around her neck," I said a few minutes later.

Trist made claws with his hands and pulled his lips back to show his teeth. "I'll guard these fake pearls, with my life! Oh. Nevermind."

"Dork," I laughed.

"Bitch." He said it so fondly.

Yeah, it was morbid. But after two years of terror running my life, it was a miracle to be able to laugh about it. Hell, it was a miracle to have Trist to talk to, to be able to say, "Hey, I see that, do you see that?" And Trist always did.

The value of that cannot be understated. I guess, despite my telling Dr. Able to piss off, there was some part of me that feared I was really mad, that the damage to my brain had left me a little cuckoo for Cocoa Puffs. Most of the terror of seeing the dead is *seeing the dead*. But part of it, a bigger part than I'd realized, was the fear that they were something I'd cooked up from my own sick brain, that they weren't there at all. So it was huge to have Trist confirm I wasn't crazy.

If I wasn't crazy, then the dead were just something external that we dealt with, you know? Like a garbage strike or Republicans in the White House. Rather than a sickness inside me.

We held hands on those walks. Capitol Hill was Seattle's gay neighborhood, so no one cared and it felt great, like we were in this together, Trist and I, and no one could hurt us. I taught Trist how, if you pretended you didn't see the dead, they ignored you. And he taught me that not all of them were irrational and stuck in a time warp.

There was a dead guy we sometimes saw near the shops on 15th, panhandling. Why he would panhandle when the living couldn't see him, I didn't know. Old habits die hard, I guess. Trist called him Goober, and his face was gray, probably from a heart attack. But he saw Trist and called him by name and spoke out loud to Trist like an ordinary person. Trist looked around, as if to make sure no one was watching, then introduced me. Goober appeared to have no interest in following or haunting us.

Maybe Goober had known Trist before he died, and that's why he remembered his name, but that doesn't explain why, after he'd met me, he knew my name too. It bugged me.

"How come Goober is like that?" I asked Trist one night when we were sitting on the couch. I rubbed his bare feet, which were in my lap. He still tended to be cold, even though I was doing my best to put weight on him. "Most of the dead I've seen, they're lost in their own world. If they see you at all, they think you're someone else, someone they knew. But not Goober."

I was thinking of Jess. Though Jess hadn't actually known who I was—he called me "Tony," after all—he had been rational when I talked to him, spoke back to me, responded to my questions. That's why I hadn't even realized he was dead until... yeah.

Trist sighed. He was lying back on the couch in my gray sweatshirt—he loved that thing. He looked up at the ceiling and wiggled his toes in my hands. "I think it has to do with whether or not they've accepted that they're dead. Like, people have a tendency to stick around, especially if their death was sudden. I think it takes a while to get over the shock of it. They just keep going, you know? They obsess on whatever it is that's on their minds. They eat, change, walk in the park, ride the bus. It's almost like they're dreaming. I guess maybe that's how your subconscious, or whatever, works things out. You know? Like, supposedly when we dream, our brain is trying to work out problems we have during the day. So maybe the dead are in a kind of dream, trying to work out the problem of, well, being dead."

Trist might not have a college degree, but he wasn't stupid. He'd spent a lot of time in the Capitol Hill library because it was free and a safe place to hang out. He loved to read. He did a lot of it at my place.

"And someone like Goober, he's dead but not dreaming anymore?"

Trist shrugged. "I think some dead choose to stay here, even after they've gotten over the denial. They could go to the light, but they just don't want to for whatever reason."

"Go to the light?" I straightened out of my slouch, my hands tensing on his feet. My heart beat went up so fast, I felt a little light-headed. "Do you really believe in that?"

Trist looked at me, a slight frown on his brow. "I don't have to believe in it. I've seen it."

"You've *seen* it?"

Trist nodded, his brow still furrowed. "Haven't you? You see the dead but you've never seen one go into the light?"

"No. I thought—I figured that was all bullshit."

"It's not, Neil. It's not bullshit." Trist spoke firmly.

"But… then why are there so many dead stuck here?"

"Like I said, I think it's part of the dying process. Though I have seen people go to the light as soon as they croak. It depends. And there aren't that many dead. Not really. Not if you compare it to all the people who ever lived."

My logical brain latched on to that. He had a point. Though I always saw the dead when I went out, there weren't nearly as many of them as the living. And if everyone who'd ever lived stuck around when they were dead, forever, I'd see a lot more, right? There'd be more dead than alive.

And while it's true, I did see some ones from past generations, never *really* old ones.

"Neil? What are you thinking?" Trist prodded me with his toes.

I wanted to say, "So there really is a purpose to this all?" I wanted to say, "You mean, this isn't all some cosmic joke?" But I was afraid of sounding like an existential teenaged girl.

I finally settled on: "What happens when they go to the light?"

"I don't know for sure, but I think it's good. The people I've seen go looked really happy. And there's always an angel that guides them over, and the angels look nice."

"*Angels?* You've seen angels too?"

My tone made it sound like I didn't believe him, which I instantly regretted. Trist sat all the way up, taking his feet off my lap and putting them on the floor. He turned his face away.

"Sorry," I said. "I didn't mean that. Of course, I believe you. But… what do they look like? Where did you see them?" It was a lot easier for me to believe in dead people than angels.

He folded his hands over his knees. "I've seen a few people die in the park. And once, when I was at the ER, I saw an old man go. If you hang around a hospital for a while, you'll see it."

"So some people just get the light right away?"

"Yeah. I guess if people have been sick awhile, they've made their peace with it. I dunno. I think you have to go through denial and anger and all those phases no matter what. If you don't have time to do it while you're still alive, then you have to do it after you die. Until you have, you can't move on."

It was at that moment that I knew I loved Trist. I was seriously in love with the man. Not just because he was attractive. Not just because he could see dead people too. Not even because we had great sex and I enjoyed his company. He thought about things deeply, like me. And, wow, I just went like a ton of bricks. Who knew metaphysics could be sexy?

"So, um, what about angels? What do they look like?" I managed.

"They look like people." He gave me a small smile. "Just like the dead do, except I've never seen an angel with blood and gore and all that. And they're fully conscious and they can see you. And they have a kind of peaceful happiness, you know? You trust them. They come to take people to the other side. Like an escort service." He snorted at his own joke. "I think they were probably people once, but now they've got a day job for the man upstairs or something."

"I want to see it," I said impulsively.

I truly did. I needed to see it for myself. It wasn't that I didn't believe Trist, but this was big. It was huge. If there really was a heaven, and there was more to look forward to than roaming around like a broken record, that would… well, it would change everything. That would make seeing the dead a lot less depressing, for one thing. And maybe I could better get on with my life knowing it wasn't all bleak sailing ahead, that there was a God or at least a really choice retirement plan.

Trist was studying my face. "Are you sure, Neil?"

"Yeah. You said we could see it at a hospital?" Two weeks ago, the idea of hanging around a hospital would have been a no-go for me. But with Trist and an actual purpose in mind, I thought I could deal.

"Yeah. The ER at Swedish, for example."

"Okay, let's do that. Maybe this weekend? I bet they're busy on a Friday night."

"Okay," Trist said carefully, his eyes solemn on mine.

"Okay. Can I have your feet back now? My lap is cold." This, actually, was a total lie because Trist's feet were always like shoe-shaped blocks of ice. I still liked to hold them, though.

"I think we can do better than that," Trist said with a sexy leer. He put his hand on my leg and sank to his knees.

And yeah, it was *way* better.

7

THAT FRIDAY night, we walked to the Swedish hospital. It was quite a few blocks from my apartment, and it was March, so we hadn't yet hit the long daylight hours. Walking in the dark with Trist was okay, though. We both wore hoodies and ignored the dead, holding hands as we went. I chatted aimlessly about anything I could think of to calm my nerves. Trist was never as afraid as I was, despite having been attacked by the dead in the park. He seemed to understand my fear, though, and he kept the conversation going when I faltered. Whistling in the dark.

Already, I couldn't imagine how I'd got on without Trist. But enough of that.

We sat in the waiting room at the ER, choosing a couple of seats in a corner where we wouldn't be noticed.

"How are we going to see it?" I asked. "Even assuming it happens. Won't it happen back in the actual ER area?"

"You just sort of feel it if there's an angel anywhere around. And if one shows up, it's because someone is dying. And we'll go find it."

As plans went, it wasn't quite detailed enough for my logical brain, but I bit my tongue and decided to let Trist run the show. After all, he'd seen this before.

Actually, there aren't as many dead as you'd expect hanging around a hospital ER waiting room. I guess that makes sense. People who died in the hospital probably didn't die out in the lobby. And I know *I'd* rather be just about anyplace else. The ER is worse than the DMV. It's like the DMV with sick people and potentially lethal germs.

We were there about two hours when Trist suddenly sat bolt upright, his head tilted to the side as if he were listening.

"What is it?" I whispered.

He put a finger to his lips. *Shhh.*

I shut up and looked around. I didn't see anything, but I noticed all my body hair was standing. There was a sense of electricity in the air. I imagined I could practically hear it snap. I had felt something similar when seeing the dead. Edward for one. But this was pretty strong.

"Come on," Trist said urgently.

He got up and headed for the double doors to the inner sanctum. There was a receptionist desk just before it, with two sturdy-looking, no-nonsense nurses. I was sure they'd stop us. But Trist was ahead of me. He just kept his head down, hands in his pocket, and walked casually as if he knew where he was going. So I did the same. Before I knew it, he'd pushed through the double doors, and I followed. No one stopped us.

Beyond the entrance to the ER proper, there was a wide white hallway with doors on either side and, farther down, another intersecting corridor. A nurse in blue scrubs hustled from one room to the next at the end of the hall, but otherwise there was no one in sight. Moaning came from one room, and a low conversation from another.

Trist paused and did that head-tilt thing of his. "This way," he said, grabbing my hand and heading for the crossing corridor, where he turned right.

I wondered what would happen if we were caught. My heart was thumping away in my chest with fear. But I doubt they arrest you for breaking into the ER. We could always say we were looking for someone. We'd be less conspicuous if we weren't holding hands, but I wasn't willing to let go of Trist. Because I *was* afraid, and it didn't have anything to do with getting caught by the nurses.

That sense of crackling energy grew stronger, and I nearly pulled away from Trist and marched in the other direction. I'd changed my mind. I didn't want to see the light. Why did I need to see it in person? I didn't! I'd seen it in the movies. And I believed Trist had seen it. I didn't have to see it *personally*, like some doubting Thomas. In fact, I wanted to just slap a ribbon on the whole thing and call it a winner. I was good.

Trist halted in a corridor in front of a closed door. "Here," he whispered. He tugged on my hand, pulling me in close to him. His face was shining and he wore a big smile. I'd seen him smile before, but never like this, like a child looking up at the lights on their first Christmas tree.

Not me. Me, I swallowed down terror, even as I felt the energy in the air bubble with positivity. It was too many conflicting signals. I backed up against the wall opposite the door, taking Trist with me. We huddled there like teenagers.

There were butterflies in my stomach, an angelic host of them, flapping away. My throat and mouth were utterly dry. "Do you… you really think there's an angel in there?" I pointed a weak hand toward the door.

Trist nodded. "Yeah, can't you feel it?"

"I feel *something*." I wasn't sure it was something good. I couldn't help thinking of *The Prophecy* series, where angels were homicidal motherfuckers.

"Shhh. Just wait," Trist said with a happy grin.

We waited. A dozen times nurses or orderlies passed by us, but they didn't pay us any attention. I guess they assumed we were there with a patient. Twice a nurse went in and out of the room we were waiting by, her face tense. Then a doctor came out. He was young but radiated confidence. He must have been in the room the whole time. He held the door open, and an older man came out into the hall, his face wrecked with grief.

"I'm so sorry, Mr. Johnson," the doctor said. "I wish we could have done more for your wife."

"No, her pain is finally over now. She wanted to go. I just don't know what I'm going to do." The poor guy was a mess.

"I understand," the doctor said sympathetically. "We have someone you can talk to about it, and about arrangements, if you like."

"Can I just… sit with her awhile?"

"Of course. Take your time. Again, my condolences, Mr. Johnson." The doctor put a hand on the old man's arm and then left him, striding off down the hall.

The old man went back into the room, shutting the door behind him.

I squeezed Trist's hand so hard, it had to hurt. "What now?"

"Just wait," Trist said, his voice all awed. "He's in there with her. He'll be out soon."

"I'm not sure this is such a good idea," I said, meaning, *I'm going to be sick. Fuck, I'm scared.*

Trist looked at me worriedly. "It's okay, Neil. I promise. But if you want to leave—"

Too late. A man in white stepped through the closed faux-oak door into the hall.

His loose pants and long-sleeved shirt were soft and a bit glowing. He looked Hispanic, his skin a soft mocha color and his hair straight and thick and long, past his shoulders. He had a big moustache. He was sort of ageless, and his face was very kind.

I was looking at an angel. Don't ask me how I knew, I just knew.

He saw us right away and gave us a smile. He had the kindest brown eyes I'd ever seen. I gripped Trist's hand tighter still.

A half-dozen thoughts entered my head as I stared at the angel—everything from falling to my knees, to asking him if he could cure my unwanted "gift," to joking about him helping the Seattle Mariners. But the moment passed, and he wasn't here for us anyway.

A woman stepped through the door after him. She was stick-thin, with white hair and blue eyes. She was maybe seventy and still pretty, even though it looked like she'd been ill a long time. Her expression, however, was one of delight and anticipation. "Can we go now?" she asked the angel. "I'm so excited to see Mama and Daddy and Jean."

"Right this way. They told me to take extra special care of you, and I will." He held out his hand with a smile.

The lady reached out, and when they touched, the hallway was bathed in light.

I gasped and shut my eyes, expecting the brightness to hurt. But after a moment, I dared to open them. There wasn't a portal or tunnel. It was just pure light without any source at all. It was so dense and bright in the hall that when the angel and the dead woman walked into it, they just vanished into the whiteness like it was mist. The light remained.

"Wow," I heard myself say in a shaky voice. "Wow. I mean, holy fuck."

I felt stunned. I felt grateful. I felt an indescribable sense of rightness and joy. This was the real deal. This had actually happened. This was death as I'd always hoped it would be, BC, before I'd fallen into a well of ugliness.

I couldn't believe Trist had shown me this. It was an amazing gift. I couldn't speak, so I just turned to him and gave him a hug. His arms went around me and hugged me tight. He kissed my hair. I wasn't crying or anything. At least, I didn't think so. I was just overwhelmed, adrift on a tide of happiness. Hey, you don't witness something like that and not feel moved.

"Hi, Edward," Trist said.

I pulled away in surprise and looked around the hall. The light was still there. And Edward had appeared now too. He stood a little ways down the hall, in front of the brightest part of the light. It back-lit him in a dramatic way. That bowler hat! Killer.

Edward gave us a little wave. "Hello, Trist. Hello, Neil." His voice sounded so ordinary and his expression was mellow.

"Hey, I can hear you!" I pulled away from Trist to face Edward, wiping nonexistent tears from my face. It felt like I should be crying, even though I wasn't.

"That's good, Neil. That's very good. You're making progress." Edward smiled, though it still had a sad tinge to it. "I'm so happy you found Trist and the two of you have each other."

"Oh God." I'd nearly forgotten that was Edward's doing. "Thank you so much! Trist is—well. I don't know what I'd do without him. And I never would have found him if it weren't for you. It's amazing that you brought us together. And that you had the gift too, when you were alive."

"I did," Edward said hesitantly. "Though my gift was a bit different than yours. I guess it prepared me for what I do now."

"Oh?"

"Neil…." Trist sounded worried. He put his arm around my shoulder and gripped me tight.

"What?" I looked at him, confused.

He was biting his lips, frowning.

"It's all right, Trist," Edward said. "Neil, are you ready to go to the light now? I think it would be a good time."

They were such gently spoken words, not threatening at all. Yet they sent terror spiking through me so strongly, I slammed back against the wall.

"What the—no!" I shouted.

Trist gripped the sleeve of my sweatshirt, hard. "Neil, it's okay!" Trist's words rang in my head, but I was staring at Edward.

He just stood there, looking at me with that patient look of his, that look that said, *Yes, Neil. You know now. It's fine. It really is.*

"Neil!" Trist said again.

In my head, I was running, but I must not have moved, because Trist clutched me to him. "Hey, listen! We don't have to go anywhere. All right? We can go back to your place. I'm not leaving you. It's all right. Don't be upset."

But Pandora's box was open, for better or worse, and I couldn't pretend my mind hadn't gone where it went. I pushed back and looked around the hallway. Down a few doors, away from the light, there was a window that looked very reflective. I walked over to it briskly, stared at myself in the glass.

I saw my shocked-looking face. It took me a moment to see it, but... yes. The edge of the door was visible behind me—*through* my body.

Neil Gaven. Twenty-eight years old. Was dead.

I wasn't Christopher Walken. I never had been. *I* was Bruce Willis.

"How is this possible?" I demanded of Edward. "I don't understand!"

"You hit your head on the board while you were windsurfing, Neil. You drowned," he said, calmly and regretfully.

Trist was practically wringing his hands with worry. "Don't force him!" he said to Edward. He turned to me. "It's okay, Neil. I didn't bring you here for this, believe me. I just thought... if you saw it, you might not be so afraid. I'm sorry. I'm so sorry."

I waved my hand at Trist. I was too full of questions to blame him. "But... I saw a psychiatrist for a year! I was in the hospital! I remember!" I told Edward.

"It was a dream, Neil. I suppose you were using the dream of a doctor to try to cure yourself. But it didn't work. It couldn't work. So you gave up that fantasy."

"Are you saying I made it all up?" I tried to think about AC 1, that first year in the hospital. Now that I tried to focus on it, the memory was a bit soft around the edges, like melting butter. I could remember a white room, a bed, nurses.... All a bit generic, no? And shock therapy? Dr. Able. *Dr. Able.* What a stupid name. Guess that should have been a clue.

"But… I've been living on my own for a while now. I work—I even have monthly one-on-ones with my boss!"

Edward just smiled sadly.

Crap. Did I? I took the bus downtown once a month. *First Tuesdays.* Was that my mind's way of forcing me out of my apartment at least that often, trying to make me face reality? And did I not actually talk to John at work?

It seemed impossible to believe I'd made up those conversations, but then I thought about what we discussed. The Gravalu project. The endless Gravalu project.

A chill went down my apparently incorporeal spine. I'd been working on Gravalu *before* the accident, hadn't I? There was no way any project would take two years. And if I'd actually been in the hospital for a year, Hora Systems would have turned that project over to someone else to finish long before I got out. The Gravalu project couldn't possibly be real.

Oh my God. Like the dead I'd seen in the streets, I'd spent hours in my apartment at a keyboard, tapping away, working on a project that wasn't actually there. I was going through the motions of a life I was no longer living. Just like they did.

I slumped against the wall, my heart a ball of bitter lead in my chest. "I don't *want* to be dead. I was just starting to live!"

Trist came up to me and gently took one of my hands, as if worried I'd reject him. But I let him take it and squeezed back. God, he felt so solid!

"Are you real at least?" I asked him miserably. "Or did I make you up too?"

"No, babe, I'm real," he said earnestly. "I'm real and my existence was shit until I met you. I love you, Neil. I don't want to lose you, not ever. Please. We can pretend if you want. Whatever you say."

I looked him over, studying his face, his chest. I took the hem of his hoodie and T-shirt in my hand and lifted them up a bit. The dark bruises were still purple against his pale flesh. They hadn't faded at all. Why hadn't I noticed?

Because denial is a hefty bitch.

"You too?" I asked. God, not Trist. I could be okay with me being dead, but not Trist.

"Yeah," he said. "I was worried that you'd figure out that I was, but not accept that you were, and end up hating me or something."

"That night you told me about? When they beat you up, hit you on the head with a wrench? You died then?"

Trist nodded, his eyes filled with pain. "It was cold that night. So fucking cold. It took me hours to die. I was alone in the park. It hurt so bad, but knowing that I was dying was worse—" He shook his head, unable to finish. "It's okay. It's over now."

God, I couldn't bear it. You see horrible things happen to people in the movies, but it's different when it's real life, when it's someone you love. Trist was beaten up in the park and he suffered alone, died alone. I couldn't stand the fact that it had happened. I practically jumped on him and hugged him for all I was worth.

"I'm so sorry! If only I'd talked to you before, when I used to ride past you on my bike. You would have been safe at my house that night and I—" I wouldn't have been acting like an idiot, risking my neck to try to impress a guy who never was serious about me. I wouldn't have died in Puget Sound.

"You knew you were dead? When we met?"

Trist nodded against my hair.

"Then why didn't you, um, go to the light before? If you knew?"

Trist hesitated, then hugged me tighter. "I lived alone for so long, Neil. I refused to die alone."

"Gentlemen?" Edward's voice. We broke apart enough to look at him. "Will you stay here awhile longer, or are you ready to go? It's your choice. But I promise, it's much nicer on the other side." He smiled. "No more seeing dead people, Neil, or living like a hermit. And Trist, it's beautifully warm and sunny."

"How does this work?" I asked, straightening my spine. "Can we be together over there? Or will we... forget the way we feel about each other?"

I didn't want fucking streets of gold. I wanted Trist.

"Oh, there are many couples in heaven," Edward assured us. "You won't feel any differently about each other, I promise. Though I think you'll both be much happier. And there'll be much more pleasant things for you to do together. I hear the windsurfing is excellent, Neil."

"Oh, yeah, let me jump all over that one," I said sarcastically.

Trist looked at me and bit his lip. "It's up to you, Neil. We can stay here if you want. Though... I have to warn you. I'm surprised your old apartment hasn't been rented out. It probably will be eventually."

Shit. I hadn't thought about that! My landlady, old Mrs. Turner, had probably just not bothered renting it out after I died. She was really getting up there in years. But Trist was right. Eventually she would rent it, or she'd pass away and her kids would sell the house. I couldn't imagine sharing my home with living people.

That would be weird.

Besides, I'd spent enough hours in that dark place to last, well, a lifetime.

"I'll go," I told Edward. "If Trist will go with me."

Hell, yeah. It could be better, right? It was definitely an adventure.

Trist looked at me for a long moment, and then he smiled. He nodded. "Yeah. Yeah, let's blow this popsicle stand."

"Let's do it," I agreed.

So we held hands tightly and, together, we stepped into the light.

ELI EASTON has been at various times and under different names a minister's daughter, a computer programmer, a game designer, the author of paranormal mysteries, a fanfiction writer, an organic farmer, and a profound sleeper. She is now happily embarking on yet another incarnation, this time as an m/m romance author.

As an avid reader of such, she is tickled pink when an author manages to combine literary merit, vast stores of humor, melting hotness, and eye-dabbing sweetness into one story. She promises to strive to achieve most of that most of the time. She currently lives on a farm in Pennsylvania with her husband, three bulldogs, three cows, and six chickens. All of them (except for the husband) are female, hence explaining the naked men that have taken up residence in her latest fiction writing.

Website: www.elieaston.com
Twitter: @EliEaston
E-mail: eli@elieaston.com

By ELI EASTON

Blame it on the Mistletoe (Audiobook Only)
Closet Capers (Dreamspinner Anthology)
Heaven Can't Wait
The Lion and the Crow
A Prairie Dog's Love Song
Puzzle Me This
Steamed Up (Dreamspinner Anthology)

GOTHIKA
Claw (Multiple Author Anthology)
Bones (Multiple Author Anthology)
Stitch (Multiple Author Anthology)
Spirit (Multiple Author Anthology)

SEX IN SEATTLE
The Trouble with Tony
The Enlightenment of Daniel
The Mating of Michael
Sex in Seattle: Books 1 and 2 (Author Anthology, Print Only)

Published by DREAMSPINNER PRESS
www.dreamspinnerpress.com

Unfinished Business

by B.G. Thomas

"Now I know what a ghost is. Unfinished business, that's what."
~~ Salman Rushdie

1

THERE WAS a girl wearing a Siouxsie and the Banshees T-shirt and walking down the center of the street. Mike Ellsworth couldn't remember when he'd last heard someone even mention the goth rock group. What's more, the shirt looked clean, brand-new.

Except, of course, for the blood. When he looked closer, he saw it was coming from a gash on the side of her head. She was very pale.

"My God," he said with a gasp. "Are you all right?"

Stupid question! Of course she wasn't all right.

And the girl? She cringed but continued on by without responding. When he turned, he saw she was walking right past the remains of his car. There were two police officers there now (when had they gotten there?). They didn't pay any attention to the girl. Ignored her! She was bleeding. How could they ignore her?

"Can't you see her?" he shouted. His heart was racing. He felt cold and clammy. Almost faint.

The police officers—one a woman with very short dark hair, and a man, stocky, older, meaner-looking somehow—were looking at his car. They were looking at him. The him still in the car. The him that looked dead.

2

MIKE WAS the one who had texted Joel, of course. He was only about eight blocks from their hotel—he would be in the room with his lover in no time—so why couldn't he have just waited?

But he was so anxious. It had been six weeks since they'd last seen each other—six long weeks—and he was as excited as a kid on Christmas morning. His last trip had been cancelled due to a flu that had landed half a client's employees at home in bed. Soon he'd be with Joel—holding him, *fucking* him—and, God, he was hard as he typed on the tiny screen.

Hey Baby. Guess where I am? Mike spelled it all out. He sucked at textspeak.

A few seconds later, his cell phone made that *ba-bleep!* sound, and when he looked, the response was *RU N lobby?*—because Joel was a master at it.

Sometimes it took Mike what felt like forever to figure out what Joel was saying—IMO, SMH, AFAIK, LMK…. Mike considered himself lucky that he knew LOL. And for months he'd thought it meant "Lots of love." It was Lori, with an eye roll, who set him right.

"Laugh out loud, honey. When you're typing away and you laugh, you write that down. You put it in your text."

"Why?" he'd asked, totally perplexed.

"Because you're *talking*. It makes the conversation more real."

Whatever, he'd thought then and thought now.

But "RU" and "N" was simple enough to understand, and with only seven blocks to go, he typed, *I will there be soon. Are you naked yet?*

No came the almost immediate answer. And then: *Where RU?*

About six blocks now. He grinned. *Get your clothes off. I want you naked in bed when I get there.*

And the quick response: *Stop texting and driving*, and, *I <3 U.*

Texting. God. How many times had he gotten on Lori for the same damned thing? How many of those stupid e-mails—and, more recently, posts on Facebook—had he seen with the photograph of a crumbled car and the caption: "Was that last text worth your life? Share this if you agree! Don't text and drive!"

Later he thought, *Stupid way to die.*

Mike ended his texting days with *See you soon*, instead of *Me too*—he just wasn't ready, not even for that—and then there was the incredibly loud sound of a car horn. He looked up and was astonished to see he had just sailed, easy-peasy as can be, through a red light and there was a car heading directly toward the driver's side of his rental. He froze, mouth falling open, and time seemed to slow down. The other car hit his, and then there was flying glass—a million tiny pieces seeming first to float and then to dance in the air—followed by the most horrible noise and pain like he'd never felt before.

And a second later, he was somehow standing beside the cars.

He was dizzy—he almost fell over—felt all light... headed? No.... That wasn't quite right....

A woman was tumbling out of the car that hit him, and she was moving in slow motion as well, like the shards of glass, and her eyes were huge, her mouth working like a fish—he almost laughed at her comedic expression. She pointed. Gawked again.

He turned to see what she was pointing at, and what he saw would have made him scream if his throat hadn't seized up, preventing him from making any sound at all.

What he saw was himself.

The woman's car was deep in the side of his, and he was looking into his own staring eyes. There was blood. Quite a lot of it.

Everything that had been moving so slowly now froze in place. Nothing moved. There was no sound. Nothing. He couldn't move. He could only look into his own face—trying to make sense of it, denying what he knew.

His face was so pale.

Dead.

Somehow, time reasserted itself then, the world moving at its regular pace, the noises of traffic were back—shouts, a car horn, a motorcycle.

The woman who had hit him was standing next to her own car, hand touching the door, her eyes blinking, lips moving, but no words coming out. Then she slumped to the pavement.

Mike ran to help her, but to his surprise, he couldn't move her. Not an inch. Even the loose fabric of her blouse. It was as if she had been carved from stone. A statue.

Dreaming. I'm dreaming. Got to be....

She was conscious, she hadn't passed out, and she was staring at him—but not at him. She was staring at the him in the car. She was looking right through the him kneeling before her.

She doesn't see me.

This is crazy. This isn't real.

His heart was pounding and he staggered to his feet. He almost fell. He felt... how to describe it? Light. Almost as if he might float away. He could hear the wail of sirens.

Cops. They'd fix everything.

The woman, half sitting on the blacktop, half slumped against her car, was crying now. She was still staring at the him inside the car.

No! That's not me. It can't be me....

How *could* it be?

Mike turned, and there were more people now—gathering around, some moving in from the sidewalks, some climbing from their cars—and a few went to help the crying lady. None of them noticed him. They flowed past him like a school of fish.

Not real. This isn't real.

He looked back and saw two police officers had arrived. They were looking at him. At the *dead* him.

"Help me," he said.

"I'm going to see if I can find a wallet," the mean-looking cop said, and walked to the other side of Mike's car. He opened the door and bent in.

Touching me. He's touching me and I can't even feel it.

After a moment, the cop came back around. "Mike Ellsworth," he said. "From Sacramento, California. Age—ah—forty? Looks like he's married. There's a picture of him here with a woman in a wedding dress. I *don't* think he's the father."

No, I'm not the frigging father! He shuddered. There was something creepy about the man looking through his wallet, checking into his privacy, looking at his wedding picture.

"Don't see no kids."

I don't have any kids, Mike thought. They'd stopped trying after the second miscarriage. Lori wouldn't.

The woman looked in the car. "He's got a wedding ring on."

Mike felt that weird sensation again. *Like a goose walking over my grave.*

That's when he saw the girl walking straight up the yellow double lines in the center of the street. She looked maybe sixteen or seventeen, was just a little plump, and had dark brown hair parted down the middle and hanging to either side of her blood-smeared face. The gash on her right temple had gotten her Siouxsie and the Banshees T-shirt bloody, although you could only really see it where the white design was against the black. The lap of her light gray pants was bloody as well. She was coming right toward him, but like everyone else, seemed not to see him at all. If he hadn't stepped aside, she would have walked right into him.

"My God." He gasped. What had happened to her? But even though she cringed, she gave no other indication that she had heard him and kept going. She was passing his car now, as well as the two cops, the man and the woman, and they looked straight at them, both him and the Siouxsie-girl. No. *Through* them. They took no notice of either of them.

"Can't you see her?" he cried.

Nothing.

The woman who had hit him (killed him) staggered, nearly fell, and when he instinctively reached out to help her, he saw she might as well have been made of bronze. She was moving, but he could no more affect her, move her, even let her know he was there, than the puff of a breeze. Not *even* that. She would feel a breeze.

I can't touch anyone! They can't see me! They can't hear me!

His head began to swim, and he broke out into a cold sweat, heart still racing. *Sit down. Got to sit down!*

The lightness was sweeping over him again. Not light-*headed*. But somehow… light. He leaned up against a lamppost, trying to regain his composure…

…only to see something else that made no sense.

There was a woman walking down the sidewalk, with bandages all over her. *What the hell?* She was dragging an IV pole behind her, complete with a plastic bag filled with some kind of clear liquid.

So strange. It was all so strange.

The cops had his cell phone now. The woman was looking at it. She shook her head and faced her partner. "Password-protected. Fuck. Why do people do that? I mean, who was this guy? A secret agent?"

Of course he had a password. He was having an affair on his wife of so many years. With a man! What else could he do? He couldn't very well take the chance that she'd see his frequent calls to a man who lived in Kansas City. She'd wonder who he was.

Joel.

God, Joel!

He should be with Joel now. In his arms. In his bed. Their bed. Fucking. No. *Making love.*

Except he hadn't been able to say it, had he? Hadn't been able to say a simple thing like "I love you too." Hadn't even been able to text the little less-than symbol and the numeral three.

And now it's too late.

Too late? Too late for what? This was a dream. Had to be.

Except in that moment, that second, Mike knew it wasn't.

I'm dead.

It hit him then, and it hit him hard—hard enough to make him stumble and nearly fall to his knees from the grief of it all.

Joel. *Gone.* No. *He* was the one who was gone. He would never see Joel again. Never touch him. Kiss him. *Never* get the chance to tell him that he loved him.

Would Joel ever even know what happened? No one knew about Joel. No one would call him. Why would they?

God! Joel!

And then….

—*Swish*—

3

THAT WAS the only way to describe it.

Swish.

One minute he was on the street, trying to understand what the fuck was happening, and the next he was in a room.

What the hell? How the hell did I get here? he thought, as yet another wave of light-headedness swept over him.

Mike looked around him. He was in a hotel room—the Meridian Hotel, of course, familiar from the dozen times he'd stayed here. He was standing by floor-to-ceiling windows that looked down into the Kansas City streets and that did nothing to help his dizziness.

And when he turned away… there was Joel.

Joel was lying naked on the bed, and the sight—as always—took Mike's breath away. He was on his stomach, perfect round butt raised, one knee pulled up just a bit to show off its perfection even more. He could see just a hint—a delightful hint—of Joel's balls hanging in their hairless sac (Mike liked that Joel shaved his scrotum for him), reminding him that this was no woman waiting for him. Not that he could have mistaken those wide shoulders, the deep ridge of his back, and the narrow waist for anything but a man.

Waiting for him.

Joel shifted. Shifted again. Turned his head, and Mike could see the smile on his beautiful face.

He's posing. He's waiting for me to open that door so that this is the first thing I see. Strangely, Mike felt himself getting hard. How could he help it at such a sight?

Who knew a ghost could get a hard-on?

Ghost? *Really?* A ghost? There wasn't a better explanation?

"Joel," he moaned, and his heart lurched and his eyes filled with tears. Tears! Him! Who would have thought? "Oh, Joel."

He walked to the bed. Looked down at his beautiful lover.

Lover. My lover.

"Joel," he whispered as a tear fell from his eyes.

Joel sighed.

Mike froze. *Did he hear me?*

Joel rolled over on his side. Looked at the clock on the bedside table.

"Joel?"

But no. Joel couldn't hear him. He reached for his cell phone. His movements were all grace and beauty, even though he was only lounging on the bed. His skin was so smooth, the muscles flexing beneath. His hair, thick and wavy brown, was pushed back from his face. He looked at the phone with beautiful brown eyes. There was a shadow of a beard on his jaw—because Mike loved Joel's balls smooth and his face just a bit rough. Joel did so many things to please him.

"I like to make you happy," Joel would say.

Beautiful man.

Joel raised an eyebrow and used a thumb to brush the small screen of his cell phone.

God. He's looking to see if I've called.

I can't call.

Joel tapped at the screen and raised the phone to his ear.

Calling me! He's calling me.

"Joel...." He reached for his lover. Touched his arm, that lovely skin, dusted with the softest of hair. But it didn't feel soft. It didn't even move.

He can't hear me. He can't feel me. He doesn't know I'm here!

Mike groaned.

Oh God.

He's calling me. Doesn't know what's happened. Doesn't know I can't answer. He probably thinks I'm parking the car or something. He doesn't know!

The cops! he thought. The phone will be ringing in their hands!

And then....

4

SUDDEN, HUGE, gigantic pain! He was somewhere else—had been ripped from where he was. People.... Looking down at him, mouths moving, no sounds....

—Falling—

5

HE WAS on the street again. What the fuck just happened?

He was standing right in front of the police officers. The phone was ringing in the woman's hand, but she could only look down at it helplessly. She shook her head. Looked at her partner.

"Thirty-six, eighty-five," he said, then cried, "Joel's birthday."

He walked up to the pair and shouted it—"Three, six, eight, five!"—even though he finally *knew* they couldn't hear him. No one could.

I'm a ghost.

He shook his head. This couldn't be happening. It made no sense. It was like something out of a Patrick Swayze movie.

The phone stopped ringing.

Joel....

It was too much. Much too much.

"No!" He strode up to the police officers. "Three, six, eight, five!" he screamed.

The woman flinched. "What?"

"I didn't say nothing," her partner said.

She gave him a funny look. "Yes, you did. It was a number. Three and six?"

He shook his head. "No, I didn't."

Her lovely dark brows turned into a single line, her forehead furrowing. "Yes. I *heard* it."

Wait. What was she saying? Numbers! Had she heard him? Mike moved closer. Got in her face, even though she looked right through him. "Can you hear me?"

Nothing. Her expression didn't change.

"Damnit!" he shouted and then saw that time she did react. She gave a slight recoil, as if he'd poked her.

"You okay, Daphne?" her partner asked. He had a gold bar over his right breast pocket with the word Townsend. His name.

Mike looked at hers. Brookhart.

"I-I don't know," she was saying. "I thought I just heard something. Swearing."

Oh! Oh God! His heart raced. "Yes!" he shouted, and she drew back against Townsend.

Oh God, oh God! She could hear him.

The cell phone number. "Three, six, eight, five," he shouted.

She jumped again.

Mike trembled with excitement. For some reason, *this* woman could *hear* him. Now if she would just try his cell.

"Daph," Townsend said, "you're freaking me out. What's going on?"

She glared at him. "Don't fucking call me that."

"Use the goddamned password!" Mike bellowed. "Three, six, eight, fucking five!"

Her brow shot up and she looked down at the cell phone in her hand.

"Yes!" he cried again.

"What are you doing, Daphne?" Townsend said.

She ignored her partner and tapped at the little screen on the phone. "Well, I'll be damned."

Mike nearly yowled with excitement.

"How the fuck did you do that?" Townsend asked.

She shrugged. "I... I don't know...."

Now if only she would....

"Well, look here," she said. "He was on his way to meet someone. Told him to...."

She stopped talking, and Mike blushed when he realized what she'd read.

Be naked and in bed when I get there.

"What?" Townsend asked, looking over her shoulder.

"Do you frigging *mind?*" she said, moving the phone so he couldn't see it. "It doesn't matter. What we know was that he was texting someone when this happened."

"Fucking texting and driving," Townsend said with a scowl.

Don't I know it, thought Mike. *Stupid goddamned way to die.*

"I'm going to call the... person," she replied, and Mike was hit with two things.

One, she was being discreet, for which he was grateful. Two—*two!*—she was calling Joel. She would tell Joel what had happened. She would....

And then that hit Mike too. It was if his stomach had turned to lead.

Oh no.... Oh, Joel. Oh, Joel I am so sorry....

Daphne dialed.

And then....

—Swish—

6

HE'D MOVED again!

Once more he felt dizzy, lightheaded. How was this happening? Was *he* doing it? This... this *moving?*

Joel wasn't in the room, but the minute his cell rang—the theme from *Mission: Impossible*—he came striding out of the bathroom—all gorgeous and godlike, a force of nature, cock swinging—and snatched up the phone. "Mike! Baby! Where are you?"

And, of course, Mike knew what he was about to hear.

He moved to Joel, reached out to touch him, drew his hand back. Couldn't stand the idea of touching his beloved and feeling only a statue.

Watched.

"Who is this?" Joel asked.

Oh, God. What have I done?

"You're a police officer? Where's Mike?"

It was horrible to watch.

The color drained from Joel's face first. Then he sat down hard on the end of the bed. If it hadn't been there, he might have hit the floor. Mike had reached out to help him, but, of course, it was like trying to grab a falling safe.

I can't effect anything anymore.

Joel began to shake. "W-What are you saying?" He listened for a moment and then closed his eyes. "Oh God. God, please no…."

Mike went to his knees and reached out—touched Joel's. Yes, it was like touching a mannequin. But he *needed* to touch the man he loved. He squeezed. Squeezed stone.

Oh God.

"No. I—I'm not… I…. Yes…." Joel shook all the more. Tears were spilling openly down his face. "The Mmm…. Meridian Hotel. Room 708. Y-Yes. I'll wait."

Joel dropped his hand between his knees. The phone fell to the floor, and then so did he. He collapsed into a heap. "*Nooooooo!*" he wailed. "God, please, no!"

There was nothing Mike could do.

7

A KNOCK on the door. Joel was sitting on the floor. He had stopped crying, but he hadn't dressed yet.

Mike had tried to talk to him. Even tried the yelling that had worked with the woman cop, Daphne Brookhart. It hadn't worked.

The knock came again. Joel looked up. "Wait," he said, and then louder. "Hold a second."

Joel got up and went to a suitcase that was open on a stand inside the closet. He grabbed a pair of black jeans and stepped into them, then pulled a sweatshirt over his head. He didn't bother with socks or shoes. He went to the door, peeked through the little hole made just for that, and shuddered. Seemed to waver for a second. Then he opened it.

The woman police officer was there, but not the man.

Mike stood watching, clenching and unclenching his hands. Thank God. She was the one who could hear him.

"H-Hello," Joel said. Tried to say.

"I'm Detective Brookhart with the Kansas City Police Department. Are you the gentleman I spoke with on the phone?" She looked down at it. "Joel Kauffman?"

He nodded.

"Any relation to *the* Kauffmans?"

"N-No," he replied. "Not hardly. God decided to give me to the poor Kauffmans instead."

"May I come in?"

"I'll let you in if you tell me you've made a mistake," Joel told her. "That he's not d.... Not... deh...."

Joel couldn't even say it, could he? Mike felt as if his heart would just fold up in on itself. It was awful. It hurt so badly. Who had ever had to watch something like this? Watch someone tell your lover that you were dead?

"I'm sorry, Mr. Kauffman. I-I can't do that."

Joel staggered again, and Mike had to keep himself from darting forward to help. He *couldn't* help him. Ever again. In fact, all he'd done in the end was hurt this sweet, kind man. He was doing it right now.

Luckily Dt. Brookhart *was* able to help Joel—and she stepped in quickly and took his arm and led him to the bed. "Sit down," she said. It was obvious she was concerned, and it felt as if it were more than just professional. It brought out a loveliness Mike hadn't noticed before. But, of course, he'd had far bigger concerns, and the fact that she had made no move to look feminine didn't help. She had short but curled hair—what might be considered an efficient style, especially for a cop. No makeup. Not even the simplest of earrings. So different from his wife, who was all dresses and skirts and low-cut blouses and appointments at expensive beauty parlors, never one hair out of place unless it was for effect.

"Can I get you a drink of water?" she asked.

Joel pointed at the dresser. "There's a bottle of whisky over there. How about some of that instead?"

Imagine. Joel drinking whisky. He'd bought that for Mike because Mike couldn't take it on the plane with only one suitcase, and he did like to travel light.

"Sure," she said, not so much as batting an eye, and went to the dresser and picked up the bottle. Johnnie Walker Black Label. Not Mike's very favorite, but Joel was a regular working-class guy—barely making more than minimum wage. That he'd paid something like forty dollars for a 750 ml bottle meant a lot to Mike, and for some reason, that almost brought on the tears again.

Mike didn't cry. Lori would have approved, he thought. Strange that Joel could bring out any emotion. Had made him feel more alive than he ever had in his entire life.

Trouble was....

I'm not alive. And with that thought came that strange "highness" again. Disembodiment.

Disembodied!

He laughed. *Laughed.* At a time like this.

Had anyone ever given the concept of "disembodied" more validity?

"Ice?" Brookhart asked.

"Yes, p-please," Joel answered and pointed again. "There's some in that bucket thingy."

God. That hand. That arm. Mike caught himself staring. He was reminded of his LSD days in college. How fascinating normal, everyday things—like hands—could be. But, of course, he was very familiar with Joel's hands. So perfect, smaller than Mike's own, but still masculine. He loved the light spattering of hair across their tops. Carefully trimmed nails without being manicured. Those hands had touched him, held him, rubbed the pain of all-day meetings from his back, stroked his cock....

Brookhart brought Joel a glass, and he took a surprising swig, coughed, grimaced. He'd never gotten a taste for whisky and said so.

Brookhart shrugged. "I'm a Bud girl myself." Although "girl" is never a word Mike would have used to describe the woman.

Mike felt a sudden weird disorientation. A... ripple. God. He staggered. What was that?

"May I ask you a few questions, Mr. Kauffman."

"Joel, please," he said. "But can I have another of these?" He held out the glass, ice clinking.

"Of course," Brookhart said, and got it for him.

When Joel was sipping the second one—sip, wince, sip, wince, and Mike continued feeling that drifting other-world-ness again—Detective Brookhart began her questions.

"I'm sorry Mr..... Joel. But there's something I need to ask. How well did you know Mr. Ellsworth?"

Joel blushed—so did Mike—and focused his attention on the glass in his hands. "I think you can guess."

"Yes, but I need to *know*."

"Why?" he asked, head snapping back. "What does it have to do with anything?"

"Because he was chatting with you when the accident happened. That will need to go in my report."

"But why?" Joel jumped up, and tears sprung to his eyes.

Mike looked away. He felt like a voyeur. And why not? Wasn't he? He felt like he should leave, but if doors were anything like people, would he have a chance of opening it?

I need to do one of those "swish" things again. Trouble was, he didn't know how he'd done it.

Brookhart sat on the edge of the bed. "Joel. Correct me if I'm wrong, but you and Mr. Ellsworth were having an affair." It was a statement really. Not a question at all. She had read the texts, after all.

Get your clothes off. I want you naked in bed when I get there. Hardly the kind of thing one straight man said to another.

Joel's eyes darted back and forth.

Brookhart placed a hand on his shoulder. "I can leave what you two said to each other out of my report. Who knows, maybe a lot more. You can tell me, although from the texting, it's pretty obvious."

Joel looked down at his drink. "We couldn't stop, you know? It was like that line in *Brokeback Mountain*. About not being able to quit you?" The tears were flowing freely now, and they stabbed in Mike's heart. "I loved him. And he didn't say it, *wouldn't* say it back. But I know he loved me."

Now Mike wanted to cry once again. He suddenly felt quite solid, quite... rooted. *Here.* Very *here* in this room with his lover—his lover—and the police detective. "I did," he said. "I do." At last. Out loud. And Joel couldn't hear it. The pain that came then was immense.

"Yeah. I get it. I find it hard to say myself. Probably lost me the love of my life. She couldn't take it."

Joel looked up. "She?"

Brookhart nodded. "When I read the texts, I told my partner to stay with the bod—with the car until the ambulance got there."

Joel's brows shot up. "Ambulance? Does that mean there's a chance...?" Hopeful.

Brookhart shook her head. "I'm no doctor, but I don't think so...."

Joel closed his eyes, drew in a shuddering breath. "I told him not to text and drive. More than once. He told me he had to for business so why not for pleas...."

Joel stopped talking, but Mike knew what he was going to say. Pleasure. Mike had said it more than once.

Brookhart squeezed his shoulder.

"We met a year ago," Joel said. "He comes to town once a month to teach... and consult... this software stuff." He shrugged. "I never quite understood everything he did. He invented it. Did you know that? Or he helped...." He smiled. "So smart." Another shrug. "We never talked much about work...."

In fact, they didn't talk much about his "real" life at all. Mike bit his lower lip—*hard.* Trying to feel. Not feeling much at all.

"We hardly talked about his other life at all," Joel said quietly. "I knew I should have stopped seeing him. He felt so bad the first time that I was shocked when he called me a few weeks later."

Mike plopped down on the desk. The chair was tucked in, and with no way to move it, the desk was the only place to sit. And it was sit down or fall down.

Joel was right. He'd felt so guilty the first time. Not only because he'd cheated, but because he'd finally broken down and had sex with a man. Not that he hadn't been tempted before in nearly twenty years of marriage. He had. He'd had plenty of chances. He wasn't movie-star gorgeous, but with his square jaw and deep brown eyes and full head of brown hair, he'd never had a lack of suitors—female or male. But he'd *always* known that if he cheated once—even once—he'd have crossed a line he couldn't *un*cross. And that after he'd done it once, there would be nothing to stop him from doing it again. Somehow he'd resisted by the very skin of his teeth.

But then he met Joel. One look across a crowded room, and it was done. He knew. Knew this man would be the one.

"I had to go to this training thing through my company," Joel was saying. "Well, not had to. I wanted to. It would be good for my career. But once I saw Mike, that was it. I hardly heard a word he was saying. I knew…."

Mike closed his eyes. *God. God, God, God!* This hurt! Hurt so fucking bad. Hurt to lose Joel and have him *right* there in front of him.

Goddamnit, why didn't I tell him how I feel?

"I can't believe I'm telling you this," Joel said.

"It's okay," Brookhart said.

"He felt so bad that first time," Joel said. "T-The next morning. I did too. I don't cheat. I don't *help* people cheat. He told me it was a mistake and he couldn't be with me again. It hurt to hear, but I knew he was right. He was married. We shouldn't have done what we did. But that night we were in his bed again. Every night that week. And then every time he came to town after…. God." He let out of sob. Wiped at his face. "Mike, I love you!"

"I love you too," Mike exclaimed.

And Dt. Brookhart jumped as if she had been goosed. Looked around her, eyes staring wide. She rubbed her arms. Shivered.

My God, he thought. *She really* can *hear me!*

Mike jumped to his feet. "Tell him!" he shouted. "Tell him that I love him. Please. Tell him I love him!"

"I love him," she cried.

"W-What?" Joel asked, obviously surprised.

Brookhart jerked, looked at him, and then shrugged, gave him an uncomfortable-sounding laugh. "*He* loves you… loved you… I'm… I'm sure."

Joel's eyes rounded. "How would you know?"

She opened her mouth and closed it. "He'd been seeing you for a year, hadn't he?"

"Maybe he just liked to fuck me," Joel said and raised his palms and covered his face.

Mike winced. Joel didn't really think that, did he? "Tell me you don't think that," he said to a man who couldn't hear him. Yes, he liked to fuck Joel. Loved it. Had never dreamed there could be such exquisite pleasure. But it wasn't just Joel's ass and how it felt to be in him. It was a connection he'd never known two people could have.

"He certainly wouldn't let *me* fuck *him*," Joel said, standing and walking over to the full-length windows. He leaned his forehead against the glass. "Maybe he was just some married dude getting his rocks off on the down-low."

"No!" Mike groaned. *Not* just getting his rocks off. Yes, they were a secret. Yes, it was true he wouldn't let Joel… fuck him. Because being fucked somehow made it all entirely too real. That he *was* gay.

But of course he was, wasn't he? And what a fine time to admit it. He'd always been homosexual. But he had things he wanted in life. Being gay would have made those things harder to get—harder to have.

He'd seen it through the years, over and over. Women, gays, recently the transgendered. Same words. "We might not live in the times we would wish for, but through our work and by our example, we can forge the bridge to those better times."

But Mike didn't want to be a bridge-builder. He didn't want to be a pioneer. An example. The guy to break the mold. He didn't want to be the token gay. He didn't want to be the one to show people that gays were just like them. That probably made him a coward.

If times were different…. If it were fifty years from now, it would be different. When Mike had started his career, there were far too many businesses that wouldn't have had a thing to do with him if they'd had even a clue he was gay.

And through the years, he'd watched things get better for gays. Saw them coming out. Saw laws change. State after state passed gay marriage.

But by then it was too late. He was married. He was married to a woman who was his partner in every way. What was he supposed to do? Leave her?

So instead he resisted having sex with a man. He resisted and resisted.

Until Joel.

And now it really was too late.

Oh, it hurt! It hurt so bad.

I've fucked everything up. For Lori. For Joel. *And for me!*

"Are you're *sure* he's dead?" Joel asked.

Brookhart sighed. "Pretty sure. I'm sorry. Not a doctor, but—"

Joel turned from the window, a hopeful expression on his face. Mike didn't. He knew things Joel didn't. That he was dead. He was here, wasn't he? Invisible? And even if he was revived, what kind of brain damage would he have?

Oh, Joel. Baby. I am so sorry.

Brookhart shook her head. "Don't. Don't do that to yourself. I'm not a doctor. But I still couldn't find a pulse. And I'm not a rookie. Hoping will only make it worse."

Joel looked away. "How could it be worse!" There were still tears wet on his cheeks.

"Let's talk about the wife," Brookhart said.

Joel let out a long breath. "What about her?"

God, thought Mike. *The wife, Lori. I've fucked everything up....*

"Can you tell me which one she is in his phonebook, for instance?"

"Her name is Lori." Then: "Hey! How'd you get into his phone anyway? Mike has it... *had* it password protected. *I* don't know the password."

Brookhart shrugged.

I screamed it at her, Mike thought.

"I don't know. I just got this sudden... hunch? It worked." She scrolled through what Mike realized must be his contacts while Joel gave her a surprised look. "Lori, you say?"

Joel nodded, wiped at his face, and stepped away from the windows.

"Ah. Here." Brookhart sighed. "Christ, I hate this. Worst part of the job."

"What's the best part?"

"Helping people," she answered immediately. "Letting them know a loved one is dead is the worst."

Oh no! Mike thought as Joel let out a moan and sat back down on the bed. *She's going to call Lori.* Again Detective Brookhart was calling someone to let them know he was dead. *Dead.* Mike fell back against the desk. *Lori! I'm sorry!* "Lori," he whispered.

And....

—Swish—

He was in a bedroom. But not his own. Not their own. But Lori was in the bed. With a man.

8

MIKE STUMBLED backward in surprise, almost tripping over his own feet. Lori was lying on her back—a sheet pulled high enough so it was just concealing her breasts—staring at the ceiling. The man was Greg Beachley. He lived down at the corner of their block. They'd invited him to the house for a party a little over a year ago, soon after he'd moved in. Mike remembered his last name even though he'd only really talked to him that one time. It was his job to remember names. Greg had seemed nice. Lori had even talked about him that evening when they went to bed. How nice he'd seemed.

Nice.

I guess Lori thought he was nicer than I did.

Greg was on his side, propped up on one elbow and gazing down at her. "I love you," he said.

"Christ," Mike muttered, and looked away. Looked back. He couldn't help it.

"Say it, Lori," Greg continued.

"Say what?" Lori asked.

"That you love me." He smiled. It was a nice smile.

Mike had never found the man to be attractive, his near-complete baldness probably a part of it. It wasn't a turnoff, but not something Mike found sexy. Maybe it was his fear that his mother would pass her father's baldness to him. Maybe that was why he found Joel's thick hair so beautiful. But Greg did have an amazing body. Mike had suspected as much when the guy jogged by in the mornings as Mike was leaving for work. The sheet on his side was pulled down to his hip, showing off a muscular chest and part of a solid, round buttock. *God! I'm checking out his body... I am gay.*

Of course, Mike preferred Joel's sleekly muscled body to Greg's bulky physique. But Lori had chosen a lover well.

Mike's eyebrows raised at an abrupt conclusion. *Always when I am leaving for work. Was he waiting for me to leave?* If he felt any anger at his discovery of his wife's cheating, it rose up and wafted away in less than an instant. *How ironic,* he thought. *I wonder which of us was first.*

Greg shifted his leg and brought it up over Lori's, the sheet pulling away and revealing his ass completely. *I need to leave.* This *was* being a voyeur of the worst kind. *I need to "swish" out of here....*

But how? He couldn't even walk out of the room. The bedroom door was closed. *How do I do it?* he wondered. *The "swish?"*

"Come on, Lori." Greg gave her a little poke in the side. "Say it. Say that you love me. I know you do."

"If you *know*...," she said, sitting up, letting the sheet fall and not hiding her breasts the way she always did with Mike, even after all these years of marriage. "...then why do you need me to say it?"

"Oh, Lori," Mike said aloud. "We're two of a kind, aren't we?"

Two people that had fit together rather well. He, successful, the cofounder of software that more and more clients wanted to use for their businesses. Those clients being impressed by the fact that he, one of the owners of the company, was willing to travel all over the country to train people on how to use it. The personal touch. The truth was, he liked to travel. To get away….

And Lori? She was the perfect businessman's wife. She was lovely—with long brown hair, expressive brown eyes, full lips, a delightful laugh, and creamy white skin. She had a nice figure (she ran three to four miles on the treadmill every evening), her breasts were neither large nor small. "Perfect," she'd declared them. She was just the kind of woman a businessman wanted on his arm.

She kept a perfect house, ran it like a business. She was a consummate cook (if he brought clients or associates home for dinner, she took pride in preparing the meals), was an excellent conversationalist (often impressing those clients and associates), and had an exceptional mind for business as well. She'd spotted great investments, discovered new clients, and hadn't it been her idea that he take those opportunities to travel and teach his software?

God…. Could she have been cheating on him for years? Was that why she'd suggested it? Almost insisted on it?

Lori climbed out of the bed and walked, carefree, to the bathroom door.

"Lori," Greg called after her.

"I need to use the ladies' room," she said and closed the door.

Greg climbed out of bed, and Mike looked despite himself. He couldn't help it. And yes, Lori had indeed chosen her lover well. Greg went to the bathroom door. "All right. Don't say it. Break my heart. We've only been seeing each other a year now."

Well, that answered that question. Who knows who was the first to have an affair. But they'd been seeing their respective lovers for almost the same amount of time. Ironic.

It occurred to Mike that he was taking all of this pretty well. Not only the fact that his wife had a lover, but that he was… well, dead. Not that it was easy. But going from death to thinking it was a dream to accepting all this as real, everything that was happening…. Why, he made the move pretty swiftly.

There was a long pause, and then the door opened, Greg nearly toppling into her arms. They laughed.

"Oh, Greg."

Just say it, Lori. Tell him. Don't be like me.

But then she *was* like him. It was why they'd been perfect partners, even if not lovers.

Greg kissed her, and she fought it for only a second and then melted against him. She pulled back after a long moment that Mike really hadn't been able to watch. He only looked back when she said, "All right, Greg. I lo—"

Her cell phone rang.

Oh no. Mike stepped forward. *Don't answer it, Lori!* "Don't answer it!"

But she did, of course. Even in the arms of a lover, she had to at least check to see who was calling. What if it was business?

"Shit," she said. She was seeing his name on the screen. He knew that. She sat down and pulled the sheets high. As if he could see her over the phone. As if he wasn't dead.

"Don't answer it, Lori...."

"Hello, dear. You all checked in to your hotel?"

Pause.

A pause that turned out to be horrible.

This woman who had just been about to say, "I love you," to her lover.... Her face. She began to shake. "What?"

Greg went to her. Mike wished he could have. "Are you all right, baby?" Greg asked.

She looked at him, eyes wide and filling with tears. "Oh God."

Mike turned away. He couldn't stand it.

"Yes. Yes, I can come. I'll see if I can get a flight out today. If not, tomorrow."

"Lori, what's going on?"

"Yes. Please. How do I get ahold of you?"

Mike looked back as she pressed the phone to her chest. "I need a pen and paper, Greg. *Now.*" Her tone brooked no argument.

Greg, looking very concerned, nodded, went to his bureau, and got what she asked for. When he handed it to her, she wrote.

"Yes. Thank you Officer. *Detective.* I'm sorry. Brookhart? Is that h-e-a-r-t or h-a-r-t? Yes. I have it. Thank you." She shuddered. "I have a friend here. I'll be all right. I'll see you soon." She signed off the phone. Looked at Greg.

"What is it, baby?"

"It's Mike," she said. "He's.... He's dead." And then she burst into tears.

It was too much. *Too* much.

Mike turned. Ran heedlessly to the door. And....

9

THERE WAS that sudden blinding pain again!

God! He clutched his chest.... Or tried to. He wanted to scream at the pain. He couldn't seem to do anything. *Light!* There was so much light, and he didn't know where he was and....

10

MIKE STUMBLED (he was on his feet again) and nearly fell into an unfamiliar street.

"Sit down," he said out loud. "I've got to sit down."

Before he fell down….

Funny, he thought. That a ghost should need to sit down. That he could get dizzy? That his heart could race? That he could feel sweaty and clammy? How could he feel anything at all?

"I'm f-fuck-ing *dead!*" he shouted in despair and felt the tears coming.

He spotted the steps of an old apartment building. Where the hell was he?

Mike walked, swaying, to the steps—they were only about fifteen feet away. He thought he could make it. An old woman with two big shopping bags was sitting there, wearing a scarf over her head and a coat despite the warm weather.

The steps were wide, though. Room enough for him. Hell, he could sit down in her lap, couldn't he? She'd never know. Of course, that would be too creepy. Obscene, somehow.

Mike made it the last few feet and plopped down right next to the woman. He looked around. He had no idea where he was. Why was he here? The other times—when he'd "moved"—it had been to go *to* someone. But this time he'd just gone away. But why here?

Was it because he had needed to get away so badly?

All that pain?

I'm a coward.

But it wasn't that. Not really.

No one should have to see what he'd been seeing. No one. Why was this happening? Why hadn't he… passed on?

"God-fucking-damn," he said.

No sooner had the words left his lips than he heard a sound—*No… It couldn't be*—and was assaulted by the sharp smell of urine. God! Had the old woman—he turned to look at her—had she just pissed herself?

"Shouldn't swear," she muttered.

There was a part of him that wanted to bite her head off. *Not swear? Really?* But….

But that part was an old part.

Something from Before Joel.

Joel cheerfully gave money to every beggar, every person who walked up in a parking lot and said, "Excuse me, sir, but can you spare a dollar? My car ran out of gas and…."

The first time—when Mike and Joel had come out of a convenience store with a couple of huge ice teas—Mike had scowled at the stinky old man and been ready to rip into him. It was always a dollar. It was always "ran out of gas." They were always late for something. But before Mike could say a word, Joel had given the guy *two* dollars.

"Good luck," he'd told him. "Wish it could be more."

"God bless you, sir," the old man had said.

"Are you crazy?" Mike had snarled once they got in the car. "Why did you give him *any* money?"

"Mike!" Joel had said, a look of utter surprise on his face. "What's *two* dollars to you? It won't buy a Big Mac. It'll help him a lot."

"But you *know* he's only going to buy booze or drugs with it," Mike shot back. "He isn't going to get any gas. He's not late for *any*-damned-thing."

Joel shrugged. "I *don't* know that, Mike. You don't either. And it's not important. I did what my heart compelled me to do. It's up to him what he does with it."

Mike had been stunned by the remark. And as the months passed—as he witnessed more of Joel's compassion and generosity, as he was bathed more and more in Joel's kindness and love—something happened to him. The stone around his heart began to crumble. The disappointment in life began to fade away. He began to find his happy childhood self again.

The part of him that was disgusted with an old woman unable to keep herself from urinating right there on the steps of the apartment building had been transformed by a sweet, loving man named Joel Kauffman. How humiliating for her. The poor woman. And when that old lady told him not to swear, in honor of Joel, he instead said, "I apologize."

"Apology accepted," she replied.

Both their heads snapped in each other's direction. "You heard me!" they chorused.

11

MIKE LEAPED to his feet in surprise. She saw him! She heard him! And he didn't have to scream at her.

She was crying, looking up at him with an expression of amazement. "Mary, Jesus, Holy Mary, Mother of God...." She looked at him in... was that wonder? "You hear me.... It.... It's... I...."

Confusion. He saw confusion in her dark eyes.

"…been so… long? Has it? I'm…." She shook her head, looked away furtively, then looked back. "So confused…." She was staring at him now, tears running down her face.

Christ! Am I making everyone cry?

"Hail Mary, full of grace," she continued. "The Lord is with thee." She was pulling something from her blouse. A rosary. "Blessed art thou amongst women, and blessed is the fruit of thy womb…."

"Ma'am," Mike said, sitting down now, instinctively touching her arm, and just as he was about to draw it back, he was amazed to find her arm was soft, pliant…. Not a statue. Not some plastic mannequin. *Real!*

The old woman's eyes went wide as well, and she looked down at his hand, then slowly—slowly—touched it. Her fingers felt cold. "Holy Mary…. Mother of God… pray for us sinners…. Now and at the hour of our…."

"How?" Mike asked. *How can she hear me? Why does she feel so real?*

"…death."

He rested his other hand on hers, not knowing the last time he'd wanted to touch another human being more.

"I… I…." She swallowed. He could hear it. "They look right *through* me. Like I'm not even here." More tears. "And sometimes…." She shuddered. "Sometimes they walk…."

Before she could finish her sentence, it happened. A young woman in a bright floral sundress dragging two children behind her—four years old? five?—walked right *through* the old woman.

Mike fell back in wonder.

"Mommy!" said the little girl. "I smell *pee-pee*!"

"Norma Raye Menser! If you've pottied in your panties…!"

"No, Mommy," she cried with great indignation. "I think it was the old lady again…."

Mike looked up after them, almost at the top of the short flight of steps, with surprise. The mother, barely old enough to be one….

Smack!

Crying….

"I told you to stop telling stories about that old lady. There is *no* old lady! How many times—" Their voices cut off as they went into the building.

The little girl said she sees the old woman. At least sometimes. Why?

It's because she doesn't know it's impossible yet, he thought. But with slaps like that, she soon won't be able to anymore. She already hadn't seen the old woman that time…. The *dead* woman.

He turned to look at her, and the expression on her face was awful. Mike leaned toward the woman, reached for her hand, hesitated, then stroked it anyway. "Ma'am...." *Surely. How to say this?* "Surely you *know*?"

"Know?" she asked, eyes wild. "Know what?"

He could see it. See it through the confusion showing in her eyes. She knew. She had to.

"Ma'am—"

"Rose," she said. She leaned forward, resting her weight on her knees. "Rose Silveira. I have to get upstairs. Make dinner for Paulo. He'll be home soon. He works hard. He'll want his dinner...."

Mike took a deep breath—then wondered about that, breathing—and continued. "Ma'am. Rose. You want me to call you that? Rose?"

She nodded. Sniffed.

"Rose. You're...." He almost said "dead" and then changed his mind. Changed the *way* he was going to say it. "You're like me, Rose. You and me. *We're*... dead."

The hurt on her face—no, the *fear*—was almost too much to take. She shook her head once. Twice. "N-No."

He nodded. "That's why some people, that woman and those two kids, were able to walk through you."

She shook her head again. "*No.*" Forcing certainty.

"That's why you can hear me," he continued. "Why I can hear you."

She looked at him. Pleading. Then slowly it came. Sad knowing. "Dead...?"

And suddenly, *he* wanted to cry. *Joel.... What have you done to me? What is with all this crying?* "Yes," he said in a voice barely above a whisper.

Her eyes filled with tears again. "You're dead too?"

Yes, he thought. "Yes."

"H-how? *How* did you...?" She stopped.

"Driving and texting."

"Tex-ing?"

"You know... *texting*." And then he saw she *didn't* know. How long had she been dead? "I wasn't paying attention while I was driving. Someone T-boned... I mean, someone hit me."

She took a shuddering breath—making him wonder once more about ghosts breathing (did they need to?). He set the thought aside. "I—I'm sorry...."

"It's...." What was he going to say? That it was okay? It *wasn't* okay. Not in the least. It was horrible. It was worse than horrible. All the things left undone. Unsaid. All that unfinished business. "Thank you," he said instead.

She didn't say anything for a long time. Then she sat up straight, letting out a tiny gasp. "Oh…. Oh, no. Oh *my*…."

"Rose?"

"Dear Jesus… I *remember*." She looked back at him, eyes huge. "I remember!"

"Remember what?"

"The stairs! I was carrying groceries." She looked down at the bags at her feet. "*These* groceries! And I fell… I fell down the steps. That's the last thing I remember before…." She looked confused again. "Falling." Bewildered. "Then I was walking home. Over and over. Oh, my sweet savior…. Over and over…."

He took her hand again. "I'm so sorry."

She looked at him. "It's…." She paused. "Thank you."

They sat in silence for a while, and then she said, "Now what?"

He shook his head. Shrugged. "I don't know, Rose."

She nodded.

"What happened to… what did you say your husband's name was?"

She smiled. Her expression was sweet. Heavenly. "Paulo. Oh, my Paulo. He died. Years ago. In the war. And I just kept going on and on and on…. Going on until I couldn't even go shopping down at the corner…." She pointed, but the only thing he saw there was a drug store. For a second she got that puzzled look again. Then she shook her head. "I keep shopping and coming home, and I'm so old and feeble that I can't even make it upstairs without peeing on myself." She turned red, an expression of total humiliation.

And I thought of yelling at her…. Thank you, Joel. For letting the light back in my soul. Why didn't I tell you that I love you? Why?

"It's okay," Mike told her. Because that much at least was true.

"I *miss* him," she said quietly. "I've waited *so* long. Too long maybe. Stuck here so long… *before* I fell… and then after. I don't want to be stuck anymore. I want to see him. I want to go to Paulo…."

"Oh, Rose." What did he say? "Have you tried?"

She shrugged. "How? I wouldn't know how."

He opened his mouth, only to shut it again. How indeed? If he knew, would he be here? Why was he here?

But he didn't want to go. *I want to be with Joel. Tell him I love him. Apologize to Lori for being a shitty husband.*

That gave him another thought, though. "You want to go, Rose? To Paulo?"

"Yes!" she said. "I told you…."

Of course she did. She wanted to go. He was the one who wanted to stay!

"Then go, Rose."

"How?" she cried.

Swish, he thought. "Think about him," he said aloud. "Stop thinking about being stuck here. Stop thinking about how you'll never see him again. Think how you *will*. Think of him. *Think* of him, Rose. Think about how *much* you want to *be* with him."

"Think of Paulo?"

He smiled. "Picture him in your head, Rose." He squeezed her hand. "What did he look like?"

Her smile was beatific. "Oh. Oh, so handsome. Tall. Blue, *blue* eyes. He had this dark brown hair, and he would comb it down the middle. He used all this stuff in his hair that made it look wet. Before he joined the army of course. To fight the Nazis."

Nazis. God. That long?

She sighed a long, happy sigh. "He was lovely. Not just handsome. *Lovely*. The first time I saw him.... He helped me. I had fallen at the curb. Tore my stocking. And then he was just right there! He was helping me up, and I looked into his eyes, and that was it. I was in love, and...." She looked at him. "People say you can't know with one look. But I did. With one look."

He smiled. He'd seen Joel across a crowded room and he had known with one look. "I know."

"You do?"

Mike nodded. "I do."

And then her eyes flew wide. "Oh!" It was almost a shout. "Dear Jesus! Paulo!"

She was looking past Mike, and when he turned, there was nothing there. Then, just as he was looking back... he saw.

Light.

It seemed to be forming out of the air. Brighter and brighter and... there was a man... stepping out.

He was tall and wearing a uniform that didn't hide a muscular yet lean body. He was smiling and holding out his hands. "Rose. My Rose," he said.

Mike felt his arms crawl with gooseflesh.

"Oh, Paulo!"

Mike looked back, and the old woman was gone. Instead, he saw a woman of no more than nineteen. She was wearing a blue dress with long sleeves, the hem at her knees. Her waist seemed impossibly tiny and the dress was cinched tight to show off her figure. She wore a little hat that matched her outfit almost exactly.

There was a run in her stockings.

And then she was walking down the steps, reaching. Reaching and…. She stopped and looked back. "Thank you," she said. She was beautiful.

Mike nodded, his heart speeding up.

"Do what *you* need to do," she said then. "Your business. So you don't have to be stuck anymore."

He couldn't talk. Couldn't reply. He gave her a single nod instead.

Her smile grew, and then she turned… and walked into the light.

It closed. Almost like a door. She was gone.

And Mike was alone.

12

THE FIRST time he'd seen Joel was across a crowded room—and Joel had been looking at him. There were at least fifty people there, and quite suddenly Mike found he could hardly breathe. Of course he didn't know Joel's name at the time. All he knew was that the young man looked young. He couldn't have even been thirty. And he was gorgeous. He had thick, dark wavy hair that was somehow combed back from a sweet but decidedly masculine face. There was a shadow of a beard on his jaw, which seemed to help bring out the deep brown of his eyes.

Oh God, those eyes. Looking at him.

Their gazes locked, and suddenly Mike forgot how to speak.

He'd had been talking to a man who reminded him of Cannon from the old television series from the seventies. It was before his time, but his mother used to watch the reruns on one channel or another. This man was bigger, though, and older-looking, and he had very bad breath and was very boring. He was saying something about how glad he was that Mike was here to teach them and—that's when Mike saw Joel (and those eyes!) and his brain froze. The whole *world* froze.

Somehow he managed to tear his look away from the stunning young man and pretend to be interested in what Cannon was saying. It was only more than a decade's experience of feigning interest that let him do it.

Luckily, Joel sat at the back of the room that day Mike was teaching. If he'd sat up close, Mike wouldn't have been able to teach anything. But sometimes their eyes would meet again, and it was like ripping his eyes out of his head when he turned away.

Then that evening, cocktails. It was part of the event. A cocktail party on the top floor of the building… and there was Joel. Joel was *looking* at him. Their gazes found each other, and he was nodding at Joel and then wondering what the hell he was doing. He excused himself to go to the restroom and then… there was Joel. Standing next to him.

There were three urinals. Mike had taken the left one. Joel took the middle. Against the unwritten law. Straight men didn't do that. They were the type of urinals that started at the floor and then climbed up the wall like shallow, narrow bathtubs set on end and then placed into the wall. There were no partitions between them.

He tried not to look. Tried. Tried but failed. He glanced down out of the corner of his eyes, saw Joel's penis, and almost let out a tiny gasp.

It wasn't huge... but it wasn't small. The circumcision scar was so perfect that at first Mike wasn't sure if Joel had a foreskin or not. But then he realized how long he was looking, and when he thrust his gaze back at the wall in front of him— the urinal in front of him—he quite suddenly knew it was too late. Joel had to have noticed he was checking him out (staring!). He'd looked too long.

He shook, tucked himself away, and when he turned to leave the room, Joel was looking at him. Unabashedly *looking* at him.

"What?" Mike said with too much force, and then Joel was blushing, turning away. Mike found himself missing those eyes.

Mike fled the room and went back to the bar and ordered a shot of whisky— Crown Royal XR—and slugged it back fast. Then he ordered a second on the rocks, turned, and there was the gorgeous young man he'd seen in his class.

He was about ten feet away, and he looked sad and confused and... desperate?

Then Cannon was talking to him again, and he could smell the man's breath even over his own brand of alcohol. He walked past the man, an inch from pushing him out of the way, and went to the young man instead.

"What?" he said, voice cracking. He thought the young man might cry.

"I—I... I'm.... Sorry? I thought... I thought maybe...."

"Maybe *what*?" Again, too harshly.

Now Joel's face was so red it was alarming. "Look... I'll leave. Please don't say anything to my boss...." He turned and started walking away, and the leaving was dreadful. Like a huge chasm had opened up between them and Mike might slip right off the edge and fall right in.

"Wait," he said, and worried that once more he'd said it too loud. Would people be looking? He dared to check, but no one seemed to be paying him the least bit of attention.

The young man froze, turned, and gave him that questioning look again.

Oh, God, thought Mike. *Oh God, oh God, oh God....*

He felt dizzy and excited and scared, and he quite abruptly realized he was getting hard.

If you don't stop right now....

That was the moment.

That was the second.

Joel was looking at him with those big, stunning brown eyes, and it was like they were the chasm he'd felt earlier—like he could fall into them.

Turn away, he thought. *If you don't turn away….*

But he couldn't. He could *not*. It was already too late.

So he nodded and walked past him and, heart pounding, left the bar and went to the elevator banks—not daring to see if he was being followed. He pressed the button, it lit up, and still he couldn't look. He simply stared at the doors. There was a *ding!* and it wasn't the elevator before him. When he turned to see which one it was, there was Joel, looking as scared and excited as he felt.

Oh God! Am I really doing this?

Mike nodded again and went to the elevator and entered, and Joel was right behind him. Someone called out, "Can you hold that?" and luckily the doors closed before whoever it was could get there. He pressed the button for his floor.

Then he was alone with Joel, and when he looked at him, the young man moaned.

"Oh God…," Joel said. It was like a sigh.

Mike began to shake and realized he still had his drink and—fuck!—he downed it and then stepped toward Joel. Joel took a step. Mike took a step, his heart slamming so hard, it almost hurt.

Joel took a step.

They were so close, they were almost touching. He could smell Joel. Mint and maybe rum and, underneath that, a musky man-smell. He echoed Joel's sigh.

Joel took one more step, and Mike was a breath from panicking. Was Joel going to kiss him? Right here in the elevator?

There was that *ding*! again, and the doors opened. He gulped and moved his head in a way to indicate they should leave the elevator.

God! Was he going to do this? If he didn't stop this *right now*, then the thing he had fought from doing for his entire life… would be done. He needed to stop this. But then the thought came again.

It was already too late.

So he didn't say anything. He walked to his room, heart trip-hammering, and he fumbled for his key—one of those weird credit card-like things—and passed it through the slot and the tiny little *bleep-bleep-bleep* was so loud! Everyone would hear!

Mike pushed into the room and *felt* Joel following, and when he turned, the young man was *right there*.

He was shaking now, visibly, and when he saw *Joel* could see how afraid he was—how stupid and inexperienced he must look!—his face heated in embarrassment and he almost bolted and….

Joel smiled a sweet little smile and took one of those steps. The last step. He reached out and laid a hand gently on Mike's chest and sighed and that was it.

Mike took him in his arms—or did Joel take him in his arms? He would never know. After that it was all sensation and light and power and gasps and a roaring in his ears—and sweat. There was sweat. He kissed a man for the first time, and had he not been in the arms of a very *strong* young man, he might have fallen, legs nearly buckling.

The kiss was so different!

How? Why? Why would it be different?

But it was. God, it was so different. Maybe, partly, it was that slight stubble of beard—he'd never felt anything like that with a woman, now, had he?—and partly it was the strength of that mouth that took his.

But that wasn't all of it....

They were breathing into each other's mouths and taking off their clothes. Mike was wearing his suit, and it was taking fucking forever to get it all off. Joel was wearing a polo shirt that swooshed right off over his head, and his raised arms revealed two patches of hair as thick as that on his head. A man's armpits, no mistaking that. And a strong, rounded chest with more hair, a triangle of it, so soft-looking (begging to be touched) going across from nipple to nipple (they were a lovely dark tan) and down to just below those pectorals. Then it was a smooth, flat, bare tummy, and then more hair swirled around his shallow navel and disappeared into his slacks.

Inviting.

For some crazy reason, Mike thought he would cry at the beauty—God, yes, beauty!—he beheld, and he looked up...

...and Joel was smiling at him and then kissing him.

Mike wasn't sure how they made it to the bed, but their pants had fallen to the floor and then their underwear and then—*God!*—there was Joel's penis again, except this time it was hard and standing so tall, throbbing in need. Somehow they were on the bed, crawling, shimmying, crab-walking back, and holding each other, their hard cocks crushed against each other one second and battling the next. Somehow he kept from having an orgasm. They were kissing, and Joel was doing magic things with his fingers and his hands and his lips and his tongue.

Oh! They were turned so they were head to feet (when had that happened?), and Joel was lying half on his belly. When he took Mike deep into his mouth, it was only Mike's desire to see Joel's cock that kept him from cumming instantly. He desperately pushed at Joel's hip so he rolled slightly onto his side, and there it was—Joel's erection. It throbbed, so alive, and without the slightest hesitation Mike took Joel's cock into his mouth.

It was exhilarating. The feel and the heat and the taste of Joel's cock. Salt and musk and sweet. Soft skin with an iron hardness beneath it, the head felt as smooth as glass against his tongue. Joel was leaking heavily, and Mike almost panicked again (*That's semen! That's man! You've got a cock in your mouth!*), and then he simply surrendered to it and moaned and relished that fluid.

They sucked and thrust, and suddenly Joel was warning him that if he didn't stop!—but Mike only grabbed Joel's impossibly narrow hips and pulled him deep, not even gagging, and Joel was pumping his seed into Mike's mouth in great jets. That pushed Mike over the brink, and he was quite suddenly having the most powerful orgasm of his life. He didn't even know he'd swallowed all Joel had given him until later.

They lay gasping after, using thighs as pillows, and when they could finally talk, it was a great rush of words and stories and explanations. How Mike had wanted this since high school, had almost done it with a boy who looked at him all the time (like Joel had looked at him), and then the boy got beat up, bad, in the shower in the school locker room. They pissed on him after they were done, and then that boy tried to kill himself.

"Can you imagine?" Mike's father had said, clearly disgusted. "The shame he's brought on his family? And now he won't, he *can't*, amount to anything in life. People will *always* know he's a cocksucker. They'll know he got *pissed* on. They'll know he tried to kill himself."

Never amount to anything.

Mike had plans. *Big* plans. He was already, even then, getting ideas for what he could do with his computer.

In college, he met Lori, and she let him know that they were getting married as soon as they graduated. Her family had money. They weren't Fortune 500, but they had *more* than enough, and they wound up investing in their kids—Lori and Mike—and his whole life got away from him.

And it wasn't like he wasn't happy. Not really.

Joel understood. He hadn't been beaten up in high school and he hadn't been pissed on, but the boys knew about him and they called him homo and faggot and fairy. He waited until his freshman year of college to see if they were right—well, he *knew* they were right—and when he finally went to bed with a man (a senior who taught him all kinds of things), that was it. Joel *knew* he was gay and he'd never even tried to be with a girl. When his father found out, Joel was disowned.

"I'm not paying one more cent of your education, you fucking freak!" his father had said. "Thank God your mother is dead or this would kill her!"

Which only made Mike marvel as the months passed and he saw Joel was such a good, kind, *happy* man. Somehow he didn't let his past rule his entire life.

First, though, there was that terrible morning when he woke up in an ocean of guilt. Guilt that he'd cheated on Lori and hadn't even given her a thought before tumbling into bed with Joel.

"We can't do this again," he'd said, and Joel told him he understood. But as the day passed, Mike knew there was no way he could leave things the way they were. He had to be with Joel again. He was. Again and again as the week passed, and then, after that, every time he came back to Kansas City.

Mike knew it was wrong. Not being with a man—nothing had ever felt so right in his entire life—but that he was cheating on his wife. He knew that was reprehensible.

But when he was with Joel, everything was right.

But now? Now it was too late.

Too late to tell Joel that he loved him, more than life itself (and wasn't that thought ironic?). Too late to make amends. To tell Lori. To see if there was any way she could forgive him for cheating—and hadn't that turned out to be ironic as well? She was doing the same thing. Having an affair!

My fault. She cheated because I wasn't the man she needed. I didn't fulfill her. My fault!

But before he could have another thought, before he could reflect any more on what was happening to him, the world turned inside out.

That's just what it was like, what it *felt* like. Falling and exploding outward, and then noise.... Noise.... *Noise!* Pain. Pain *beyond* imagining. And Cold. Metal? Lights! *Blazing* lights. Silhouettes.... *God!* Was this it? Was he going to... the next place?

And...

13

...HE WAS somewhere else.

14

IT WAS some kind of junkyard, and he was lying in the dirt. The pain was gone, thank God, and he sat up and saw he was in the middle of a salvage yard. He was surrounded by a great valley, a canyon of the remains of cars and trucks and SUVs. He lay half in and half out of a row of these remains, looking down a large aisle, and saw there was row upon row of vehicular carcasses. They were perched upon empty wheels, two in front and one behind, and when he went to pull himself to his feet, there was a quick and senseless bolt of fear that he might topple one. But these cars, these remains of cars—stripped as they were of doors and hoods and rearview mirrors and fenders and bumpers and headlights—were still, nonetheless, massive. Thousands of pounds—tons of metal—they wouldn't fall over that easily.

Certainly not for the weight of a ghost.

What in the hell am I doing here? he wondered. And *why* too. Why was he here? He wondered that.

He stood and then, with an unexpected chill, he *saw* why.

The car he had used to help himself to his feet….

It was *the* car. *His* car.

"Oh God," he said with a sob and lurched back away from the thing. There was still dried blood on it.

Oh no! No!

He shut his eyes and swiveled around so that… *thing*… was behind him. He couldn't look at it.

How long? How long had it been? He had somehow lost time…. How much? How long did it take an insurance company to declare a car totaled and then to get it to a place like this?

A graveyard, he thought, and that chill rushed over him again.

A week? A month?

God…. Had he been away for a month?

His eyes flew open and he thought of Joel—alone and grieving—and Lori—feeling guilt for having an affair when that was what he had done! And there wasn't a goddamned thing he could do!

Too late! Too fucking late!

He dropped to his knees and then fell back, and the only reason he didn't go all the way into the dirt again was that he'd come down on a big tire.

So he sat.

He was surrounded by dead metal and dead dreams. There were other things too. Car hoods lying out like platters for a giant, a rearview mirror revealing a cloudy sky through shattered glass, a steering wheel, a kid's pink-and-blue sneaker, a container of suntan lotion, pop bottles, a squashed Red Bull can, a single Lincoln Log, a pair of panties….

Mike sat in a graveyard of dead and empty cars.

Except, they weren't all empty, were they?

There were feet sticking out of an old Ford not ten yards away. Someone picking something out? Finding that part they needed to fix their own car?

But when the man wiggled out from the car, his right arm was missing. It was bloody. He had pale skin, and one of his eyes was filled red with blood. He was still bleeding.

Mike let out a startled cry and almost fell backward off the tire. He scrambled to his feet and backed up against the car (his car... *the* car).

The man looked at him, his eyebrows coming together. "You can *see* me."

Then a woman stepped out from one of the rows. Her head was cocked at an impossible angle, almost level to her shoulder. There wasn't much blood, but it was quite clear to Mike, in his new way of knowing things, that she was dead.

Ghosts. They're ghosts.

She opened her mouth and something came out, but it was hard to tell what. She was trying to talk. The words were garbled, but then—and only because the man without an arm had just said it—Mike came to understand what she had said.

You can see me.

Gooseflesh ran up Mike's arms and the hair stood up on the back of his neck.

Then there was another. And another. And another.

They came out of the aisles and rows, and he saw they were all dead. An African American man whose body was twisted into a horrid S, a little girl in a blood-drenched Snow White costume, an old woman with a gaping hole in the middle of her chest, a boy wearing nothing but dirty underwear and one pink-and-blue shoe.

"You can see me," they said.

Not us. They didn't say, "You can see us." In fact... it seemed as if none of them could see each other at all.

"Can't you see each other?" he cried. "So many of you? Can't you *see* each other?"

They came in close and tight, jostling one another, but seemingly totally unaware they were elbowing one another aside, nudging, bumping heads, crowding in.

"How can you not see each other?" he shouted.

A few of them looked around curiously, then back at him—trying to understand, maybe.

"You're *all* dead!"

Now there was a host of expressions: confusion, surprise, anger, shock, and incomprehension.

"What'd you say?" said the black man with a jaw that wasn't moving the way it should. "What're you sayin'?"

"You're dead," Mike said, trying to back up more but totally unable to. The car was one of those immovable objects—not that it wouldn't have been had he been corporeal.

"Dead? I ain't dead!"

"*Look* at yourself," Mike all but howled. "*Look* at yourself! No one can get their body like that."

The man looked down at himself, and a shocked expression spread over his face. "Oh… oh Christ! Oh dear God!"

"You need to move on!" Mike cried. "You're *supposed* to move on! *All* of you."

The black man looked scared now—in fact, several of them did.

"What?" said the black man. "I need to what? Help me!"

Mike shuddered and wanted to scream. He wanted to cover his eyes—he wanted to gouge them out—but he could barely move. "You've got to go, you've got to move on…."

"Move on where?" the man cried.

"Haven't you lost someone?" Mike asked in a frantic desperation. "Someone you love? A wife? A boyfriend? A mom? A dad?"

"Mamma?" he asked, and a tear began to run down his cheek.

I'm making people cry again. That's all I do. Make people cry.

Mike pushed the thought away. "Did she die?"

"Y-Yeah," he said.

"How?"

"She died when I was a boy. She died having my brother."

"C-Can you remember her?"

The man paused. Fell back a half step. "Y-Yuh." So horrible watching that broken jaw try to make the words….

"See her," Mike said. "*See* her! *Remember* her."

"See her?"

Mike nodded vigorously. "*See* her. Think of her. You're dead. Now you can finally be with her…."

All this while the others crowded close, unable to see one another but unable to get closer either. But they were feeling something. Mike could see that!

"*See* her," Mike said again.

The black man paused, his focus going distant, and….

A light played over his features.

"Mamma?" he said, and then exclaimed. "Mamma!"

And then just like that, he grew bright… and then just winked out.

He was gone.

The others pushed in to take his place.

And one by one, he told them… helped them….

Told them to remember their wives and husbands and mommies and daddies and sisters and cousins. And one by one, they went away.

15

MIKE HAD no idea how long it took. They kept coming even after the crowd was gone. It went into the night and through the next day, although not as urgent. Not as heavy.

One by one, he helped them pass on.

He told the little girl to remember her mommy and her daddy, and then she smiled and it was glorious and she was... gone....

He helped a nun recall her sister, her real sister and not one of the nuns at the convent. She cried when she realized she was dead—had died in a van belonging to her convent, along with several sisters. Then she slowly finished with her tears, and not long after that, she was smiling and calling out to someone named Carol, and she was... well, gone.

Mike helped the boy with one pink-and-blue shoe remember his parents, because he didn't want to think about his uncle who had done things to him and had been doing them when they were hit by a semi.

Bit by bit, ghost by ghost, he helped them go away—to wherever they were supposed to go. And while sometimes Mike saw the people *they* saw, or maybe the white, white light... he had no idea where they *were* going.

And when he had an hour's freedom, he tried to think of someone *he* loved. Someone he could go to. Someone who might be waiting for him.

But in the end, exhausted and worn in a way he'd never dreamed possible, he saw there was only one person he'd ever loved in his entire life.

Joel.

And Joel was alive.

A few more of the dead came to him. Some were more work than others, especially these at the end. Maybe that's why they were last. It had taken them longer to know he was there.

Finally, *finally*, he was done.

Then, all alone and tired beyond any imaginings, he thought of Joel again and....

And then....

—*Swish*—

16

HE WAS with Joel.

Joel was sitting in a chair and reading out loud. It was a romance book, of all things. Why was he reading a romance book?

226 | B.G. Thomas

"My God," Joel read. "And her eyes widened, and the warm color ebbed from her cheeks...."

And then Mike saw something that was the biggest shock of all. Nothing that had happened had prepared him for this.

Joel was reading... to him.

Mike froze, unable to even think.

Joel was reading to *him*. A him who was lying in a hospital bed, surrounded by equipment and tubes and wires and a *beep—beep—beep....*

Mike tripped this time, over his feet, and fell to the floor and looked up (his body was no longer visible) and saw Joel reading.

"That looks ghastly!"

He... he wasn't...? "I'm not dead?" he asked aloud.

"He can't hear you, you know" came a voice, and both Joel and Mike turned to see a nurse standing in the doorway.

"They've proven," Joel said, "that people in comas can hear. I don't want him to be alone."

Coma? I'm in a coma? I'm... I'm alive?

The nurse, a big woman with pale skin, shook her head. "Honey," she said. "He's not *in* a coma."

Wait. What? Not in a coma? Then....

"What the hell is he, then?" Joel was all but shouting.

She sighed. Took a step into the room. "He's *gone*, sweetie. It's only the machines keeping him alive...."

Machines?

Joel was shaking his head. "No...," he whispered.

The nurse came into the room and pulled a chair beside Joel. She laid a hand on his—it quite suddenly reminded Mike of him touching the old lady on the steps of the apartment building.... Rose—and said in a soft, kind voice, "He's brain-dead. Whatever made your... friend... what he is... was... that part of him is gone. It's only the machines keeping him alive."

Oh God, thought Mike. This was worse than anything he could have imagined.

"Please...," Joel said, and once more his eyes filled with tears. "No...."

This was almost too much to bear....

"And as soon as this man's wife can think straight, she's going to—for your friend's sake, at least—she going to let them turn the machines off...."

"No!" Joel shouted. "No!"

And Mike wanted to scream. He wanted to scream just so he couldn't hear the woman!

Machines keeping me alive?

Then with a horrid sense of clarity, it all came to him. It made sense, didn't it? The machines. Maybe it was the machines themselves keeping him here... why he couldn't move on like all those other ghosts....

And the pain he'd felt.... They'd been trying to revive him....

The cop—Brookhart—had been wrong. She said she hadn't detected a pulse. But she'd also said she was no doctor....

But it had been too late by then, hadn't it? By the time the ambulance—the EMTs, all of that—got to him, it was too late. Machines were all that was keeping him alive. That part of him that was... well, *him*... it wasn't in his body anymore.

It's me here... standing outside of myself.

God, Mike thought—watching as Joel lowered his face into his upturned palms and sobbed—*I wish I could talk to you one more time. Tell you how sorry I am. Tell you how much I love you. I wish! Oh God, I wish!*

Then Mike had another thought.

Brookhart. The cop. She could hear him! He would go to her. Get her to tell Joel! Yes. Yes! He had to. Had to go to her.... But how?

Mike closed his eyes. Took a deep breath. Think of her. Picture her. See her in your mind. Brookhart.... *Daphne* Brookhart. *Please. I need you.*

He could hear Joel crying, tearing his heart out. Mike's throat seized up. *God... please....*

Daphne Brookhart! Please! Please....!

And just when he thought it wasn't going to work....

—Swish—

17

MIKE WAS standing in... a locker room? He looked around and blanched. Brookhart was in her bra and panties. *Shit!* He looked away, embarrassed—until he realized she couldn't see him.

But that didn't make any difference, did it? Doesn't everyone want their privacy in a situation like this?

No. Fuck that. Sometimes there were more important things to worry about. He turned back around (relieved to see she had her uniform blouse almost completely buttoned) and walked up to her like he'd been doing this for years.

"Brookhart," he shouted.

She reeled back, arms pin-wheeling, and crashed against the lockers. "What the fuck?" She looked around her, wide-eyed and now alert. "Who's there?"

Mike steeled himself for the insane. "Detective Brookhart," he said in a much softer, but still firm, voice. "Can you hear me?"

Her eyebrows lifted so high, they seemed to want to disappear under her curled bangs. "My God," she said with a gasp.

"You can," he replied in relief. "You can hear me."

Those brows came together, eyes flashing. "Who is this? Townsend? Is this a trick?"

Mike shook his head, then chuckled under his breath. She couldn't *see* him. "No. It's not Townsend."

She squinted, looked left, right....

"I'm here in front of you."

Her hand shot out, slashing back and forth. It was most disconcerting when that hand passed right through him.

"I think you better sit down," Mike said.

She did. Heavily. "What's going on?" she asked in a whisper.

He sat next to her, and when he spoke—"This is going to be hard to believe"— her head swiveled quickly in his direction. She really could hear him. He wasn't even yelling anymore. "I'm...." Funny. It was still hard to say. Of course, he hadn't been able to actually speak to anyone before, had he? To a living person? Besides a shout or two? "I'm dead, Detective Brookhart."

"Dead," she said. It was a statement and not a question.

"Yes," he confirmed.

"I see." She swallowed. Nodded. Her expression unreadable.

"You don't believe me. I don't blame you...."

"I didn't say that. But here at police headquarters is not the place to be caught talking to myself. Get out of here. Let me get fricking dressed."

He stood, surprised at her willingness to at least play along. "Okay. I'll wait outside."

"You do that," she said grimly.

So he did. He left the locker room, and it was a relief—it was only a matter of time before he saw someone with a lot less clothes than Brookhart. And it wasn't that she was a woman. Or it was. He wasn't upset by female nudity. It was just that this wasn't his place. It was rude. It was wrong, spying like this....

Although it would have been a convenient ability all those times he'd wanted to see a man naked, wouldn't it? He laughed at that.

Mike waited outside the locker room, and when she came out, she whispered from the corner of her mouth. "You here?"

"Yes," he answered. And then so she wouldn't have to say anything else, said, "I'll follow you outside?"

Brookhart gave a nod, and he did just that: followed her. They passed through the station, past desks and the lobby (where two cops were dragging a shouting prisoner inside) and out into the parking lot. She kept going, setting a determined pace, and he found himself amused that he was having trouble keeping up. She got to a car, paused, opened her door, and then asked, "Can you get in?"

And just like that, he was inside, on the passenger side. It startled him, and just as she was asking again, he called out, "Yes. I'm inside already." *Not sure how, though.* Seemed he was getting better at the "swish" thing.

She climbed into the car and started it, put on her seat belt, adjusted her mirror, looked, and pulled out of her parking space. "Are you Mike Ellsworth?"

He gasped. "H-How did you know?"

A small smile crept to her lips, and she gave a tiny nod. "I don't know. I just did. You're Joel Kauffman's lover."

He stiffened, then relaxed. "I—I am." First time he'd ever said it. And it was as a ghost. To a cop.

"Last week—you told me to tell him that you loved him."

He nodded, realized once more that she couldn't see him, and answered, "Yes. I did."

"I didn't appreciate the way you did that."

"Sorry. I'm new at this. I've only been... dead... a week? Is that what you said?" He'd lost a week?

"Yes."

"Damn. Something happened to time...."

Brookhart stopped the car at a red light and then actually turned in his direction. "All kinds of weird shit is happening."

"Tell me about it," he said, thinking of dying and teleporting and old women and bright light and ghost-filled salvage yards.

"You know you're not dead, right? I mean, I thought you were. That's what I told your lover. Joel. Sweet kid. But then I found out that they'd revived you. Had you on machines...." There was a honk behind her, and she glared into her rearview mirror. Started the car up again. "I called him right away when I found out they revived you. Surprised the shit out of me. No doctor, but damn. Now I wish I hadn't told your friend. He's been at the hospital all week, talking to you, reading to you, telling you jokes."

Mike closed his eyes, rubbed at them, and fought back a sudden sob.

"You're not dead and... you *are.*"

"Yes," he managed. "Those machines... the ones that are keeping my body alive. I think they're...." He paused, grasping for the words for something there really were no words for. A science they didn't teach in school or on anything except horror movies and maybe that silly show *Ghost Hunters*.

"Is that how you're here? The machines are keeping you... anchored somehow?"

"Yes!" he said. That was it. "I think so. How are you taking this so calmly?"

She shook her head and gave a sigh. "Weird things have been happening to me lately. I've seen some *weird* fucking shit. Shit you wouldn't *believe*...." She laughed. "Then again, you might."

"Tell me about *that*," he replied. "I saw an old dead lady, and after we talked, she went into this light to be with her husband. Then I was in a salvage yard, and there were more ghosts. Lots of them. All crowding around me. I thought I would go crazy. Hell. Maybe I *am* crazy."

"I can imagine...."

"Can you?" he asked.

"Like I said... I've seen some crazy shit. Would you believe voodoo gods?"

"Really?" Mike said. Voodoo gods? Really? But who was he to question?

"What happened then?" she asked. "To those ghosts."

"I helped them," he said, and shuddered. "Helped them see they were dead. Then one by one, they... went away."

"I see. Well...." She laughed again. "I don't see *any*thing."

"I wish there were some things I couldn't see. Like Joel crying in the hospital. It was horrible. And my wife?" He let out a laugh. "I've been feeling so guilty for what I've been doing with Joel, and yet the happiest I've ever been in my...." He almost said "life." He went on. "Guess what? She's having an affair! And from what I've been able to figure out, I think we both started cheating at the same time." He shook his head. "Quite a pair, my wife and I, huh, Brookhart?"

"Daphne. If you're going to talk to me from beyond, then at least call me by my first name."

"If you'll call me Mike."

"Why the hell not?" She shook her head.

"I'd shake your hand but...," Mike said.

"Yeah. Except it wouldn't work?"

"Not that I've been able to figure out."

They drove for a while in silence, and then she asked, "You still there, Mike, old boy?"

"Yeah," he said. "Still here."

"Why *are* you here?" she said. "With me, that is? Why'd you come to *me*?"

"Because you're the only one who can hear me," he exclaimed. "Why is that? *How* can you hear me?"

She shrugged. "Don't know. Maybe seeing flaming voodoo shit did something to me."

"I'm just glad you can," Mike said.

"Can't say I agree with you, Mikie."

He sighed. He hated to be called "Mikie," but somehow, right now that seemed to be the last thing in the world he needed to worry about. What was that popular book a few years ago? *Don't Sweat the Small Stuff*? And a nickname really was small stuff, wasn't it?

"What do you want? Is it just to chat? Because I'm betting it's something else."

His breath caught, and he let it out slowly. "Yeah. Something else."

"You want me to talk to Joel, don't you?" She flashed him a look—even if she couldn't see him.

"Yes," he said. "Please. I'll go away then. At least from you. I promise. Help me out, and I'll never bother you again."

She rolled her eyes. "Do you really think it's a good idea for me to talk to him? Couldn't it make things worse? And how do you know he will even believe me?"

Mike bit his lip. Hard. He barely felt it. "I don't see how it could be much worse. And wouldn't you want to hear from someone who... well... died? Someone you loved?" It was certainly clear now how much Joel loved him. He didn't deserve such love. *No. Don't think about that.* "You ever have any unfinished business you wish you would have taken care of?"

She gave a slight jolt, her hands gripping the steering wheel, then relaxing. She was quiet for a long moment, and just as Mike was about to say something, she finally did. "My sister. She died. We'd been fighting. *Bad* fighting, Mikie. She called me some... names. I called her some back. Then she... she died."

Were Brookhart's eyes getting wet? Cast-iron Brookhart? Was he making *her* cry? The powers of being a ghost!

"I always wished I could'a said I was sorry. Wished I could have told her...."

"I'll bet she knew," Mike said.

"How do you know that?" she snapped.

"Things are... different here," he tried to explain. "Perceptions. If she didn't just go directly to wherever we're supposed to go, if she hung around, I'm sure she was trying to tell you she loved you."

She stiffened again, relaxed. "You think?"

"I do."

"She—she isn't hanging around now, is she?"

"No," Mike said. "I don't think so. There's no one hanging around you that I see...."

Brookhart let out a long sigh.

"Look," Mike said. "I need to tell Joel something. He'll believe you. But I *have* to tell him. And I have to tell Lori something too."

She shot him a look, then got a frustrated expression on her face. "This hearing you and not *seeing* you sucks!"

"Believe me, I understand. Seeing people but them not being able to hear me sucks pretty bad too."

She let out another long sigh. "I can't believe I'm doing this…."

Mike sat up straight. "You'll do it?"

"Do I really have a choice? I mean, if'n I don't want to worry about you showing up in the ladies' locker room again. Did you see anything, Mikie? Get your jollies?"

Mike laughed. "Not hardly!"

Now she was laughing. "I know. I'm too skinny. That's what Townsend tells me all the time."

"Townsend's fat," he replied. "And that's not it. You're fine for a…. I'm gay, Brookhart…. Daphne." He'd done it. Really done it. Said he was gay out loud. And she was the only person on earth who could hear him.

"Thank God. It's the only reason I'm not squicking out myself."

"Squicking?"

"Never mind."

"So you'll do it?" Mike asked, trying not to squeak like a little girl.

"Like I said, it's that or worry about you showing up when I'm showering."

And he was so excited, the "swish" thing happened, and he was there, right there, with Joel.

18

JOEL WAS slumped back in a chair. Asleep? Where? Mike looked around him.

A waiting room. *He's not in my room.* He looked back at his lover. His beautiful lover.

He was lying back, head resting, and it took a moment for Mike to figure out if he was indeed asleep or not. But then Joel shifted and sat up just enough for him to see the puffy, red eyes.

Mike wanted to throw himself on his knees before him, beg him to be able to hear. Hear in his voice. Hear how much he adored him. How he didn't know if he could keep…. Keep what? Living? Keep living without him? Well, that wasn't right, was it?

He went to Joel anyway. He did get down on his knees. He reached out and touched his hands, with those veins on their backs, the light spattering of hair, those perfectly trimmed nails. It didn't matter that he couldn't feel the soft skin, the silky hair, the *warmth* of him. Didn't matter that he was like a bronze statue. He *had* to touch him.

"I love you, Joel. I love you more than... more than anything."

Joel sighed. "I love you, Mike."

Mike started, looking up into those beautiful brown eyes. Had Joel heard him? But they were staring blindly, and Mike figured it was far more likely that Joel was just saying the words. Words that both warmed and hurt his heart.

If only he had said it. Done something about it! Told Lori a thousand years ago why he wasn't the lover she deserved. Was it why she had sought out a lover herself? Had she needed someone to love her and make love to her the way he had needed?

Was he a piece of cheating shit?

Or maybe... maybe he was just human? Or at least he had been?

Well, now he had a chance. If not for him, at least for Joel.

For Lori. To give his blessing?

That's when she arrived. She cleared her throat.

Both Mike and Joel looked up.

But it wasn't Detective Brookhart.

It was Lori.

She looked stunning. Of course. Every hair in its place. The dress was a dark blue instead of the bright colors she usually wore this time of year. Appropriate. Her makeup was perfect too, wasn't it?

No. Wait. It wasn't. It was smeared around her eyes. She'd been crying.

"Excuse me," she said. "I'm...."

Joel looked like he might bolt.

She held up a hand. "No," she said. "It's okay. May I sit?"

Joel trembled, then nodded. "S-Sure."

She did, like a lady, folding her hands over her lap so the skirt wouldn't ride too high. Joel looked at her, his eyes filled with, perhaps, the very questions on Mike's lips. "I'm Lori Ellsworth."

"I—I know who you are." He glanced away, trembling.

Mike felt like he was dying. Crazy.

"And you are?"

Mike looked back at her.

"I'm Joel."

"Joel?"

"Joel Kauffman."

"Any relation to the—"

"N-no," he said. "God decided to.... To g-give me to the...." He stopped, unable to finish his old joke. "Not related."

"So...," she continued. "I.... You're the young man who's been sitting with Mike?"

"I... what? Why would...."

"You *are* the young man who's been sitting with Mike." This time there was no question in her voice. "One of the nurses. She told me how you sit with him for hours. You read to him."

Joel sat up. "I...." His voice caught, full and thick. He coughed. Cleared his throat. "Yes."

It was surreal. Watching. Not being able to add to the conversation. Once again feeling like a voyeur. Like he was some kind of Peeping Tom. Spying on them. He should leave. But how could he? How the hell could he?

"They asked me if you were his brother," Lori said. "Mike doesn't have a brother."

"N-no," Joel said.

She gave a nod, looked down at her hands, then up at him. "The nurse said Mike was.... She said she thought *you* were his... friend."

Joel swallowed and nodded back. "I—" His voice caught again. "I am."

Lori wet her lips with her tongue. "We've never met."

Joel shook his head. "I live here in Kansas City. We met in one of his classes."

She bobbed her head once. "I see. And you've known him for how long?"

"A year," he said. "We got to know each other about a year ago."

"In a class," she replied.

"Yes."

"He's your... you two are close?"

Joel nodded stiffly and gripped the arms of his chair.

God. He was a terrible liar. But that was one of the many things Mike loved about Joel. He was the definition of honest. Honest people made terrible liars.

"Mike never mentioned you."

"Oh?" Joel said, his voice cracking.

She shook her head. "No."

"Hmmmm.... He talked about you a lot. Told me you were beautiful."

Lori's throat made a funny little sound. Not a gasp. Not a sigh. Something in between?

"Perfect is what he said. He was right. You are. Perfect."

"Mike said *that*?"

"Yes," Joel said. He sat up taller, and Mike heard Joel's back pop. Waiting room chairs. Torture devices. Mike had sat in one or two. He could imagine how

Joel's back must hurt, and he longed to rub it. But he couldn't, of course. Couldn't comfort him in any way. And there was Lori, of course. Just what was she doing? Why was she talking to Joel?

But a part of him knew. *Friend*. The way she said it. The way the nurse had said it.

"Do you want to get some coffee, Joel?"

"Coffee?"

"Or how about something a whole lot stronger?"

Joel trembled again. "I think that sounds good."

Lori stood. Perfection.

Joel stood. Beauty.

"I saw a little bar just kitty-corner across the way."

"Okay," he said. And they turned and left.

Mike stood. *No! Wait!* Brookhart would be here any minute.

But they were gone.

Mike decided to wait. As much as he wanted to hear what Lori and Joel would be talking about, he needed to wait. He had to get Brookhart to them. At least he knew where they would be.

He turned back to the chair and almost sat on a woman who hadn't been there before. She was covered in bandages, and he couldn't imagine why she had been let out of her room....

Mike gave a soft moan.

Oh God. She's dead. Of course she is. I'm in a hospital. The place would be filled with ghosts, wouldn't it?

He looked up, looked around the room.

There were more of them now. Bloody, broken, hobbling, shuffling.... An African American man, his white shirt bright with blood; an old man, half dragging a broken leg; a woman walking and pulling an IV pole behind her like a reluctant dog on a leash. She looked familiar.

It hit him. He'd seen her (a week ago?) on the street when all of this had first happened.

Dead! They're all dead!

And if they realize I can see them!

That's when he saw Brookhart. He was at her side so fast, he thought it might have done his "swish" thing. "We have to get out of here."

Brookhart jumped. "Dammit," she hissed. "You have to stop fucking doing that!"

"Sorry. But *I* have to get out of here. The dead, Daphne. They're everywhere. If they know that I can see them...."

She nodded. "But what about Joel?"

"He's with Lori—"

"Oh, boy…. He's with your wife?"

"They went for a drink. Across the street."

She nodded. "I know the place. A lot of their customers wind up here. Let's—"

Mike didn't hear the rest of what she was saying. He was already in the bar.

19

THE TWO of them were standing at the bar, Lori waving for the bartender. In charge, of course. "What do you want?" she asked.

"I—I don't know…."

She clenched her jaw. It was subtle. If Mike hadn't known her for years, he wasn't sure he would have seen it. "What would you get if you were here with Mike?"

"A rum and coke," Joel said.

She turned to the bartender. "A rum and coke for my fr—"

"Johnnie Walker Black," Joel said.

Lori flashed him a look. Interesting. Her expression almost slipping. It didn't take knowing her for years to see that one. "Want to up the game?"

"Excuse me?"

"Live a little? How about getting something better instead?"

Joel got an almost hurt expression on his face. "Johnnie Walker Black isn't good?"

Then Lori surprised Mike again. She smiled. "Sure it is," she assured Joel. She'd done what Mike had seen her do hundreds of times: read Joel's face like a book. "Mike loved the Black. But when the mood struck, he'd get something even better, okay?" She looked back at the bartender. "What do you have in a really good whisky?"

The bartender told her.

She nodded. "That sounds wonderful. Two," she said. Then looked back at Joel. "Doubles?"

"What the hell, live a little," he said, and his voice caught.

What I always said, Mike thought.

"Mike says that a lot," Lori said.

Joel agreed.

The bartender handed them their glasses, and Lori paid, along with a generous tip. The bartender raised his brows. "Thank you, ma'am."

Lori ushered them to a corner table. There was only one other customer this time of day, but she was in business mode. Mike saw that clearly. She didn't let people know her business.

They sat. For a long moment, neither said a word. Mike could see Joel was waiting for her.

She held up her glass. "To Mike."

Joel held up his. "To Mike."

They drank, and Joel's first swallow surprised Mike. Barely a wince. And it was a good swallow. Then again, it was really good whisky.

Mike found himself suddenly craving a taste of the whisky himself. He realized it was the first time since all of this had happened that he'd wanted anything to eat or drink. But now? Now he could use a drink. Could almost taste it. Smooth, woody, smoky....

He sat next to Joel. Put his arm around the back of the chair. Anything to feel close. When he looked over at his wife, though, he felt funny. Like he was flaunting his love for someone else. It didn't matter that she couldn't see him. It didn't even matter that *she* had someone else. This "wrongness" and "rightness" at the same time had been a source of anxiety from the very beginning. If only he'd had the courage to be a bridge-builder. To be out from the beginning.

But then he would never have had met Joel, would he?

"Are you in love with Mike?" Lori asked quite suddenly. Mike all but gasped. Joel did. It was not the subtle touch she usually used, but sometimes she just went for the kill.

Joel just looked at her, mouth half open.

"Oh, come on, Joel. We're both adults here. I can see it on your face. I can see it in your eyes. The nurse was hinting all about it. 'Friend.' Please!" She took a good drink of her whisky.

"I—I...."

"It's okay, really." She reached out and uncharacteristically touched his hand. This was not one of her "we're all friends here" touches that she would use to good effect in business. This looked truly sincere.

"What?" Joel asked, clearly confused.

"You're gay, aren't you?"

He nodded. Joel was not one to deny himself.

"And you're in love with Mike. As far as you're concerned, it's love." Again, not a question. "If Mike and I weren't married, you would want to be with him."

Joel sat up straight in his chair. Raised his head high. "If he would have me, yes. In a minute. But he *is* married to you."

"Was," she said with a sigh and took another drink. It was enough to finish her glass, and she waved the bartender over. "You too?"

"What the hell."

She raised two fingers, and the glasses were set before them in an instant's time. The power of a big tip.

"That's good," she said when the bartender left. "That you love him. Mike deserved to be loved. I've never given him what I should have. I've felt guilty about that through the years. The things is, I don't think I had it in me. To love."

Mike's mouth dropped open. *What?*

"My parents taught me through their 'unlove' that practicality is what mattered. And until…" She paused. "…recently, I didn't think I was really capable of love."

Greg, Mike thought. *Greg!*

"The question is, did Mike love you back?"

Mike held his breath—a purely unnecessary act, of course, but he had a lifetime's habit behind him, even if he wasn't alive anymore.

"Lori, I don't speak for Mike."

"And Mike *isn't* speaking. In fact, his doctors are trying to tell me to turn the machines off—"

"No!" Joel said, nearly knocking his glass over. He froze, then slowly relaxed. "Please Lori. Can you wait? Just a little longer…?"

She didn't move. Didn't say anything for what felt a very long time. "You really do love him."

"More than I've ever loved anyone in my life."

"And you won't tell me if Mike loved you."

Joel took another big swallow of his whiskey. He grimaced for a moment.

"Careful, slugger," she said.

"Lori, did Mike *ever* tell you that he loved *you*?"

"No," she admitted. "Well. Maybe a few times in the beginning." She looked away for a moment—but as if to somewhere else. Into another time, perhaps? "Maybe." She shrugged. "It was really never about that for either of us. We loved each other in our own way."

Joel didn't say anything.

"So he never told you he loved you?" she asked.

Mike felt the tears coming on. He was such a fucking idiot. *Why didn't I tell him?*

Joel shook his head. It was an answer. Did it answer her unasked question? Lori wasn't stupid.

"Did you sleep with Mike?"

And she'd done it! She'd asked! Joel's eyes went wide and he sat back. God! Now what?

"I believe I can answer that question."

They all turned.

It was Detective Brookhart.

20

JOEL RECOGNIZED her, of course, and Mike saw that Lori did too. But she would, wouldn't she? She was the one who had called Lori. They must have met when he lost that week....

They asked her to sit, and again, Mike could see Lori didn't want her to. That's what the years had done. They could read each other easier than any book. They even had a language of sorts. Could express essays in a glance. They were a team, if not the most loving of couples.

"How can we help you?" Lori asked.

Brookhart looked decidedly uncomfortable. Whatever cop-face she might have developed through the years—and Mike imagined all cops must have that skill—it wasn't present this afternoon. "Well.... It's like I said." She coughed. Cleared her throat. "I think I can help you."

"And how is that?" Lori asked.

"Well, you wanted to know if your husband was sleeping with Joel."

Joel jumped. "Detective Brookhart!"

Lori was nodding. "Yes. I did want to know."

"Detective...," Joel moaned.

"It's all right, Joel." Brookhart turned back to Lori. "I can answer all kinds of questions."

"You can, hmmm?" Lori raised a carefully plucked right eyebrow.

"Ask me something," Brookhart said. "But ask me something that only Mike... Mr. Ellsworth would know."

"Are we playing a game, Detective?"

"Sure. A game. Ask."

"All right, then," she said. "What's the combination to the safe?"

"Mike?" Brookhart said.

And Mike gaped at her. She really was jumping into this. No messing around.

"*Mike?*" Lori asked.

"Our anniversary," Mike said.

"But then I don't know your anniversary, do I?" Brookhart asked while Lori came close to losing her composure.

"June 16, 1997," Mike said.

Brookhart repeated the date. "So I assume the combination is 6, 16, 97?"

Lori's mouth all but fell open. Then her control took over. "Good guess. Tell me something else."

"You need to ask," Brookhart said, and leaned on the table.

Lori narrowed her eyes. "What did my father say when Mike asked for my hand?"

Mike sighed and told Daphne the unromantic answer.

"Really?" Brookhart asked. "Harlequin Romance that is not."

"Who are you talking to?" Lori asked.

Joel said nothing. He just sat there. Pale. Almost unmoving.

"Really," Mike confirmed.

"Your father said that he thought he could approve. It would be good business. And that you both had good genes, and that even though your children wouldn't continue his name, as far as he was concerned, everyone would know they were of Pitcairn blood."

Lori's hand shot out and knocked her half-full glass to the floor with a crash of broken glass. She didn't even seem to notice. "How the fuck did you know that?"

Fuck, thought Mike in surprise. Imagine. Lori saying "fuck." He wasn't sure if he could count on one hand the times she'd used the word.

"Well, I'm glad you're both sitting down. The reason I knew...." She paused. Mike could see her steeling herself for this. "It's because Mike is here with us now. And I can hear him."

"What?" cried Joel.

"Bullshit!" Lori cried in turn.

"Seriously," Brookhart said. "You don't think I know how crazy it sounds? How crazy it is? In fact, until I was able to answer your questions, I wasn't entirely sure I hadn't lost my mind." She lounged back in her chair. "It's a goddamned relief, is what it is."

"You expect me to believe this?" Lori demanded.

"Mrs. Ellsworth. What do I have to gain with this? Besides maybe getting my ass in hot water? I didn't want to do this. Your husband begged me."

"I didn't beg," Mike said.

"Oh, you begged, all right, Mikie boy."

"Mike hates that nickname," Lori snapped.

"He does?" Then glancing to her side. "Do you hate that nickname, Mike? You should have told me."

"Yes," Mike admitted. "Never did like it."

"Then why didn't you tell me?"

"Stop it!" Joel said with a groan. "This is crazy."

She looked over at Joel. "You, sweetie, are the main reason I'm here."

"Me?" Joel had gone dreadfully pale.

"You," Brookhart confirmed.

"Why me?" Joel asked.

"We'll get to that in a minute." She looked back at Lori. "Ask me something else."

"No. You tell me something. You tell me something that you couldn't know."

Brookhart sighed. "Mike?"

Mike thought about it a moment. "Tell her, yes, that I am having an affair with Joel."

She told Lori.

Lori nodded. He was relieved she didn't jump on what Brookhart said. She let it go. She only nodded. Then she looked at Joel. She actually gave him a half smile. "I thought so." As if she believed Brookhart was talking to a... ghost? To whatever he was.

"And tell her that she needs to tell Greg that she loves him."

Brookhart looked back his way, again—even though she couldn't see him. "You sure?"

"I'm sure," he said, determined.

Brookhart sighed. "Mike says you need to tell Greg you love him."

Lori's mouth fell open.

"Tell her she deserves love."

"He says you deserve love."

"Tell her that I'm sorry that I cheated on her, and I should have been honest from the beginning."

Brookhart told her.

"But then, you *were* cheating on me."

Brookhart told her, and that's when Lori lost it. Lost it for *her*, anyway. Tears ran down her cheeks. "Mike?"

"He's really here?" Joel asked. He was crying too.

Actually, it looked like Brookhart's eyes were wet as well.

"Y-Yes," she told Joel.

Mike told her what to say next. He was crying too, of course. Openly. And why not? Only Brookhart could hear him.

"Joel. He says for me to tell you that he loves you. That he's sorry that he never said it. That he couldn't even text you the little heart symbol. He says he is sorry that he was texting and driving, and that he should have listened to you. He said that he's sorry that he didn't cherish you like he should have. That he kept you a secret. He said he wished that he could salvage everything. And that if he'd only told Lori"—Brookhart nodded at Mike's wife—"then they could have parted amicably, and she could have been with Greg and that he—Mike, that is—could have been with you. He's sorry for all of that, and he will love you until the end. The end of whatever comes."

And then they were all crying—even if Brookhart was doing the best at not losing it—all four of them.

There were more questions after that. And Mike answered them. But then something very peculiar began to happen.

Mike began to feel… drunk. He found himself drifting like he hadn't since this all began. The voices of his loved ones—of Lori, of Joel, the voice of a cop going beyond the call of duty—began to fade. It was growing harder and harder to hear.

My God, he thought. Was this it?

No! Not now!

But that anger didn't seem to make any difference.

"God! Brookhart!"

The detective jumped. "Mike?"

"I'm…. God… I'm fading!"

He felt like he was swimming. The bar dissolved away. It grew dark, then shockingly bright.

The light? he wondered. Had he done what he was supposed to do? Was that what had really been holding him here? Was he going on…?

21

HE WAS on a city street again. A familiar street. The very place he had died. The traffic wasn't as heavy. It was afternoon—after the lunch break and before rush hour—and look there! That driver was texting and driving. Mike wanted to scream at him, tell him to stop before he got himself killed.

Was this last text worth your life? Share this if you agree! Don't text and drive!

And look…. Across the street. The woman with the IV pole, dragging it behind her, banging and wobbling and probably the only thing keeping it from keeling over was that it wasn't real.

And then….

"It's you."

Mike jerked around and looked. Who should it be? Why, the girl wearing a Siouxsie and the Banshees T-shirt. She was just as pale, the blood from the gash on her head flowing just as freely. But now there was something more. The blood in her lap. It was spreading.

He stepped back.

"No," she said. "Please."

"What do you want?" As if he didn't know. He wiped the tears—still wet— from his face.

"I've heard about you. That you can help us. Help the dead."

"I—I…. Sometimes." He took another step back and stopped himself. She had heard about him? How? Then something else occurred to him. "Wait. You know you're dead."

"Fuck, yes," said the girl. "Known it for a long, long time."

Mike shook his head, confused. "But that's how I help. I tell them they're dead. They don't know, you see. It's like they say in those horror movies. They don't know they're dead, and when I help them see it, they go on."

She shook her head, which only made the wide gash on her head bleed all the more. "No. Not *all* ghosts. Some of us *do* know. But some of us can't rest until something has been done."

"Done?" he asked.

"You know. *Just* like in the movies. I was murdered. And no one knows it. They never found my body. They don't even know I'm dead. I've probably been on the back of a milk carton, if my parents ever even told anybody I was gone."

Mike found himself needing to sit again. Instead, he leaned against a light pole. "You were murdered?"

"By a trick," she said. "A john."

"You were…."

"I was selling myself," she snarled. "Get over it. I had to. You do what you have to do."

"And you want me to…?"

"I need someone to know. To find my body. When they find my body, I can rest. I can die. *Really* die."

"And you think if I see it… your body… then you can move on?"

"It don't hurt to try," she said.

True. It didn't hurt to try.

"Where?"

"Funny you should ask," she replied. "Not far. Not far from here at all." She reached out to him.

"You want me to…."

"Just take my hand, mister. And we'll go together."

So he did.

And….

—Swish—

22

THEY WERE standing outside an old building that looked a lot like a brownstone.

Mike looked at her and she nodded. "This is the place," she told him. "He buried me in the backyard. But he keeps my finger in his bedroom."

"Christ," Mike said.

"Tell me about it," she replied.

A second later, they were moving—*swishing*—and they were in a bedroom. She pointed and he looked.

There on the headboard—it was the old type, with a couple of shelves and two little cabinets on either side—lying right out in the open, was a finger. Except there were lots of fingers. They were dried. Mummified, somehow. But they still smelled. Sweet and something more. Like gasoline.

"God…," Mike said, and tried not to puke.

Could he puke?

"See?"

"B-But which one is yours?" he asked.

"The one with the snake ring." She held up her hand. "See?" Her middle finger was missing. How had he not seen that before?

So he looked. He looked at a good dozen or more mummified fingers, and yes, one of them had a snake ring.

"I see it." He turned back to her.

She looked up at him. Waiting.

"Well?" he asked.

A look of total grief spread over her face. "Fuck…," she cried. "Nothing's happening. You're not fucking enough! I must need someone *alive* to find it. To find me! Now I'll never get out of here! I'm stuck forever."

But then Mike thought of something.

Maybe he could help.

23

WHEN MIKE went to Brookhart, she was sitting in the waiting room of the hospital. "Daphne?" He didn't yell at her. He kept his voice down.

She flinched only the barest amount. "Mike?" she asked, sitting up.

"Yup," he replied.

"God. We thought you were gone." She seemed genuinely happy to hear him.

"Not yet."

"Well, I better go tell them. They're both in there, making the decision to pull the plug."

"Pull the plug?"

"You know, buddy. Turn off the switch. The machines keeping you alive." She stood and started for his room.

And Lori was letting Joel help make the decision? Simply incredible.

Then he made a decision of his own. He made it fast.

"No."

She stopped. "No?"

"No." Determined.

She turned around. "You sure, Mikie?" she asked, forgetting or not caring that he didn't like the nickname, and that people were looking at her talking to seemingly no one. But then, it was a hospital. All kinds of things happened in hospitals.

"I'm sure, Daphne."

"Why, Mike?"

He sucked in a shuddering breath, quite certain he might cry again. Him. Who before all this happened hadn't cried in… well, he couldn't remember when. "Because I've done almost everything I'm supposed to do. I've told Lori I know she's having an affair and that I'm happy for her—I wish her the best. She can take my money and not only be the killer in business she is, but she can also have someone who loves her."

Mike stepped closer to Brookhart. To Daphne. A woman he felt, strangely, was his friend. "I finally told Joel that I love him. Now the *only* thing *else* I want him to know is that he needs to move on. Find love. Find someone who will shout their love for him from the rooftops. Can you—will you tell him that?"

She wiped at her eyes. "Y-Yes, Mike."

"And now there's only one last thing."

"Okay. What's that, Mike? Tell me."

24

MIKE SAW it all. It couldn't have gone better. Not for anything. He thought later that if it had happened in a book, people would have said it was too happy an ending. Corny, maybe. But hell, that didn't mean things like that *didn't* happen in real life, right?

Brookhart's partner went along. She wanted to make sure she didn't do anything wrong—anything that could get her into trouble. Townsend would make sure of that. He liked to get the bad guy. And he wanted to make sure the bad guy didn't get away because of some stupid, bumbling mistake.

They didn't have a search warrant, of course. How would they have gotten one? Excuse me, judge, but a ghost told me that one Wayne Jeffries has killed at least a dozen people—one of them a seventeen-year-old girl who he buried in his back yard? Sure!

But they could ask questions.

Mike was right there.

Brookhart knocked on the door of the old brownstone. There was no doorbell, just a hole where one had once been. A moment later, it was answered by someone right out of a George Romero movie. Or maybe that guy who played Lurch in the early nineties movie remake of *The Addams Family* instead.

He was tall, balding, with stringy, greasy hair on the sides. He had deep circles under his eyes. He looked like he was sixty if he was a day. And there was something wrong with him. Something besides the fact that he was a killer. A jaundiced color to his skin.

He's sick, thought Mike. *Really sick.* Disease *sick.*

He turned to Siouxsie-and-the-Banshees-Girl (who turned out to have the very real name Kelly). "You went home with *him*?"

She rolled her eyes. "Mikie, baby…."

"Don't call me that!"

"You let *her* call you that," she barked.

"She's tougher than you."

"Please! I could…."

"Would you two shut the *fuck* up," Brookhart growled.

Two? Mike thought. *She can hear us both now?*

"Two? What are you talking about," Townsend asked, looking meaner than ever.

That was when the guy from *The Addams Family* had answered the door.

"Mr. Jeffries?" Brookhart said.

He stood there, not saying a word.

"Is that your name?" she asked.

"Yes," he said in a gravelly voice.

"I was wondering if I might ask you a question about a girl named Kelly McCarthy—"

He ran. He threw the contents of his mug of beer at them and ran into the apartment. Which, of course, gave them probable cause.

Detectives Brookhart and Townsend entered, guns raised. Wayne Jeffries shot first.

Thankfully, he missed. Mike wasn't sure what he would have done had Daphne been hit. It wasn't clear who shot Jeffries first. Both Brookhart and Townsend fired, and by the time they were done, he wasn't going anywhere.

They found the fingers.

And seconds later, a girl named Kelly McCarthy, who was a very big fan of Siouxsie and the Banshees (thank goodness—she'd had to wear that T-shirt for a very long time) began to fade.

She smiled. She leaped at Mike and she kissed his cheek and then she was gone....

His heart leaped as well, and he turned to Brookhart (who couldn't see him) and he didn't even try to stop the tears.

"Thank you," he said.

That's when he saw the light.

"Oh God.... Brookhart!" he called.

"Mikie?"

He could only smile. "The light. I see it!"

"Mikie?" Brookhart said again.

"Who are you talking to?" her partner asked.

"You'll tell him?" Mike asked. "You'll tell Joel?"

She smiled a grim and determined smile. No tears. "I will."

"Who the *fuck* are you talking to?" Townsend growled.

Mike smiled. He'd done it. He'd done all he was supposed to. He'd told his wife to love Greg. He'd told his lover that he loved him. He'd helped a lot of people. He'd helped a girl named Kelly McCarthy leave the world after who knows how long.

He found he had only one regret: that he didn't get to hold Joel in his arms one more time.

But still... he moved into the light.

25

MIKE ELLSWORTH wasn't the only one who was surprised when he awoke with a huge, hurting gasp in the bed of a hospital just as the doctors turned off the machines that had been keeping him alive.

26

SIX MONTHS later, Mike was standing on the roof of One Southwest Tower off 39th Street, not far from downtown Kansas City. It used to belong to a business associates organization that had been around for years. Since then it had been converted to high-quality condos. They were gorgeous.

Mike walked to the edge of the roof.

"What are you doing?" Joel, his fiancé, asked.

He grinned, then turned and shouted out over the city. "I am in love with Joel Kauffman!" His voice echoed. It was a wonderful sound.

Joel laughed and threw his arms around Mike. "Me too."

Mike stuck out his lower lip. "Say it."

Joel laughed again. "I love you, Mike Ellsworth!"

Mike smiled.

"Lori and Greg will be here soon," Joel said.

Mike nodded. "Yeah. But they'll call first." They had to. The building had security out the ass. They wouldn't even get through the gate, let alone into the building, without calling up first.

Funny. Who would have imagined dinner with his soon-to-be ex-wife and her fiancé? Who would have thought Greg would turn out to have a mind for business himself?

How stupid would it be to break up such a team?

"Well, I'm going downstairs," Joel said, and planted a kiss square on Mike's lips.

"I'll be down in a minute," Mike said. "I have… something to do first."

He was looking at a man in a three-piece business suit standing about twenty feet away. The man was climbing up onto the building's ledge.

Joel turned in the direction Mike was looking. He cocked his head and then gave Mike a knowing look. "A minute?"

"Ten at the most," Mike assured. "Believe me. I got this."

"I believe you," Joel said, and left Mike to his real business

B.G. THOMAS lives in Kansas City with his husband of more than a decade and their fabulous little dog. He is lucky enough to have a lovely daughter as well as many extraordinary friends. He has a great passion for life.

B.G. loves romance, comedies, fantasy, science fiction, and even horror—as far as he is concerned, as long as the stories are character driven and entertaining, it doesn't matter the genre. He has gone to literature conventions his entire adult life where he's been lucky enough to meet many of his favorite writers. He has made up stories since he was a child; it is where he finds his joy.

In the nineties, he wrote for gay magazines but stopped because the editors wanted all sex without plot. "The sex is never as important as the characters," he says. "Who cares what they are doing if we don't care about them?" Excited about the growing male/male romance market, he began writing again. Gay men are what he knows best, after all—since he grew out of being a "practicing" homosexual long ago. He submitted a story and was thrilled when it was accepted in four days. Since then the stories have poured out of him. "It's like I'm somehow making up for a lifetime's worth of stories!"

"Leap, and the net will appear" is his personal philosophy and his message to all. "It is never too late," he states. "Pursue your dreams. They will come true!"

Website/blog: bthomaswriter.wordpress.com
E-mail: bgthomaswriter@aol.com

By B.G. THOMAS

All Alone in a Sea of Romance
All Snug
Anything Could Happen
Bianca's Plan
The Boy Who Came In From the Cold
Christmas Cole
Christmas Wish
Derek
Desert Crossing
Grumble Monkey and the Department Store Elf
Hound Dog and Bean
How Could Love Be Wrong?
It Had to Be You
Just Guys
Men of Steel (Dreamspinner Anthology)
Red
Riding Double (Dreamspinner Anthology)
A Secret Valentine
Soul of the Mummy
Editor: A Taste of Honey (Dreamspinner Anthology)
Two Tickets to Paradise (Dreamspinner Anthology)
Until I Found You

GOTHIKA
Bones (Multiple Author Anthology)
Spirit (Multiple Author Anthology)

SEASONS OF LOVE
Spring Affair
Summer Lover
Autumn Changes

Published by DREAMSPINNER PRESS
www.dreamspinnerpress.com

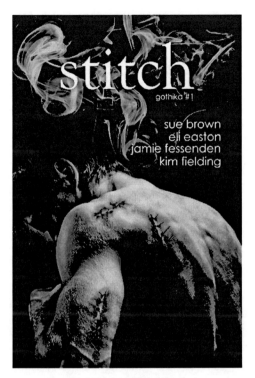

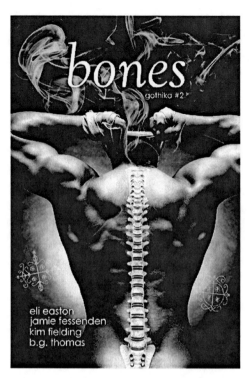

Gothika: Volume Two

Vodou. Obeah. Santeria. These religions seem mysterious and dark to the uninitiated, but the truth is often very different. Still, while they hold the potential for great power, they can be dangerous to those who don't take appropriate precautions. Interfering with the spirits is best left to those who know what they're doing, for when the proper respect isn't shown, trouble can follow. In these four novellas, steamy nights of possession and exotic ritual will trigger forbidden passion and love. You cannot hide your desires from the loa, or from the maddening spell of the drums. Four acclaimed m/m authors imagine homoerotic love under the spell of Voodoo.

The Dance by Kim Fielding
The Bird by Eli Easton
The Book of St. Cyprian by Jamie Fessenden
Uninvited by B.G. Thomas

www.dreamspinnerpress.com

Gothika: Volume Three

Beasts lurk in the shadows of wild and forgotten places and in the hearts and souls of men. They are the stuff of dreams and nightmares, but are they feral and savage, or just misunderstood? Creatures of myth and legend stalk these tales of dark desire and animal passions. Three men come face-to-face with such creatures and find they are much more than they seem. While there is danger, there might be unexpected benefits as well, if they can accept the impossible and dare to venture into the primordial regions where nature and the beasts still reign. Three acclaimed authors of gay romance explore the boundaries between man and beast and the place where their worlds overlap.

Isolation by Jamie Fessenden
Transformation by Kim Fielding
The Black Dog by Eli Easton

www.dreamspinnerpress.com

CPSIA information can be obtained
at www.ICGtesting.com
Printed in the USA
LVOW10s1115071117

555290LV00009B/114/P